Trajan's Arch

Trajan's Arch

Michael Williams

SEVENTH STAR PRESS

Cover art and design: Enggar Adirasa

Cover art in this book copyright © 2019 Enggar Adirasa & Seventh Star Press, LLC.

Editor: Karen M. Leet

Published by Seventh Star Press, LLC.

ISBN Number: 978-1-948042-75-8

Seventh Star Press

www.seventhstarpress.com

info@seventhstarpress.com

Publisher's Note:

Printed in the United States of America

Second Edition

For Joshua and Shane

PROLOGUE

Lake Geneva

10/12/92

Dear Jasmine,

I went back to Mass yesterday.

I know you've never held to processions and vestments and incense, and that I obliged you, in the time we were together, by not holding with them myself.

But there you are. I've always loved the pageantry, even in those times when my believing faltered; and Jazz, this is not one of those times, for I'm believing like a pro these days. And right now, "attending" is the word for it, kneeling and watching as the priest and the censers and the crucifer pass me down the center aisle (for it's as High Mass as I can get in southern Wisconsin, you'd better believe it). And knowing how it goes, how it's going to end and that it will be a happy ending, all of that is reassuring: it's like one of those dreams you have where you realize you're dreaming and it's all good, where

1

you can look behind the purple and the smoke, and when the priest lifts the host over the altar and the Body of Christ breaks in his hands, the cracking sound like bones breaking at two millennia's distance...

Well, you know me and my symbols. My love of the things that dance behind things.

I even went to confession, which I still think you, of all people, should approve of, though I know your thoughts on priests and the consolations they offer.

I wanted you to know you were right in a way, at least about this priest, and I know that changes nothing except that you enjoy being right, and as always I want to bring you joy.

Because this priest told me that struggling against unpleasant ties would make me stronger.

But I am coming to believe that sometimes, struggling only makes you tired.

You are right about the stories, too. They weigh heavy for a manuscript barely an inch thick. Trajan typed them on an old manual Remington. I remember seeing the typewriter, even if I never saw him at it—one of those gray monstrosities whose frame was as durable and ugly as the old Chrysler he let sit in his driveway. Back then I'm sure it was harder to put stories together: you had to invest more in a manuscript when cut and paste meant scissors and glue.

Well, that Chrysler fell apart at last, and the Remington fetched six dollars at the estate sale, according to my mother. And the manuscript has seen better days, too. It's starting to yellow, the edges of the pages softened and powdered after twenty years of lying around. And now, when I look at it, I understand why there aren't any marks in the margins, not a word scratched out or altered. It was part of Trajan's brilliant laziness, his reluctance to retype, to pretend or intend to retype.

It is a sleekness I can understand, but I just can't figure, except to admire it and wish that I could do it. And to wish that those stories were mine.

You asked about my work. Well, it's on the same table, bursting out of boxes and accordion files, covering over reviews of the first book, letters from my mother and from you, and covered in turn by *those damned freshman essays on "How I Spent The Summer."*

I know. It's October. I'll grade them soon.

I promise you the work is getting along. A second novel is traditionally a hard thing to do—just ask Barry.

Or, then again, don't.

It's sitting here on the table as I write you, the chess knight I was sent, for some reason, with Trajan's manuscript lying on top of it like a preposterous paperweight, as though from the distance of death my old friend is still sitting on my substance. It looks like someone ransacked the room, the same words on file cards and legal pads and typed in a delirium of fonts, like something Jack Nicholson would have done in "The Shining;" but there's a method to this boy's madness. I'm pretending that looking at the same words in a different way, or maybe in a different hand, will change them and move them across the page.

Trajan always said to let something dwell with you before the words start, and in a way I am doing that. A hundred variations on a hundred words, so that they have ceased to stand for something, and no matter how they lie on the page, you would never call them finished.

Neither would Barry. Neither would this new editor. She's calling regularly now, and I can't help wishing I'd done this before. I'm almost thirty-eight, and midway through only the second book.

And not midway. I don't know who I'm kidding—certainly not you.

And not Barry, either. Lately the calls have gone through the transformations my writer's group talks about, and it's just like they told me. The friendly calls have already moved to polite questions, then to the sympathy for second novel blues, then to things being about Barry instead of me, to maintaining that his job is in a kind of jeopardy, his own ass on the line in the "predatory world of publishing"…

His phrase, not mine.

But I am farther down the food chain than Barry Green, who has a dozen clients and can afford to lose one, especially a mid-list novelist where his ten percent is barely cigarette money. It's like something inside him has given up on the process, has been saying things so that, when the time comes, he can tell someone that he said them.

Recently, when it moved to "Call me, Gabriel," on the answering machine, I did a bad thing and sent him some stuff, claiming it was the first half of the novel. I gave in to the pleading that changed to command, the command that moved quickly into flat statement. It was a kind of appeasement: he read what I sent, marked it down as "pretty good," then asked for the rest, so I've just been stalling for time the last month, trying to think of something before the calls begin again.

All this damned while, Jazzie, I've had the temptation. Trajan's stories sitting silent and solitary on the table. Miss Vivien's been dead a while, too, so nobody knows about them but me. They've invaded my writing space. It's like my own work surrendered to them, retreated from their quiet and serene resolution, like somebody moved the black chess piece from his square to my own. All of them are there—the first one about the Filipino prodigy, the one about the calmed ship, and beneath it the story about the girl who channeled the Jacobean dramatist...

And of course the longest one, the one he did not finish, about home when the last century turned, and the father who tried to guard his child against the past and all the ghosts that lived there.

Other than the last one, you would think the manuscript was a finished draft, or pretty near finished. It has the smoothed-down look of submitted work. The pages are as neatly arranged as the day the lawyer handed them to me, and the same old binder clip holding them together like a plot line or the frame of a story.

But of course there is a faint patina of rust around the jaw of the clip. The bubble and stain of the first page, blistered by the condensation of beer cans. I tried to match the clip to the rust when I put the manuscript back together, but it didn't fit the same way: things don't happen like that, don't click together like the jewel boxes the writers' workshops always talk about. So it sat there, in the middle of intangible loose ends, waiting for me to do something.

I used to think I knew why these stories were bequeathed to

me. I'm not so sure anymore. After all, Trajan was one for the quiet surprise, the sudden appearance of something out of nothing and the reversal of something into nothingness before you could grasp it. He was all about that kind of moment where everything becomes translucent, and the shapes of things are revealed as cloudy, unstable, barely masking the wonders beneath them.

I know what you're thinking. That's Gabriel. The old Hibernian song and dance, right?

These mornings I stand at the window, trying to remember moments like those, the frost branching and flaking on the far side of the glass, the southern Wisconsin landscape sealed away, stunned by a week of impossibly early snows falling on the living and the dead. Even the parking lot is as blank and white as an untravelled page.

Trajan Bell has been a distant thought, his spirit embedded in a generation of ice. But he's coming closer, Jazzie. He's stalking years and miles, and I pour myself a whiskey against all that finality and closure but also against his coming, and all the while my memory drifting toward an irrecoverable time back in Kentucky when, over twenty years ago, August Street was transformed by his first arrival.

I'm going back there over Christmas. Mother wants me to sign some things, to settle some scores with the old man's estate, and I have some scores to settle as well, and even though I haven't told you it all, I suppose you've guessed the outline of it.

Jazzie, I'd like for Dominic to join me. His gramma will warm to him this time, I'm sure, and he's fifteen now, old enough to fly from New York by himself if you or Benjamin would take him to the airport. If you can't see free to do it, please give him my love and tell him that his Da never figured on things working out like this.

Fondly,
Gabriel

P.S. Please say it's his Da. If he's calling Ben "Dad" now, there's nothing I can do, but please save a name and a place for me in his memory, Jazzie: a thing that dances behind things. I'd love it if you did that much.

O N E

O WHAT can ail thee, knight-at-arms,
  Alone and palely loitering?
The sedge has wither'd from the lake,
  And no birds sing.

1

Trajan Bell came to August Street in 1968, appropriately in August. Three hundred miles north, the country was preparing to tear itself apart in a political convention. Doctor King and Senator Kennedy were both months dead, Nixon had lockstepped into the Republican nomination, because, well, it was his turn. The war continued in abstract jungles, and an appalling numbness spread across the whole country.

The journalists would have you think that everyone was seized by history; that every action was played out against some momentous future. But on August Street, if you were thirteen years old, history was like a faint rumble of thunder over the hills of Indiana across the river—close enough to hear, but far enough not to trouble the hearing.

And there were three of them waiting, all of them thirteen years old in that hot, unmindful summer. Their neighborhood was young as well, spreading south of Louisville in one of those grid works of working-class brick ranch houses straining at middle class, three bedrooms branching off a hall where you'd have to turn sideways to pass somebody, and a garage only if you were especially lucky or your father especially handy. Each of those few garages, it seemed in that time of smaller childhoods, housed the dreams of a male eighth grader, his ambitions yet to be broadened by high school. Someday, each boy believed, the garage would be converted, metamorphosed into a room of his own, a roof that was not his parents' but still safely close to their kitchen table.

August Street ran east and west, intersected by Flora, Scarlett, and Echo. To its west lay a tree-canopied thoroughfare—Gethsemane Lane, named after the Baptist church where it intersected the highway—that brushed the edge of the subdivision on its way to the river. The names had seemed exotic to Gabriel when his mother and he first moved to the neighborhood—names of goddesses or witches, or something vaguely mythological. And indeed, the two boys who were there to meet him, Delano Robinson and Joey Hardy, who examined his bicycle and the wiry sling of his throwing arm and found both worthy, were tuned to the subtleties of the crossing roads. They could see the differences it would take Gabriel months to learn. He learned them nonetheless, and the mysteries receded, and later he even discovered these streets were named for the developer and his three daughters, and by that time he was scarcely disappointed to know it.

But the summer of 1968 was sliding into that part of August where school became a prospect. There was still a week or so of vacation left, and the grass in Del Robinson's back yard was worn into base paths, disputable bald spots over which the boys debated the safes and outs of hotbox, where they foretold, over the sudden whir of cicadas, just what team would face their glorious and favored Cardinals in the Series two months away.

Into this noise came Trajan Bell, his arrival inauspicious enough to go unnoticed, if it weren't for the fact that the life of a thirteen-year-old boy in that place and time was not much more than anticipating and paying loose attention. When the van made a left turn off of Echo and passed by the three boys as they straddled their bikes in Gabriel's driveway, it immediately became the talk of weeks.

It was the 22nd , three days before Joey's fourteenth birthday, and the movers were from some Yankee company: there was a map of New England on the sidewall panel, and the license plate was Massachusetts, which Del announced as Massatoosutts until Joey pointed out the spelling. From a safe spot across the road, the boys looked at the map like it was alien country. They looked for Boston on it, the familiarizing home of the Red Sox, whom their Cardinals, of course, had sent to defeat in the previous Series.

The van pulled into Miss Vivien Bell's driveway and idled, the fumes from the exhaust buckling the humid air, and for a moment it almost seemed like the vehicle had slipped behind a veil of water as the movers, two enormous black men, stepped from the cab and opened the truck.

This was new country for the boys as well. August Acres was all white except for the Rowans, who did not technically live in the subdivision but in a solitary house half a mile up the Louisville Road. As a matter of fact, aside from Clarence Rowan's quiet presence in left field on their Babe Ruth team, their only experience with black people was through television, so Gabriel's first thought, before he pushed it under as the thought of a silly kid, was that these men must be pro athletes, that somehow Miss Vivien Bell had football connections he had yet to understand.

The men moved quickly and silently. One of them glanced across the street at the boys, then reached into the bed and wrestled a tall book case out of the truck, just far enough so that the other man could shoulder its end. Together they hauled it into Miss Bell's perpetually empty garage - she didn't drive, of course - and from where they were going with it, Gabriel imagined they'd have a terrible time turning it to enter the narrow door that straddled garage and kitchen.

Del must have been thinking the same thing, because when the men came out immediately, climbed into the truck and emerged with boxes, he thumbed the stupid little bell on his bicycle and said, "Them colored guys is movin fast. They left that bookcase in the garage, I guess."

Joey looked at him and smirked. "No shit, Sherlock. Now

11

what we got to figure is whose stuff it is that Miss Vivien is storing."

"Then how 'bout we check it out?" Gabriel asked, because each of the boys had his role, and it was always Gabriel's to say that.

***

Now, from the distance of five hundred miles and twenty-five years, an icy rain rising off a desolate Wisconsin lake to rake against his windows, Gabriel saw more clearly why he was the chosen one—the one who figured in this story.

Del had the high sense of wonder. Had once lost a game for their Babe Ruth team because he was sitting in right field drawing a doodlebug from its hole with an onion. He would lose himself in the surprise of things, and he marveled all the more because he had trouble catching on. Del was in the slow track at school, a thing that Gabriel and Joey were slow to understand themselves. In the summer of '68, they still envied their friend because, when 8-A's field trips had been to the orchestra, his class had gone to the potato chip factory.

Joey, on the other hand was all A's without studying, except for penmanship; and, as Joey said, "penmanship's for suck-ups, anyway." Always ready with a funny, biting comment that put someone or something in its place. Joey saw the density of things—always did—how one thing you tried could touch a switch or a cord in another, how things were related on their insides. Two dozen years later, when the AZT wasn't working and his cells started going haywire, it was that knowledge of insides that took him quickly. But in 1968, intelligence and insight held him back: he would comment and judge, but he never took the first step.

Of course, he had Gabriel to do that. The boy whose major part in the story came from the fact that he was probably less gifted than his friends.

So Gabriel was the one who crossed the street first and stood behind the open van. One of the movers looked at him and nodded, then continued with his business. He watched as the man drew forth still another cardboard box, the words "Philosophy and Esoterica" written in soft lead pencil on the side.

"*Esoterica?*" Gabriel whispered to Joey, who stood at his shoulder now, a head taller and smelling of the neat's foot oil he had just used to break in a new glove. "Ain't *esoterica* some kind of nekkid pictures?"

Joey shook his head. "That's *erratica*, dumbass. And what you think Miss Vivien would be doin' with nekkid pictures to begin with?"

The other boxes followed, some of them labeled with more recognizable words—*history* and *religion*—while others were numbered, as if Miss Vivien was setting up a library in her garage. This seemed altogether possible, as the old woman had all the qualities the boys had come to expect in a librarian.

She had been there in 1965, when Gabriel moved to August Acres. Del and Joey both claimed she had been there when they arrived, and they had been in the neighborhood a couple of years before Gabriel got there. Joey, with his capacity for scorn and his constant invention on the spur of the moment, even spun out a story that she had been here longer than any living creature in the neighborhood, longer even than the trees, and that indeed she had been one of those trees at one time, that you never saw her barefooted because her old toes still resembled the roots out of which she had risen.

Del had laughed at the story, but his eyes went serious when he laughed. After all, it was his house that was next to hers, and in the first week they were neighbors, Miss Vivien had confiscated his basketball when it wandered over her privacy fence in the wake of an ill-aimed hook shot. Del's dad had negotiated its return, but not before the old woman had brandished a pistol and explained in some detail how she was prepared to use it.

From then on the neighborhood had been warned: Miss Vivien was a local hazard, as close to a fairy-tale witch as there actually was such a thing. She floated in that uncertain space between mean and harmless old-womanhood and something more magical and sinister; it had taken a little courage to stand in her driveway, to watch as the garage filled up with its new and peculiar contents.

"These come all the way from Boston, then?" Gabriel asked one of the movers.

He nodded and hoisted another box.

Now it was evident that the van contained only books, and already the small garage was half-filled. Gabriel moved toward the door like he was approaching the mouth of a forbidden cave, peering into half-darkness at the words and numbers inscribed on the boxes. For a moment, the shadows seemed softer, almost welcoming, and he took a step onto the smooth concrete of the garage floor, following the stacked boxes up to where they seemed to brush against the rafters…

Where something glowed above the topmost box, hidden by the cardboard on which it rested, but still bathing the low rafter in a slanted, bronze light.

"You best not go in there, young man," rumbled a voice behind him. "Miss Bell, she done told us not to let no boys poke around in there."

Gabriel turned abruptly, but both the movers had their backs to him, and he was never to figure out which one had warned him. But he wasn't studying the movers, and that night, after the van had pulled away, he wondered about the light, about what poking around might have uncovered in that dark and beguiling place.

***

Gabriel's bedroom window overlooked August Street. If you opened the venetian blinds and if the moon was just right (as it was that night in late summer) it would bathe and illuminate the front of Miss Vivien's house. It was a vantage point he'd never valued until that night, when he imagined there was actually something to see over her way.

Red brick and striped green awnings. In the distance and in the bleaching light of the moon, the colors were in his memory rather than his eyes: the house was outlined in grays and silvers, blending into each other in the bare, uncomplicated moonlight. Gabriel was sure he had seen her house before in the same light, but for the first time it seemed mysterious, estranged.

In the front yard, the leaves of a water maple fluttered from silver to dark and back to silver, as if something imprisoned in the tree was desperately signaling for help.

Gabriel reached for the cord of the blinds.

Then the light went on in the side bedroom of Miss Vivien Bell's little house. And the blinds of that room drew back.

A tall man was standing in the window. His hair spread in wide disarray around his enormous head. His glasses, catching light from somewhere, glittered like tilted mirrors in the heart of his wide face. Then he looked straight at Gabriel's hidden window, waved and moved forward, his shoulders filling the window frame until he blocked the light and darkened to a black silhouette.

It was like a body rising out of black water, afloat on a shadowy current, emerging and sinking as it swept away into a deeper darkness.

Calling to Gabriel as it floated away. It was creepy, what the image of the man had made him think. He wondered where he got it, where it came from. Only gradually did his thoughts settle on the man.

Who was this man? Where had he come from?

Gabriel turned from the window and slipped guiltily into bed. It was like he had been found out, caught doing something somehow wrong.

He watched the ceiling for a few minutes or hours, the moonlight tilting over the patterns in the low acoustic tiles, and the occasional rush of headlights across the room as though something in the heart of his house was sending search beams toward the heaven, only to have them blocked by shabby architecture and the mundane night.

¶¶.

By late morning, as the boys convened in Del Robinson's back yard, Gabriel basked in the safer light: standing on the makeshift baseball diamond, so close to Miss Vivien's house, the world seemed salvaged, no longer estranged. He thought he might have dreamed it all, from the hazy van to the strange apparition in the old woman's window. But then the stories converged, each of them rising from the watchful houses on August Street, as regular and accurate as Del's remarkable fastball, and Gabriel found himself listening to them all, his gloved hand stinging as Del threw to him again and again. Gabriel tried to piece the stories together into something that made sense. Something that did not threaten him.

Del's father worked for Dean's Dairy. He came home with new kinds of ice cream, even before the A & P or the Winn-Dixie stocked anything more exotic than Neapolitan or French Vanilla. Del's dad liked to be the first with things, the bearer of novelty and knowledge, and because of his job and the fact that he joked with the boys, he was the favorite of the two available fathers. (Lieutenant Hardy, Joey's dad, had squandered all the glamour of being a police detective by simply not being around, except in brief down times laced with bourbon and melancholy). It was up to Mr. Robinson, then, to tell the boys that Miss Vivien's son was moving back home.

"It don't seem to me that Miss Vivien should have a son," Del objected, drawing a laugh from his old man.

"I know what you mean," Mr. Robinson said with a grin, lighting a Pall Mall and staring over the privacy fence at the roof of Miss Vivien's house, the sunlight directly overhead, beating down on the shingles so that they seemed to be settling, emerging out of mystery. "Seems like Miss Vivien should of just skipped a generation—gone straight into being a grandma without stopping to be a mother."

The smoke cascaded from his nostrils, and Gabriel could tell something was up with Mr. Robinson, though he knew in his deepest intuitions that it would not come out, that Del's dad would brush against it and let it settle in the back of the mind.

Already, better than his two friends, Gabriel knew the slow, conversational dance of other boys' fathers when they gave you advice, how it was different in tone and chemistry from the smothering tirades of Irish mothers. Gabriel's own father was a disembodied voice on the phone somewhere up in Michigan, hard to match with the picture on Gabriel's dresser that his mother insisted he keep there out of her abstract sense of fairness. His father called less frequently since they had moved to August Acres—only on Sundays now—and when he called, the pauses on the phone line were longer. But he still made Gabriel laugh when he called Mother's scoldings "the old Hibernian song and dance."

So maybe Gabriel listened more closely to Mr. Robinson, who leaned against the privacy fence and lit a new cigarette with the butt of the old one. "Well, I'm hearing different things about this Bell boy," he said.

His eyes passed over the boys, then settled and locked on Gabriel.

"Y'all aren't messing around in Miss Bell's yard no more, are you?"

"Nossir," the boys lied in unison, and Gabriel dropped his gaze from Mr. Robinson's soft brown eyes.

"That's good," the man said. "Seems to me that's a good idea, dontcha think, Gabe?"

∗∗∗

Miss Vivien's son was widowed, they were saying. Or he was never married.

He was a professor of sorts in New England. Or he was a preacher or a mad scientist.

He was the oldest of three children, or the younger of two, or in one version, which Gabriel resisted, Trajan Bell was an only child.

He had traveled in Europe, in the Navajo Southwest, in Tibet or in the polar wastes.

He had come back because Miss Vivien had taken a turn for the worse, or he was in some kind of trouble and was lying low.

There in the rising heat of Del Robinson's back yard, the boys discussed the possibilities. Gabriel set down his glove and told them about the night vision at the window. Told them so quietly that his friends stopped tossing the baseball, approached him and leaned toward his whispered words—Del freckled and slack-jawed and Joey catlike and surmising.

"Then he *is* a mad scientist," Del deduced. "Coz he's got hair like Alfred Einstein."

Joey shook his head, turned his Cardinals cap bill-backwards and leaned his ear against the dried vines of the privacy fence. The cicadas ratcheted in Miss Vivien's maples, and for a moment it seemed that the branches sagged above the fence as though the locusts themselves were gathering in numbers to warn and protect the Bells from spies and intruders.

"We gotta get better intelligence," Joey insisted. His father had fought in Europe and Korea, so Joey talked in terms of *intelligence* and *recon*. "I can't hear or see a damned thing from here." He crouched beside the fence, picked up a dried branch, and diagrammed a plan in the dust.

"So what I figure is this. Robinson, you can get in there one of two ways. Grab hold of that limb there and climb up into Miss Vivien's tree, or you can go in through the corner."

The boys all kept the secret of the corner, where one of the planks in the fence had come unmoored from the nails and could be raised and lowered, tilted back and forth like the trunk of a car. On several occasions they had used it to retrieve baseballs, but today, with the arrivals at the Bell place, no entrance to Miss Vivien's yard seemed quite secure.

"Why's it gotta be me, Joey?"

"Coz it's your yard, Robinson. And you're the shrimp here. Me and Rackett have trouble getting through the corner any more."

Del nodded. He wasn't positive Joey was right about this, but he suspected that it was close to the truth. You could see him glimpsing the layers of the situation. He was unconvinced.

"I just don't know why we gotta know this stuff, Joey. Ain't that I'm scared or nothing, but it just don't make sense. Can't we leave it alone or something?"

Joey's eyes were serious. "Leaving it alone ain't an option, Robinson. What if Miss Vivien's son is like a murderer or a spy or a pervert or something?"

"That don't make me want to go over there much," Del replied quietly, and for a moment Joey seemed backed against things, as though his own imaginings had undermined him. Then, he picked up Del's glove, smiled, and tossed it over the fence.

"There's your reason, Del Robinson," he whispered. "Just tell me what you see on your way back."

***

Gabriel stepped in because of the doleful look that Del gave him, the way his friend seemed to recede into the shade of the overhanging branches like he was being drawn into dusk.

"You gonna owe me one, Del," he sighed. "I'll go instead, I reckon."

Joey looked away, suppressing a smile.

"There's always ice cream if you find the glove, Rackett," he called after Gabriel as the boy rounded the fence toward the corner

Twenty-five years later, Gabriel would remember his own misgivings as he followed the fence line through the canopy of dried branches, a stick no thicker than his thumb gathered ridiculously to his back pocket as a kind of protection.

He told himself it was noble. That he was doing right by his friend. That it wasn't really the nosiness his mother said got him into trouble, because he knew the lay of Miss Vivien's back yard and there was nothing to nose about, not really....

It had something to do with his mother, broguing her worries to him as she gathered the teacher's checks and the sporadic child support together at the kitchen table, its short leg leveled by a folded piece of shirt cardboard.

If you're for getting killed, Gabe, I won't be having the wherewithal for yer burying.

So cover lightly, gentle earth.

But nobility, curiosity, rebellion—all of them vanished into the shadows as Gabriel left the sight of his friends and approached the corner, the dislodged rail, the hard ground tunneled a foot beneath it from the boys' previous ventures into Miss Vivien's back yard.

They'd best find a new ball field, Gabriel thought. If Miss Vivien had a man around the house, the fence would be fixed for sure.

He turned sideways to crawl through the hole in the fence. For a brief, uncomfortable moment, the stick in his back pocket caught on the fence, levered and gouged into his buttock. Then he kicked through, was free in Miss Vivien's back yard, the stick snapped in half in the opening behind him.

And the whole world plunged into green silence.

***

The cicadas were still now, the light fragmented. Gabriel could hear Del and Joey on the far side of the fence, the sound of their voices a modulation stripped of words, like a murmuring overheard through glass or from a back room.

Then another sound rose slowly, above the mutter of his friends' voices. It came from the house, and it, too, was a wordless music of voices, a high, and tremulous woman's tone like a pipe organ, within which the tenor of a man's voice wove in response.

Through the yard Gabriel crept, the uncut grass brushing his ankles. He skirted the overgrown push mower, scuttled over the cracked pavement of Miss Vivien's patio, and headed toward the stand of water maples at the far end of the yard. Del's glove had lodged neatly between two branches on the farthest tree, and Gabriel reached for the lowest branch, swung himself into the tree, and scuttled like a ghost through the musty, entangling network of twigs and leaves.

Below him, the sounds had died away. It was as though he had climbed away from them, that his path through the green toward sunlight and the glove was taking him out of mystery, back toward a familiar high ground.

He steadied himself on a thick, rough limb and reached into the shadows for the glove. His fingers closed around it. He had to tug to pull it free, and with a snap and rattle of leaves, it was there in his hand, as he rocked back from the effort of his pulling. His feet struggled for purchase, his arm wrapped around the limb beneath him, and he rolled beneath it, still clinging to it for balance, his legs flailing vainly until, slowly, he realized he was not that high off the ground, not really, and could drop from the branch without danger.

Tossing the glove down into the leafy dimness, Gabriel lowered himself until he dangled by his hands only, then confidently, silently, slipped to the ground.

It was a longer drop than he had expected. He landed feet first, felt the shock in his shoulders and teeth.

Looked around him for the glove.

He thought he saw it lying between the exposed roots of one of the trees, larger than he remembered it and mottled with sunlight. But when he took a step toward it, whatever the thing was at the shadowy foot of the tree suddenly stirred and lurched into the high grass with a quick, undulating movement that made Gabriel jump back.

A man stood, bathed in light, on the cracked pavement of the patio. Clothed in a pale homespun suit that was not really white, not yellow, not gray.

Pale, Gabriel thought again.

What is the color of pale?

For a moment, he thought it was Miss Vivien's son, the man in the window. But the raggedly cropped hair, the beard, the glittering bird eyes…and again the pallor.

Then the man grinned at him, a gapped grin, and in its wake what was either laughter or the call of the cicadas, Gabriel could not tell. He stared at Gabriel with those bright, depthless eyes, and something in the boy recognized the face, the creepy smile, but again from where he was uncertain. The man made a gesture—a crude movement with his right hand that began as a wave but ended with a sudden, grotesque turn of his neck, as though he held a rope in it and was strangling himself in a rain of sunlight.

And then he was gone.

A strange, skidding sound followed his departure. The light in the center of the yard folded and steamed, so quickly that Gabriel could not put sight or words around it, but the high grass furrowed and thrashed in the wake of something, and with a high-pitched cry that soared out of hearing, a wind rustled the reeds near the fence.

It left behind the sour stink of rats, but somehow Gabriel knew that was not what it was, though it was something, indeed, that did not belong in sunlight.

He caught his breath, shaky with the thought of it….

And a hand fell onto his shoulder, strong-fingered and

heavy and pushing him to the ground. Thinking of the pale man, Gabriel twisted his shoulder, trying to escape, but his knees buckled, and he fell face first....

The man from the window stood over him.

"You all right, young man?" he asked, his voice reedy and melodic, tumbling from shadow and a silhouetted shock of wild hair.

Gabriel tried to speak. Thought better of it.

This man was wearing a white shirt, baggy jeans and suspenders. His hair was like Gabriel remembered it from the window—a spray of dark brown and gray that rose in all directions as though he had just escaped cartoon electrocution.

He crouched beside Gabriel. There was something heavy in his movements, a slight pivot and limp, as though crouching was not high on the list of things he liked to do. And yet from eye level, his face looked more monstrous and yet more vulnerable. He was younger than his wild hair implied....his late thirties, perhaps or early forties. The eyes behind the glasses were watery, like he had been rubbing them too long. The stubble on his unshaven chin was mottled with gray.

Gabriel did not know whether to be afraid or amused. He was a little of both, and smiled weakly as he shrank from the man, tried to gather his legs under him.

Then the man returned the smile. The two front teeth buckled slightly toward each other, and something in his face softened, as though he were learning the expression, or trying to remember it.

"Next time, son, just knock at the door and tell me that the glove's come over into the yard."

The man looked up into the leaves. "Of course, when I played baseball as a boy, it was the ball we threw rather than the gloves. Perhaps the rules have changed with all these expansion teams?"

Gabriel shook his head. "Twins is the only ones worth much of anything," he replied, before he realized how stupid it was to answer.

But the man snorted merrily. "Sox fan myself. All that poetry and loss."

Gabriel wanted to ask him about the pale man, then. He started to, but something—perhaps his own sense of what was proper—checked the question. If you were nosing in someone's yard, it was probably bad manners to ask him questions about what you rooted up.

Now the man—Miss Vivien's son, evidently—stood laboriously, ruffed Gabriel's hair, and ducked behind the tree, producing Del's glove and holding it to the light, like a magician's climax in a sleight of hand trick. He tossed the glove to Gabriel, who thanked him under his breath and stood on one leg, uncertain as to how he was supposed to leave Miss Vivien's yard.

"Go back the way you came this time," the man said, leaning against the maple. "But remember what I said the next time you lose something over here. I'll mow right away, and prune these trees when it's seasonal, and fix the pavement soon enough. But as for now, my mother's back yard is not the safest place for a boy."

He caught Gabriel's gaze, raised an eyebrow.

It was not as friendly of advice as he wanted it to sound. He checked himself, ventured the smile again.

"The name's Trajan Bell, son," he said. "You can call me Trajan."

Gabriel nodded stupidly, backed away from him, turned, and headed to the opened corner of Miss Vivien's yard. He squeezed into the shaded fencerow, his breath shallow and fast, and he broke into a run as he hurried to join his friends. Behind him, the board at the fence corner creaked loudly and slammed into place, but still he did not look back until he emerged breathless in familiar light, Del reaching for his glove and Joey rolling his eyes in exasperation at all that delay.

25

August slipped toward Labor Day and the beginning of school, with no sign in the air of approaching autumn. Gabriel tried to catch a further glimpse of the spectral man in the yard, though the image floated to the surface of his dreams, and several times troubled the bright heat of waning summer.

One time, passing down the back fencerow of Miss Vivien's property, he had heard the cicadas hush suddenly. Then the smell of wet wool rose out of the shade and the heated air, and below that smell something sour and wild, the rat-smell he remembered from that day he had retrieved the glove from the back yard.

He burst out into September light, gasping, and the world staggered upright again. He knew not to look back. He headed in a run across Echo and sprinted back toward Scarlett until he ran out of breath and the image of the man in homespun receded into the overhang of leaves and rubbish behind the fence row.

He was afraid to go behind Miss Vivien's now. It felt like unhallowed ground on the far side of the fence.

But he had not figured Trajan Bell, the strange mixture of allure and menace. His fascination with the man was more steady: each morning Gabriel would look out the window toward

Miss Vivien's front yard, and it was not long before the changes became apparent—the awnings and pavement conjured back into shape, as though a new house was rising out of the memory of the old.

Still, the heat was foremost in Gabriel's thoughts—that smothering Ohio Valley mugginess when it seemed he was breathing through wet rags, when the grass-stain smell of his own sweat hung in the motionless air, and he felt like the season had stopped. In the hot mid-afternoons he would find birds lying on the asphalt, their feathers matted, their beaks agape as though the temperature and accompanying death had ambushed them, rushed at them out of the cloudless midwestern sky. At first, he felt sorry for them, but as the week passed on, the sight was so familiar that it baffled pity, and he fell back into his routines, all foreboding banished.

The week before school began, Del Robinson, his brindled, stiff-bound composition tablets under his arm like a scholar's on "Ozzie and Harriet," had to go back early for the first of his seasonal remedies.

It was what they did in high school for the backward ones, Joey said. They would assure that Del could read well enough to follow assignments and to be bored along with the rest of them. What it meant for Joey and Gabriel, however, was later, less frequent visits to their makeshift ball diamond, and more distant imagining about what was going on behind Miss Vivien's privacy fence.

Trajan Bell was as good as his word, it seemed. From his vantage in the middle of August Street, Gabriel caught the smell of cut grass, heard hammering, and in the late mornings before Del's bus returned, he could hear something that sounded like digging if he approached Miss Vivien's house from the other side from the fencerow. Trajan was unearthing or burying something, and it made Gabriel think of the pale man in homespun, of the laughter and vanishing he had tried to bury somewhere in his own thoughts, but had emerged twice in dreams nonetheless, leaving a sour smell in his room when he awakened.

A week after their meeting in Miss Vivien's back yard, Trajan had moved to the front. It took only an afternoon's work for the boys to see that he was a skilled carpenter, and that he was building some kind of ramp or incline that began at Miss Vivien's driveway and rose over her porch steps to the front door. They had heard before that the old lady was confined to a wheel chair, but they hadn't seen her in months, and this was the first confirmation that maybe she was. That maybe Trajan was staying longer than just to fix up things around her house.

That Saturday, early and before his friends awakened, Gabriel made a point of riding his bicycle back and forth in front of what the adults were now calling *the Bell place,* as though it belonged to two people now, and Trajan had staked a tentative claim just by working on it. At Gabriel's third pass of the property, Trajan, who was completing the incline in the front yard, looked up and waved and called to him.

"Oh what can ail thee, knight-at-arms, alone and palely loitering?"

Gabriel braked the bicycle with his feet, frowned, and leaned against the handlebars.

Trajan was halfway up the incline, sodden with sweat in the already-hot summer morning. His long white sleeves were rolled up to the elbow, and dark, salted crescents sagged at his sides. Producing a blue bandana, he wiped his forehead and smiled at the perplexed boy.

"That's just Keats, young fella. He never hurt anybody."

Gabriel walked the bike closer, lowered the kickstand and approached the ramp on foot, his hands deep in his pockets. Almost as if the conversation was over, Trajan turned away from him, fitted the railing at the top of the incline, and hammered it in place with half a dozen sharp, accurate strokes.

"You guys don't believe in autumn down here, do you?"

Gabriel shrugged, looked at his feet. "Thought you was from down here."

Trajan looked over his shoulder. "Not in ages. You can stop being *from* a place, no matter what people tell you."

29

Gabriel looked up into the bulbous, red-rimmed eyes. "When you stop bein' *from* one place," he asked, "do you start bein' from another?"

Trajan smiled, set down the hammer. "Now that's a good question. My take on it is that you don't. You just kind of come unfastened. Make sense to you?"

For some reason Gabriel thought of the Sunday phone calls. "I guess it does, sir," he said.

"None of that 'sir' stuff with me. I think it's ok for a guy your age to call a guy my age by his first name. That is, if it's all right with the parties involved."

"OK...Tradejin."

"That's Trajan. Marcus Ulpius Traianus Bell. Name of a Roman emperor. Don't know what my mother and father were thinking when they did it."

He rolled his eyes, and Gabriel snickered a little. "I was named for a guy in a story," he offered. "I'm Gabriel."

"Ahhhh....the affable archangel? Or was that Raphael?"

"Dunno. I think I was named out of some other story."

And indeed he was. Gabriel's mother was Irish, from Galway, which he had visited only once when he was very small, and which he remembered only for its cold winds and driving rain and the place called Salthill where his grandda lived. After his father left, she had gone back in anger to being a Conroy, to his grandda's name and Gabriel's own middle name, so it made for questions in the classroom. Every once in a while, especially on Mondays, she'd be after Gabriel to change his name as well, but he had learned to be quiet about it, to let her go through the Hibernian song and dance, so that Tuesdays would be better, and then the weeks would pass without it coming up again.

The fact that they were both named for people in stories made him like Trajan more, and he leaned against the bottom of the incline, peering at the handiwork and considering it to be pretty good for a mad scientist, while the man picked up the hammer and returned to the job.

The wood wasn't like any Gabriel had seen before. Too

hard to be pine, and different from oak or ash or butternut. Almost like walnut, except for the odd, spicy smell that lingered around it and almost gave him a headache and a scattering of dark purple blotches. It was like it was already weathered, a little pocked and furrowed beneath Gabriel's fingers, and it had lost the smell of new wood as well. He figured it was some Yankee wood, and decided not to seem ignorant by asking.

He had other questions, maybe not the ones he wanted to ask, but they would pass the time and keep him by the incline.

"So, your mom gonna need this to get around, Trajan?" he asked finally.

"She doesn't think so, Gabriel," the man replied, almost cheerfully, gripping the rail and standing to examine his handiwork. All the while his broad back was to Gabriel and wings of sweat sprouted from the white cotton of his shirt. "She's decided to accept her confinement. I used to be the family gimp, I guess, but now she's housebound and has to get used to it."

"Then, why…"

Trajan leaned against the railing and regarded the boy with bemusement down the gentle slope. "This is what I call an interior incline, Gabriel," he explained, lowering his voice and glancing toward the windows. "It's imagining something else for her. I don't suppose that makes much sense, does it?"

Gabriel was inclined to believe it didn't, but he nodded politely, raising his eyebrows as if he understood.

Imagining something else. Pale homespun cloth flashed briefly through Gabriel's memory.

Homespun cloth and dead, glittering eyes.

"Uh…and you and your mom…are the only ones living here?"

"Of course we are, Gabriel. Not much room in these little houses, now is there?"

31

***

He talked to Joey and Del about much of this later. How Trajan had greeted him with something that sounded like poetry, which Del said sounded kind of sissified. Joey said nothing about the poetry, but wanted to know about the wood, and kept asking until Gabriel threw up his hands and swore at his friend, saying he had told him all he could god damn it, and if he wanted to know more about it go check it out for himself.

Joey laughed then, and reckoned he would.

That evening Gabriel looked up the Emperor Trajan in the encyclopedia, looking for something or other that might connect him to the strange man who was building and pruning a small brick house south of Louisville. This Trajan was a builder as well, the encyclopedia told him, popular and successful, and there was a photograph of some arch in a place called Beneventum—a huge structure, it looked like, standing all by itself in the midst of dry and bare surroundings.

The arch was cool, Gabriel decided. It looked like something out of Greek mythology, and was built in honor of the emperor's triumph over Dacia. Even though Gabriel had no idea where Dacia was, it was a name he relished and committed to memory.

Then he looked up Gabriel as well, finding nothing about the character he was named for. The angel Trajan Bell had mentioned was there, however. An archangel who "according to the Gospel of Luke, was the angel of the Annunciation: *And in the sixth month the angel Gabriel was sent from God unto a city of Galilee, named Nazareth, to a virgin espoused to a man whose name was Joseph, of the house of David; and the virgin was named Mary* (Luke 1:26-27)."

Gabriel knew that story. It had nothing to do with him. And while he speculated about the confusion of names, wishing the real Gabriel was in the encyclopedia so he could read something about him without having to read Mother's long and boring story about Ireland, the phone rang, and his mother said it was Joey Hardy on the line for him.

"Don't be all long and tying up the line," she warned him blearily, warned him as she always did, as she handed over the receiver.

"Rackett, you gotta see this," Joey blurted out, almost before Gabriel could say hello.

"What do I gotta see?"

"That Yankee wood on Miss Vivien's incline. You gotta see it."

"Maybe you forgot that I was the one who told you about the Yankee wood, Joey."

"You gotta see it, Rackett. You gotta see it…*now*."

***

It was always easy to slip out on Mother at night. Perhaps that was why he did not try it very often.

Mary Conroy had worked teaching drama for as long as Gabriel could remember, a part-time job at St. Frances Cabrini School. It was hard work, as she constantly reminded him, because her students were all girls, and could he imagine directing a play when you had to ship the boys in from Epiphany or St. David's? And part-time was just as demanding as full, but when a woman had a growing son she had to give him her best time, what they were starting to call *quality time,* which was why she had never taken a professional theatre job more worthy of her talents. Because of the nights, you know. And yet on most nights she would come home weary, and some of those nights she would just go into her room, and if she came out she would be all distanced and it would take Gabriel two, three times of calling her to get her attention.

It was one of those nights. There was a production of *The Tempest,* she told him, and God only knew how she would find a Prospero among students she had never even met. It was even more a mystery to Gabriel, who knew only that *The Tempest* was something by Shakespeare: a boring one without the swordfights and full-scale slaughter at the end. So he stood at the half-open front door and told Mary Conroy in a quiet, conversational voice that he was going out to see Joey Hardy for a few minutes. That he'd be back before bedtime.

Of course, he meant *her* bedtime when he said that; they'd agreed on that, since Gabriel would stay up hours past his mother, especially on the nights he felt distracted. She nodded at him, waved in his direction, the table at her elbow littered with notes and the paperback play, with pills as multicolored as derelict seashells, her watery attention on the television screen, where Patrick McGoohan fled a sagging white balloon through an eccentric Welsh village, the dialogue lost in sound of the air conditioner rattling in the window.

Joey lived two houses down August Street, farther from Miss Vivien's than Gabriel. But by the time Gabriel was outside, he could see Joey's tall, lean figure under the faintly glowing street lamp. It was barely after eight, having passed from late afternoon to dusk. For the life of him, Gabriel could not see how the two of them could approach Miss Vivien's house without being in full view of anyone who was watching.

And now, at dusk, Gabriel again recalled that afternoon a week ago in the enclosed back yard.

There was a chance that not all watching eyes would be friendly.

Joey was almost frantic when Gabriel caught up with him. He dragged Gabriel toward Miss Vivien's yard, whispering as he tugged.

"I was going over there just to look at the wood. Just gonna take a look at it and go, coz I thought it was prolly mahogany or teakwood—you know, they make decks out of teakwood and it's not like them Chinese carvings…"

He shook his head quickly, like he was trying to jostle himself back into memory.

"But…it was…oh, hell, Rackett, you gotta see it, there's just no way around it, you gotta…"

They had reached Miss Vivien's driveway. The lights were out in the house, but Gabriel suspected that the old woman, at least, was at home. What was it Trajan had said?

Housebound and had to get used to it?

So he was quiet as they approached the incline.

"Dammit, Joey," he hissed, his whisper almost lost in a high evening wind that was starting up in the maples. "Dammit, you don't need to tug me like I'm on a leash or somethin', I'm comin'!"

Joey was insistent, implacably silent. With a strength that was uncanny in a boy so thin, he hauled Gabriel up the incline toward the little platform, toward the very spot where Trajan had stood that morning, talking about lonely knights and affable archangels and inclines of the imagination.

"There!" he whispered triumphantly, pointing at the rail. "You're right when you say it's not like any wood you seen before, but it ain't Yankee wood and I'll be switched if I can tell you what it is...."

He swept his hand across the platform, and the branches and leathery leaves that had sprouted from the railing glowed a silvery green in the last of the dusky sunlight. Four-lobed flowers blossomed in the darkness, and reaching into this new greenery, Gabriel's fingers rested on firm, black berries.

He held them up to the moonlight, to Joey's widening eyes. One of the berries had burst in the picking, and its dark juice stained Gabriel's hand.

Caught up, almost hypnotized by this sudden, unnatural blossoming, neither of the boys would have noticed the sputter of moths against the street lamps, the possible shifts of the night wind bearing cooler weather from the west, or, if it happened at all, the blinds in Miss Vivien's window part slowly and narrowly and someone observing them with mounting interest.

TWO

One cold morning at the tag end of September, Gabriel awoke to a whirring sound at his window. A wasp had found its way between the pane and the blinds, and lying on its back, stung the air vaguely in its death throes.

The first few weeks of school had distracted him. It was high school, after all, and a striking change from what he was used to: the building was large, three-storied and slate-gray, confusing to navigate and filled with older, menacing students. Joey and he had only two classes together, and alphabetized; they sat rows apart, while Gabriel only saw Del on the morning and afternoon bus ride.

Del was making different friends already. He hung with the shop boys, who wore T-shirts with packs of Luckies rolled up in the sleeves. The games of catch in the Robinson back yard were less enthusiastic, and even the old common ground—the celebration of the Cardinals—was muted this year, because the team was *too* good, had left behind all competitors in the dazed and hitless National League.

Maybe it was just that the season was over, Gabriel said. Maybe it was just that Del's attentions had to be elsewhere, for of the three of them he was the most athletically talented, and the baseball team held fall tryouts so that it could start winter training with a full squad.

Surely, that was all it was, he told Joey, as they walked together from the school bus, crossing the corner of Del's yard farthest from Miss Vivien's property, the old diamond overgrowing with the last vestiges of autumn weeds.

Joey, however, wasn't buying.

He didn't argue it, like Joey usually argued things. He just shook his head and settled his eyes beyond Gabriel, like he was watching for something that hadn't arrived yet: something that perhaps he had yet to imagine himself.

That afternoon, Gabriel waited for both of his friends to no avail. Both boys had left the bus at different stops—Del with the shop boys over on Echo, and Joey with some Junior, his hair down over his forehead, who knew about the Beatles' new White Album; even though, Joey said, it hadn't been released yet.

It was disconcerting, boring to be alone. Gabriel sat on the basepaths in the Robinson's back yard, wearing his glove but with nothing to catch, wondering if he was being outgrown. He was the youngest of the three—the only one not yet fourteen—and it seemed to him that his friends had somehow been more ready for the change of schools than he had.

For once his mother had assured him. Mary Conroy had seated herself heavily on the sofa as Gabriel watched *Mayberry RFD*. He was thinking how the show wasn't as good any more, how the town wasn't the same without Andy and Barney and the characters he had watched ever since he could remember, when his mother leaned toward him, a kind of softness in her face that Gabriel did not associate with her except when it came with a faint whiff of evergreen, of juniper, as it did that night.

And there's none of your little friends about, Gabriel? That happens when you change schools, love.

He knew he was too old to bask in the voice, in the Irish accent and the astringent smells and the tenderness, but he found himself doing so, found himself halfway between embarrassment and pleasure, and safety and assurance, like in the days before he started school when his mother had read him the melancholy poems about the deaths of children and together, sitting on his bed, they had brimmed with tears over abandoned toys and the dolor of empty cradles. Back when he had adored her.

They've not moved on, his mother told him, wrenching Gabriel back to the present. *Not yet, and not yet entirely.*

Sure, but it's that kind of a bond that's made for the breaking, and you'll be ready for it when it comes.

For a moment, the poetry of the past continued to blur with a mild and current sadness, and he felt as if he had glimpsed Del and Joey through a great lens of distance and loss. But he would be prepared when the time came: his mother seemed to be sure of that. And even though Gabriel was inclined not to believe his mother in much of anything, this time he believed her, so he lay down on the sofa, his head in her lap, a mild melancholy washing over him as he watched Aunt Bea and the rest of the people of Mayberry, his thoughts trying to get around the new cast, the new situations.

✳✳✳

For the first time in several weeks, Gabriel thought of Trajan Bell.

After its eerie night of blossoming, Miss Vivien's incline had returned to its everyday shape and form. The boys had returned the next morning, only to find no evidence of its fertile magic, and they had sworn to one another that yes, they had seen the leaves and the black berries. As a kind of proof, Gabriel showed his hands, the dark stain still on his palms.

Like stigmata, he said. But Joey, being Protestant like everyone else in the neighborhood, did not understand, and it took too much time to explain it. *Just stains,* he had said then.

But stains that stand for something.

Joey had understood that, but the peculiar metamorphosis of the incline had been the last secret they had shared. Two weeks into school, Joey had taken up with the older guys, who were impressed, Gabriel figured, with what he knew about music, since by that time in August Acres every other garage was becoming a venue for amateur bands, and the sounds of "Gloria", "Louie Louie," and "96 Tears" echoed through the neighborhood like the three-chord fanfares of loud armies.

He could hear it now, this brisk fall afternoon, "Magic Carpet Ride" cresting above yet another garage over on Scarlett. He hummed along with the song for a moment, but his thoughts beached against hard lonesomeness, and he sat down, leaning against the privacy fence.

"*Let the sound take you awaaaaaayyy,*" he sang softly, his voice dying into the rustle of branches on the other side of the fence, the crisp and definite click of shears, the slow, half-labored breathing. He sat and waited, listening as Trajan trimmed the tall dry grass at the base of the fence. At last, he heard Miss Vivien's back door open and shut, and the concealed yard fell silent.

On an impulse that he would later remember with dread and gratitude, Gabriel Rackett tossed his glove over the fence, went to the front door of the Bell place, and knocked.

✳✳✳

Trajan was slow to answer the door. When he did, he leaned out into the light, half startled and half wary, blocking the threshold with his commanding frame.

Gabriel stammered as he explained how the glove—this time his own—had found its way over the fence. It was obvious that Trajan wasn't buying it, not for a second, but he nodded anyway and motioned Gabriel in.

"C'mon through," he urged. "You can help me find it in the yard."

The boys on August Street had only recently been allowed to enter each other's houses. When Gabriel and his mother had first arrived, Mary Conroy had waded into this unwritten code, and had noticed the reluctance of Joey and Del to be invited in. There was a standard maternal opinion, it seemed, that your own child in someone else's parlor was a loose cannon waiting to fire on carpets and furniture and other valuable things, so it had been a rite of passage to be allowed into Joey's and Del's rooms.

Gabriel paused at the threshold. Miss Vivien's house smelled of cigarette smoke and mildew. The parlor walls were lined with bookshelves, makeshift plywood and cinderblock contraptions that were taller than Gabriel himself and brimming with paperbacks. In the center of the parlor sat a tall library table, littered with papers and books, spine-up and covers propped like pup tents. Ever curious because of Mary Rackett's litter on the kitchen table, Gabriel squinted at the titles.

He found them alien, illegible. In Spanish or French or something coded. Indecipherable.

But for Gabriel, the greater mystery lay around him. The room was architecturally identical to one at home (because *all* the houses in August Acres shared a floor plan), but transformed by its furnishing into a space more shadowy and fetid and masculine.

Trajan gestured grandly toward the interiors of the house. "Come on through," he urged. " *'Abandon hope, all ye who enter here.'"*

He laughed, but Gabriel was perplexed.

"Is that Keats again?" he asked, his hand still clinging to the knob of the front door.

"Naw, but it's poetry nevertheless. You can tell by the way the words rise up, can't you? Quickly, now. And please forgive the disarray. I wasn't expecting your glove to…drop in, and even if I had been, I'm not much on tidiness."

Gabriel followed the big man toward the kitchen. A hall branched off to his left, which he knew, from the floor plan of his own house, led to the bathroom and bedrooms. In the kitchen it was warmer, something simmered in a large pressure cooker on the back of the stove, and the smell of tobacco gave way to a sweet, muddy whiff of cabbage.

"Guess you'll be havin' corn beef with that?" Gabriel asked, nodding toward the stove.

Trajan opened the back door. "Nah. Vegetarian here. No

41

eggs or beans, either." He smiled. "Kind of a Haight-Ashbury thing, I know. So don't look at me that way. I get enough of that from Mother."

∗∗∗

The glove was in full view, lying in the bare, shaded ground beneath one of the water maples. But Gabriel nearly forgot what had brought him to Miss Vivien's when he saw what had become of the back yard.

Only the maples had stayed the same. Their leaves were edged with the first yellow of autumn, but beneath their branches Trajan had planted a whole grove of trees. Gabriel recognized only a few of the species: oaks and ash, the deciduous trees he had grown up seeing in this part of the country. There were others familiar, though he did not know their names, and others as well—more fragile and slender, some bare in anticipation of the coming fall, others evergreen, displaying the leathery leaves and dark berries Gabriel remembered sprouting from Miss Vivien's incline.

All of them circled the broken patio, ranged concentrically like an amphitheater of trees, bending toward the ragged stones like they were listening. And there on the patio, the source of the music Gabriel had heard when he sat against the privacy fence—an acoustic guitar, its body shimmering deep red, like ripe fruit caught in the shadowy autumn light.

Cherry wood, Gabriel thought. He stepped lightly. He knew he was in the presence of something.

"I heard you playing a while back," he said quietly. "You're pretty good, Trajan."

Trajan's brusqueness seemed to evaporate. Quietly he retrieved the guitar, sat heavily down on the porch steps, and motioned for Gabriel to sit beside him. Gabriel shook his head, but Trajan gestured again, this time more insistently.

"It's just Bach," he explained. "He can't hurt you, either."

He rested the guitar on his right knee. Tuned it momentarily.

And the leaves seemed to rustle behind the whine and stretch of the string.

It was the first time Gabriel had noticed that Trajan was missing the tips of three fingers. On his right hand: middle, ring, and pinky. And yet those fingers, foreshortened and damaged, raced heavily over the strings, awkwardly at first, then picking up a surprising grace as the music began to take form.

And the music from that red guitar seemed to rise out of darkness, not looking back, ascending into the expectant branches and filling the little grove with music. For a moment the sunlight flashed green on the branches, a warm wind rustled the maple leaves, and Gabriel thought that spring had tricked him by returning, by skipping winter altogether…

As he listened, he scanned the rest of the close, shady grove. On a stone bench beneath the mystery tree, someone had set a heavy marble chessboard, its pieces scattered through several rows of squares. Though Gabriel knew little about the game, he knew enough to gather that the game was in progress, and to be struck by the strangely carved pieces—samurai warriors, he guessed, rather than the curiously abstract chessmen he had grown up seeing, where you could recognize only castle tops and horse heads, the rest looking vexingly alike.

For a moment, Gabriel wondered who was playing the game. Miss Vivien didn't seem like a chess player, and Trajan had assured him that only mother and son lived here. Later, he would learn about chess by correspondence, how a game could last for years with its players far away in place (and in time, when you considered the days it might take for letters to arrive), but even then he would not know whose game this was, who sat on each side of the board.

His thoughts, stirred by the vivid and dire shapes of the chessmen, came back from reverie and settled in the garden, in the music, in the big damaged hands coursing over the guitar.

Bach, Trajan had said. High-toned music that Gabriel resolved to discover, wondering if Bach had written something besides the piece he was hearing. He lay down on the patio, rested on his elbows…and…

"Marcus!" the voice shrieked from inside the house.

Trajan set down the guitar.

"You pick up my Chesterfields at the store?" Miss Vivien shouted. "You! Marcus!"

"Yes ma'am!" Trajan called back to her. He motioned toward the half-forgotten glove.

"You'd best be going now, Gabriel," he said, his eyes wide and suddenly weak, his temples flushed with autumnal reds and oranges, as though, despite the quiet and the serenity of only a moment before, he had been caught in some strange and furtive transgression.

"When she starts in, she never lets up."

✳✳✳

"She screeches like some old bird," Gabriel told Del and Joey, as the three of them sat in his room the next afternoon.

For some reason at the bus dock, the old friends had sought out one another, had flocked together like they had done at summer's end. It was odd, but Gabriel didn't question it, because he was brimful of things to tell them—about Trajan and the garden, the chess set, the guitar, the shrill intrusions of Miss Vivien.

"She calls him Marcus, too," he said. "And I looked it up later, and you know that was the old emperor's first name, too, so I reckon that he got the whole name loaded on him and it makes you wonder why, don't it?"

But it seemed that the other boys, who were never as fascinated as Gabriel with the doings of Trajan Bell, had brought their own stories to this reunion.

Del, it seemed, had passed through the late-season tryouts for the school baseball team. It was astonishing—it surprised all three of them, in fact, because they had heard the fathers' stories about a year or so of waiting, that it was the reason for junior varsity, that as good as they were (and Del was the best of them), a last season in Babe Ruth League was the preparation for the glory fields of high school.

But Del's arm was the great exception. The fastball would dance and rocket from his hand, and the curve—Del had learned a curveball over the summer, despite all the warnings that it was disaster for a young arm—well, the curve would drop like a dime in a pay phone.

He couldn't hit. He fielded his position like the pitcher's mound was mined. But all of that was beside the point when the ball blazed past you and you swore that, given a second, given warning and a swift turn of the bat, you could have hit the pitch. You could have, really. But already both Gabriel and Joey knew that their friend was outpacing them, that there was something of a gift in the way Del held a baseball, in the quick and flexible whip of his arm that bent back and shuddered forth like the wind-tossed branches of a sapling.

It was golden and promising, his arm. It was the blossoming of three boyhood dreams, and they all seemed to know that it was for Del to enjoy, because it was this dream he had kept on dreaming, but that it was also theirs to enjoy as witnesses. And not only because he was their friend, but because it was the beginning, it seemed, of a glorious story.

And that day, Del was luminous. Gripping the baseball, turning it over and over in his right hand, his index and middle finger exploring the raised seams. It was all he could do to listen or pretend to listen, as Joey wrested the conversation onto music and *his* older friends, and Gabriel sat back, watching the dust motes lift and settle in the afternoon light.

Gabriel stood, moved to the window. Joey was going on about a garage band over on Gethsemane, a *concept band*, he called them, whatever that meant. "Zuice," or something like that. It was supposed to be clever, a Greek god's name spelled in a funny way. The lead singer and guitarist went to St. David's, the Catholic high school a few miles up the highway—Gabriel's spirits always sank when he heard the name, because he had been supposed to go there before the support checks became intermittent—and Joey was talking about how cool the guy was, how they let them grow their hair longer at St. David's, and how this guy understood that the old three-chord rock and roll was already passing and that a new kind of music would take its place, *a music that would endure like classical music, but it would be our own.*

Like Bach, Gabriel thought, and opened the blinds. He could tell that Joey was saying words that were *not* his own, and it seemed like a change that he didn't want to consider. He looked out the window, and saw the door to Miss Vivien's house ajar.

Trajan stepped out onto the deck. Slowly, with what seemed to be a bit of a struggle, he guided a wheelchair through the open door, a lanky, white-haired figure seated in it, fumbling with a scarf and gesturing at him with a lit cigarette. Trajan pivoted the chair and guided it down the incline toward the driveway and his car, which waited with the door wide open on the passenger side.

Gabriel frowned. He didn't know Miss Vivien traveled anywhere. He had imagined her as stationary, contained: a sort of resident spirit in Trajan's house. Because already the house seemed like Trajan's, transformed from a brick box in an identical row into something a little larger and less familiar, its drab front window shadowed by unseasonably growing holly, the spiny leaves covering dusty glass and weaving up and around the incline.

But there she was, and Trajan was taking her somewhere. His limp more pronounced because he was in a hurry, he wheeled Miss Vivien around the car, hoisted her into the passenger seat. Miss Vivien was flailing one gangly arm, waving a Chesterfield and railing at her son. Through the window Gabriel could hear her voice, muted by the glass, a kind of sawing and wavering timbre like a fiddle played from unfathomable depths.

Gabriel caught only shards of phrases.

Myself…she was saying

If not you first. And you better behave back here.

Trajan Bell bent to help his mother into the car, his shoulders bunching as though her weight were suddenly, briefly unbearable.

Lake Geneva

10/22/92

Jazzie,

I understand. It was great of Dominic to phone anyway. At fifteen you have things to do, I guess, and a holiday is a holiday, though don't forget he would be "spending it with family" if he was with me. Maybe he can visit in the summer, when the lake is warm and there's less visiting to be had.

You can let Ben see this, by the way. It will astonish him to see that I am agreeable. But seriously, I've been thinking about my teen years lately. About home and August Acres. And especially about Trajan. I know you think you heard it all back in the day, and maybe you're tired of hearing me rehash it. I know you're tired of me living there. But there are new things, Jazzie—things I am not able to explain just yet, because I am not able to understand them myself.

Yesterday, when I was looking for those student essays that had all of a sudden vanished from the table, I found the chessboard. It was in the bottom of the closet, Detached from memory, forgotten like all those things I told you about seeing in Miss Vivien's back yard. Yet here it is; and I don't remember putting it there. Maybe it surprised me more than the stories.

Because it was part of the package, you remember.

They sent me the board along with the stories. And the solitary samurai knight. Or did I tell you that as well?

And it set me remembering: the dim, smoky interiors of the house, the back yard that was and was not the same, the strange haunted music from Trajan's guitar and Miss Vivien's creaking interruptions. And the table in the shadowy parlor, the papers under the books, like Trajan was concealing something and not concealing it, at the same time.

I did not receive the chessmen. Just the one. And like you said at the time, it seemed like a strange thing to separate the pieces from the board. Or from each other.

But, then again, I knew the history of that solitary piece. But I didn't know the game. And still, I'd seen it played just enough to find the empty board melancholy, even desolate.

So I went to a hobby store the day after I found the board—a place called The Dungeon, for God's sake, there in that beaten-up three-story building on the corner of Main and Center—and I looked at chess sets.

I needed to populate the board. To make it look dwelt upon.

And yet none of the chessmen seemed right for Trajan's board. There was no samurai set to buy: just Sherlock Holmes and Civil War, Lord of the Rings (which I was tempted to buy for myself) and Alice in Wonderland. For a moment I thought about an Ancient Roman chess set, with emperors as kings and legionaries as pawns— it would go with his name, after all—but the pieces seemed too rough and unwieldy for the board.

I settled on a traditional set—they call it Staunton—and I brought it home. I tried to remember where the pieces went. Pawns in the front row, Castles on the ends, and the king somewhere in the middle, though I was still not sure about the king, whether you put him on the left or the right.

So I looked it up in the same old encyclopedia, the black and red Collier's that Mother used to have on her shelves. After all, the game hasn't changed since the Eisenhower administration, either, so whatever I found would probably be enough for decoration.

It made me remember some things, Jazzie. Like looking up the Emperor Trajan, the picture of the arch.

So I tried to remember Trajan Bell through the mist and cover of years, and was surprised to discover that the image had blurred at the edges, that my Trajan was not much clearer than the old emperor.

I recalled a face at the window. The dark, scuttling sound of something in the back yard. For some reason, a prevailing mist over Dixie Highway as it dwindled, in a long line of traffic, toward a vanishing point that was the heart of the old city.

And the board, of course. The game in progress beneath a stand of evergreen.

I'm sending you Trajan's story about chess. Because you asked. Because Dommie is learning the game, and it makes me uneasy that he is, for silly reasons. And because, eventually, you'll see the story anyway, and then I wonder what you'll think.

By the way, where the king sits depends on your side of the board.

Fondly,
Gabriel

P.S. Tell Dominic I'll mail his present before I head to Kentucky

49

$\mathcal{VI}$

Giuoco Piano
A Story by Trajan Bell

He understood Alejandro Flores only when the boy was weeping for his lost knight.

They were all staying at the Midtown, there at the corner of Main and Winooski, in the desolation of a Burlington snowstorm. Not the best hotel in the city, of course, but even the best chess players in New England were used to shabbier accommodation, and the rooms were warm.

David Corydon's room overlooked Main Street and the entrance to the hotel. Taxis coasted through the snow soundlessly, their headlights dim in the Vermont overcast. They were the only way to St. Michael's, to the hall where the tournament was held, and so David found himself outside the warm room, propped against the side of the building, looking longingly in the window at the bald light and the steaming coffee of the diner, waiting in the early Thursday morning for the cab that would get him to his match on time.

He saw the boy, then, though he had no idea who it was beneath all the clothing. Same hotel, apparently, and bound for the same destination. Fur-lined hood on his parka. Bundled against the weather.

Corydon took it for a high-school kid. Which, of course it was, but taking the boy for that was taking him for less, or we wouldn't have a story.

When the first cab arrived, David slipped in ahead of the boy. Who held back politely, even deferentially, then huddled against the diner window, his face obscured in the thick fur of the hood.

By Saturday evening, David would wonder if even this was part of the boy's strategy, if he had somehow known who David was, even in the carefully orchestrated moments of that first and snowy encounter. If the kid was setting the trap even then. But of course he wasn't thinking that now, as the taxi pulled away from the hotel and the hooded teenager shrank back beneath a snow-weighted awning. Instead, David began imagining the string of matches before him, the Alejandro Flores that awaited him at St. Michael's, as the real boy receded into the snow-struck streets behind the scudding taxi.

∗∗∗

David Corydon was a good player, even when you measured him against the world at large. Twenty years in Middlebury College's Starr Library, only thirty miles south of Burlington, had left him with little to do but master the depths of the game. His career in chess had been a circle: he dominated his competition at Middlebury from enrollment to graduation, then moved up the road to UVM, where he competed statewide, then regionally, as he studied for his masters in library science. The library position was waiting for him with the degree in hand, so after two years it was back to the alma mater with little or nothing ventured. He had followed the path of all but the most exceptional players: a quiet and cloistered job supplemented by his occasional prize money, not good enough for a sponsor or for international travel. Not good enough for anything beyond sporadic flashes of brilliance at state and regional tournaments. It added up to the kind of minor celebrity that gets you noticed at school auditoriums and rented union halls, by a handful of people who could not name a member of the Boston Red Sox or a single Beatles song, but people who knew other names—those of strange and solitary figures like Fischer and Petrosian, Botvinnik and Spassky and Tal.

It was not much to speak of, but it was all the fame David Corydon needed.

Over the last year, he had first heard the name Alejandro Flores. A Filipino prodigy — fourteen or fifteen-years-old — whose father was a Bennington professor. No doubt the Flores boy was a typical professor's child, smart and sheltered and over-stimulated. David resented him from the beginning, when he began to hear of Alejandro's brilliance in some matches down in Bennington and Marboro, how the kid was dismantling players twice and three times his age with a cool and measured poise.

"The maddening thing about him, David, is not the boy himself," Shepherd Frame had insisted in exasperation over the phone, when the boy had beaten him in a match down in Rutland. "Alejandro is actually quite silent and sweet. It's the damned father's exulting afterwards."

Frame had a Class A FIDE ranking, so he was the kind of opponent whom Corydon could beat on a regular basis—a solid, occasionally intelligent player with no higher ambitions. Corydon himself had been an Expert for a decade, the Master title always dangling elusively out of his reach. He had yet to shake the greater hopes.

And here was this upstart, this Alejandro Flores, rising through the ranks like a young god in a tired pantheon. David knew that Frame, with his great fondness for young boys, would romanticize the kid into an abused and pressured figure, the father a tyrant, a dying king schooling the young prince for the throne like something out of a fertility myth.

It was just the kind of story that Frame would bask in, weepy and amorous, fit for the speaker of a bad Housman poem. David, on the other hand, had already imagined the boy as a little monster, some kind of prodigy deprived of a childhood, with all the viciousness and sullenness of adolescence and none of its charm.

Or that was the image of menace David Corydon chose as he rode in the cab toward St. Michael's in the rising snow. The observer in him resented all prodigies, those boys who complete and accomplish while the observers watch. But the competitor in him was wiser, and competitors know first what we all know eventually: it's less complicated to prepare for menace. An opponent you render monstrous in your imagination is easier to face, can be taken down without remorse or second thought.

Corydon was listing the boy's intolerable qualities as the cab turned off 89 into the St. Michael's campus. It was inevitable that he and the Flores boy would meet, unless a terrible mistake cost one of them an early match. And it was easier to imagine Alejandro in simple, abstract colors, like the geometrical movements over the chessboard.

Because that's the way a lot of chess players see the game. Their vision extends beyond the pieces.

Corydon had learned to anticipate five, six, sometimes seven moves ahead—not the clairvoyance of a Grand Master, probably not nearly as prophetic as the boy he would eventually face. But he had enough foresight, enough to know that chess is a better game when stripped of distracting emotion, when the pieces, mathematical and relentless, rise into diagrams, diagonals and verticals and angles above the wood or plastic of bishop or pawn.

It was like they left their bodies then. Like they rose and converged on a plane where they were energy, or where they were purified of the carved horses and the castles and the mitres that constrained them. They became like wizards, or like Dante's suicides freed by a strange act of grace, afloat over the bondage of the imprisoning trees.

David Corydon shook his head. It always made him laugh when poetry came on the scene. But it was no time for laughter. He descended into himself, watched the flick of the windshield wipers as the cab coasted on a patina of ice to the south of the awakening city.

The Herrouet Theater on the north campus of St. Michael's College was prepared for the matches—tables, clocks and boards designed to give each pair of the sixteen invited players their own private audience. Corydon was guided to his table, where he took the light into account, then examined the board. He lifted the black Staunton knight to test its weight (always the black knight, his one concession to the world of superstition among chess players) and seated himself in each of the chairs.

It was good enough, this setting. Better than most. He felt the rising anticipation of the approaching match—a man about his own age with the impossible name of Dragon, whom he had bested on five occasions and expected to thrash again. Flores could be the next match, but Corydon tried not to look that many moves ahead. Instead, he urged himself to be content in the light, in the pleasant heft of the piece, in the diagrammatic board that hung on an easel behind the table, a grid-like abstraction of the chessboard, with "Mr. Corydon" above the white pieces and "Mr. Dragon" below the black.

He breathed in the smell of pine and polish, lit a cigarette, and headed for what the school called the hospitality table. "Tea, please," he called out to the distracted college girl near a pair of battered percolators. She seemed entranced by a long-haired boy in a fatigue jacket, so David turned to the modest array of muffins and sticky buns, wondering which ones of them had not been placed out the night before by a lazy student volunteer.

"Here's your tea, sir," a soft voice beside him murmured, and Corydon turned to face a stunning Asian girl, her hair raggedly cropped at mid-ear and only the slightest hint of liner to enhance her dark eyes, a dusting of makeup (or perhaps only the flush of cold weather) to ruddy her flawless features.

"Thank you, my dear," Corydon replied. His hand shook slightly as he took the cup from her. She was radiant, dressed boyishly, in the flannel shirt, baggy jeans, and brogans that were standard Vermont college issue. Around her neck a pendant—a pawn from a Japanese chess set, as far as Corydon could tell. A samurai archer, bow drawn and aimed into the air, into a celestial nothingness. Despite the setting, despite the fact that she was far too young, Corydon found himself staring at the pendant, how it hung precisely at the topmost button of the shirt, moving softly with each restrained exhalation.

Her stare was direct—honest, but not brazen—and he breathed again only when she turned away.

She looked over her shoulder to assure he was watching her leave. She was not disappointed, and her smile confirmed that Corydon would not be disappointed, either. In fact, he was incredulous that someone so dark and dazzling could award her attentions to a man over twice her age.

By Monday, he could not imagine how mistaken he had been. How he could have been fooled so completely by so little artifice.

By what, in fact, was probably no artifice at all.

$$***$$

He made short work of J.T. Dragon. Corydon felt like St. George as the little man across from him squinted and smoked, the air above the table blue with their coalescing fumes. Some of the more squeamish observers left the hazy room ten moves into the game—perhaps because of the smoke accumulating over three hours of play, but more likely because the game was over by then. A knight fork, two moves away, and little J.T. had missed it until it was inevitable, until the best he could do was trade Corydon's knight for his rook.

J.T. Dragon tipped his king on the seventeenth move. Swore a little under his breath.

It was over.

Tomorrow Dragon would play white, and of course he would have the resultant advantage. But they both knew—*everyone* knew—it would not be enough. J.T. had reached a kind of ceiling to his game, that kind of mediocrity that passes for excellence in the larger world. But you know it for what it is when you see it over the tight, smoky boards of championships. It's what happens to men in middle age—all but the luckiest of them, or the most persistent or rare. And there was luck indeed, Corydon figured, in having lasted this long, having reached your forties before your patches and unravelings were on display.

Corydon did not bother to size up his next opponent, although he overheard in conversation at the hospitality table that Alejandro Flores was dismantling someone over in the farthest room. So he relaxed in his victory, scanned the sparse crowd for a sign of that striking girl, but the room had reverted to a men's club, as was often the case at chess tournaments. Slowly he sipped a second cup of tea and contemplated what to have for lunch after such an early conclusion to his day.

"Hush!" whispered someone beside him. "There he is!"

He knew instinctively that he was the subject, and strained his ears to eavesdrop. The conversation was at a distance, but between two elderly men, one of whom was hard of hearing, it seemed.

Flores, he heard the other man say. *Flores and Corydon. Next round.*

Corydon was suddenly tired. Not from the exertions to defeat J.T. Dragon as much as from the anticipation of what lay ahead of him—the tournament brackets that would lead him toward Alejandro Flores all too quickly and soon. It seemed unfair: they were clearly the best two players in the tournament, and you should save such pairings for the final days, so that the games could culminate like a good story, in the battle between hero and villain.

Not that the boy was a villain, mind you. He was merely exceptional. If there was a villain in the piece, Corydon decided, it was the evil father, who, like the stepmother of the fairy tales, held the child beneath some kind of enchantment.

He laughed at his own thought. Shepherd Frame, it seemed, was too romantic an influence.

But that night, back at the hotel, poring over a second Scotch and a dog-eared paperback on the Sicilian Defense, Corydon's thoughts drifted like ash from a bonfire, afloat to the floors above, where he knew that Alejandro was lodged for the night, probably over books of his own, plotting the course of his coming games.

Eventually, Corydon dog-eared the page in the book. Pouring a third stiff drink, the glass tilted in his right hand and a cigarette drooping ash in his left, he stepped out of his room into the glaring light of the corridor, leaving the door ajar. Almost furtively, he took the stairwell to the floor above, setting the Scotch on the landing and opening the door to the hall.

A solitary naked bulb sputtered over his head, and the path before him wavered in shadow. A voice spilled out of a room at the end of the hall, muted and indecipherable, as though he was hearing it underwater. Feeling a strange combination of excitement and prurience, like he was an inebriant spy in an old, flickering movie, he moved on tiptoe to the source of the sound.

Someone was scolding a child. The voice, domineering and harsh, hovered around the far door like smoke, its tone unmistakable though the language was unfamiliar. The child answered in English.

"I still won, didn't I?"

A flurry of incomprehensible scolding, like an incantation, then the child:

"I'll be ready. It's hard. You don't understand."

Corydon leaned against the door, an uncanny heat rising to his forehead.

He understood. No matter the language, which he guessed was Tagalog, he understood the drama in the room.

Back to the landing he crept, the voice behind him sinking into wavering light. He picked up the glass and headed down the stairs, only half wondering that the ice in the Scotch had melted in the cold stairwell on this colder night. It was almost refuge to reach the room, the veiled interchange between the boy and his father drifting in his half-drunken imagination. Flinging open the door, halfway to the bed, still translating from the fierce, incomprehensible language, he brushed his foot against something on the floor.

He looked down, wobbled a little. His eyes focused.

An ivory chessman lay on the worn carpet, its carved bow pointing toward the window.

His sleep was fitful and erotic, peopled by unfathomable voices, dark eyes, and fleeting movements across a lamp-lit board. Once he woke with a start, imagining the wingbeats of some lost, disenfranchised dove outside his window in the impossibly frigid night.

✳✳✳

On the next day, Dragon went down like his namesake.

Sputtering and smoking, J.T. rose from the board by the fourth move. He began to circle the table. He lit another cigarette.

Corydon sipped a cup of tea, serene and smug as an English baron. The game was still young, but J.T. was already about the task of beating himself. It was only a matter of moves: Corydon could wait out the morning, let Black bring an already crumbling attack against the firm battlements of White's Sicilian Defense.

This one was inevitable.

And it was all Corydon could do to stay with the board. Several times he reeled in his floating thoughts. It was too soon to think of Alejandro Flores. Come back to the here and now, he told himself.

And there it is, in a nutshell: the dilemma of any chess player in the wide, middle-range of gifts and insights. When do you look ahead, and when do you rest in the solidity of wood or marble?

By the twelfth move, the gallery began to fill. Younger people slipped into the chairs behind J.T. and Corydon. J.T. propped his chin in his hands, glared at his disadvantages.

Corydon, on the other hand, felt the low simmer of excitement. The match before him was over. Three, maybe even four moves down the road, it would be clear to J.T. Dragon that the advantage of first move had not availed him.

But the late arrivals in the gallery signaled the news. There was no doubt that this wave of young people had come from another match.

As J.T.'s hand hovered over a pawn, then withdrew, as the little man squinted and reached into his pocket for the pack of cigarettes, Corydon let his mind float into another room of the theater. He imagined it there: a young boy his thoughts had barely outlined, leaning back in a chair. Behind the kid loomed the shadow of the dark, protective father, but it wasn't the old man's moment, not by a long shot. As his opponent tipped the king and rose from the table, Alejandro Flores steepled his fingers and forgot to smile, the short work of the morning a prelude, a clearing of thoughts.

The signs were in the room and in the air. They were on for tomorrow.

***

Corydon returned to the hotel, spent the evening with *Chess Review* and the *Thomas Mann Reader*, an anthology suggested to him by Shep Frame. He wasn't much of a reader: he claimed that a library who employs a bookworm is like a tavern that sets up its most regular drunk as a bartender, but he knew the comparison made no sense, or not much. It was a side effect of chess, he figured, that your thoughts broke free of your eyes in a search for patterns and tendencies, and after half an hour with this Mann fellow, Corydon set up his board and played through one of young Fischer's superb, incisive games—a King's Indian Defense from the late 50s. His attention moved from notation to pieces, then back to notation with a rising amazement and respect. The game, like the work of any genius, he figured, made sense when you looked back at it: the growing pressure on Olafsson, the point at which the older player is simply doing numbers, counting pawns, thinking that a piece-for-piece exchange will balance it all out, forgetting that position is paramount...

That indeed position can be everything.

David Corydon set down the magazine, contemplated the end game. There was something about the pawn at K7—at the edge of the chessboard's quiet chaos—that got his attention and kept him awake.

He lifted the piece closer, examined the dark purple blotches in the wood. He had ordered the set on impulse from an Oregon wood carver—one of the few excesses in a librarian's austere life. Bay wood, myrtle... whatever you wanted to call it.

Mountain laurel was the name he preferred. Laurel, for the ornament of the victors.

He inhaled the sweet, residual odor of the pawn, his thoughts entangled in the approaching match.

∗∗∗

Flores arrived late for the first game.

Corydon could not help but be amused at this oldest of strategies, intended to ruffle the opponent, to set off timing and temper.

Well, he had seen it before. Old theatre, like a comedy from Shakespeare.

He smiled, lit a cigarette. Just to let the spectators know that stagecraft could not harm David Corydon. That even though Alejandro Flores had a promising future, the future was not yet, was not this game.

That instead of the boy taking David Corydon to the theatre, David Corydon was about to take the boy to school.

Of course, even those who have paid only passing attention to the story so far know what is about to happen. For the last few days, the spectators had done what spectators always do, as readers of the last few pages must have glimpsed the second of Alejandro Flores' strategies. In fact, at this point David Corydon is the only one vulnerable to surprise, and you must be asking yourself, not "what is about to happen?" but "how in the world could Corydon have avoided knowing it?"

For Alejandro Flores was the beautiful Asian girl of the previous days, a boy so lovely he had captured the heated imaginings of Shepherd Frame and, with the least of disguises—a disguise so spare it was probably not even intentional—had unsettled the thoughts of his opponent, who gaped at him now across the chessboard, the ash lengthening and bending on the end of his neglected cigarette.

"If you'd put that out, please, Mr. Corydon," the boy recommended with a soft smile, moving his pawn to K4—an unexceptional opening to this most exceptional game.

Corydon was befuddled. He had not stopped to ask, those days ago at the courtesy table. There had been no need to ask, he had been sure of that. The boy had seemed so easily and comfortably feminine that they both had played to the illusion. For a moment the chess pieces were incomprehensible, carved pieces of wood on a geometric floor, and Corydon forgot how the bishops moved.

For a moment, he glimpsed what his own life was like— would continue to be like—outside this marginal game. The files and rows of the chessboard faded into the files and rows of the library—the institutional furniture and dust and fluorescent lights. The walk home to Weybridge Street in the desolate cold. And the cycle of days and years in which that had been (and would continue to be) not only familiar country, but the only country there was.

Corydon leaned back in his chair, snuffed his cigarette on the table to the distaste of his opponent, and collected himself.

But it was almost too late already. Alejandro's pieces had seized the center of the board and, within the first eight moves, the boy was a pawn ahead—an advantage that generally spelled victory in a match at this level. Alejandro smiled at him across the table, long brown fingers poised over a knight, as if he might or might not move it.

What was his next intention?

Corydon caught himself guessing, anticipating three and four moves in advance, but the pathways were cloudy. He could not picture the pieces in those future positions.

There was tomorrow, Corydon told himself. A chance to start everything again. Only one game behind—steep, but not impossible odds.

So be it, he was about to say. His hand moved toward his king, his finger extended to topple the piece—the traditional gesture of resignation, or surrender.

But something widened in those dark, fathomless eyes across from him, which looked up, back to the board, and up again.

Corydon withdrew his hand, looked over his shoulder.

An Asian man of about his own age had entered the room.

The Bennington professor. The father in question.

Corydon fastened his eyes on his opponent. Whose move it was.

Alejandro rested his cheek upon his hand, turned suddenly sullen and fifteen, all of his radiance flying from him with some kind of spiritual centrifugal force. He was diminished, no longer girlish and beautiful. With a swift, almost undetectable movement of his fingers, Alejandro brushed his eyes, leaving a dark brown smear on his eyelids as though he had not slept for several nights. And his next move, an obvious attempt to create a knight fork and force Corydon to choose between queen or rook, was a tactic born of insomnia—a move that if, countered properly, would reverse the tide of the game entirely.

Corydon waited a while, inspected the board. Surely he was missing something. A rising murmur among the spectators told him that some of them had seen a mistake as well. But was it a mistake? Or was it a disguise—yet another layer in the boy's exceptional calculations?

Remember that this was one of those players, after all, whose vision of the game had moved beyond the simple relations of pieces into fields of force, a sort of abstract understanding that was half geometry, half instinct. Alejandro, Corydon knew, could glance at a board from across the room, see only the arrangements of black and white, and tell you within a second—a solitary second—who was going to win.

I was about to resign anyway, Corydon told himself. No doubt he has an ambush for me, something I'll see a dozen moves up the road, if not sooner. I can resign then. What difference between last move and the next?

But it seemed apparent—unless Corydon was missing something and missing it grievously—that the mere entrance of Alejandro's father had thrown the kid off game. How or why that would have happened this time was a mystery to Corydon: after all, the old man supposedly accompanied his son to every match, hovering over his shoulder like a boding raven

The kind of thing that happens, he had heard, with promising boys who had difficult parents. But it seemed a special shame that a boy of Alejandro's talent was about to lose like this. For his brilliance to come up against a child-devouring father, like some old myth that Corydon tried to remember for a moment, his eyes drifting away from the board to the downy curve of the boy's jaw.

No.

And no. Alejandro Flores had to learn the hard lessons, providing this was one of them. The cost of the game was everything, and he might be only fifteen, but he was old enough to know that.

Corydon brought his bishop slanting in from a far file, removed Alejandro's fumbled knight. For a moment his stomach tightened at the possibility that there was some nuance he had missed. Then despite himself, contrary to all his charity and experience, Corydon looked up into his opponent's eyes...

Which were brimming with tears, as Alejandro Flores examined his developed pawns, held his hand momentarily above his one freed castle...

Then moved to the king, tipped it over with a clatter, and stalked from the room, the Asian professor at his heels like some hungry, avenging ghost.

✳✳✳

As you might expect, David Corydon would go on to win the

tournament. But that night, he mapped out a strategy for the next day.

Tomorrow Alejandro would play black, would be on the defensive. Corydon hovered between planning a gradual, stately offense—a *giuoco piano*, or 'soft game' as they called it—or moving to something swift and relentless, something to throw the boy back on his heels and to use his father to advantage.

He decided to walk around the Midtown Hotel to clear his mind, to plot the opening moves.

Burlington had fallen into the deepest cold. It was the kind of crisp, dry New England air in which your nose hairs freeze and bristle, so Corydon wrapped a scarf around his face. Three young people were seated on the stoop outside the diner, their parkas pulled tightly over their faces so that Corydon could not tell who or what they were.

College students, he supposed. From what he understood, while St. Michael's hosted the chess tournament, the Byrds were up the road, in concert at the larger University of Vermont. He was glad that his pleasures were quiet, as the snow at the edge of the sidewalk creaked aridly beneath his boot.

Crossing Main Street, he headed for the storefronts that faced the hotel. The clouds had given way to clear skies and moonlight, and had it not been for that, David Corydon would have missed Alejandro Flores' ascent to the roof of the Midtown Hotel. It was the boy's shadow he noticed, after all.

Or he knew it was Alejandro, no matter how bundled the poor child was against a cold that, in moments, he had no intention of feeling. He recognized the parka as that of the considerate teenager from Thursday morning, but he knew it was Alejandro by the gentle curve of the boy's leg, as graceful as a laurel branch, and as out of place in a world of winter.

It should have alarmed Corydon, to see the boy on high, but by this time he was less accustomed to thinking ahead. For a moment, a foolish passage of poetry drifted in and out of his memory...

> Smart lad, to slip betimes away
> From fields where glory does not stay
> And early though the laurel grows
> It withers quicker than the rose.

It was stupid stuff. He would have to ask Shepherd Frame about it.

All the while, as he mulled over the sight of the boy above the fourth story windows, outlined against the northern sky, the words from the poem giving Alejandro Flores another shape and meaning, it did not occur to David Corydon that the boy intended to jump, than anything more than accident had brought him to that place and height.

A cold breeze lifted from somewhere in the southwest, borne no doubt off of Lake Champlain and slicing a frigid diagonal over the city. Alejandro leapt off the roof, into the embrace of the icy wind, and for a moment David Corydon lurched toward the sidewalk, cried out and extended his hand in an old gesture of resignation...

And just as suddenly, Alejandro Flores was carried aloft. Buoyed by the wind, he rose above the hotel, his thin arms constrained by the absurd bundling of his parka. Corydon lifted his hands to the spectacle, as the boy seemed to cartwheel in the night air and discover his bearings, now lying face down on the current of wind, which bore him northward: toward Montreal and a new language and freedom. Corydon watched from below, the faint sound of approaching sirens in his ear.

VII

You could hear it in the middle of October on any afternoon that you walked down Gabriel's part of August Street.

The regular, almost ritual slap of Del's fastball against his father's glove, and Mr. Robinson's encouragement, half plea and half bluster, until those sounds were quickly becoming all that Gabriel knew and remembered about his friend.

He didn't even talk to Del any more. Their common ground of the Cardinals had disintegrated into embarrassed silence when their unbeatable heroes, unbeatable indeed through the first half of the World Series, emerged from a rain delay in the fourth game as a different, shaken team. It was like they had crawled from underground, that the light was too much for them, and the anemic Detroit Tigers, behind the suddenly invincible left arm of a fat, jug-eared pitcher named Lolich, caught up with them and beat them in seven games.

How about them Cardinals? they had asked, greeting each other until the rain and the fourth game, when the greetings and the conversation dwindled into an embarrassment that had something—but not quite everything—to do with the changed fortunes of their team.

Miss Vivien came back, of course, from wherever it was that Trajan hauled her on that September afternoon. For a month afterwards, Trajan's work on the house seemed to pause; in the midst of this new stillness, Miss Vivien's place took on a resemblance of solidity. For a while, it promised and boded less, its Roman brick serene, like an undisturbed pond.

It made Gabriel wonder if something was swimming beneath the surfaces.

Late in the month, as he helped Mr. Hardy put up Halloween decorations in the absence of his son (Joey, as usual, was cup bearer to Zuice), he received a kind of answer. Up the street he saw Trajan on Miss Vivien's incline, broad shoulders and unruly hair, baggy sweatshirt and sagging jeans, shears in hand as he leaned over the railing to trim the chaos of holly.

He said his good-byes, quick and polite, to Mr. Hardy. Hands in pockets, he rambled up August Street to the corner, where he could hear at last the ticking sound of the shears as they sliced through thorny leaves and thin branches.

"Hola, Gabriel," Trajan said, the name strangely accented in what Gabriel guessed was a Spanish pronunciation, although he was paying so little attention in Spanish I that he could not be altogether sure.

"Hola," he replied, and Trajan must have sensed the current in his voice.

"Autumn's a sad time of year," he said, still shearing the holly. "'While barred clouds bloom the soft-dying day,' and all that."

"Keats?"

Trajan turned, ghosted a smile. "Right you are, *hombre*."

Gabriel smiled back. "Sooner or later. You know what they say about the blind hog."

"Gets his acorn. Something like that." Trajan set the shears on the incline. "So what's doin' at old Jeff?"

It surprised Gabriel to hear Trajan refer to the high school—"Jefferson High School" on the façade and in the phone books—by the name the students used. Trajan was far too old to know that kind of thing, was surely forty and maybe even older. It also seemed like a kind of privilege, like you would almost let an old guy call the school "old Jeff" if he had gone there or something, but Trajan had come down from New England after all.

But then, Trajan had spent some time around here, hadn't he?

So it was partly from surprise that Gabriel answered weakly, his hands deep in his pockets now, clutching two quarters and the house key. He thumbed the smooth teeth of the key as Trajan sat down on the incline and regarded him.

"Everything all right, Gabriel?"

It was more of a statement that a question. Gabriel nodded.

Trajan picked up the shears and turned them in his big hand, examining the blades as though he was looking for some kind of damage or flaw. "You know," he said at last, "I remember when I first started over there. It was a—"

"You went to Jeff, then?"

Trajan laughed softly. "Back in the Bronze Age. We wrote with a stylus on wax back then, so the excuse was always 'my little brother melted my homework'. But I still remember it, remember that the hardest thing about going there was all the changes at first, how high school seemed so different from junior high, and how everybody pretended it was just like going to the next grade, but it wasn't, not really…"

He waved, like he was brushing away the thought.

"And sometimes…" Gabriel began, wondering if he should go on with this, wondering how much he should say about his new and peculiar sadness. "Well…. sometimes you don't see the guys like you used to. Sometimes it gets…"

"Lonely?" Trajan asked, his broad face framed by the open blades of the shears.

"I guess," Gabriel replied. "Well, no…not really. Just… well, just weird."

Trajan nodded, and turned back to the trimming.

They sat together silently for what seemed like a long time to Gabriel. He thought, as he waited, that Trajan was waiting for something as well. Something stilled in the air around them, like a kind of vacuum that was filled by the rising whir of cicadas, a sound that rose above them, seemed to whirl, then ebbed away.

"But you know," Trajan said finally, "high school to college is even a bigger leap. Like a long sea voyage at the bow of a ship you are certain could sink at any moment. And then, when you come back…"

The rattle of the insects circled above them and stilled, as Trajan's voice trailed into silence.

Gabriel leaned forward, propped himself against the railing.

"It's…it *is* hard not seeing the guys anymore, Mister…. Trajan," he said. "It's like we didn't fight or nothing, but things have changed."

Trajan nodded. "I understand. Better than you think."

He set the shears down again.

"I had a friend like that once, Gabriel. When I was up north. This was a really special friend. My Georgia Peach."

Once again, Gabriel felt as though he was on the edge of mystery. The October wind seemed to calm around the two of them, to create a pocket in which the past and its impossibilities could happen.

"I don't know," Trajan began, his eyes fixed on the horizon, on the Indiana hills and the slow descent of the autumn sun. "I don't know whether you are old enough to know this kind of thing, Gabriel. Oh, never mind. Do you think that I should trim this holly lower? Or is this about right, do you think?"

"What about your friend?" Gabriel asked, his curiosity drawn forth. "What about your Georgia Peach?"

Trajan smiled, and though the smile seemed only sad and haunted, there was something beneath it that was unsettling and familiar. Gabriel imagined hot weather and a kind of shadowy, sour smell, but he brushed aside his imagining, and it was Kentucky autumn, and Trajan was clipping the holly, and the smell of crushed evergreen brisk on the temperate air.

"Another time," Trajan said. "A time when you're older."

Gabriel reddened. He hated that kind of dismissal. The

tremor in the air had passed, and he was quickly forgetting it, and he felt more insulted than threatened now, as though he had been benched in an important game, or kept back a year at school.

"But I will tell you this much. Because you may not be old enough to know it, but you're old enough to live it, it seems. At least to come upon a parting in the roads, like they say—a place you can't go back to, even if it seems like you're being offered the chance."

His eyes lowered now.

Gabriel had no idea what he was talking about, but he figured it must be important.

"I know," Trajan said softly, and in that softness was a kind of admitting. "You're thinking what you wouldn't give for last season: for the heat and the dust, and for baseball stretching endlessly before you—before the *three* of you, over in that yard next door.

"Well, it doesn't matter what you'd give for it. Doesn't matter how much, because the price of turning back is pretty much everything, Gabriel."

"What do you mean, Trajan?"

Trajan picked up the shears once more, turned back to the trimming, his broad back shedding wings of sweat onto his white shirt. "Never mind" he muttered, the dismissal almost lost in the forest of holly.

"Well, you brought it up," Gabriel insisted, still smarting a little from uncovered truths. He wished that Trajan would just leave off about his friends, would just mind his own business, and with that thought he turned back toward the street, toward his house, and it took Trajan's calling him a third time to bring him back.

"I'm sorry, Gabriel. It just doesn't seem like a story for you. Not just yet. Maybe not ever."

Gabriel folded his arms, stared at the roof of Miss Vivien's house. Trajan propped the shears against the railing, leaned against the incline and produced a cigarette.

"You brought it up," Gabriel said again, struggling to strip the touchiness from his voice.

"I know, Gabriel. It's only that…"

Gabriel shrugged, manufactured a smile. "It's cool, Trajan. Whatever you wanna tell me or not."

He started toward the house again, and again Trajan called. Gabriel stopped but did not turn around.

"You can't tell that I told you this, Gabriel."

Gabriel turned. All of a sudden, it sounded more interesting. Trajan smiled again. Gabriel knew he had been tested.

But it would be years before he knew whether he had passed the test.

He stepped back into the yard, as though he was walking across a crust of ice and there were depths below him that he had yet to understand. "Why not, Trajan?" he asked, and prepared for whatever would come.

Trajan pushed his glasses onto the bridge of his nose, regarded Gabriel over the taped and tortoise-shell frames.

"'Coz I asked you to? That's not good enough? I know this seems like mystical claptrap to you. You'd better go on."

Gabriel shrugged.

Trajan picked up the shears again. For a moment it was as though he grew larger—deeper, as Gabriel would describe it later—the shears glittering in the tame October sunlight as though they were wet with something thicker than sap or dew. "Let me tell you about my Georgia Peach, then," he said. "But remember that stories cover other stories, and that some of what you hear is meant for you and some of it is just me telling you what happened. It's up to you to figure it out."

Gabriel crouched by the incline. "What do you mean, Trajan?"

"It's up to you to figure it, Gabriel. Like I said. But this one—this story—took place up in Vermont. We were the only two Southerners I knew of, because up there Kentuckians were Southerners, pure and simple—none of this regional hair-splitting and haggling we do down here. And Artie…well Artie was well traveled, with a family that had spent time in Europe and Burma and even in Tibet. So I guess neither of us was the Southerner that everybody thought we were.

"But that's neither here nor there, Gabriel. Let's just say it's what drew the two of us together, Artie and me."

In the pause that followed, Gabriel tried to think of this Artie. To imagine someone, unaccountable and remote—someone who had left Trajan's story before Gabriel had even entered it.

And *Artie?* he asked, and *Artie?* again, until Trajan explained what it was short for. Then Gabriel thought of the forest goddess Artemis, then of Jim West's sidekick Artemus, then of disguise and costumery, of stories covering stories, until his wits jostled a little, and Ross Martin, packing derringers in a paisley vest, transformed into a goddess in a white tunic, carrying a green and golden bow. And it was with the goddess that Gabriel's thoughts settled, when Trajan said that his own Artie was a blonde, and said it with a certain tenderness that made Gabriel just a little embarrassed to look at him.

Again, he tried to think of the goddess. In a little white tunic, a moony crown on her blonde hair. He wrestled back to the image again and again, but it wouldn't stick, not really.

So Gabriel gave up, uncomfortably.

He looked closer, toward the railing he had seen blossom in vine and leaf that time in August. He listened to the story, his eyes coursing down the beams, looking awkwardly for bud or branch in the sleeping incline.

"I'd visit Artie's dormitory room, or Artie would visit mine," Trajan continued softly. "It just depended on whose roommate was late coming in, or sometimes away for the night. But it was better in the snow of that first year in Vermont, both of us bundled up by late October, our coats so thick and heavy it was hard to know who and what we were, and if we hadn't been waiting for each other, we might not have recognized each other, if you understand what I mean."

Gabriel nodded. But of course he was not sure he

understood. Not sure whether Trajan understood, either.

"There was something about Artie and the outdoors," Trajan continued dreamily, shifting his weight and stretching his long legs down the incline. "Something about the way the wind seemed to calm down in front of us, like the two of us together could part its current. And Artie was the best of audiences, someone with an ear for the guitar and a tolerance for a voice that was already tired of singing. You have to remember that this was before the Beatles, before Elvis even, and so my serenades were old Tin Pan Alley standards. Things like "Shine On Harvest Moon" and "Bye Bye Blackbird," and older songs, like Stephen Foster, that reminded us both of home. It wasn't much, but it was all I could do any more, 'cause I set down the guitar when I was about your age, was tired of all that classical training and of Mother's telling everyone how much she paid for lessons.

"But this was different. This was because I wanted to play for someone...

"So maybe Artie's ear was more tolerant for a reason, you think?"

Gabriel nodded absently again. He had visited Galway twice, and his father in Michigan for half of one summer when he was nine, but never had he sought out reminders of August Acres. And as for the songs...well, "Love Me Do" was as far back as Gabriel went, so that even when Trajan mentioned Elvis it was history—an oily, leering semblance sacred to his mother, enshrined for another generation like the dead President and his Senator brother.

"Well," Trajan continued, lighting another cigarette with the glowing butt of the first one, "Artie and I stayed close through that first winter. It was something new for me, being away from Mother and all, so at last I could pick my friends as I saw fit. And Artie was the first one to call me 'Trajan', and I was so glad to get rid of that 'Marcus'.

"But I was even gladder for Artie. For the long walks in the daytime, and blankets and coffee into the shank of the night."

Trajan paused. It looked like he was edging against

something, looking back over a distance. Then thinking twice about it, and turning away.

"But it doesn't let up by March, Gabriel. The snow, that is. In Vermont it arrives in the fall and settles, and it's sometimes into May before you see green ground again. The time was that when somebody died up there, they iced them until late May or early June, when the ground softened enough to drop them the required six feet. That was way back, though—don't look at me like that. Nowadays they have the machinery, of course. It doesn't matter if you die in winter or at midsummer.

"There's a small town—a village, really—south of the college. It's called Ripton, and right outside it was where Robert Frost had his cabin. But at the college there was this gossip about it, this underground notion that it was the incest capital of New England. Maybe even of the world. And maybe I shouldn't be telling you this…"

Gabriel shook his head. "Go on."

He wasn't sure what Trajan was talking about. But he liked the fact that it seemed to be forbidden.

"But I didn't put stock in it, not until the next spring. Around the time they used to break ground for the bodies out in the cemeteries, Ripton would fill up with people down from the mountains, coming to the store for the first time in the year. These albinos with cornsilk hair and watery, red eyes. I've heard there were worse specimens, but I can vouch for the albinos."

Gabriel had seen an albino rat once. He struggled to imagine how that paleness and frailty would fit on a human form.

But Trajan was not finished. "Outside of Ripton," he continued, "up State Road 125, which branches east toward Breadloaf just north of Mt. Pleasant and Satan's Kingdom, there's a shock of woods that is still pretty thick, even though the environs have been cleared away almost to the Windsor County border. Artie used to think that it had to be the woods that Frost was calling 'lovely, dark and deep' in that poem of his, and if you think I'm a fool for poetry, Gabriel, you should have known Artie…

"But anyway. Anyway.

"It came to early March of '47, Gabriel. The time you'd be expecting more than a hint of spring—maybe the outright buds on the branches and certainly not the forsaken stretch of snow you'd see off of 125, at the spot where we parked my Chrysler— it was almost new back then—and headed off for a walk into the woods.

"You know this is gonna be fateful, don't you?

"You know it's not gonna end happy?"

For a moment, the October wind seemed to rise, bearing with it the whiff of burning leaves and, from over on Flora, the sounds of Zuice cranking up, ripping the first few chords of "Jumpin Jack Flash" into the suddenly still autumn air.

"So do you wanna hear it?" Trajan asked. "You still can turn back from this."

When Gabriel did not respond, he continued.

He wanted it told, Gabriel guessed.

"So there we were. And what you never expect is a rising snow in March. Warmer weather, yes. It was above freezing when we began the walk, and the snow was glazed and sweating underfoot—slippery going, and even more slippery, we guessed, after nightfall, when the temperature dropped again.

"We were gonna hunt. Or I was. I was big on the bow and arrow back then. I still take it out when the seasons change, but I'm not shooting at anything these days. I was hunting, and Artie...well, Artie was there to be with me. We had no plans to be out after dark. We walked on the edge of the woods, and eventually Artie did what Artie usually did, beckoned and encouraged me deeper into the first dark line of trees.

"I said no, that time. I knew we should be headed back toward the campus. You could see it in the sky, in the iron depths behind the overcast, and there was no promise for sun in the whole horizon. I wanted to get back, to the blankets and the coffee and the safety of my dorm room, back to Keats and the Burlington radio playing Chopin down the dial and over the static. Back to the nights I had grown accustomed to loving.

"But instead I followed that green parka into a deeper green, because it was Artie, and no matter what you think, it was Artie who called the shots between us.

"By that time the snow had begun, spitting wetly as the temperature dropped, swarming and stinging my face like a legion of inept bees. Once I lost Artie in the swirl of snow, and it's funny how you panic the first time something happens, when later—when it's the real thing—you're almost uncannily calm. That first time, though, I was alarmed, followed a shadow into a cluster of evergreens, dried vines clutching my ankles and that kind of cold that happens in Vermont, so cold that the hairs in your nose freeze when you inhale..."

"I never been in that deep a cold," Gabriel said, because he had to say something, because it was getting colder and colder on the sunny incline.

Trajan nodded. "...and there's no knowing what I mean, not really, until you are. And it was frightening, a little, with Artie dipping in and out of sight until it wore me out a little, until I figured it would be best to stop, stay where I was.

"Be a still point in the turning woods.

"It was then that the deer came out of the brake."

Gabriel frowned. "The deer?"

"I know it was March. Way out of season, because you hunt deer in the fall, Gabriel. But you know that."

Gabriel nodded, though he had no idea when the deer seasons were.

"Here was this buck," Trajan continued. "The best buck-hunting country was downstate around Rutland, so this fellow must have strayed north till he was miles out of his stomping ground. He just walked into the clearing, Gabriel, and the season slipped out of my mind, and I'm thinking this is a chance that you don't get often, that I could drop him with a bow, with a single clean shot...."

"Well, did you?" Gabriel asked. It did not seem like a part of Trajan he wanted to think about, something sly and predatory.

"No. I didn't shoot. But there's something exhilarating—

exciting, I mean—about having a creature in your sights. You see it differently, then. In all its…you know what 'frailty' is, Gabriel?"

Gabriel nodded, a little impatiently. "I know, I know. So you didn't shoot it?"

"Artie started calling me right after that," Trajan said. "There'd been…an accident."

Suddenly the deer vanished from Gabriel's thoughts. "An accident?"

"An injured leg. You know it was March, and the snow and the footing…"

Trajan's voice trailed off, his eyes averted. But he continued.

"I found Artie from the shouting, lying in the brake not far from me. Maybe the accident had rousted the deer, I don't know. But at any rate, Artie and I linked arms so we wouldn't lose each other again, and we turned about and headed out of the woods. The trouble was, we had lost the way out. The trees arched over us, all cavernous and shadowy, taking on ice and bending branches like they were weeping in sympathy with us, and turned around in that gloom we couldn't tell that the light was failing. The thin ice under our feet, sinking in snow to our ankles, and then to our knees.

"Only around then did I start to get scared, Gabriel. The temperature was dropping steeply, and the dark was closing in. I was looking for light in the snow, and it wasn't there. Then Artie says, 'Go on ahead of us, Traje, I'll keep up with you, don't worry.'

"Man, I didn't like it at all, not at all. But I knew why Artie had said it, because obviously I was the bigger and the stronger of the two of us, and I could plow through the snow and leave a trail behind me, and the purchase would be easier, and you couldn't miss the trail, even in a blizzard."

Trajan leaned back against the incline railing. He was listening for something. Behind him, the house seemed to lie in silence and secrecy, as undisturbed as those snowy woods he was talking about.

Dark and deep, but not lovely. Gabriel could tell that Trajan did not relish hearing a call from back there.

He tried to imagine Artie in those long-ago woods. Tried to picture long blond hair under a toboggan, a slight form wreathed in a heavy coat. For some reason, he could not see it, maybe because he was imagining it wrong.

After all, Gabriel had never seen snow that deep.

"Well, that's when it got worse," Trajan said, his voice more hushed, hovering in that middle country between conversation and whisper. "I could hear Artie behind me until about the time I saw sunlight, or what I thought was sunlight, catching the snow among a stand of birches. I scrambled toward the light, but the bank leading up to it was slippery, and I must have made enough noise with thrashing and hollering to…

"Well, to raise someone on the road. And it turned out that it was good I did, at least for me. Because I looked back once, saw Artie, then a green outline, then nothing in the shadow of the trees, and I lost my footing and went over backwards. I remember the sky dappling shadow and light, and then nothing else until the hospital in Rutland.

"It turned out to be a spring blizzard. The '47 blizzard, for that matter. Fifty inches in Readsboro, to the south of us, over a three-day period. A kind of storm-of-the-century thing, and while we had been in the woods the first six inches had fallen, it was happening that fast.

"I came to, and asked immediately for Artie. The doctors seemed surprised. *You mean there was someone else in the woods?* they asked, and one of them sent a nurse away. They told me about my incredible luck: that there was a long-running boundary dispute between the Leonards and the Gryffins, and one of them—I think it was a Leonard—was driving his pickup down 125 and making sure no Gryffins were on his property, and of course he sees the Chrysler at the side of the highway, and he gets out to look around, and by my incredible luck I'm not a hundred yards from the car and the road, so it doesn't take him that long to find me.

"The luck, it turned out, was not so incredible that I wouldn't lose three fingertips on my right hand and the two small toes on my left foot, but when all was said and done it was a miracle, they said, near a miracle. And all the while I'm looking up into this lamp, and I'm thinking about Artie, and I gave one of them the description, from the green parka to the peach-yellow hair. And they begin to allow that it wasn't the miracle they had hoped it was, at least not for one of us.

"They sent out a search party. Out in the midst of the snow that would end up topping three, four feet in our part of the state. Not a trace of Artie. They started at the edge of the woods, where you would start if you were hopeful, and when they found nothing, not even tracks, some of them went in on cross-country skis, because I don't think they had snowmobiles back then, Gabriel, or at least I know they didn't in central Vermont.

"And it's funny how the giving up begins. They set forth other stories—how Artie might have found a trail out of the woods, or followed the creek bed. How you might be surprised, you know, because people turn up after a week or so if they find a farmhouse or even sometimes a sheltering barn. And they're telling me this, and everyone knows it's a story, that we're agreeing to believe it as long as we can."

"I'm sorry, Trajan," Gabriel offered in the long pause that followed, a silence broken only by the lift of the wind and Miss Vivien's calling, plaintively but not urgently, from somewhere in the recesses of the house. "Did they ever find...find Artie?"

"They found some bones two years ago," Trajan said quietly. "But I could have told them the bones weren't Artie's. And I can't tell you why, Gabriel, except to say sometimes there are intuitions between people—you know, how one of them knows what the other is thinking or doing even with miles between them?"

"Kind of like fortune-telling or ESP?"

Trajan smiled, and again it seemed unaccustomed, like he was rehearsing for something. "*Kind* of like that, Gabriel. Like when you're with your friends...Del and Joey, right? And how one of you laughs 'cause he knows just what the other one's about to say?

"Or better yet…it's kind of like playing chess with someone long distance. In the mail. What they call correspondence chess, where you think about the strategies, the tactics, the thoughts of the heart in someone miles away, who might not even be around unless…unless you call."

Gabriel nodded, his thoughts only half on the example. Miss Vivien was becoming more insistent.

"Well, it's like that, Gabriel, and the feeling is something that doesn't quit. Something I expect you'll hit upon every now and then when you're older. But let's just say I knew it wasn't Artie's bones when they made the discovery in '65, and in spite of that, it's taken me all this time to come back."

The look he gave the front door was veiled, covered over by memories and by other thoughts. Gabriel was afraid to ask him how he knew the bones weren't Artie's, and what that had to do with his returning to Kentucky.

"So…" he said at last, as Miss Vivien's calling from the house became suddenly shrill—something about cigarettes again, and something about the television. "So…even though you knew how it wasn't Artie…how did they figure out?"

"You can tell about bones," Trajan said, grasping the railing and drawing himself heavily to his feet, "if you find enough of them, that is. And they found some that told them it was someone else…different age and different sex, and toes missing on a foot that seemed to indicate…well, *may* have indicated that the one they found had gone through frostbite years before. Kind of like I did.

"But maybe that's a story for another time, and maybe it isn't."

Miss Vivien shouted from the parlor now. Something about "Otto's" and "medicine" and "trifling with your little friends on the porch." Trajan flushed, raised and lowered his hand slowly as though he were trying to soothe his mother, to quiet and appease her with a gesture she could not see. But as he turned toward the doorway, he pivoted toward Gabriel, gesturing in the same way toward the boy, so that Gabriel could not tell who Trajan was calming, who was the object of that vague and bootless signal.

"I'll talk to you later, Gabriel," he murmured. "I'll talk to you…sometime."

The wind seemed to rise as the door opened and closed behind him, and Gabriel sat a while longer in the cold sunlight, until a rustle of the blinds at the bedroom window brought him to his feet. He hurried across the road, alert to the eyes at his back.

He knew better than to turn around and face them.

***

…and of course this was not the last time we had that kind of talk, Jazzie, though you always seemed to think I was at Trajan's heels every day during the fall of '68.

I have looked back on it, in biography and history of those short intervening months between the time I met Trajan Bell and the last Halloween. You could say that 1968 ended around the time of his arrival in Louisville, because all that strikes me in that stretch of September and October was the flight of Apollo 7 and the release of "Night of the Living Dead"—two events I did not think about when they happened, and which would not register for years.

Instead it was a time of privacy and growth, and Trajan was only a part of it. After all, it was in those two months that I picked up and abandoned the guitar and read Lord of the Rings for the third time. It was also the time when I brought home a 'D' in algebra, and while lying on my bed with my nose in The Two Towers, listen to Ma propelled by a handful of pills and phoning Mr. Yankton, a crusty old math teacher who told her the truth—that I was distracted and lazy, and therefore, in her eyes, the heir to generations of male Racketts and their attendant Rackettude.

And though Trajan was only part of those months, he was an advisable part. You are right after all, about his influence, but still wrong, I believe, in thinking he was bad for me. He was a respite, an interval, a waking, and seasonal dream. It's hard now to reconstruct how and when things happened back then, but of course events are not like stories, so maybe I've put one incident before another or cobbled together several different encounters, all to make it sound like things were headed toward some moment or climax or meaning. I am not sure about that.

What I am certain about, on the other hand, is that Trajan was there with stories from his own life and from the larger venues of other peoples' histories. I would not have put it that way, but I could tell he knew that he had dodged a bullet in that frozen New England woods, and though he came out of it muted and scarred, he came out of it and knew he had survived.

It was like the old emperor, he claimed. Like Marcus Ulpius Traianus, who had found himself in the city of Antioch at the time of a disastrous earthquake. It seems the emperor was passing the winter in that city, and of course it was like he was a magnet that drew every nation—soldiers, ambassadors, merchants and lookers-on.

Well, he drew them into disaster this time. The story goes that there had been thunderstorms and ominous winds—the kind of thing that any Roman fortune-teller worth his salt was accustomed to reading--but it seems they missed this one, that no one would ever have expected the ground itself to rebel, capsize and buckle. First there was a great bellowing roar, then a tremendous quaking. Buildings leaped into the air, rocked and tilted like bereft ships at sea. According to Trajan—and this is my Trajan, not the old "dux et imperator"—the timbers, tiles and stones crashed together horribly, and you could see the dust all the way to the real sea, to the ships safely out on the Mediterranean.

There were stories he told me about this quake, and at the time I marveled how close Trajan could get to the insides of history, and it never occurred to me that he might be making up part of the story. Making up the trees lurching out of the ground, roots and all, and the thousands of people trapped in the tumbling buildings, buried for days until finally, crushed or smothered, they died.

When it was over at last, the people of Antioch recovered the survivors—a woman who had lived for days feeding her child and herself on her own breast milk, and another infant who had lived by suckling its dead mother. They had seemed too intimate to me, these survivals, and I remember thinking at the time that survival should be more heroic than this, should bristle with swordplay and fire and drama, not this strange and embarrassing link to nurturing.

Which was why the story of the emperor's escape was more to my liking then. Old Trajan, it seems, was trapped in a building and made his way out through a window. But the story went that "some being of greater than human stature" had come to him and led him out with only a few slight injuries. It was a god, Trajan said (this is my Trajan and not the Roman emperor), or at least a ghost, and it made him wonder what else the emperor had brought out of that ruin.

Because there is a kind of passage, Jazzie, that we talked about that September, that October. Turns out Trajan Bell had been in Tibet, had been in the Southwest in the Anasazi ruins, and he saw the same heart and pattern wherever he went. Yes, it was then that he explained the Bardo Thodol to me—the Tibetan Book of the Dead—and I know you have never bought in to his explaining, that it was all too simple-minded for you, but remember I was still thirteen at the time. So maybe it was my understanding that was the simple part, and not the way that Trajan explained it.

Because he told me that it was always the same passage, the same journey, and it didn't matter who took it—if it was Orpheus or Moses, Odysseus or Aeneas, Dante or Mulian or me or you. What happens is you slide away from yourself, from the here and now, then you travel the country of the gods, and only then do you come back, like you've climbed from the window of a collapsing house, guided by or tugged by or pushed by some being of greater than human stature.

It was the journey Trajan had travelled, or thought he had travelled, in that blizzard south of Ripton, Vermont. Dismantled, left for dead, straight through the country of the gods to where he was born again, and living to tell of it all, the country of the gods still lingering as images in his remembrance.

VIII

Gabriel's first Halloween in August Acres had been his last in costume.

His dad had left by then, of course, and the costume wasn't much to speak of—something Mary Rackett (soon to be Mary Conroy again) had thrown together with an old, almost translucent sheet and a pair of scissors.

She had called it "the ghost of shame" and tried to make a joke of it.

Gabriel had laughed, too, but on the next Halloween he had simply not dressed for the holiday. Sat home that night, watching Rat Patrol and Felony Squad, as kids two, three, even four years older walked past his shadowy house toward the neighbors'. There the porch lights were on and large plastic jack-o-lanterns sat on the steps, filled with candy and placed in the trust that nobody would take more than one piece. He felt shut out of the festivities that year. Ghosts and pirates, angels and Confederate army officers drifted by the window, while Gabriel basked in the blue light of the television and thought, for the first time, what it meant to grow *out* of things instead of *into* them.

But this year was different. Joey and Del had caught up

to him, it seemed. Now Gabriel's abstaining from Halloween three years running seemed foresighted, incredibly cool to his friends, and as the holiday approached, they found themselves drawn together, their separating lives bridged one more time by the season and by the memory of the season.

So they decided to roam the neighborhood together, aiming for sheer disruption. Because each of them recognized *this* change, had seen the older guys go through it on Halloweens past. Even if they did not understand the other changes—the things that made them strange to each other and to themselves—they knew the shape and color of this night. This was no longer the country of children, but the teenaged Halloween at last: the chance for wandering in darkness and for petty vandalism. And that was easy. That was a place all three of them still had in common.

Somehow Gabriel put thoughts around that very idea, as his two old friends approached from opposite ends of the street. They had both outgrown him in a matter of two months, it seemed.

Or at least, if they weren't actually taller or larger, they had come to look older in the rise and tumble of that particular autumn.

Del was becoming more broad and solid, shaped by weights and wind sprints as the baseball team moved indoors for its winter conditioning. His right elbow already buckled outward, ever so slightly. Even though the new wisdom was that throwing a curve ball wouldn't hurt you at all, the slight tilt of Del's arm, like he had stopped himself in mid-turn of a doorknob, was something that worried Mr. Robinson, despite what the coach and the doctors were saying.

Maybe it's too early for junk, Gabriel had heard the old man say from the Robinson back yard. *Maybe just stick with the heat for a couple of years.*

But in that advice there was a question, Mr. Robinson's voice rising at the end of the sentence like he wasn't sure, like someone or something was slowly taking his boy away, and he was coming to suspect that *someone or something* was Del himself.

And Joey…well, he was prodigious. Each day he became more exotic and rare.

Zuice, it seemed, had begun to play dances in the South End of Louisville. Once or twice, frats at the University had hired them. The boys would load up a U-Haul and tug their equipment up Southern Parkway, spend two hours setting up and checking sound, and come home with forty dollars split five ways and, if they were lucky, a cup from the keg. They learned their licks in front of audiences too drunk to listen, much less to dance, but for Joey it was the Beatles at Shea Stadium or the Who at Monterey Pop. Joey'd come back with stories about Ninth and O, about Sylvania Teen Club or some Lutheran Youth Dance up in Shively, and he'd make it sound like the grand tour, like the band was cooking so hot that the bricks wept. It was too obvious that Aron—the lead singer of the band—was his hero, and Joey had taken to wearing his own hair dangerously long for their part of town, and especially for a public school where the principal was an old navy ensign who ran the halls like an admiral.

There they were, Gabriel's vanishing friends, both of them larger in autumn twilight, headed for earth's wide bounds and ocean's farthest coast, but converging one last time on this evening of All Saints' with flashlights and soap, toilet paper, two books of matches, and paper bags filled with eggs and dogshit.

Del nodded at Gabriel. Joey was carrying a bag, flashed his old friend a two-fingered peace sign. They both were growing away from him, from each other. But here they were on Halloween, and Gabriel said to himself, *it is like old times*. Then he thought what a weird thing that was to think when you were thirteen.

***

The first stop was a two-story house at the corner of Flora and Echo. It was the only two-story house in the neighborhood, built there before August Acres rose pretty much out of nothing in the building boom of the early sixties, and because of its size, the boys had told stories about it, had imagined it haunted. They came to find out that it was owned by a dark, ill tempered, crew cut man of about Trajan's age, who had a German wife. Joey had almost persuaded Del that the man was hiding Nazis, until Mr. Hardy explained to his son that the man was Sergeant Bolgia, was ex-military, and the German woman was what they called a war bride.

It was a disappointment. But you could still imagine the Nazis if you approached the house in the half-light of a Halloween evening, and Gabriel clutched the roll of toilet paper tightly, in the back of his mind prepared at any moment for guttural voices and machine gun fire. A glance at his friends told him that, despite their recently discovered cool, Joey and Del were checking the trees for snipers.

They paused on the sidewalk, ducked behind a squat taxus shrubbery. Joey opened the bag, drew out the rubbery masks.

"Our intrepid disguises," he announced in a low voice, and Gabriel knew at once that the word *intrepid* was Aron's. He held the mask up to the light.

Three grinning pigs. The amiable, cartoon Disney faces. Gabriel's mask was crowned by a sailor hat that popped back into shape when he put on the intrepid disguise.

"Aron got these for me," Joey announced. "At Caulfield's."

His two companions whispered, "cool" in a kind of Greek chorus. Caulfield's was downtown, on Third Street. Joey was the first of them to have a friend who drove, who knew his way by car downtown.

And there were three masks. One for each of them.

Joey had been thinking of this, and of them, for weeks.

It made it better somehow. Shadows returning, and a kind of shimmering light on the stripped branches of the trees in the Bolgia yard. There was something Gabriel had missed in this, and as they whispered and strung the trees with paper, it occurred to him that what he had missed was more than the fellowship with his old friends, was more than the holiday. He could not put words around what it was, not exactly, but he knew that his bones understood it.

Like knowing what they would say before they said it. Like a game by correspondence.

Masked and grinning, they rushed up August Street in the shadows, the paper in the branches almost luminescent behind them. They passed Del's house, and stopped in the middle of the street.

Miss Vivien's house stood before them, the streetlamp in front of it fluttering.

"Our next target, Rackett," Joey whispered, his grip on Gabriel's arm tightening expectantly.

Gabriel looked at Del. Who looked away, his floppy mask, sporting an engineer's cap, averted.

"C'mon, Joey," Gabriel protested thinly. "There's lots of other houses. This one's…next door to Del and all…"

Joey rolled his eyes. Or you could imagine that was what he was doing, even in the darkness and even under the mask.

"You don't give a shit about that, Rackett. You're just a wuss, 'coz it's your boyfriend's house and all."

It was just like Joey. He lived farthest away from the Bells', had the least chance of being caught and no reservation about risking his friends. But it was more than that this time. This time there was an ugliness in the words, like Gabriel had opened an underground door—to a cellar, perhaps, or a bunker—that had been sealed for years, only to hear a stale whisper, perhaps poisonous, rising to meet him out of the dark.

He didn't like it, nor did he like Joey much at that moment. But Del was looking away, he was outnumbered, so Gabriel knew they were headed for Miss Vivien's now, ready for tricks instead of treats. And the image of Trajan's cleaning dried soap from the windows, melancholy though it might be, came up against the urgency, the sheer pleasure of the three of them—the Three Musketeers—bound together on dark adventures, and adventure won out over regret.

They debated whether to approach the house from the back. It was much darker in the shaded and fenced back yard, proof against being spotted with whatever paper or eggs or burning bag of dogshit Joey had planned for the Bells.

But Gabriel was reluctant to go there, of course, given the same darkness, the faint metallic stink of something in the close air by the fence. The memory of broadcloth and black, glittering little eyes. It was why he lingered at the front of the house, watched the fluttering street lamp optimistically, hoping that a trick of nature or current would extinguish it, that they could approach their mischief from the incline.

But the light sputtered once, then burned steadily. Out of the shadows soared an unseasonable moth, pale green and the size of Gabriel's hand, and though he knew that luna moths were harmless, the size alone lent the creature menace. It beat its wings against the glass casing of the light, and standing far below you could hear the erratic spattering sound, like a cold, exotic rain. The moth seemed to cartwheel in the night air and discover its bearings, to lie face down on the current of wind, and then tumble off into the intertwined, bare branches of Miss Vivien's maples.

Let's skip this house, Gabriel wanted to say, but Joey's scornful words about *wusses* and *boyfriends* goaded him. He could not back down. Could not even consider it.

Nevertheless, as they passed along the fence between the Robinsons' and the Bells', as they turned the corner and crept along the back row, the overhang of weeds and shrubbery almost bare now, the faint moonlight filtering through a spider web of branches, Gabriel made sure Del walked before him in their little column. Trajan had repaired the hole in the fence, after all, and to get into the Bell's back yard, you had to climb these days. If Del was in front when they reached the best spot—the lower branches of a tree that abutted the fence—Joey would insist he climb over first. That alone might be enough to cool Del's spirits, to make him object to this whole uncomfortable business. It would be two of them, then, against Joey. The odds would be better.

They reached the spot in the fence line, and it was even more ready than Gabriel remembered: the maple flush against the planking, two branches overhanging, thick enough to support a boy's weight. Again it seemed that it would be Del who would have to test them first.

"You won't wuss out like Rackett, will you?" Joey whispered.

Gabriel started to protest. He knew Joey was all talk, would take it back if pressed. But it didn't seem worth the argument. Something in Gabriel wanted to hold on to this night, and at any rate, Del was clambering through the branches already, sufficiently dared into action. He crested the fence, outlined against the shadowy spilled oil of the sky, and suddenly he seemed far aloft to Gabriel, appallingly out of reach.

But over he went, and you could hear the rustle of his feet on dry leaves, and Gabriel could breathe again. Del muttered something, and Gabriel grasped a branch and pulled himself into the moonlight.

***

The back yard had changed even more since Gabriel last visited. Trajan's careful arrangement of flagstone and cracked pavement was overgrown by the last grass of the season, and his grove had died back into autumn. Only the evergreens remained unchanged, of course, but beneath them, as far as Gabriel could tell, the chess game had progressed—the pieces in a different, sparser arrangement, and captured chessmen scattered around the edges of the board.

Del and Gabriel waited against the fence until Joey dropped over beside them. The three of them scuttled through the yard and crouched against the wall of the house.

"Not the dogshit this time, Joey," Gabriel muttered. "I'm not gonna go with that."

Joey smiled then. He had too many teeth, Gabriel had always thought, but there was a fullness to his smile, almost cartoonish, and it reminded Gabriel why he liked his friend, why he would do dumbass stuff to please Joey.

He saw the soap in Joey's hand.

"Simple and traditional," Joey whispered. "Boost ya to the window, Rackett?"

As Gabriel set his foot into the stirrup of Joey's linked fingers, Del Robinson suddenly became all advice.

"Write 'fuck' on Miss Vivien's window, Gabe," he urged. "Or draw a big ol' pecker on it. She'll freak for sure!"

Joey shook his head. "Minor league, Robinson. We're making a splash here. Needs to be somethin' major flashy, so that boy of hers will take notice."

"I don't particklary want him to take notice, Joey," Del insisted.

Gabriel rose toward the window. "Whaddya want me to write, Joey?"

"*Klaatu,*" Joey said. Repeated it, then spelled the word for Gabriel.

"And what the hell is that?"

"Some alien says it in an old movie. Aron seen it on Fright Night, and says it was really cool."

"And what does it mean, Joey?"

But suddenly Gabriel's foot slipped from Joey's grasp, and for a moment he dangled from the sill.

"Damnit, Joey!" he hissed.

"Somethin's out there, Gabe. Look out there. In the far corner by Del's yard."

Gabriel started to turn, to let go, to make the short drop from the windowsill, but then he felt something buoying him from underneath.

He was standing on Del's back.

Slowly, Del rose to his feet. Gabe pulled himself up toward the window and shifted his weight, until he sat on Del's shoulders. He pivoted and looked out to the fence line, at the spot where Joey was pointing.

"I don't see nothin', Joey," Gabriel said. "Reckon you're spooked or somethin'. Don't wuss out like me, ya hear?"

He heard Del chuckle softly below him.

Joey looked out at the fencerow for a long time. From behind you could see the anger in his shoulders, the way his neck stiffened and stretched.

"Never mind," he muttered. "Just write it and let's get the hell out of here."

Gabriel turned to the window. For a moment his hand paused on the pane as he tried to figure how to make a backward 'K'. Beyond the glass the room was dark, the doorway to the hall gray from some lamp he could not see, perhaps from the bathroom or from the parlor.

He worked at the word uncomfortably, the thought of Trajan and Trajan's story nagging at him. His hand shook as he raced through the first several letters.

"Hold steady, Del!" he hissed.

"I am!" came the reply from between his ankles. "It ain't easy to prop you up, ya heavy-weight bastid!"

Despite himself, Gabriel smiled, and made the crossing stroke of the "T" before he saw her fill the light of the doorway.

Miss Vivien slumped in her wheelchair like a drowsing monarch. A cigarette burned between her fingers, and her glasses, usually a part of the face she presented the world, were hooked over the arm of the chair like some kind of steering apparatus. She had wheeled herself into the doorway and sat there aimless now, looking back over her shoulder at something in the hall, preparing to turn into the bedroom but paused as though she had second thoughts about moving, about movement in general. Bringing her cigarette to her lips, the old woman took a deep draw on it, and her face filled with the borrowed light of the glowing ash.

Slowly she turned to face the window, and Gabriel stood frozen on Del's shoulders, the soap dropping from his hand as the old woman's face seemed to widen and glow, to rush toward him as it filled the window pane, glowing a faint orange in the light of the cigarette.

For a moment Miss Vivien looked years, centuries younger. Something in her hand glinted as she raised and leveled it.

Gabriel pivoted on his perch, trying to turn away. He lost his balance and fell from Del's shoulders onto the hard, leaf-littered earth.

Out near the far corner of the yard, Joey looked up, startled.

"What is it, Gabe?" Del asked, his pig face grinning at the boy on the ground. But Gabriel scrambled to his feet, grabbed him by the arm, and tugged him toward the tree and the fence and escape. For a moment Del resisted, as though he was rooted among the oaks and laurels, but a pull from Gabriel roused him at last, and the two boys raced for the back of the yard, propelled by a fear neither one of them could name.

Through the grove they raced in a couple of bounds. Del was behind him somewhere, he knew, from the sound of breathing and the snap of a bare, dried branch, then abreast of him as Gabriel, for some strange reason beneath his thought, swept by the marble chessboard and, snatching up a black, samurai knight capsized at the game's edge, stuffed the piece into his pocket and ran, full tilt toward the spot in the fence and the welcoming, drooping limbs.

Joey joined them at the corner, and a swift boost launched him over first. Gabriel followed, clutching the top of the fence, pulling himself up by a narrow branch that cracked and slipped as he crested the boards.

He looked back then, straddling the planking, and lowered a hand to help Del.

Something loped out of the shadows, ragged and on all fours, pale and tattered and shapeless, picking up speed as it rushed toward them.

Del extended his arms, grabbed Gabriel's wrist and started to climb.

As the thing took shape. Part man, part smoke, part something feral and appalling, more movement than substance, the still point in its roiling face two black eyes glittering like the dead wings of a beetle.

It rumbled hungrily as it rushed them.

Gabriel cried out as the thing struck his friend, thrust a

long, angular tendril into Del's back.

A sour, metallic smell boiled the air.

Gabriel pulled, dragged Del over the wall in a fetid trail of smoke. For a moment the pale thing curled like a burning leaf over the chest of his friend…

Then darkened, then vanished.

Del swore, shivered, and scrambled to his feet.

Joey was ahead of them, halfway to the Robinson's yard. Crashing through branches, into light and back into shadow.

"Del?" Gabriel whispered.

"Yeah, I'm OK."

"What the hell was that?"

Del shook himself, like a dog coming out of the water. "Whaddya mean, Gabriel? I just…I just followed you on account of you was running."

Gabriel leaned against the fence, gathered his breath.

"Why, Gabriel? Whaddya mean?"

"You sure you're OK, Del?"

Del wrapped his arms around himself. "Fine, Gabriel. Just a little cold, is all. Just real cold. You're a turd for spookin' me like that. I mean, what the hell you…."

But Gabriel was tugging him again, along the fencerow, toward the yard and Joey and the light, leaving behind them the smoke and the smell…

And the black, glittering eyes.

"What is it?" Del asked. "What is it, Gabriel?"

"Shut up, Del," Gabriel urged, pulling his stronger friend through the tangle of limbs and high, dry grass. "Shut up and get the hell out of here."

IX

Very seldom did Gabriel go downtown by himself. The city was perceived by his suburban neighbors as the center of crime and clamor, their judgments both racial and rural. Gabriel had come to Old Louisville with his mother, and occasional field trips would bring his class to the downtown area, to the orchestra or to a holiday production of A Christmas Carol.

Mostly, though, for his trips with Mary, it was to Mass at St. Louis Bertrand. On occasional warm summer Sundays, they would follow the service with a stroll several blocks south to the park where the amphitheater lay, and where Mary could dream of Shakespearian roles and sit on the tiered benches with her restless son.

An actor named George Castille had promised her a role in his next production of Hamlet—an opportunity that never came while Gabriel lived in the city. In the summer of 1969, when Gabriel was fourteen and reeling from the events of that momentous season, Mary would bring him to the park to see Castille as Fernando in a histrionic version of *The Tempest*. Gabriel would remember little of the performance except to wonder why his mother had wanted to stage it at her school to begin with; he did, however, think he saw Trajan there, standing in the leafy shadows with several well-groomed young men, and he supposed that Trajan didn't see him, for his friend was gone when the lights went up.

But that summer was yet to come. November 1968 brought a bus ride to high Mass with his mother, then a strange encounter back home that passed for a higher form of celebration.

✳✳✳

They did not hear Mass on All Saints'. On major feast days, Gabriel's mother was not content with squat suburban churches, so they waited until Sunday the 3rd, when they caught the downtown bus at the highway and rode it to Broadway, where Mary hailed a cab that took her four blocks south to St. Louis Bertrand.

She went there for the Irish and the altar, she claimed. It was a journey her son didn't half mind, staring out of the cab window at the three-story houses, at the decrepit dry cleaners and the steeple rising over the roofs ahead, the call to Mass quickening on the bells as the driver pulled in front of the church.

As usual, Mary tipped the cabbie outrageously. Gabriel's father had always maintained that his ex-wife never fathomed the currency exchange, but Gabriel, having lived with her longer, knew it was something more than that. There was an Irish docility he had yet to put words around, and despite the violence of their history that gentleness was the other side of half his people, half his inheritance. That being said, he always winced to see the money change hands so generously, imagining the end of the month.

But it was the third after all, and month's end was far away. Gabriel's spirits lifted as they entered the church by the north door, past the Knights of Columbus and sodality pamphlets into the nave. Dutifully following his mother, he dipped his fingers in the water and crossed himself, smelling his fingertips curiously as the first words of the Mass sang in the vaulted ceiling.

Everything but words prevailed on Gabriel when he heard Mass. The comfortable smells of mildew and old wine, and on the feast days, the incense. The high, arching voice of the priest as he sang the Introit (which Gabriel had missed today because the cab had stopped at two lights). He even wished that Mass was still in the Latin he was fast forgetting, so he could slip away from familiar language and float in its music as well, setting aside the long bus journey with housewives and colored soldiers from Fort Knox, the smell of diesel fuel and the strange narcotic sleepiness of morning sun through the tinted windows. It was peaceful to rest in the mysteries of the old church and the yellowed, gothic woodwork of its interiors, the sunlight glimpsed through the muddy stained glass as though the world outside was violet and red.

The blonde wood and the mustiness and the shadowy light reminded him of the incline in front of Trajan's house. Gabriel remembered the tendrils of dark leaves, how Joey had marveled and cupped them in his hand.

And all of a sudden, he felt bad for Trajan.

Who had enough to concern him, living with a mother who was old and disabled and probably wounded in some unexplainable way.

It made Gabriel sad to think of it, and to think that he and Del had been fixing to write *fuck* on the windows of someone like that. He thumbed the samurai chessman in his pocket, and for a moment he considered the confessional. But it would be too much trouble. If he went in on his own, his mom would know he was up to something, and Mary wasn't in the habit of making him go in at St. Louis Bertrand.

He looked across at his mother, who was returning his glance. Obediently, he rolled the rosary beads over his fingers and looked to the altar, where the priest was elevating the Host.

Which becomes the body and blood of Christ.
And don't let your friends tell you otherwise, Gabriel.

Gabriel smiled despite himself. Like he and Joey and Del would talk about something like that.

But maybe with Trajan he would.

The possibility struck him as he folded his hands and slipped into the communion line. That this was something Trajan was here for, or something that he would know about. Things changing into things, by magic or by miracle, like leaves sprouting unbeckoned from treated wood, or apparitions afloat in a tiny suburban yard.

***

Years later, when Gabriel looked back upon the week that followed, he was both surprised and not surprised that he had missed its history. On Tuesday the long-awaited election took place, and Richard Nixon, claiming a "secret plan" to end the Vietnam War, stepped into a presidency that would shape the course of Gabriel's country for decades to come. By the end of the week, the one secret about the war was Johnson's: B-52 bombers were saturating the Cambodian borders, and, unknown to many Americans, the conflict was spilling into neighboring countries.

But all of that seemed remote, inaccessibly adult, as he watched for the signs of life and change across the street. Part of him regretted not having confessed on Sunday; the events at Miss Vivien's house over Halloween troubled him, and he had begun to think that the apparitions in the yard had something to do with his own bad feelings.

It was almost with eagerness that he rushed out into the yard when Trajan appeared on Saturday morning. Buttoning his jacket against the suddenly crisp fall air, he stopped at the curb of August Street, tightening the laces on his Chucks and looking through his scattered bangs toward Miss Vivien's incline.

Sure enough, Trajan was watching him as well. Looking down on him from the incline. Something in his stare revived the mystery and alarm that Gabriel had felt in Miss Vivien's yard on Halloween night, but as soon as Trajan turned away, so did the feeling, and Gabriel knotted the laces, crossed the street, and approached the frost-crusted ramp.

Trajan was holding a bow.

Gabriel thought of simply saying hello, then moving on to next door as though he had been headed for Del's all along. But it was too obviously not so, and he didn't want to appear furtive or guilty around the Bells, given the events of last week. Besides, Trajan only *sighted* his target with the bow, didn't he? It was not to shoot but to sharpen seeing.

Gabriel stopped, leaned on the railing, and Trajan asked him if he wanted to go hunting.

"Not to kill anything," the older man added hastily. "You know I don't...and not because it's a seasonal thing. Not anymore. You understand?"

Gabriel was completely baffled, but he nodded.

Trajan smiled. Held up his right hand. "At any rate, you've seen my fingers. If anyone does any shooting, it'll be you."

Vowing to himself he would do no shooting, not yet, Gabriel went home, put on his boots, then met Trajan at the westernmost end of Flora Drive—where the familiar road made a T intersection with another street that had no name yet, because it marked the boundary of a new development, a subdivision that would stretch from Gabriel's neighborhood over leveled or vanishing woods, ending at the banks of a creek that bordered the public golf course.

The new subdivision was undiscovered country. Del, the hunter among the three boys, had explored it some in the previous spring, pronounced it a bleak place, only a nesting ground for doves and rabbits and the occasional exiled raccoon. But part of the boys knew otherwise, for it had been woods when they arrived here, and the stories about those woods were, of course, things that each of them remembered.

In 1963 the Ohio had spilled its banks, and Del's people had helped stack sandbags at what was now this T intersection, because the creek had overflowed and the golf course itself was flooded under what Del claimed was a fathom of water, though Joey and Gabriel suspected he liked the word "fathom" because he had boated over the seventh hole on his way into the clubhouse.

Which was underwater as well, the pro shop littered with the flotsam of empty golf bags, the dirty current brushing against the top of the bar in the lounge, where the color television, the first one that Del had ever seen, lay submerged in the wash, its antenna protruding pitifully into the damp air.

Or so Gabriel imagined it when Del told the story, and some imaginations were even darker—the story of how last summer a naked man, hairy and decked in weeds, had rushed out of the creek bed and attacked a foursome of women golfers as they stood on the sixth green (Gabriel had wondered why Joey was the sole source of this newsworthy item), or how at night birds as big as dogs took wing out of the starved trees at the border of the subdivision.

It was those trees that Gabriel and Trajan were passing now, his broad shoulders swiveling as he broke through the high, dried weeds and pampas grass on his way toward the creek bed. The pampas grass scraped against Gabriel's thighs like a blunt knife, and he wished he had worn his levis instead of the thinner khakis.

"So what's been up, Trajan?" he asked, surmounting a slight shiver in his voice because, yes, it was cold in the field, no houses to baffle the wind, and for the first time it felt like winter weather here.

Breasting the higher weeds now, Trajan did not seem to have heard him. But as Gabriel started to ask the question again, this time a little louder, he was interrupted by the answer.

"Working for Humphrey and cleaning the windows. Neither of which did much good, I'm afraid."

Gabriel tried to think about Vice-President Humphrey, the kind of clownish cheeriness that his mother had said was *all we got against that gobshite Nixon.* It made him chuckle, snort to hold in his laughter, the image of the comical Humphrey and his mother's Irish swear word.

Trajan heard him clearly this time, turned to face him, the bulbous eyes unreadable behind the thick glasses.

"So you were for Nixon?" he asked testily. "Or maybe that

redneck Wallace?"

Gabriel was overwhelmed by the strange question. It was like he stood inside a cave, in shadow, with a sunlit Trajan staring back at him and neither of them seeing the other, not really, and the cold wind stilled suddenly so you could hear the rush of a car west on Gethsemane, headed toward the river, its rumble rising and falling as it passed.

"No..." he said meekly. "No. I voted for Bobby Kennedy."

Trajan shrugged, the look on his face unchanged and unfathomable. "Well, Bobby Kennedy's dead, and you can't vote anyway. Looks like we both lost out."

Trajan turned, began to walk again, the field of weeds widening behind him. Gabriel stood by a downed water maple, wondering what had got into his friend, what Trajan knew about the last week, anyway.

It looked like he was sinking into mud, like the fat boy in Del's story—Jeremy Ricks, who went frog gigging alone in the aftermath of the flood, and vanished entirely, never to be seen again.

Del said there was no Ricks family in the neighborhood because they had moved out of sorrow.

It was a lie. Gabriel could tell by the eyes, by the looks that Del and Joey had exchanged.

"Wait up, Trajan!" Gabriel shouted. The wind rose, and he closed the ground between himself and his friend, and Trajan turned to meet him. In his heart, the boy was sorry for the Halloween venture, the word scrawled on the window, the stolen chessman and the victory of Richard Nixon...but he did not know what Trajan knew, and he feared that too pointed a question would unmask his own guilt, like a confessional door accidentally swinging open.

He swore himself to silence. Especially now that he walked side by side with Trajan, not behind him, and whatever tension there had been seemed already past, and Trajan was off on another subject, promising to show him something by the edge of the creek.

***

He would always remember the moment when the world dropped away.

Trajan was gesturing to him, down there in the creek bed, shaded by overhanging dry branches, as though tangled in a web of shadows. Gabriel knew he must descend to see it—whatever it was—but he knew that the slope of the bank was steep, that it would be a hard return up into familiar sunlight.

His reluctance was more, too, but he could not say it. Could not even put words around it. He thought, bizarrely, of his long-dead grandfather in County Galway, of Trajan's Artie and of Bobby Kennedy, none of whom had a face that could rise to his recollection, even when he had seen the pictures. Behind him, somewhere back in August Acres, a few bars of a rock song flared from a garage and vanished—not enough to title it, or even to guess where it was headed.

Gabriel held his breath. He took a few steps downstream (or in the direction that downstream would be if there were more than a trickle in the dry bed of the creek), but there was no way to get down the bank except to slide. So he clutched the branch of a felled oak that gabled over the creek bed, lowering himself down the incline toward his waiting friend. Sliding a little in the crusted mud, stripping the oak branch as he dropped down the bank, he landed in the creek bed on his knees, bathed in a stillness that seemed like November at the time—cold and humid and inexpressibly hushed, a stillness he would come to understand later as inside him and outside him, late autumn blended with his own expectancy.

Trajan was upstream in the creek bed, his bow propped against the bank. He was crouching like some Indian over a dark scattering of twigs and ash, trailing his finger through the debris like he was scrawling something on the ground. Gabriel dusted dried leaves from his hands and approached his friend in the close, shadowy air.

Peered over his shoulder.

"Looks like bird…doo to me, Trajan. Why? Is it something else?"

It was a large splash of droppings, spread over an outcropping of limestone.

"I suppose that's all it is, Gabriel. In the old world they called it *fewmets*, I believe. But you gotta look at the size of it. What's that telling you?"

"A big bird or a bad supper," Gabriel replied.

Trajan snickered. "Let's stick with the big bird. Take the bow, Gabriel."

Gabriel did as he was told. The weapon was heavy, and his hand shook a little as he turned it and ran his fingers over its taut string.

Birds big as dogs in the starved trees.

He looked again at the droppings, but Trajan was underway, climbing back up the branch and out of the shadows. Gabriel fitted an arrow to the bow and followed.

The trees along the banks of the creek were flimsy and bare. You could see the opposite bank where the ground rose steeply, and beyond the rise a small red flag hung limply from half a visible pole—the cup at hole six, the summoning banner, or so they said, for naked, weed-covered men. But at least in the winter you could see them coming up the bank. And surely if there were a big, man-eating bird in these parts—a hawk or a buzzard, Gabriel thought—you could see it coming as well, and from far off.

But there was nothing to see, frankly, except for a yellow backhoe, not in use on a Saturday, a capsized RC can on its hood, alone and melancholy on the opposite bank like a prehistoric creature headed for extinction. A moment before, Gabriel would have paid no attention to the dormant machine, but now, with the shadowy creek bed behind him, everything was strange portents and apprehensions, and he felt like he was being offered a glimpse into something that he would rather have declined.

That he would have liked to be not ready for this as well.

Trajan stepped over the branches of a desolated bush and

followed the bank, Gabriel close behind him. Blocked upstream by the construction project, the creek was little more than a dry, frost-encrusted trickle, but it became stranger still at this point, where the construction crew had been paving the bed as a gesture of flood control, imagining no sandbag walls around August Acres, no floating televisions in the clubhouse any more.

"Pay attention," Trajan urged softly.

"To what?"

"To the woods, Gabriel. Or what is left of the woods. Your ancestors and mine lived in dread of the woods. It was a place of chaos, and a place where the devil walked by night and day. There are stories of travelers abducted by the Fair Folk, who we now call the fairies but are more dangerous than the Disney ones you know, or the ones that used to barter for your teeth."

Trajan sounded dramatic and a step away from things, like a voice in a junior high film. There was something else in his speaking as well, a density that, years later, Gabriel would locate as condescension. But as for now, the sound of his voice was merely watery and distant, part of the ungovernable strangeness of this place and this journey.

"But those people didn't know all the stuff we do, Trajan," Gabriel objected, straddling the crest of the bank, bracing himself with his right hand, holding the bow aloft in his left because it just seemed wrong to set it on the ground.

"I don't think that's the whole of it," Trajan said, sliding toward the concrete bottom of the creek bed. "I'm not so sure that *knowing all the stuff* gets us any place. Because…well, never mind."

Gabriel sat down on the hard clay of the bank. He was a little afraid of Trajan now. Crouching in the shadowy valley of the culvert, like a hungry ghost.

But he wanted to hear the rest.

"Trajan, you're doin' it again."

Trajan looked up at him. "Doin' what?"

"'Never mind' don't work with me, Trajan. Got to be more than 'never mind'."

Trajan nodded somberly. "Because, then…because that stuff is still happening, Gabriel. Nothing's changed because we turned on the lights and are blinded for a long moment. People are abducted everyday: by the fair folk or the foul, it doesn't really matter. And the devil or the angel is still walking through the woods, no matter how you pave or develop it. No less there because you don't see them right off, and maybe more there, because you have to… to triumph over everything in order to know they're here."

Gabriel interlaced his fingers behind his head. Resting the bow on his stomach, he looked up into the November clouds and puzzled at Trajan's mysteries. He was not ready to let on that he didn't understand, and to be honest, something in him yearned to believe that his friend was right.

"But how would you know, Trajan?"

"Get up, Gabriel. Get down here. Time to be moving before it gets too late. How would I know what?"

Gabriel scrambled to his feet. "How would you know if they were there? I mean, the fair folk or the foul folk or the devils or angels? How would you know?"

And again Trajan turned to him, the big eyes watery beneath a baffle of dirty glass. "You tell me, Gabriel."

Then the owl burst out of the brush on the near bank.

***

Years later, Gabriel would marvel at how he was not surprised at all, how everything—the spontaneous outing and the bare landscape and Trajan's guiding them on a path along the bank, not to mention the very fact that he had been given the bow, that the weapon was in his hands—led to this moment, when Trajan hissed now! and he raised the bow and sighted it on the big bird, knowing all along that he would not shoot, was not supposed to shoot.

And over the nocked arrow the owl took shape out of undergrowth and damaged light, as white as an apparition and as silent after it burst, startled, from a tangle of dried branches. Its wings extended, dappling white into a rusty yellow, part bird and part smoke, motionless in a powerful glide, it skimmed the creek bed and veered right, sailing off over the desolate construction ground, leaving behind the smell of burnt leaves and the afterwash of rain.

Gabriel watched the big owl over the arrow point.

"Queen of the ghosts," Trajan whispered, placing his hand on Gabriel's shoulder.

The owl soared out of sight, and Gabriel turned to Trajan.

"It was like she—"

"Not yet, Gabriel. Don't let her rise into words just yet."

"What do you mean?"

"Keep her in thought," Trajan insisted. "Keep her image there. Do not even name her parts, or call her what you think she is."

"But the—"

"No." Trajan shook the boy a little, bracing his hands on Gabriel's shoulders. "Not yet. And not even yet."

So Gabriel stood there, bow still lifted in the aftermath of what he understood he had seen. The bird sailed back into sight once, and from an abiding distance the ground over which she passed seemed to shimmer as the morning sun caught on the crystals of frost still lacing the dried grass in her wake. Gabriel's thoughts settled, letting the image and recollection of the owl pass away, beneath understanding, into a place where she lit and perched in the darkness, and when he returned to her later, she was indeed the Queen of the Ghosts.

✳✳✳

The big white owl soared through his thoughts as Gabriel followed Trajan back into the neighborhood. He noticed the differences among the squat, brick ranch houses—how the dried grass breathed and bristled in the yards at the end of Flora Drive, and how the high sun sparkled on the windows, melting the thin residue of frost.

More color than he had imagined. More variety. He lingered on the sidewalk before a house he had always imagined unremarkable, and he remarked on it as Trajan caught up to him. It was like something within him had taken hold of it, the green shutters that no longer seemed uniform and drab, the abandoned flower pots on the porch out of which thin, dry stems protruded and tumbled over the ceramic lip. He remarked on it and began to transform it like the words of the priest transformed the bread and wine.

He started to try to explain, but Trajan interrupted him.

"It works the same way here, Gabriel. Don't let it rise into words just yet. Do not put your thoughts entirely around it."

And Gabriel nodded, did as he was told, and for a moment he brushed against the edge of discipleship.

✳✳✳

Miss Vivien was seated on her wheelchair at the top of the incline, her broad, bony shoulders wrapped in a dull green shawl. Cigarette smoke tumbled and weaved from her big hand, and she leaned forward, the lines of her sharpening as the two adventurers approached.

"You should of told me you'd be all day, Marcus!" she scolded as they entered the yard. "I don't want to sit around 'till all hours worrying about what kind of trouble you get into."

Gabriel looked down at his shoes. "I expect I should be going, Trajan."

"Maybe you should, Gabriel."

Trajan started up the incline, but his mother waved him away, beckoned Gabriel.

"Aww, don't let me spoil the fun, boys. Come on in and visit."

Trajan turned Miss Vivien's wheelchair toward the door. "It's all right, Mother. We kind of have things to do, anyway."

"Oh, I don't see what's so important about what you're

doing, Marcus. Bring your little friend in, and take him around back if you like. I've seen this one before, and it ain't been long since I did."

Behind the thick glasses, Miss Vivien's eyes were unreadable, even though she smiled and waved and gestured. Trajan frowned at Gabriel, and then guided the boy through the musty living room, through the kitchen and out into the yard.

Something had changed. The son was trapped in the mother's prison; the wizard of the desolate fields now locked in the trunk of an oak, asleep forever. All of a sudden there were distances. The books and papers on the table had been scattered about, a small sheaf of typescript stacked at one corner, and the kitchen smelled of cigarette smoke only, a solitary Chesterfield still smoldering in the ashtray on the table.

The trees were bare now in Trajan's lonely grove, their branches intertwining in a kind of low vault over the circle of broken stones. The chessboard beneath the evergreens was virtually bare as well, only a half dozen pieces left on the board. The guitar was no longer there. But perhaps the weather was too cool and damp to leave it out. In its place was a lawn chair, its flimsy aluminum frame bound with frayed plastic tubing.

Gabriel backed toward the chessboard. He had the secret, guilty intention of replacing the samurai knight among the scattered, taken pieces, but now, standing beside the board, he discovered to his dismay that the captured chessmen had been whisked away, perhaps boxed or otherwise secreted. Bleakly he dropped the knight by the board, certain that when Trajan discovered it, he would know why it had been missing.

Trajan sat down in the chair. He was sweating, which seemed odd for this chilly weather.

"She has to have someone minding her," he said softly. "She doesn't realize how vulnerable she is, you know?"

It was the kind of question Gabriel knew he did not need to answer.

Nor did he need to answer the next question.

"So I guess I know where the soap on the windows came

from last week?"

Gabriel looked away. "I'm sorry, Trajan. I didn't want to do it, but—."

He stopped before he betrayed another friend, but Trajan was brushing the air, smiling.

"Don't worry about it, Gabriel. What is it? 'Boys will be boys'?"

And then he recited the Keats, the line about the loitering knight-at-arms, and Gabriel knew he had been found out, all of him, and the grove and the autumn and the declining year tightened around him irrevocably, like something was watching him from the branches.

He mumbled an excuse, a goodbye, to which Trajan nodded without listening. Still, the two of them sat in the yard a while, ill at ease, and when Gabriel left for home, he sat in front of the television, watching Notre Dame lay into Pittsburgh 56-7, and finding himself not rooting for the Irish, perversely mourning each Notre Dame touchdown and secretly enjoying the quiet disloyalty.

Gabriel woke in the early evening. There was no sign that his mother had come in, so he slipped off into his bedroom and lay down a while, staring up to the ceiling where he had recently taped a poster of the Barbara Remington cover to *The Fellowship of the Ring*. In the shadowy room, his eye followed the psychedelic branchings of the tree from the center of the poster into its upper corners, where huge globules hung ripe from the branches and geometric birds took off in a kind of nether-land between the tree and the pink mountains looming in the distance.

It is not going to be like that for me, Gabriel told himself. Drowsy, his fingers interlaced behind his head, he laughed a little as his memory slipped, and he was not sure what was not going to be like what.

His mother came in from rehearsals an hour later and passed the door of his bedroom. She looked in for a moment, saw her son sleeping, shrugged, and walked back to the living room where she poured a glass of gin, shook a pair of yellow pills from the bottle, and sat before the blaring television, Jackie Gleason's dancing girls forming a shifting kaleidoscope of legs on the screen.

X

10/29/92

Jazz, I expect that Ben is up in arms because I write to you so much. If you're showing him the letters, I can see why, because they aren't that much about Dominic after all. There are two reasons for that, one of which has everything good to say about you, and another that says nothing good about me.

I know Dom's in good hands, Jazzie. That he's better off in a family with two incomes, like the judge said. And hell, he's better off financially in a family with either of your incomes, just one of them, than in a family with mine.

But we both know that isn't all of it, and that the real bottom line is that you're a better Ma than I am a Da, and I could go into all that psychobabble about how the role wasn't modeled for me but it would be irresponsible, you know it, and it's beginning to dawn on me how much of a lie it would be when I look around and see all the fathers that leave the scene of the accident and the mothers who can't handle the sons, and that it isn't good for anyone except the Ritalin industry, and it's then I can't feel sorry for myself thanks to Trajan. And even if his plans for me were impure, like you've always claimed, well so be it, goddamn it, because he only tried to guide me.

That was what the trip in the woods was all about. And it happened just the way I always told you, right down to the bow and the owl. It was like standing on the edge of myth, Jazzie, and with myth looking back at you.

It was the last time I entered the woods except one. I went back after the thing with Del, and this time there was no Trajan, and it was the last thing I did with Joey for years, that dead-of-night walk to listen to Zuice, and maybe that woods is the source of a loneliness I am trying to understand even now.

So that is what the rest of this letter is about, Jasmine. You are the one nominated, because there's no one else to tell this to until Dominic comes of age.

Joey called me on a November night in '69, about a year after I went into the woods with Trajan. By then Joey and I had passed through the freshman year and all those losses together, and I had figured I would not hear from him for some time, because the whole Del business lay in the back of how we knew each other, and neither of us was all that comfortable with the other anymore. But here was Joey calling, and I was glad to hear from him and a little scared.

He wanted to go out to the Country Ball Room, which was left over from when the golf course was part of a country club. You probably don't remember seeing the place. They tried it as a library later and none of those things—country club, ballroom, or library—worked in our part of the county.

It hadn't reached the point where the place had entirely lost its promise. Back then, the Ball Room took in a bunch of local rock acts, and once in a long while it drew a band from outside—Sir Douglas Quintet had played there, I think, on their way up- or downhill, and maybe the Lemon Pipers once, though I'm not sure about that. But I am sure that on this night it was Zuice, and Joey had some score to settle with Aron—some big, dramatic falling-out that I didn't understand then because boys basically got angry with friends then buried the hatchet, and that was the way such things operated.

I had to sneak out to go, because Joey wanted to wait until about 1 or 2 in the morning when the band was breaking down. So it was out the window at around midnight, and the only lights were the streetlamps and a window at Miss Vivien's, because Trajan was always up late. Joey was waiting for me, of course, out on August Street, and we stood there for a second watching the lights in Trajan's house.

There was something in Joey that never knew what to make of Trajan. I used to think it was because Joey had been the brains of our operation till Trajan showed up, but a few years ago—you remember the last time I saw Joey—I began to wonder if it wasn't something more submerged, something that he hadn't put thoughts or words around yet. At the same time, he was fascinated by the wooden incline, by the way that, if the moonlight was to catch it just right, it seemed to be branching and blossoming, like it had done that night in late summer when both of us approached it and burst the berries in our hands.

And I swear that, out of season and out of nature, a lesser light from Trajan's bedroom window edged a jungle of new branches, peeking through leaves like damaged sunlight. I was all about pointing this out to Joey. I guess I wanted familiar adventures rather than the one he was promising, but he was setting off straight up August, to the little lane that connected our subdivision with Gethsemane Lane. Then west along the wooded road, and the November air that night was so brisk that the music seemed to freeze on it as it reached us across the golf course, the creek, and the development.

I remember asking him what the deal was with Aron, and why it needed dealing with at this hour. He brushed away the question, and when I wanted to walk on the left side of the road facing traffic, he herded us right, and it made me nervous.

There was another Baptist church about a block north of us, a less respectable one where they didn't wear ties and where Del's family had gone. By the time we got there, I could hear "Within You, Without You" coming from the club in the distance, and I was wondering what kind of music that was to dance to, with the sitar and everything.

We passed the last baffle of bare trees, and the music swelled, and we entered the lot. A car was pulling away, older kids who shouted at us and spun their tires on the gravel with a shredding sound. The band was playing "Inner Light" by then (why Zuice covered all those George Harrison Hindu songs eluded me then) and in the midst of the noise Joey turned to me and said something.

He was shivering, and I moved closer and saw that the fool just had pajama bottoms on, underneath a long, thin raincoat that had to have been his mom's. I started to say something, to suggest that we go back, but he was off again to the side of the hall, where you could watch the band through a line of windows.

There was no way we were getting in. First of all, they were serving alcohol, and even though nobody in the band was 21, they were checking you at the door.

Second, it cost a dollar fifty.

So we stood in the cold, by the window nearest the band, and watched Aron, his blond hair covering his ears entirely, impossibly long for Kentucky and the year. He guided the band into something off Wonderwall—I don't know what, because, like I said, that Indian stuff all sounded the same to me. And apparently it sounded the same to the people in the hall, a little too alien for a crowd schooled on the Kingsmen and Four Seasons. They were standing around, warm in the slanted light, and Aron on the stage weaving through flashes of red and green, a bad high school light system and a song out of place.

Joey's face was pressed against the window, almost for warmth as much as to see what was going on, like an insect looking for the light. He had wrapped the coat tightly around himself and he was muttering something, something I lost again under the cadenced throb of the music.

On his face was something I had never seen, picked up in that last year of absences. I knew it was to do with Aron, but I didn't know what it was until a lot later, and even then, you didn't think such things about your friends, not in your teens when your whole masculinity struggled for purchase, and certainly not in Kentucky, where it was unthinkable for a boy to look at a boy like that. I knew it was something forbidden, and that was as far as I got on that night, except I knew it was uncomfortable to look at. I felt like I should back away, step out of the light and leave it to Joey. And he must have known I was looking on, because he turned and shook his head in disgust.

I thought the disgust was for me at first.

"Let's get out of here, Gabriel," he said, a little loudly so I could hear him over the nasal drone of Aron's old Fender Stratocaster trying vainly to sound like a sitar. "I should of known better than this."

"Yeah," I replied dimly. "Next time wear more than your jammies."

Joey looked at me like there was a whole world I had not taken into account, and I suppose he was right, Jazzie.

I suppose I was lucky not to have my heart broken until I was old enough to reckon with it.

"Let's just go home, Gabriel," he said, his voice mournful and higher than I remembered it. "Let's go. I reckon I got years to figure this one out."

It was very late. We left the dance, Aron's voice soft and adenoidal over the heavily reverbed music, again a George Harrison song—"Blue Jay Way," if I remember right.

"Please don't be long," it urged. "Please don't youuuu be very long...."

We hurried back toward the neighborhood, the streetlights sputtering like candles over Gethsemane. I wondered what it was that would take someone years to figure out, and I thought there was something I should say to Joey, but for the life of me I could not get my thoughts around it. Once it seemed like I had it, I put my hand on his back, but he shouldered away from me like he was slipping off a coat, and I thought what I had to say was nothing much, anyway.

And then, ahead of us at the edge of the lamplight, something moved in the middle of the road. Something pale and writhing, turning once in our direction with a red glitter of eyes, then turning away, setting back to its work.

It made us stop. Slowly, because we had to get home after all, we approached it from the left side of the road, the tree line and the development at our backs as we sidled around it. I was thinking of strange visits, of the previous year and the things I had seen...

But it was two dogs humping in the middle of the road, a white mutt humping a brown bitch that looked like Del's old dog Molly, the one who had vanished after the game. But there they were, going at it, the male swiveling his hips as he thrust, his forepaws draped over the bitch's dark fur.

"Oh, shit!" Joey moaned, like it was something worse than I expected. I started to ask him if it was Molly, but he grabbed me and tried to yank me off the road and beyond the hang of trees, to what he must have thought was the safety of the open fields.

Or maybe it was something else. Because that night was about other things as well, Jazzie, about a moment that passed so quickly it did not register until months later. Because when I wrestled free of Joey, I stood there in Gethsemane Lane for a moment, watching the dogs go at it, and then there was this blaring sound behind me, and things moving slowly as the dogs scattered in front of me and my shadow rose out of twin pools of light.

What pushed me off the road I do not know. But whatever it was, it lifted me and hurled me through the air, like the old emperor in the Antioch earthquake, and I rolled through the high grass at the roadside and looked up as the pickup careened into far gravel and found the road again, the red tail lights snaking away through the darkness. It was like being born aloft by a sudden, violent tremor, and for a moment—just a moment—a column of mist hung over Gethsemane Lane, then dissolved and spilled into the asphalt.

I couldn't stop to wonder. I was in open fields now, moon-mottled foundations of houses rising from the ground like ruins, like gravestones, and Joey breaking into a run toward the eastern edge of the development, toward the place where the neighborhood began.

I started to run, to follow Joey, but he was always faster, and the ground between us widened. By the time we reached the near end of Flora Drive I had lost him. I figured he would make for home and that I should do the same.

The window was ajar, like I left it. But something looked out of place as I started to climb back into the bedroom. I looked over toward Miss Vivien's, and it felt like the whole world tilted.

There was a man standing on Miss Vivien's ramp. Standing

there watching me.

At first I thought it was Trajan. But no: the man was gaunt. Wearing a pale duster, tangled in those strange branches that sprouted out of the inclined railing.

The light from Trajan's window framed him, shone through him.

For a moment I thought of the dog in the middle of Gethsemane. And then I thought of the Halloween a year before, when I saw something in Miss Vivien's back yard that I never told you about— never thought I would be telling you.

The man waved at me. He beckoned, and the branches grew around him and through him. And the light from the window passed over him, and he cast no shadow.

I scrambled back through the window, and I don't think I slept the next night, either.

No, I'm not crazy. I know all the explanations, and I still rehearse them. I am starting to remember what happened after I came back from the fields with Trajan, but that later night is firm in my memory, and the man was not beckoning me for then but for now. It's part of the reason I'm headed home.

It's just as well that Dominic can't come with me. Tell him his Da is thinking of him, and not to worry about the holidays. You don't worry, either, Jazzie. I'll let you both know how it turns out.

Fondly,
Gabriel

TWO

And such too is the grandeur of the doom
We have imagined for the mighty dead.
--Endymion, ll. 20-21

XI

Gabriel would find out later that Trajan had once come close to escaping, back in 1946 when he had gone to New England to school.

It was the typical story of the promising Southern boy who had reached the edge of his talents. Excellent and effortless grades, superlative test scores that were nonetheless percentiles behind his Northeastern fellows. A single mother with miniscule means of support, a father dead with the AEF in North Africa.

All in all, it added up to scholarships. One to Ohio State, and another to Rochester, where Gabriel himself would go years later. But the third was far into Vermont, in a small school that seemed, by 1940s standards, a week's journey from the damp and stifling suburbs of Louisville, and that was the school and the distance that Trajan seized upon.

Thracia College. Maybe five hundred students there in the '40s, and by the time Gabriel had heard of it from Trajan, there was nothing much to hear about. Thracia had closed its doors in 1965 amid a profusion of scandals, almost all of which were venal and financial. But for a while, in a kind of halcyon non-witch-hunt 1950s, it had been, according to Trajan, a "good little school," and after a stint in graduate school he had returned there, Masters Degree in hand, to teach Latin to the last generation of students who thought the language was worthy or even interesting.

To hear him tell it, these were great times for Trajan Bell. He drifted over the campus in a kind of sweet mournfulness, content in the minor basics of the language, delighting in the mathematics of its irregularities, the surprises of its exceptions. He taught a course on lyric poetry, then one on Ovid when he was five years into his teaching. He studied and drowsed in a sunstruck office on the third floor of Thracia's decrepit Arts building, the windowsills smelling of lemon wax and the ancient glass panes originals, the glass blurred and heat-startled. Absorbed in Ovid's great long poem, *The Metamorphoses,* where gods and heroes transformed into trees and flowers, into reptile and bull, Trajan's time was his own, and his own metamorphosis was that of a man released.

Oh, he missed Artie, certainly. After only six months of their knowing his friend's image was indelible. But sometimes in the classroom he could forget about the woods east of Ripton and the blinding snow of '47 and the loss of his Georgia Peach. Especially in the fall and spring, when Vermont changed color before and after the ice came in and settled, there were breathing times when your thoughts could drift away from your losses and the landscape would deepen and complicate.

Trajan enjoyed eight years of that. Eight years until the trouble in the school. Then the retreat, a brief stay in Michigan— not far, by coincidence, from where Gabriel's father lived—and then the summons home.

In a way, Miss Vivien's illness must have been a kind of relief. It had been there all along, implicit in every conversation, transforming and metamorphosing into new ailments and pains. From the start she was trying to draw him back and enclose him until, finally, in the summer of '68, his wanderings had ended, and he came full circle home.

There and back again.

So as Gabriel drifted in and out of sleep on that November day, his dreams were completing the long trajectory and fall of Trajan's journey.

As shallow snows settled once, then twice, on the mid-South, Gabriel lodged with his remorse, something in him estranged from his new friend, unspoken and uncomfortable, like the moments when you see your own reflection in the corner of your eye, then, when you turn to face it, discover that you are something safe again, something familiar and acceptable.

And while the winter passed, who knows what dwelt with Trajan through the winter and the early spring? Gabriel glimpsed him only a handful of times, shouted *Merry Christmas* across the street and was greeted in kind. But they both knew something had changed, as they regarded each other from a narrow, unfathomable distance.

✳✳✳

It was the winter of the burning boys.

In January 1969, a Czech student named Jan Palach lit himself afire in Wenceslas Square in Prague, protesting the Soviet occupation of his homeland. An eighteen-year-old boy named Jan Zajic followed his example a month later, and then in April, in another act of martyrdom, Evzen Plocek (forty years old, and according to Gabriel's mother "of an age to know better") doused himself in paint thinner and suffered immolation in the town of Jihana.

Gabriel noted these events with a kind of perverse fascination. He was old enough to remember the Buddhist martyrdoms in Saigon, but the burnings were closer this time— the faces of the immolated filling the television screens as David Brinkley and Walter Cronkite intoned newsmen's eulogies over these pale, incomprehensible figures.

Mary Rackett called it morbid. Until two weeks after the fiery death of Plocek, when she joined her son by the television, riveted by new accounts of the arrival of British troops in

Northern Ireland.

All in all, it was the winter when the sins of the fathers were visited on the sons. Because Tom Rackett had called back in November, had asked that his son come up and visit in the week remaining between New Year's and the start of school.

It seemed that Gabriel was to meet a new stepmother. To see a new house. And though Mary protested at first, bringing up all possible excuses from weather to air travel and to short notice, eventually she gave in to Gabriel's pleadings and to muffled phone conversations with his father, arrangements and truces that her son followed not so much by words as by shifts in the whispered tones.

Don't be expecting Brazil, she warned Gabriel, with a kiss and a wan little smile at the airport. It was one of his mother's enigmatic phrases, slipped into his imagining so that despite himself he nursed a prospect of balmy weather and women in fruit headdresses until his father and he stepped out of the Detroit airport into a January cold past his ability to imagine, its dry, icy intrusions freezing the hair in his nostrils (like Trajan had said the cold could do) by the time they reached the parking lot.

Nor was it Brazil in Tom Rackett's house. The stepmother, a mild, pleasant girl named Daphne, struck him as closer to his own age than his father's, though he was not used to reading the signs and could not be altogether sure. She was blonde, wore her hair like Joni Mitchell's, and smelled of patchouli oil, which kept Gabriel sneezing for the first two days of his visit.

Daphne and Gabriel formed an odd alliance in that week, a conspiracy of winks and eye rolls arrayed against Tom Rackett's tireless desire to please and impress his son. She had a strange accent and called a sub sandwich a grinder, but she was funny and pretty, and Gabriel, all set on hating her for replacing his Ma, found that Daphne was better company than the man he had come to visit.

On Sunday, Tom took Gabriel to see a Pistons game, which Gabriel perversely insisted on calling a "Sixers game" in honor of the visiting team. The Sixers won, 126-119, and Tom's mood soured that afternoon at the distance and surliness in his son he didn't remember and perhaps had never before seen. He became touchier still when the two of them arrived home to Daphne's announcement that Mary Conroy had called.

"It was actually kinda far out," she said. "I mean: your mom is pretty cool, Gabriel. And that accent!

"She was just checking on how you were. Wanted you to know that some old lady named Miss Vivien is in the hospital again."

"I reckon I should call her," Gabriel said, glancing at his father.

Tom Rackett shrugged and walked into the living room, but Daphne nodded solemnly.

"Your own room," his father called the room in which Gabriel stayed, but the spindly bedposts and the vanity gave it away as quarters for any houseguest, not something reserved for a visiting son. The walls were bare, and Gabriel longed for his *Lord of the Rings* and Beatles posters, but someone—Daphne, no doubt—had the foresight to have stocked a solitary white bowl with Spanish peanuts. The room, as well, had the advantage of its own phone.

Gabriel started to call his mother, but after a brief hesitation, called Information instead.

"Trajan Bell," he whispered into the phone. "August Street, in Louisville."

A long pause at the other end of the line. The operator's uncertainty.

"Then try 'Vivien Bell'," Gabriel offered, having remembered that the house was not Trajan's to begin with.

Dialing the number of a V. Bell on August Street, Gabriel second-guessed himself and hung up.

What if Miss Vivien was already back? She had a history of brief hospital stays. And he would rather not talk to Miss Vivien.

But as he lay on the bed, his hand on the phone receiver, he realized he was more afraid of talking to Trajan. That their journey together over the construction site had offered him something he felt he had turned down even before it was offered. The distances of their odd estrangement seemed both greater and less from up in Michigan, and after a short hesitation, Gabriel redialed the number, waited for the ring.

Hung up when a young man's voice answered, reedy and uncertain in the imponderable depths of static. It was an accent like Daphne's, a pair of hellos, then silence on the other end of the phone.

Gabriel propped himself on his elbows and looked out the window at the snow drifted on suburban yards. Somehow the thought of a visitor at the Bells' unsettled him. Someone familiar enough to answer the phone, but probably there only by virtue of Miss Vivien's absence. Something about that ghostly presence—that boy/man on the phone—irritated him as well, with an emotion he recognized as adult, even though he did not understand it. He would know it later as the kind of mild smoldering reserved for trespassers of all kinds, but at that moment, he knew of no boundaries and borders over which anyone could trespass.

And what he saw from the window was quiet, but not assuring. It was like his neighborhood seen through a winter glass, the snow steepled over the red flags on the mailboxes and the squat automobiles sliding mutedly by. It was only then that he began to understand his mother's warning. This was indeed no Brazil, and the images of sunlight and cockatiels he had carried with him on the airplane faded into the impenetrable white of a Michigan winter.

Daphne read his cards that afternoon.

Emerging into the Racketts' disheveled living room, Gabriel surprised her, a book in her hand and brightly covered cards arrayed along the top of the coffee table.

Her blonde hair was tied back, and she wore a white peasant blouse. Something in Gabriel ached as she looked up at him and winked.

"Our old man's gone for burgers," Daphne announced. "Says I can't feed you every night on hippie food."

Gabriel settled into his father's easy chair. "Sounds like him," he observed, propping his feet on the leather ottoman and staring at the blank television screen.

"You wanna watch the tube, man?" Daphne asked. "If you do, make yourself at home."

Gabriel craned over the chair arm. He wondered what he should call his stepmother, but he decided that he would avoid naming her as long as he could. He would not let her rise into words just yet.

"Nah. Television stinks on Sunday afternoon, unless there's a ball game."

"And a Pistons game isn't much of a game, now is it? I'd of thought a good Irish boy like you would have been a Celtics fan. You like Russell and Havilcek?"

Gabriel nodded, even though he and Joey and Del had sworn an undying hatred for all Boston teams in a prelude to last year's World Series. Something about Daphne was coaxing his consent, and he complied, sailing into her drowsy smile.

"Sure. Well, better than the Pistons, anyway. What are you doing?"

Daphne sat back on the sofa, smiled at him, and stretched. The bottom of her peasant blouse slid immeasurably up her taut stomach, revealing an inch of pale skin. "Reading the Tarot, little man. Like to watch?"

Gabriel swallowed hard. "You mean the cards?"

She laughed softly and gathered the spread images into the deck. "Tell you what. I'll do you better than just watching. I'll read your fortune if you like. How's about it?"

It was another act of compliance. Fortune-telling cards were superstitious, the priest had said, and Gabriel's skepticism, just past its novitiate, bucked at the idea of taking a step back into childhood; especially, for some reason, in the presence of Daphne.

And yet she was encouraging the step, and there was something daring about it, as though with a single stride he could move forward and backward, into a time and place where adventures were adventures and where the adventures made sense.

"This is your card, Gabriel," Daphne announced, rifling the deck and producing the image of a boy in yellow, holding a sword. The boy was standing on rocky ground, behind him swirling clouds and high above him a flock of birds.

At the sight of the birds, Gabriel thought of Trajan, of the Queen of the Ghosts, but Daphne drew him back from remembered creek beds and from November thoughts.

"This is what they call your significator, Gabe. Now shuffle the cards, and cut them into three piles, with your right hand to the left, while you think of a question you want to ask them."

Perplexed at the directions, Gabriel looked up. Daphne was reading aloud from a book on Tarot, and suddenly all the potential mystery of the moment began to ebb away. It was like assembly instructions or an owner's manual, so he obeyed her ironically, more entranced by her necklace of intertwined leather than by the promised arcana of the cards.

Quite simply, unaccustomed to the nuances of fortune-tellers, he asked what the future held for him.

Daphne leaned over the table now, squinting at the three stacks of cards, and drew one from the leftmost stack.

"I'm never sure whether I start from your left or mine, Gabe," she admitted with a soft, abrupt laugh, "so we'll go from your left. This is the card that covers you, the present situation… you know, what's happening right now."

Gabriel nodded, a little impatiently. He didn't like being talked down to any more than he liked being called "Gabe."

"And it's the King of Swords," Daphne announced serenely. "Kinda matches up with your significator, don't it, man? I guess that's to mean you're in your father's house, even though Tom is mostly a Wand."

She giggled a little as she turned a card face up and laid it across the King, but immediately her supple face was serious, even sober.

"Seven of swords, little man. It's the crossing card: the opposing force. You been liberatin' things? You know, rippin' them off. Stealing."

She shrugged at Gabriel's vehement denial, dealt four cards around the cross she had made, like the numbers on a clock or the compass points on an old map. "Beneath, behind, crowning, and before," she proclaimed in a solemn, newscaster's voice. "The things you're used to, the things that are just passing away, what might happen in the future, and what's about to happen."

Gabriel moved from the chair to a seat beside Daphne on the sofa. Suddenly the reading had become interesting in its focus on possible and definite futures. He pointed to the card beneath him. "What's the Ace of Wands mean?"

He wanted to call her Daphne, but was shy of the familiarity. Nevertheless, in some ways the girl had gypsy instincts.

"Call me Daphne, Gabe. Now the Ace of Wands—I remember that one, 'coz I seen it before when I met your father— that's the beginning of a great adventure. That have to do with you coming here, you think? Or just with life in general?"

Gabriel shrugged. At one moment his stepmother could tune in, while at the next she seemed surprisingly, disappointingly thick. But with growing certainty, now that one of Gabriel's cards had matched one of her own, Daphne raced through the remaining three on the clock face of the spread, telling him things he would remember, then forget, about the Strength card reversed, the Chariot and the Queen of Pentacles. Out of this trio of cards Daphne wove a story about how Gabriel would grow in good things and assurance, and the woman he would meet "sometime down the road" would very possibly be a wealthy one, perhaps even an heiress.

But something in Gabriel told him to remember the cards, that at some later time the names and the meanings would avail him in what would be the real story. He watched, then, as Daphne spread the last four cards in an ascending row to the right of the cards she had already set on the table. Fears, Family, Hopes, and Outcome, she called them, and Gabriel noted the Moon, the Ten of Wands, the Three of Cups…

And then, in the place of Outcome, the card of Death.

Daphne was quick to the rescue. "Don't get uptight, little man. The weird thing about the Death card is that it's not a card of Death."

Gabriel looked skeptically at the pale rider, the skull beneath the visored helmet and the sunset behind the towers in the distance. "So if it ain't a card of death, then why do they call it Death?"

He could hear the uncertainty in Daphne's voice now. "Well, it says here that the card means the change of old concepts for new, the change from the personal to the universal. You understand that, Gabe?"

He guessed he did.

"It's like this," Daphne expanded, moving closer to him on the sofa until her leg brushed against his. "In order for something new to happen, something old has to give way. Junior high ended, right? So it kind of died there, in order for you to head on to the new stuff. Is it making more sense to you now?"

Gabe was thinking of Daphne's thigh pressed against his. He had understood the card before the girl's rather fumbling explanation, and he understood a little the stirring in his trousers. Uncomfortably, he shifted away from Daphne, listened abstractedly to the rest of the reading, and then returned to the guest room, from which he would emerge to hamburgers and strange disapproving looks from his father.

It was only the next Sunday, on the plane ride home to Louisville, that he realized how Daphne's Tarot reading, in all of its subtleties and branchings, had been the closest thing to magic in Michigan.

XII

November 16, 1992

Jazzie,

None of it surprises me now. I was thinking of Daphne the other day, of how, in my second year of college, she sent me that indifferent note about why she was leaving my father for some guy from the Detroit Wheels, who, I think, had been disbanded for about five years when she met him. I wanted to think for a while that she was the Devil with the Blue Dress, but there was really nothing devilish about that sleepy vertigo, the cards and the peasant blouse.

By then I knew what Ma had meant by not expecting Brazil. It was "Breasil" she had said to me, part of the Celtic song and dance about an Island of the Blessed. Made me think of the little Frost poem that went (and I'm quoting it from bad memory) "But Islands of the Blessed, bless you, son, / I never came upon a blessed one."

But I'll give Daphne this much. The reading was uncanny in ways that she could not have foreseen, given who she was and when she did it. Surely somewhere inside her, she knew she was no clairvoyant—"I mean, don't all of us know that at some level?" I can hear you saying—but you're wrong, because just when you get to the knowing, Jazzie, and just when you've shut the door on everything else, well that's when there are noises behind the door you've shut, soft and ominous rustlings that sometimes will let other people know that the world is re-awakening.

And Daphne's reading took years to come to pass. Crazy as it sounds, the cards had something to do with this sheaf of stories on my table, and I know that you're already bringing up projection and wishful thinking, but maybe that's a part of seeing most everything, not just mysteries and ghosts. At any rate, what might be even crazier, Trajan knew the cards at some level, the very spread of swords and Major Arcana she showed me on that snowy Sunday in Michigan.

I know that when I returned to Louisville, Miss Vivien was still in the hospital. I saw the young man, who must have been the mysterious voice on the phone, glide in and out of the house at night, because I watched across August Street in the late hours, wanting and not wanting to know the business in the Bell place. I remembered the accent, hoped foolishly that he would shout aloud something in the January night, something that would carry across the street and through my window closed against the cold. But of course he never did, since what was going on over there was more secret in those times. And sure enough, one night I saw the boy loading boxes into the trunk of his car, thin and ghostly in the yellowing glare of the street lamp. Miss Vivien was back the next morning, Trajan pushing her chair up the forlorn incline like they were two figures bound together on a Tarot card, eternal and inexpressibly sad.

I didn't see Trajan up close until spring, when the thing with Del happened that I told you about long ago. I went back to the encyclopedia once, on one of those idling Sunday afternoons in February, when there were neither Tarot cards nor snowdrifts to distract me, and I looked closely at Trajan's arch. There it was, standing in the midst of a place called Benevento, and it seemed to me then, given the bare desolation surrounding the monument, that it was some huge triumphal structure in the midst of nowhere, marking a passage between the nothing in front of it and the nothing beyond. I remember thinking that surely something changed in you when you passed through it, that the world on the other side of it was somehow different, that the arch had to be a boundary of sorts.

But whatever the case—how much or how little the Trajan of my history had to do with imperial Trajan, my own Trajan seemed to know what had happened to me before I knew it myself. He left me the stories, after all—especially the one about the spiritualist/con artist, because the story is a kind of door as well.

I know I am not being clear on this. I know you are thinking "thank God Dominic is with me over the holidays, instead of with his crazy father." But the story is a door, Jazzie. I looked at it again last night, the way it positioned itself in the manuscript and in the cards, all at the same time, and then the door started to open for me, and I backed away. But I only backed away for now.

Because the noises have been rising from behind that door for weeks, and visions like a light glimpsed through latticework, or like the landscape on the other side of an arch. There's a code in the story that is not a code really; not in that sense of correspondences, like a cipher, but in a more profound sense of suggestions and symbols, like a painting you look through instead of at.

Back when the first snow of the season came, I stood by the window here and watched it fall over the maples. Beyond our parking lot there's a side street that runs back away from State 50, back toward more apartments, and beyond that, other side of the street, a steep decline into about an acre of brushwood, and the snow seemed to be filling the underbrush, clinging to the tangle of dried bramble and weeds.

And yes, there was whiskey present, three fingers of bourbon and a solitary cube of ice, and though it was the second, you have seen me on the third and fourth before, so you should know that hallucination or illusion do not necessarily follow in the wake of Messrs. Beam and Daniels. I say this because, standing in the snow-mantled lot were a host of figures, blurred by the convergence of streetlight and darkness and glittering downfall of snow.

In front of them all stood a solitary, definable figure: a bearded man, shaggy and thin and gangling, his legs outlined in front of a snow-crusted white pickup. He was dressed poorly for bad weather, his light, almost translucent jacket no match for the cold and the driving snow. It took only a moment to notice that the snow was not falling on the man, but through him. Even from this height and through the veil of glass, you could tell he was dry, that the snow settling around him was drifting and settling beneath him, as though he was made of mist or cloud.

Then the man looked at me. At once I recognized the face, the obscene smile I had glimpsed twenty-five years ago in the foliage behind Miss Vivien's house. The October Man made a gesture: a crude movement with his right hand, and a sudden, grotesque turn of his neck, as though he held a rope in it and was strangling himself.

His laughter rose from the lot and seemed to mist against my window.

In the morning, before the first stirrings in the apartment complex as people went off to work, I walked out into the lot, circled the area where I had seen the great host of shifting figures in the night, and ended up by the white pickup, parked close to the steps leading up to my building.

And whether the snow had continued long enough to cover the tracks, I couldn't tell. The ground around the truck was white, unruffled, inscrutable, and whether my late night visitor had risen from my mind or from somewhere outside me—somewhere in the icy night—I have never been certain.

That night, however, sent me back to the manuscript. Back to codes and suggestions I had been trying to avoid for years, to the stories that are mine simply because they were mailed to me. And I read them like poor, dim Daphne read my cards on a table in Michigan, both of us rash to claim mysteries as our own. One of them is a story of Tarot as well, and of the afterlife of things. And wouldn't Trajan be surprised to know the afterlife of his stories?

It's as though the old times are coming up to meet me here, rushing into a vacuum of beckonings and unfinished desires. I see a constant, dark mantling of clouds now to the southeast, on the horizon as November slips toward December and the holidays, when

I will fly back to Louisville through a welter of memory.

Fondly,
Gabriel

P.S. I'm mailing this late again—Irish Standard Time, my father would have said. Tell Dominic his Da wished him a happy Thanksgiving, and to stick to his studies after the break, because there are rumors that tryptophan causes brain damage and sluggishness in students. Even students like him.

Second Ephesians
A story by Trajan Bell

Part 1: Sybil's Masque

The Chariot is the card for those who achieve greatness. The cryptic pharaoh in a canopied cart, drawn by twin sphinxes, his vehicle emblazoned with wings above lingam and yoni

But perhaps, in the days of Mrs. Sybil Gault Lefcourt, the chariot was merely a symbol for all vehicles, for all travel. For the travel that brought her miles across the ocean, and those less defined, interior travels that brought Ephesians Munday onto the stage of her memory and thought.

Sybil Gault first entered the theatre in 1891, when she was but a girl of sixteen, at Stratford, in *The Tempest*.

Though she would appear in the same play in later years—and then as Ariel, mind you—on this particular performance she was only a dancing sprite near the play's end, among a chorus of girls swaying ethereally to the music of Mr. Haydn's Sturm.

There will be time enough, I am certain, to recount her other early ventures on the English stage. But it is the events of that particular performance that I shall relate here, as they are in keeping with her visitations and intimations of the World of Spirit, a world that often mingles with our own. And as with most experiences of travelers in the ethereal and transcendent, the venture began in unsettlement and unease.

As she joined in the dance on that evening in '91, the first of Sybil Gault's troubles was simply a girlish one, to assure that her crown of daisies did not slip from her head. The second, of course, remembering the simple steps of the dance, and aligning them with those of her fellows. It was in watching the moving arms of the girl beside her, matching gestures with those of the older, more trained dancer, that she noticed yet another girl, arriving late and taking a place at the end of the row.

This creature was squat, a head shorter than any of the other dancers, her skin pocked and curd-pale. The face and features of a Mongolian idiot, her own steps abstract and tentative, as though she were remembering them over a long span of years or reading instructions through murky water.

Something repellent there was in her smell, moreover. Later, Sybil would describe it as a whiff of the charnel house, though at that time she knew nothing of that terrible sweet odor, nor that the phrase itself was good spiritualist poetry, one that medium and mystic alike would use to describe ghostly visitation. At the time, however, Sybil thought of setting her foot at the topmost step of a rat-rife cellar, of a warm metallic stench rising out of that cool dark underground.

Watching the poor thing gesture her way through the simple dance, trying to keep up nervously and awkwardly, Sybil's sympathy transformed into a kind of contempt. The cruelty of those sentiments alarmed her, more than the girl's nature or her occluded purpose in the Shakespearian dance.

Despite herself, Sybil wanted to slap the girl. Wanted to startle and confuse her. She did not like what she wanted.

And then, the dance coming slowly to a close, the creature turned over the sea of waving arms and swirling crinoline. Her eyes were all dark, as though the pupils had expanded to fill them entirely, lid to lid, so that she stared from blackened slits and smiled stupidly, a grin ecstatic and malicious, sans teeth and sensibility.

Sybil turned from this slow monstrosity and fumbled with the music. The dance ended with her some steps behind her fellows, staggering like an idiot in the silence. It was the girl's fault, she told herself with the righteousness of a sixteen-year-old, and she vowed to take it up at curtain.

But of course, by then the creature was nowhere to be found.

As Sybil moved through the dancers, through the bustle of actors and stagehands, her anger at the creature changed to a sort of pity borne out of her own shame. For after all, there was something inexcusable in the malice she felt toward the terrible little thing. Perhaps this was a friend or relation of Frank Benson's, or an idiot girl upon whom the famous director had taken pity. Surely such contempt was unreasonable and inordinate.

Sybil searched the tiring rooms, then the whole of the backstage. Miranda flitted before her like a wraith, and Ariel as well, though at a second glance these figures were clearly and palpably actresses, solid and in the process of undress, making re-adjustments in their paint and attire about which I could never tell you, for it is unfamiliar country to me, as it was to Miss Sybil Gault at that early hour of her theatrical calling. She would grow accustomed to mask and role in later years, but now she waded through simple enigmas, through the milling cast in search of a greater mystery.

There was one patch of darkness in the wings, farthest from the lamps, and as she approached it, a smell—sour and feral—drifted to meet her out of the mottled shadows.

No doubt it was more caution than kindness that slowed her steps. Whatever the girl was, whether dancer or revenant, she had receded into that inclement darkness. She was hiding from Sybil there, or waiting for her.

Sybil stopped, at the edge of the lamplight, her reluctance mingled with fear. For a moment, she glimpsed a deeper darkness in the heart of the shadows. Something that moved away from her, that settled and crouched in a shapeless, disheveled heap that was alive, or feigning life, to judge by its movement in the core of the gloom. Again, the hot, rusted stench of some furtive creature boiled in the close air.

Sybil turned away from it, from the strange truce it was making between life and death, and it was almost a decade until that shame would slip away from her. Sometimes she would remember that turning as a kind of betrayal of what was best in her; at other times, she felt as though she had betrayed her worst impulses, and that it would have been wiser to see them through, to give them light. It would be years until she could decide which, and it would take the events in Marylebone to show her that she had turned from neither side of her nature, but from what was deeply and radically both.

Needless to say, the next production of The Tempest was short two dancers. Sybil set off by the train to London, and never worked with Frank Benson again. And yet in the years to come, when again and again she would tread the stage in this very play—as a Nymph, then as Ariel and finally as Miranda—she could never sing her songs without a shudder.

> *Full fathom five thy daughter lies;*
> *Of her bones are coral made;*
> *Those are pearls that were her eyes;*
> *Nothing of her that doth fade,*
> *But doth suffer a sea-change*
> *Into something harsh and strange.*

✳✳✳

It was six years from that moment—almost to the day—when the Ethereal would yet again touch Sybil Gault's mundane life. Doubtless something in her acknowledged its presence: the dim and perhaps ulterior promptings of beyond and beneath.

But here is the strange part, Reader. That moment in Frank Benson's theatre she had dismissed almost altogether for a spell, remembering it only when she passed by the mouths of dark alleys, when she heard voices tumble from second-story windows at sunset. It was as though something in the Mystery—or perhaps something in Sybil—prevented future encounters.

Sometimes, albeit rarely, when The Honorable and she would attend the theatre, when visiting friends backstage, Sybil would catch a whiff from a tiring room of something turning in the air, and see a shadow in the corner of her eyes that seemed to quiver for a moment, but would resolve into a cape, a property coat rack or a billing sign when taken in full gaze. But memory is a strange ghost. It haunts you at times of its own choosing, and for motives that are entirely its own.

Suffice it to say that, five years to the day, her lodgings more comfortable in Marylebone now, her daily life becoming more accustomed to the new flat, to her new husband and to his Parliamentary absences, and to her brace of servants, she chanced across a second and more enduring encounter.

Her father had moved his family to London in her infancy. Sybil remembered the first house near Tower Hill, the bridge and the bone-white parapets, but chiefly the stench and the yellow smoke, the gray water pooled in the morning wash basin, even after she had scrubbed diligently before going to bed. The lamps lit at midday against the omnipresent fog, and the stream of visitors with American accents and whispered business.

At times she wondered if her father were not a smuggler of sorts, because all the arrivals smelled of far places and sea salt. But it was nothing so dramatic, nothing of romance and piracy: he had simply espoused the losing army in the disastrous American civil conflict, and had refused the reconstruction of his conquerors. Instead of defeat, he chose decay and poverty, and Sybil's earliest days were spent hand to mouth in the Borough.

But Marylebone, where our story takes place, was another London altogether. Far west of the early squalor Sybil remembered, north of the seediness and dust in which her father located them finally, Marylebone was respectable, even posh around the Regent's Park. However, it was, for the daughter of an actress and a genuine American Confederate general, tame surroundings, despite her sudden rise in social prominence as the new wife of an M.P. At first Sybil would welcome the respite from work, would relish the security, enjoy the company of her lady's maid Becky, but soon her thoughts turned back to other pursuits. Most to her liking, she was not far from the theatre, and the Marylebone Spiritualist Association was even closer, located on Russell Square, within walking distance from her flat.

Let it be known from the outset that Sybil Gault Lefcourt (for that was her name now, in the safety of this Parliamentary marriage) took not a shilling for her readings. To have done so would have been to add fraudulence to what was at its very best an understandable pattern of deceiving. This part of London was filled with ladies who had little to do and much to ponder, and the findings of Messrs. Lyell and Darwin—not to mention the questionable Mr. Freud—had turned gentle thoughts along unhealthy and brazen pathways. Or so Sybil's husband, the Honorable Philip Lefcourt, insisted, urging her to use her gifts—both spiritual and theatrical—to restore these ladies to their customary spirit of meekness and impressionability.

Perhaps she did her duties less gladly than she should, for she employed her gifts toward the goals The Honorable set before her, being as St.Paul urges those of her sex, submitted to her husband. And yet she stood at the edge of a new century, when the glory was passing from the world, and parlour games were one sad way to recover it, so she employed her gifts theatrically, not spiritually, and certainly not in a manner that met with the approval of the M.P.

But it is a story unto itself how Sybil Lefcourt had come to such mannerly duties. A story that, perhaps at this time, I should recount.

∗∗∗

Sibyl Gault's earliest theatrical ventures were those not uncommon to a young woman of reasonable comeliness and wit, though the small role in Mr. Benson's Shakespearean troupe was testimony that the comeliness was more than reasonable, the wit sharper than common. Though the Gaults were of modest social station, as I have related, nonetheless the stage would have been forbidden her were it not for her father's death in her eighth year. A mournful and distracted mother had kept scant eye on her sister and her: her education was one of greasepaint rather than Greek, of lamplight rather than Latin. It is a wonder that Sybil learned to read at all, but learn she did, if only to master the scripts and prompts of the stage that excited her, that seduced her by the age of twelve.

By the time Sybil was fifteen, as raw and untutored a child as ever stood before a stage lamp, she had met Mr. Frank Benson, whose Shakespearian productions traveled all England from York to Shrewesbury. It was something in her appearance and demeanor that had drawn Mr. Benson to her, but I assure you that his attentions were never untoward, never more base than paternal. Under his guidance, she had played Peaseblossom, had played as well a Nymph in *The Tempest*, and later, of course, the most challenging rôle of Ariel. For a brief run, when she was scarcely eighteen, she had played Phebe the Shepherdess, and once, with great nervousness and chagrin, had stood in the part of Viola.

That was the night she had met the Honorable Phillip Lefcourt. Who fell in love with her, he claimed. And indeed, the note he sent backstage was filled with ambiguous praise of her adoption of Cesario's role, how the boy had become his master's mistress, and on and on with such airy delights that she felt herself compelled to meet him.

Now, only three short years later, his bride of a year and two years removed from the stage, she was given permission to again employ her talents, this time for the amusement of idle ladies. But by then, the employment of those talents was insufficient. An especial estrangement had occurred between the Honorable and his much younger wife, although I hesitate to blame the divisions upon the difference in their ages. Mark it as one of those situations in which two souls drift widely apart on a sunstruck, desolate sea. Each acknowledges that once, years ago, he saw the other suffused in a glorious light—nothing like this bare and merciless glitter on calm waters. But each acknowledges as well that the memorable light was imagined at best, reflected at worst.

No matter, the reasons, early in their second year of marriage, Sybil's husband took to long nights at his club, then boldly announced he would be playing chess at the residence of the Honorable Valerian Quant. Though the Honorable Philip Lefcourt had displayed neither inclination nor talent for that game in their brief courtship, Sybil knew fully well his élan at other games, other matters: Valerian Quant had a dark-haired daughter scarcely fourteen.

At any rate, when her husband released her to the stage, Sybil Lefcourt was no longer drawn to acting. Instead, it was the stagecraft and dramaturgy that enchanted her, and most of all the words that breathed life into the actors. She knew the impossibilities that a woman could write and stage her own dramas: even the melodramas, the provinces of Jerrold, Bernard, or Boucicault, were forbidden country for the female pen, and though her husband knew both Messrs. Shaw and Wilde, neither of the aforesaid gentlemen was inclined to lend assistance to the fairer sex.

Nor would The Honorable himself ply influence to aid his wife in the manly pursuit of playwriting. He would pat her on the head, like he did his spaniel, and explain that the stage was too rough a trade, that rescuing her once from gaslight and vagaries should suffice for a lifetime, given that she was a clever and resourceful girl.

That even though the theatre district swarmed with lesser luminaries than Bernard or Oscar, lesser contemporaries who might be more amiable to women and amenable to championing their causes for the fame that notoriety could bring, it was still London, after all. London, not Paris, mind you. And a whiff of scandal—any whiff, and any scandal—could be quite damaging to the wife of an M.P. (there's a good girl).

So the playwrights, as Sybil translated his warnings, would be no help to her. She was forced to improvise, and the Association on Russell Square became a likely spot for invention. It was well known that, in the old days of Good Queen Bess, the roles she played on the stage would have been acted by boys, and it had occurred to her that when the Honorable Phillip Lefcourt fell in love with his Viola, she was a girl who played a girl playing a boy, and was that unlike the layers of masquerade she would perform at the Association? And in Shakespeare's day, had her husband and she met under those circumstances, she would have been a girl playing a boy playing a girl playing a boy...

It dizzied her to think upon such matters.

The Spiritualist Association was far more simple: it offered itself, a choir of true believers wherein the fairer sex might mask and masquerade as both playwright and actress. It occurred to Sybil that these ladies were a willing audience, at home with spectacle and high drama, at finding meaning beneath the brittle surfaces of event and situation. So she must be forgiven for approaching their assembly with a scheming and indifferent heart, for she was a woman penned in a city and in a household, and we should not be too quick to judge her behaviors.

Automatic writing is a wonderful talent, Dear Reader. When genuinely undertaken, as I have come to believe it may be, it can open the doors to the Unknown and Unfathomable, giving us purchase in untraveled country. In the years that followed, wiser women than Sybil—Miss Besant, for example, and the celebrated wife of the poet Yeats—would draw the miraculous from a narrow parlor as the spirit's hands closed on theirs, guiding their pens across the page with messages from the Otherworld.

I regret to say that Mrs. Lefcourt used the practice as a hoax. Meeting with a number of the distinguished ladies of the Spiritual Association, she introduced them to one Ephesians Munday—a playwright from the time of the first King James—whose work, she claimed, had existed only in what they called prompt copies and foul papers—the manuscripts used by the players in performance. They had been lost in the burning of the Globe Theatre in 1614, but the insistent Munday, whom she had met in a session with planchette and lettered board, was bent on salvaging his name through his posthumous visitations.

That was her story. Indeed, there was conveniently little more to substantiate it beyond a passing mention in the Stationers' Register—Sybil was clever enough to do her homework, and this old record of Jacobean play performance had been preserved, reprinted and bound, and she knew her way around the Museum in Bloomsbury. Moreover, she knew her associates well enough to know that her research was probably superfluous—that gullible women need a trail of magic more than a trail of clues.

But her research, thin as it might have been, was more than a covering of her tracks. Somehow, the presence of names in an old document became a kind of evidence for Mrs. Lefcourt herself, as though she needed testament that something—that anything—lay behind the stage of her own imagining, in a dark tiring room where things scuttled and moved. If she were making Ephesians Munday from whole cloth, she reckoned, it would somehow soothe her heart and her own yearnings if there were essentials, signs to read that stood for something. If there was an Ephesians Munday behind the one she invented.

At any rate, the Register mentioned four works—a series of masques 'performed at the Black Fryars and to acclayme at the Innes of Court.' It was enough for reverie. With the names in her recollection, in long sittings with pen poised above blank paper, Sybil performed for her susceptible audience, inventing the history and ambitions of Ephesians Munday, and finally passages from his vanished works.

The four masques Munday had supposedly written, shaped by enterprise and counterfeit trances, were each supernatural and of classical bent. Now the masque, good reader, is a playlet of sorts—a short drama scented with music and dance, in its day and time a story that stood at the margin of the real, the larger story that was the play itself. The masque, Sybil explained to the assembled spiritualist ladies, was especially splendid in that it bridged the worlds of audience and illusion. When the masquers came down from the stage to dance with those who had watched the play, it was as though the play would continue through eternity, she told them, with the lines between audience and characters perpetually and unchangeably blurred.

You can imagine how much she laughed inside when she told them this.

To hear Sybil tell it, Master Munday was reaching his prominence as a writer of masques, when mystery cut short his time, leaving us with this curious legacy of four short plays.

Indeed, so that you will not consider all my doings fraudulent, I insist that the names were present in the Register.

One was *Achilles*, entered in the 1609 Register. And Sybil took the single word in hand and invention, spinning a tale for the credulous of the hero's haunting by his dear friend Patroclus, of his untimely death, and his ghostly return to demand the death of the maiden Polyxena.

The next was *Alcyone*, and another ghostly tale: her inventions were more restrained, because, unlike Achilles, Alcyone had few stories about her. Sybil picked the most famous: that of her mourning, of the loss of her shipwrecked husband, his nightly visits and her transformation into a bird at the end of the masque.

The next was even narrower: *Thyestes and his Maske of Vengaunce*. And though Sybil had no Latin, she remembered her father's library, and so she claimed it was the oddest thing, was it not, that Munday had translated and adapted Seneca's dark story of revenge? This, of course, was the easiest, for all she had to do was read a translation of the Roman play (again, she had no Latin) and 'render' it through 'automatic writing'.

And finally, entered in the Register in late 1613, there was his *Eurydice*. And of course the poor girl is known only for her tragic story—the brief, happy marriage to Orpheus, the adder's bite and her death, and her bereaved husband's vain attempt to harrow her out of the country of death.

And yes, they would talk with Master Munday, after the lectures on the Tarot and the Hindoo pantheon, the anecdotes surrounding the tulpa, that Tibetan ghost with no prior life, conjured from the imagination of the Asiatic magician. After the readings from Nostradamus and the Renaissance Platonists, when the air was still, and Sybil gathered the ladies around the table, they would hover and bode then, like a pack of perched ravens, while Sybil's pen traced over paper and the planchette skimmed the lettered board. Mrs. Murtagh, the wife of a blustery Home Rule Irishman, took copious notes as Sybil invented, improvised, and translated her impulse and her desire for expression into Jacobean poetry, which the women would read aloud in muffled light.

2. Ministering Spirits

Without another clue, she would have recognized Maggie Murtagh as a spiritualist from a simple glance at her parlor. It seems that most women with metaphysical interests, especially the Irish ones, lose all notion of tidiness.

The place was a striking contrast to the neatness encouraged by the Honorable and enforced by Becky, Sybil's Cockney housekeeper. Blankets and deep chairs cluttered the Murtaghs' parlor, and the thick curtains blocked the sunlight entirely. The socket lamps cast an almost shadowy light, next to the electrical wonders of Baker and Oxford Streets, scarcely a cry from the window.

Indeed, the whole room was dingy, as though glimpsed through a dirty window, and the faint, ammoniac smell of a cat underlay the heavy mixture of kerosene and lilac. There would always be the divining board, often lying athwart the marble tabletop—sometimes replaced by Mr. Murtagh's chessboard, or by a stereopticon with its twinned, amber pictures of Tibet or India or of Roman ruins, but always in the parlor, always in sight. Maggie would note the board as they entered the room, and if there were men present, now would come the time of gallantries, of polite departure. Often in their midst was Conan Doyle, author of the ratiocinative tales, and Thomas Parnell before and after the scandal. Occasionally, Messrs. Wilde and Douglas were among the company—this before the disasters and humiliations of the Queensbury trial.

In short, it was masculine company in which the truly remarkable and the catastrophic were about to happen, to which the spiritual adventures were merely prelude or postlude or intervening dumbshow. And when the men, led by the Honorable Edmund Murtagh, retired to the dining room, to cigars and an opened bottle of whiskey, then Mrs. Murtagh would set the device on her knees, take up the planchette, and look at her expectantly.

So it was each night, until the summer of '94, when the veil parted and Munday's ultimate masque was played out upon a wider London stage.

Her husband's coach had brought her to the Murtaghs'. The Honorable had no need of it that night, or if he did, he would need it much later, for there would be time aplenty to wander, after his wife was safely home. But on this particular night, Sybil stood in the archway between dining room and parlor, half-contemplating what the Bushmill's would taste like, and whether word would reach her husband if she joined the gentlemen, though she knew that the matter was settled, that she would join with the ladies, and derive amusements in their company.

It would be an opportune time. Slovenly the house might be, but it breathed money, and Maggie Murtagh was just the type to underwrite a larger theatrical venture.

The matter would have to be broached delicately. There were always warnings in the papers against confidence artists. And it seemed that theatrical folks were more suspect than anyone. But perhaps the matter could be broached delicately when the gentlemen retired: perhaps Ephesians Munday might suggest the possibility of patronage from his vantage point in the afterlife.

Reluctantly—because she rather liked some of the men now filing into the study, despite their rather silly female attachments—Sybil seated herself as accustomed, opposite Maggie Murtagh. She placed her fingers lightly on the planchette.

These devices were rather easy to use. Your fingers barely brushing the indicator, you would follow along with the first few letters or numbers. It was a fluid, intuitive process, waiting as your partner in divination eventually opened her hand.

Your partner was almost always a woman. The thing that Sybil liked most about the husbands of these women was their immunity from such foolishness. Almost all of the spiritualists had an idea how the Beyond would answer their questions. They looked for confirmation rather than insight; if you were lucky, the first few letters would tell you the direction of your reading, what your partner wanted to hear.

If it was what you wanted her to hear, that was well and good. Let her push the planchette wherever she pleases.

If not, you would be forced to improvise. The letters already revealed by the indicator you would slowly direct toward another word entirely: the 'm.a.r' she intended to spell 'marriage' might, under your hand, become 'martha' or 'march' or, in Sybil's case, 'Marlowe' or 'Marston'—a name that guided her toward the subject Sybil wanted to address.

In a matter of a few minutes Sybil Lefcourt could spell out intentions and expect them to be followed. Her partner would do her own work in the meantime, her desire for a spiritual guide persuading her that these were the words she wanted to hear all along.

I must confess that Mrs. Lefcourt rather liked the feel of this kind of fortune telling. The conspiracy, unspoken and even unaware, established with a willing mark. It was a masque itself, as your performance spilled onto the board and planchette into your compliant partner, as again the line between player and audience became indefinite. And even before this particular night, Sybil had noted the occasional sense that a third presence inhabited the space of the board, and that she was carried somehow into its vicinity, as in those moments on stage when, for an instant, she began to see the world through the eyes of the character she portrayed, to believe what she believed.

And though, Dear Reader, Sybil Gault Lefcourt fancied herself weathered and skeptical, she was still but twenty on the night of which I speak, and she was susceptible to many things. And in retelling the invented stories of Master Munday's stage career, playing the role of a woman inadvertently receiving mysteries, she sometimes came to believe her own fictions: that she indeed might have seen a kind of lambency behind the world, that indeed the masques of Ephesians Munday might have once filled the stage at Blackfriars or even at the court of King James.

But not tonight. Tonight Sybil was pure calculation. And she fought down a rising irritation when Miss Urania Bell lit a candle by the divining board and placed her hand as well upon the planchette. Another hand would make the job of fooling Maggie Murtagh that much more difficult.

'Do you suppose Master Munday will speak to me--to us?' Raney asked breathlessly.

'Hush, dear,' Sybil replied, with as much kindness as she might muster. 'No placing of ideas in Mrs. Murtagh's lovely head. Hands back on the indicator, Mrs. Murtagh. I only tease you. I know full well you are...receptive.'

For a moment Sybil felt a presence over her shoulder. A proximity of breath, the faint hint of whiskey and tobacco. And before she could even startle herself, a voice jostled the arcane mood.

'If it is Ephesians Munday you summon, Mrs. Lefcourt, tell him his verse is wooden and sordid.'

Sybil turned, annoyed, to face the man she had seen on the doorstep—this interloper between separated worlds.

'I am sorry, sir. I do not believe I have had the

pleasure…'

The man bowed slightly. 'The oversight is mine, then. Lysander Garvey, Disrupter of Mysteries, at your impertinent service.'

She could not prevent a smile. The man was handsome; he must have once bordered on beautiful, or more likely thought he had, like a magnificent fallen angel. But her attraction to him was blunted by the quick realization that the attraction was not mutual, that his gaze was assessing rather than admiring. Where she had seen him before was the greater enigma. She plumbed her memory, found nothing at the moment.

'Now, Mr. Garvey,' she admonished, scolding flirtatiously because somehow they both knew it was safe to scold and to flirt. 'Mystery does not brook interruptions. Nor do playwrights brook harsh words regarding their work. So if you might--'

Mr. Garvey winked, placed his index finger across his lips as though he were about to quiet a small child.

Sybil turned back to the board, the back of her neck warm and reddening. In her distraction, the indicator had already passed over two letters. Raney had written down the 'f' and the 'r', and by the time Sybil gathered myself, focusing thoughts on what had already been spelled and how she might guide the message toward yet another play by Master Munday, the planchette had raced across other letters:

Fratreme.

Garvey chuckled grimly.

'"*Fratreme*'?' Sybil was at last constrained to ask. 'Miss Bell, might one of your guides be…'

But again the indicator moved, passing across even more perplexing letters.

Fratremexpauescat?

'Why, I do believe we've Latin here!' Lysander Garvey exclaimed with a kind of mocking astonishment. 'Something about brother fearing brother, I believe, though my once formidable Latin is rusty. Best to call Sir Tristram: Perhaps great Caesar's ghost is present!'

Raney scowled at him. 'Then do call Papá, if you will, Mr. Garvey.'

Suddenly the mockery had left the room. Her hands

shaking a little, riding the indicator over the board, Sybil tried vainly to follow the flow of the letters.

Surely Raney knew some Latin. Had picked it up from her father's endeavors. Perhaps her hands were guiding the planchette more than Sybil had reckoned heretofore. But it seemed an astonishing length to go, for Urania Bell to summon a Latinate control.

But now, summoned in the flesh by a smiling Lysander Garvey, Sir Tristram Bell stood in the room. A Scotsman, knighted by Victoria for heroism in the Raj. Soldier and scholar. The wise man, the reader of omens. He stood in the doorway now. Another handsome older man—younger than Mr. Garvey but, I would surmise, passing his fiftieth year. Still a bit of the fusilier about him, and dashing in a silvery, bearded fashion with the face of a Roman emperor.

Which was entirely in keeping with Sir Tristram's reputation as an amateur classicist of some standing.

'Now, really, Urania,' Sir Tristram chided, and you could hear the slow glide of whiskey in his voice. 'You know that I do not hold with...'

But Urania pointed to the paper on which she had printed the letters. He read, and then watched as the planchette continued to move and his daughter continued to write, his face unreadable in the light of the socket lamps.

It seemed an hour. And yet the clock on the mantel had marked only a quarter of that time when the planchette slowed and stopped entirely, and Urania handed the message to her father.

Tristram squinted over the words. 'It's difficult to tell,' he began apologetically.

Edmund Murtagh had entered the room by then. 'Your reputation as scholar is at stake, Sir Tristram,' he scolded jokingly. 'I, for one, am free of such anxiety, my studies in linguam Romanam having concluded at the Masses I so dearly wished were over, and in the schoolroom when the subjunctive reared its head and scowled at me.'

Tristram joined in the soft masculine laughter. 'Oh, but there are spirits and subjunctives here, sir,' he explained. 'And no space between words, just as one would encounter on arch or sarcophagus. Once I divide this passage, I shall translate wonders.'

You could hear it in his voice. The lukewarm attempt

to summon the same skepticism and irony as his comrades. He wanted to tease, but he was not up to it.

Now the planchette quivered a last dying time beneath Urania's fingers, and the socket lights gutted and fluttered, then revived into smoky, slanted light.

'Ah...' Mr. Garvey exclaimed, in counterfeit mystery. 'Did not the room grow suddenly cold, gentlemen?'

'Mr. Garvey,' Mrs. Murtagh began to object, but Sir Tristram interrupted.

'From **the** *Thyestes* of Seneca. Early in the play, the Fury mocks the ghost of Tantalus, announces the collapse of all bonds. Brother will fear brother, she prophesies, parents will fear children, and the son the father, and the wife will plot the husband's undoing, as blood will irrigate the world...'

'My, my, Mrs. Lefcourt,' Maggie Murtagh exclaimed, her broad Irish face knotted in a skeptical frown. 'Perhaps Master Munday shows us that, indeed, his Latin was worthy to translate Seneca? For I can speak for Miss Raney and myself in telling you that Latin is...well, Greek to us.'

Her laughter, and the laughter of the other guests, tunneled away from Sybil, as though the world had dropped from the table. She felt a lightness behind her eyes, and a shudder along the back of her neck.

For Dear Reader, Sybil Gault Lefcourt had perhaps less Latin than either of the other two women whose hands helped to guide the planchette that night. If Mrs. Murtagh spoke the truth—and I have no doubt that she did—there had been a fourth story, a fourth hand on the board, a story to complement the others, and no doubt a hand that was years, if not centuries dead.

3. *Stereopticon*

That night Sybil stood at the bedroom window, her vista facing east toward Russell Square.

The events of the afternoon had unsettled her. She had pled dizziness and left soon after the Latin, carried in coach by the kindness of Mr. Garvey. The Honorable was not at home—indeed, had not been at home since the previous night—and the young girl or girls with whom he was no doubt consorting were spectral in her thoughts, only abstractions.

As for now, the masques of Ephesians Munday seemed infinitely more real.

Some would call it a leap of faith that she picked up the pen and little journal. And some would call it even more than faith—would call it a kind of foolishness—that she placed her hand above the blank page, that she emptied her thoughts of all save a simple command.

Return to me...whoever or whatever you are.

Next she would remember the morning. The sunrise over Regent's Park as it climbed into her window, waking her or not waking her...

For she was uncertain whether she had dreamt or even slept.

And whether it was sleep or entrancement, the page of the journal—the page upon which Sybil Lefcourt had set her pen and cleared her distracted orb—was full now with scrawling, with letters in a child's hand that metamorphosed slowly into a mature albeit ancient Italic script.

What evrer, it had begun, two bold words framed by inkblots and scrawling, as though her pen had struggled for purchase on the blank page.

What evrer in the signs arraied by heauene...

And then, on the facing page, a verse in Latin:

> *umbra fuit sed et umbra tamen manifesta virique*
> *vera mei. non ille quidem si quaeris habebat*
> *adsuetos vultus nec quo prius ore nitebat:*
> *pallentem nudumque et adhuc umente capillo*
> *infelix vidi.*

Then trailing into incomprehensible scrawls.

These are the very words she had copied, reader. At first she pondered returning to the Bells' and seeking the skills of Sir Tristram. But in that, of course, she should procure the involvement of Miss Urania, and that, in turn, meant questions she might not be comfortable answering.

Depending on what the Latin said.

She mulled on it. '*Umbra*' she knew to be 'shadow', and '*manifesta*' was probably 'manifest'. But everything else in the passage was opaque. Sir Tristram looked more likely each time the reading baffled her. But if this were not Latin but gibberish—spuriously, nonsensically Latinate, or little better, Latinized weather forecast or directions to a decorator—then what would be made of her talents? Could she throw herself on the mercies of Sir Tristram, confessing fraudulence when, indeed, she had duped his daughter?

Or if (and believe me when I say that she still considered this prospect remote) indeed this was a message from some sentient, external force, then what if the Latin exposed her previous deceptions?

As Sybil looked at the circumstances, it seemed that both the most likely and least likely of possibilities would unmask her. In either case, it would cause scandal. And scandal was the least welcome guest at the house of the Honorable Philip Lefcourt: indeed, she could not imagine her husband's reaction were his wife exposed as a confidence artist.

It was then that the thought of Lysander Garvey descended, like a rescuing angel, into the midst of her dilemma.

He had spoken, had he not, of his once formidable Latin. Perhaps a ghost of it remained—enough, at least, to clarify what was written in the journal.

And now, in the trance or the dream of the evening, Sybil Lefcourt had remembered the circumstances under which she had seen Lysander Garvey before. In these desperate straits, she was prepared to exchange her confidence for his own.

That afternoon, accompanied by her lady's maid Becky, Sybil paid a call on Mr. Garvey. Becky was, of course, horrified at the prospect of a lady calling unsolicited upon a gentleman, but Sybil assured her, quite truthfully for once, that it was exclusively a business matter, related to her translations of the masques of Ephesians Munday. Why, Becky could even be present in the room, if she thought it proper, Sybil told her, knowing full well that the poor girl would stammer and decline.

Sybil was sure that Becky did not believe her entirely. Of course, she was also sure that the girl would know her place, would ask no questions and reveal no secrets, at least to those who would convey them to husbands.

✳✳✳

Lysander Garvey received them graciously.

His flat on Oxford Street was decorated at the height of elegance, the most striking of its adornments a pair of pen-and-inks by Aubrey Beardsley and a pastel by Fernand Khnopff. A beautiful Asian boy in a paisley robe opened the door for Sybil, and then slipped quietly into the far room of the flat as Mr. Garvey offered tea and cordialities.

They exchanged chatter for a moment; chatter that hovered comfortably near gossip. It was soon that Sybil mentioned Cleveland Street to him, and Lysander Garvey absorbed the information without dramatic response. After all, it was a small step from meeting the boy at the door to insinuations of Cleveland Street, where many a boy could be found.

But not a boy like that one, Sybil noted. Not one who hovered like a bright apparition in the back room of the flat, his burgundy robe almost trailing light as Sybil glimpsed him through the doorway.

"Your friend keeps busy," she observed, and Lysander raised an ironic eyebrow.

"They say bad things about idle hands," he observed.

"Thai?" Sybil asked.

Lysander frowned, his hands moving to his collar. "Beg your pardon?"

"Thai...Siamese...the boy. Am I right?"

"Hardly. Khandro is Tibetan. I met him there. Sometimes I feel like I conjured him out of mist and mountains."

It seemed an odd thing to say. Sybil stammered a little, grasped at the conversation.

"Then no doubt, Mr. Garvey," she began at last, "you enjoyed the presentations of Helena Blavatsky on her travels in that region, though I fear I never met the famous Madame."

"Oh, Jack," Garvey observed dryly, using the strange pet name Blavatsky allowed to her friends but not her followers. "A magnificent fraud, that one. I doubt she ever got east of Palestine."

It was an odd thing to say about such a revered mystic. Once again, Sybil was surprisingly stuck for words.

However, Lysander Garvey was only beginning.

"Blavatsky never spoke of Tibetan witchcraft. At least not in my hearing. And it always seemed to me that she'd never have ceased talking of such things, had she known of them or even seen them. Nothing of the extraction of vital energies, or of the tulpa, of which I know you heard at that silly spiritualist club."

Sybil frowned. "So the Tibetans can invent their ghosts. Out of airy nothing."

Lysander nodded toward the room at the back, where Khandro stood by the window, holding a piece of silk up to the dim London sunlight.

✳✳✳

She knew that he knew that she knew, and from that moment a silent and mutual understanding passed between them, as Sybil poured extra cream into Lysander Garvey's bracing tea, and Becky hovered by the doorway, trying not to look at the Beardsleys.

'So what business brings me a lovely visitant?' Mr. Garvey teased. 'I am sure you know that my business is hardly theatrical, so I fear I can provide no venue for the redoubtable, albeit late Master Munday.'

Sybil could not refrain from smiling, even though she feared what the next revelation might bring. 'Indeed, it is that very gentleman who brought me here,' she replied, extending the journal to Mr. Garvey's waiting hand. 'It seems that Master Munday has left me a cryptic missive.'

His frown as he read the passage unsettled her.

'Yesterday you said, I believe, that your Latin was formidable.'

'*Once* formidable, I believe I said. Once formidable, now rusty. However, you need not fear. This is schoolboy's Ovid. Indeed, I believe Khandro himself could translate it.'

Sybil cleared her throat. 'Khandro looks untranslatable himself, Mr. Garvey. If, however, he is old enough to translate, I should be surprised.'

Mr. Garvey raised an eyebrow, and then turned to the Latin. '*It was a shade,*' he translated, '*and nevertheless, it was the shade of my husband, truly made manifest. If you ask, he had not the same face...features...as once he had, nor did his face shine as it once did. But, unhappy, I saw him pale, naked, and with dripping hair.'*

He looked up from the page. His eyes were inscrutable. 'A ghostly visitation, Mrs. Lefcourt. And your Master Ephesians Munday sent you this classical missive?'

Sybil kept silent. Becky fidgeted uncomfortably behind her, and from somewhere in the back room came the faint sound of Khandro talking to himself.

'The imperfect tense has always baffled me, Mrs. Lefcourt,' Mr. Garvey said, his gaze unwavering. 'Easily recognized, but damnably difficult to translate. The Romans made much of shadings and nuance—imperfect, pluperfect, perfect—but I say what's past is past. Do we agree?'

'I must confess my ignorance, Mr. Garvey. If this is some point of grammar, it is lost on me entirely.'

He shrugged, withdrew a cigarette from a silver box on the tea table. He offered one to Sybil, who smiled and declined.

'I see,' he said at last, smiled, and lit the cigarette. Jasmined smoke wreathed his hair briefly, and he brushed it away languidly. Now he stood, and moved slowly to the library table by the window, where a chessboard rested, the pieces already moved in the first stages of a game. He reached down and tipped a white rook elegantly, then righted the piece and stared out the window.

Becky coughed nervously.

''Tis a sad story,' Mr. Garvey said at last. 'That of Ceyx and Alcyone. But of course you know it, Mrs. Lefcourt. Or should I say that your playwright knows, or knew, it well?'

Sybil was no longer sure where this was headed. 'Oh, I know it as well as he, Mr. Garvey. Ceyx sails off, is drowned, the wife mourns him inordinately, and they are both transformed into sea birds for her tears.'

'*Inordinately*? 'Tis a curious word to use, Mrs. Lefcourt, for a widow's sorrow. But the tale is more perplexing than you—and perhaps Master Munday—have understood it.'

He looked at Sybil slyly, picked up the letter opener that lay on the library table and turned it in his hand, the smooth silver blade catching the rusty light of late afternoon. He seemed to be choosing his words carefully as he began to speak.

'You have, I assume, recalled where we first met,' he

said at last.

'Yes sir, indeed I have,' Sybil replied, though she was still fumbling in the dark of memory, persuaded but not altogether sure she did recall. 'I believe, though, that it has been seven—no, eight—years, since we met.'

He nodded. 'Those were better times,' he said. 'Before the dreadful business with Oscar.'

At once Sybil motioned Becky from the room. For she had her first certainty since the night before, when the planchette had moved into unknown country. Now she was sure that it was Cleveland Street, that the notorious 19 Cleveland, where gentlemen would go to meet much younger gentlemen, had been their place of meeting. Do not ask, readers, what had taken her there as a young girl, but rest in the knowledge that some of her stage acquaintances, especially some of the boys, had occasion to frequent the place.

Now the scandals surrounding Oscar Wilde and Bosey Douglas had made the climate of the city less forgiving for men of inverted nature, and after all it was only '97, with Oscar still in Reading Gaol and his plays still an anathema to London producers. Despite his claim, the past was not past to gentlemen of Lysander Garvey's proclivities, and the conversation was dodging, strained.

Sybil had no desire to unmask Mr. Garvey, to display the painting in his attic or, more directly, to identify the boy as a frequenter of his lodgings. Indeed, she was unsure whether Khandro was a presiding angel in Mr. Garvey's flat or simply a wayfarer. Her hopes were simple: that Mr. Garvey would not betray her cozenry out of simple gratitude for her disinclination to expose him. Though she did not express her full sentiments to Mr. Garvey (and perhaps she should have, perhaps that was her failing) she had no intention of making public whatever arrangement prevailed in those apartments. But she claims to have meant Mr. Garvey no harm, and if anyone knew today where her dear Becky resided, it is sure that the girl would confirm that Mrs. Lefcourt's intentions were innocent on this matter. For in fact, Becky's testimony on other matters before the police in the days that followed was unfailingly loyal, and her advocacy of her lady's 'plain auld goodniss' was compelling to the constables and, I can guarantee, touching to the mistress who employed her.

For this story ended unhappily, as by now you must have concluded it would end—would have no other way of ending, given the ghosts and betrayals. Mr. Garvey was, of course a gentleman, offering his carriage for Sybil's return to Marylebone. She had no choice to decline the transport, assuring him that her husband's barouche was at our call, when indeed they both knew that it was not, that given Mr. Garvey's possible reputation in some circles, her maid and she would be walking substantial distances or...

But a long account of how they returned to Marylebone is not the subject of my story. Suffice it to say that, upon returning to her flat, a surpassing weariness haunted Sybil. Something in the light had changed, and as Becky, possessed of the same strange lassitude, trundled from lamp to lamp, the parlor took on a kind of amber glory, a distanced and painterly quality like a photograph glimpsed through a stereopticon. Sybil had long ago plumbed the mystery of that novelty—how a slight variance between the photograph glimpsed by the left eye gave the illusion of depth when the mind juxtaposed it over or beneath the image that the right eye captured and held. She had the stereopticon used by confidence artists: how the huckster would set a figure in one photograph and not in the other, parallel one, and when the viewer glimpsed the scene through the glasses of the device, the single figure would shimmer with a kind of transparency.

It was one way a photographer invented his ghosts. And yet, even if Sybil knew the devices, the amber tint of the photographs had never ceased to render them mysterious and strange. It was that colour of light in which she wandered now, and she imagined somewhat foolishly an adjoining room, in which all furniture and ornament and lighting were identically the same, with one remarkable exception.

In that second room she was not present.

And the very act of thinking such a thing made her feel diaphanous and frail.

But it was more than that. She knew somehow that Mr. Garvey's photograph, though tinted the same amber and possessed of the same furniture, differed ever so slightly from her own—a shift of perspective, perhaps, or simply from the left eye to the right.

All this talk about the stereopticon may seem

incongruous, dear Reader, as out of place as an honored general lost in a smuggler's den, or a smuggler's daughter in the houses of the Houses of Parliament. As a strange, unsightly idiot girl dancing sprite-like to the choruses of *The Tempest*. But our minds entertain strange suppositions, and we move far more readily from thought to thought than we do from house to house, from station to station. And events move more strangely than our thoughts. For here is what came to pass that very night.

It was the stroke of the mantel clock that awakened Sybil, the sonorous little bell marking the hour of two in the morning. She was lying on the divan, journal open and spine-up on her lap. For a moment, brief but fraught with a great and manifest unease, she was reluctant to look at the pages, assured in some terrible recess of her mind that they would contain more words, that her conversation with Master Munday—or whoever had guided the pen in her hand on yesterday's sunlit and distant afternoon—would have continued while she slept, only to greet her on wakening with new and incomprehensible communication.

Imagine her relief to find the page blank beneath the Latin and the inkblots. But imagine as well a tremor of what she could only call disappointment. For Sybil had thought briefly that she performed on a larger stage, wrestling not against her own untruthfulness and selfishness and resentful imaginings, but against principalities, against powers, against the rulers of the darkness of this world. Now it seemed that in this—in this grandeur and scope of proportion—she might have been mistaken.

But what of the Latin? she asked herself. What of it, indeed?

Questioning that brought her, with little delay, back to the table and the journal beneath her steadied hand. Questioning that closed her eyes and emptied her thoughts, as she slipped beyond calculation and performance into a state of comfortable quietude.

In the times that followed, when I spoke to the girl, dear Becky vouched that her mistress had not left the room, that Sybil had spoken to no one since her return from Mr. Garvey's flat, and that even the conversation with the aforesaid gentleman was conducted under the watchful eye of the ladies' maid.

I fear that now I must provide the rest of my testimony. And I fear that I must provide it by denials.

Sybil did not feel 'something come over her'. Did not feel her hand move. Nor could I tell you where her thoughts ventured and strayed. It was more an abstraction, a reverie sans images and emotion, her chin propped on her hand and her eyes intent on nothing. But it was not quite that, either.

What emerged from this state—this trance, if you will—was yet another passage of verse. It was, in fact a famous speech—one Sybil had spoken on the stage herself—but that speech was rendered aslant and off kilter, invaded by surrogate words both intimate and disturbing. I record them for you in this account. You can only imagine her alarm.

Full fadom fiue thy Philip lies,
Of his bones are Corrall made:
All the girles that charm'd his eies,
Into nothingnesse doe fade,
He doth suffer River-change
Into something lost & strange,
Mantel clocks will ring his knell.
Harke now I heare them, ding-dong bell.

You will have to believe my testimony, dear Reader, and I may only trust that you will, having lingered with my story this long. But as Sybil read the last line, the clock on the mantel rang three, as though her thoughts were summoned and blocked by stage directions.

She blinked and shuddered, both at the coinciding of inner and outer worlds, and at the strange, perverse twisting of the Bard's honoured song. Was this the contrivance of her own hand? Was it the inscrutable joke of Ephesians Munday, played on his greater predecessor? Or was this a hand and voice with some even darker intent?

I am sure she entertained all possibilities. But as of yet, she had no inkling of the moment's immediate import.

It was late the next morning when Becky admitted the officers from Scotland Yard, who came bearing the terrible tidings of Sybil's new widowhood.

Apparently, it was an evening upon which Sybil's husband was indeed late in his offices. After leaving the Houses of Parliament, The Honorable had walked over Westminster Bridge, headed toward the site of the old Sanger Theatre. Where he was bound that late at night and with what purpose, neither the inspectors nor Sybil herself were able to divine.

And though I shall not speak ill of the departed—of any of the departed—rest assured that I could guess at the dead man's motive.

At any rate, they had found the body at the foot of the bridge, entangled in some flotsam that in turn was entangled amid the moorings of the structure—one of the inspectors explained these things quite avidly, explained as well the wound inflicted by several, swift stabbings with a blunt blade. For some reason, he insisted to describe the pain that might ensue from such a weapon, such a terrible death — but of course Sybil was beyond understanding, perhaps even beyond hearing.

Perhaps she was thinking back over years that seemed like centuries, thinking of Philip's face when, in another, now-vanished era and on another stage, he brought flowers to his dazzled Viola. There is always a desire to return, you know. To redeem the time. Because all days are evil.

It would be remiss, dear reader, to burden you with the depth and the fervor of Sybil's mourning. Suffice it to say she strove, in all ways, to be worthy of her husband. And it is heartening when your provider continues to provide: her inheritance left her self-sustained, and her further ventures with cards and crystals, with board and planchette, deepened well into her middle years.

In those years she came to believe that Ephesians Munday had seized his opportunity. And when an addled girl in the British Museum had endeavored to invent him, had dreamed him out of mist and paper, he had issued forth to body her imaginations. He had wrested her game from her hands and guided her toward his truth.

But was that the truth, after all? Sybil Lefcourt herself understood the layers of truth, not only how one truth lay beneath another but how, sometimes, one could glimpse two of them side by side, bleeding into each other to form a picture in its entirety out of the fragmentary ghosts of both. So it will not surprise you, I am sure, that I was on Westminster Bridge that night, and that I saw the Honourable Philip Lefcourt passing. That I knew full well the layers of truth in ghostly communications, the unspoken desires that lay beneath the words from the pen or the planchette, and the desires that lay beneath those desires as well.

I saw Philip Lefcourt, but he did not see me. And whether I acted on impulse or cold premeditation, or if some larger force compelled my hand, I am powerless to determine, even from this undiscovered country. But a pale mist encircled the two of us as I approached from behind, as I was accustomed to approach, and I am sure—or as sure as I can be in such matters—that he felt the brush of my hand against his shoulders before the knife struck, before he tumbled into the Thames and into reckoning as deep as any plummet sounds.

Or so it seemed from the Westminster Bridge, on the way to the old Sanger Theatre.

And perhaps in that theatre, not long for this world itself, the cast of this and a hundred other stories are assembling now in your mind or mine, These our actors, as I might have told you, had we the time, were all spirits of a sort, as insubstantial as the souls they courted, and like the generals and guides and sibyls of spiritualist fancies, they too are melted into air, into thin air. I am not sure on what layer of truth some of them might lie—neither the poor girl in the play, nor Ephesians Munday, nor even the strange boy Khandro imagined in a dream of mountains, but they were on the stage with Sybil Lefcourt, though they were not the ghosts that peopled the stage of her later and perhaps more vivid nightmares.

I wonder myself what became of some of these ghosts, though there are others whose whereabouts I can almost, if not entirely, guess. For I am old passing into ancient, and though I should say there are no surprises left on the globe, there are surprises aplenty in the backstage shadows of our mansions.

XIV

It was in a kind of exile and solitude that Gabriel learned the most from Trajan Bell.

As February began, he took note of the situation. Still the two of them regarded each other from opposite sides of the street, the attitude not unfriendly and yet cooler, in a kind of distancing that kept with the February weather. Gabriel spent the late winter indoors, reading and listening to music. Once again he drew forth his Tolkien and found himself in Lorien by the time March began, for the third time making the journey with the Fellowship, his paperback copies of the trilogy already dog-eared, only the first of four editions he would buy.

Gabriel had also listened closely to Trajan, so closely that dropped words and observations—off-hand comments from the strange and solitary man—had dilated in his memory. In later years he would be surprised when he realized he had spoken to his older friend fewer than a dozen times. But he followed the names that rose from these encounters—Hesse and Castaneda, Eliot and Allan Ginsberg—and began to read things that his distracted mother and shabby public schooling could not provide for someone attuning himself to mystery. It is that kind of distancing, where imagination retires upon itself in a winter of solitude, in which the lessons begin to move, out of words and lectures into habits of heart and mind.

The poetry was too difficult, a bewilderment of languages and allusions that Gabriel could not follow or catch, but the other books he grasped in a way, especially the Hesse. A simultaneous wading through *Siddhartha* and *The Two Towers* gave him perplexing dreams, and he would waken from nightmare and look through the frost-vexed window at the Bell place, where the lights were always on in what he hoped was a kind of vigilance. After several weeks, though, Gabriel discovered that the Bells were reversing the hours of sleeping and waking, that *all* the lights—not just those in Trajan's room—were on in the house, and that morning brought a deadness and closure to the place, the lights winking out in the gray February sunrise, while the dried branches on the ramp promised no spring, not for a long while, as mother and son slept away a third of the year.

So Gabriel changed some things in his own routine, to honor the changes in his friend. Since he still had to keep student's hours, he reversed other behaviors—wearing his T-shirt backwards and eating only one food for days on end, sometimes weeks. Inspired by Tolkien's appendices to *Lord of the Rings,* he began to create his own fictional world, with maps and family trees and chronologies. This unreal kingdom was peopled with elves and dwarves and ghosts—the ghosts were his addition, born from his preoccupations since Halloween. He followed the logic of including them and assured that his fictional country would be a place in which nobody died. He called it Dacia, picking the name from the encyclopedia article on Trajan's Arch. And his imagined Dacia took shape in an old spiral notebook on his desk—one he had inherited from Del that fall, when his friend had stopped taking notes in science class. He had torn out the first five pages, smudged with Del's penciled notes and doodling, and drawn his first map of the country in February.

It looked like one of Tolkien's maps, he figured. He was not sure whether that was bad or good, but perhaps an inherited notebook should begin with an inherited map. There would be stories about the place later: in fact, he was saving most of the notebook to include them.

Most of March poured into the making of Dacia. Gabriel did not know enough about the world outside his window to invent a new one on the page. But nonetheless, Dacia began to take shape, its landscape somehow familiar, but somehow made strange—partly by what Gabriel was reading, partly by the winter he had just passed through. The glimpses he had of Dacia, sometimes sketched in his notebook and sometimes imagined in that lulled space before and after a dream-haunted sleep, were views of a snowy country, like his father's Michigan, but his own terrain—a country of frost-blasted deciduous trees, old maples and oak like the groves in Miss Vivien's back yard, but oddly persistent, keeping their yellow and red leaves far into the season's turn, so that in his mind's eye, Dacia hovered always between fall and winter, the memories of life still brilliant amid icy branches.

Perhaps it was this dream of Dacia that sent Gabriel north in the years that followed—to upstate New York and, finally, the winter desolations north of Chicago, where he always felt uncomfortable but at home.

✳✳✳

The disaster that awaited Gabriel in April, that would haunt him until that Christmas Eve when he stepped into the basement of the Bell house, began harmlessly enough, with a Saturday morning call from Mr. Robinson to Mary Rackett, announcing that Del would be starting his first game as a varsity pitcher. Mary urged Gabriel to go to the game. She liked those situations in which Gabriel kept contact with old friends, chiefly because she mistrusted new friends by instinct. It seemed that a doubt of her son's good judgment always lay at the heart of her suspicions.

Gabriel was busy drawing up a family tree of ghosts. It had stumped him, however. Were the ghosts in the genealogy of elves? Of dwarves? And if they were human, should he include humans in his imagined kingdom? And what if they were simply ghosts, having been nothing truly alive before they began to inhabit the castles and forests of Dacia? Did two ghosts make another ghost as humans made another? Or as elves or dwarves did, which he had assumed would be in much the same way as humans did it? It seemed more interesting, he was about to decide, if ghosts came to life by another way—something to do with memory, he guessed, or with intense feelings. But then, who had remembered or felt the first of them into being?

It was all too complicated, this business of imagining. And so when his mother, more and more preoccupied with the May production of *The Tempest*, came to the door of his room, prepared with all her arguments as to why he should "end his revels and set down his make-believe," should go watch his friend play ball, Gabriel surprised her by not resisting at all, by scrambling into jacket and shoes and, after placing a brief call to Joey, heading off on his bike toward school.

The ball diamond lay behind Old Jeff, next to the Barns, which was what the upper-classmen called the buildings set up ten years earlier to hold the swell of Baby Boom students, the double sessions of classes that disrupted family life south of Louisville by sending most of the junior high students into classes from one in the afternoon until eight in the evening. The school still referred to the Barns as "temporary structures," but by 1969 nobody was kidding anybody else, and all of Gabriel's freshman classes were in the tin-roofed buildings his reasonably cool English teacher had described as "glorified Quonset huts."

Gabriel and Joey tried the door of their TV Science classroom and found it locked. Gabriel was relieved, and expected that Joey had felt the same, for had they found the door open they would have been required to explore inside and to turn the televisions on to "George of the Jungle" reruns, both of them having discovered, by differing routes, the riches of irony. It was good, this old connection—how the three of them would gather to celebrate baseball and lost companionship—though Gabriel knew all along that he could tell Joey nothing about the ghosts of Dacia, and he already suspected, given the night journey of last autumn, that Joey had some secrets of his own as well.

The diamond lay just beyond the TV Science building, and the two boys climbed to the top of the bleachers, watching Del go through his warm-ups. Del looked up at them and waved, but then his gaze settled back on his attentive father, leaning on the fence beside the first-base dugout, and he became all business, his stride lengthening in the bullpen and the baseball whipping with vaporous speed into the catcher's mitt.

"That's it," Mr. Robinson urged, all the laid-back humor of the man who had brought them ice cream sheared away from his voice. "That's it, Del. Bring the heat, son."

"Mr. Robinson's all weird these days," Gabriel confided to Joey, who gave him a sly look in response.

"He's got a lot riding here, Gabe. Some guy from Cincinnati come down to watch Del pitch, I hear."

"A scout? The Reds?"

Joey snorted. "Nothing close to the Reds, you dumbass. Some guy from the university up there. Mr. Robinson ain't that stupid, but Del is, and the only way he's goin' to college is up on that ball diamond."

Gabriel kept silent. He didn't like Joey's descriptions, because when Del was diminished, it seemed like it diminished everyone. What's more, Gabriel was jealous that Joey knew the neighborhood news before he even had wind of it. The prospect of Del in college reminded him of the TVs in the science classroom, of "George of the Jungle" playing while people tried seriously to learn, and he brushed the cruel thought away, intent now on watching Del take to the mound as the first inning began.

It was St. David's they were playing. The Fighting Friars. Not one of the big gun Catholic schools in the city like Trinity or St. Xavier, but still big enough to draw students and players from all over the southern part of the county. They were a good team, and Gabriel envied the boys who went there, wishing again that his mother sent him to that school instead of to Old Jeff. He leaned forward, his support for Del deepened by resentment of his privileged opponents, and prepared to enjoy the game.

Then "There's that creep Bell," Joey whispered.

What had got into Joey? Everyone seemed stranger this morning, and for a moment Gabriel longed for the peaceful and frigid hauntings of Dacia. But he followed his friend's faint nod to a place on the left field line, where Trajan leaned against the fence and watched the game unfolding.

"Hey, what's wrong with Trajan?" he asked, a little defensively, but Joey shook his head and smiled.

"Don't jump bad on me, Rackett. You got a lot to learn about creeps."

He was about to ask, to challenge his too-knowing friend, but the catcher signaled the ball around the horn, and the infield convened on the pitcher's mound, Wade Hampton Flynn, everybody's choice for All-State third baseman, handing the ball to Del, who took it a little too reverently and stepped to the pitcher's rubber.

"He's gonna ask Hampton for his autograph," Joey whispered, and Gabriel laughed in spite of himself.

By the second batter, though, Del had pitched the mockery off the field. Two rising fastballs followed by a tricky changeup, and the leadoff batter stomped back to the dugout, cut down on three strikes.

You could hear the protests from the Friar dugout.

He don't have nothin'. You guys can clobber him.

Rubber arm.

Yeah, Gabriel thought. Only took three pitches on you, asshole.

Del wound up, and the first pitch to the second batter dropped off the table.

"Damn!" Joey exclaimed, his irony sliding eagerly into appreciation. "I didn't know that Del had a curve!"

Gabriel chuckled. "You got a lot to learn about some stuff, too, Hardy."

And it seemed at that moment that the tension broke, that

the two boys leaned back in the bleachers, shedding months and perhaps years in a simple and awestruck recognition of their friend. It was one of those kinds of moments—Gabriel would have but a few of them in his life—when someone you know takes on a glory, starts to shimmer with a light that isn't borrowed for a change. Years later, when he thought of the dangers when someone steps out of a story and into the daily world, he thought that sometimes it happened just the other way—that someone you know steps into a story.

And this was the story, and somewhat the way it happened.

The batter was the opposing pitcher, some big Polish kid from out around Seminole Park, and he looked like somebody had him by the short hairs, and the somebody was Del, who rocked back, whipped his arm forward again, and delivered yet another fastball as the umpire pivoted and called the second strike.

Gabriel and Joey whooped in unison, and the cry was taken up by the Old Jeff fans. Surprised at the cheer, Del looked into the crowd, locked eyes with his old friends, and tipped his cap almost ironically.

It was enough to set the batter off. The big boy stepped from the batter's box, pointed his bat at Del, and said something harsh and menacing, lost in the rising murmur of the Jefferson fans.

Del caught it though, either the words or the body language, and shrugged, tipping his cap again for emphasis at the furious hitter. Now the batter took a step toward the mound, raised his middle finger, and shouted, "Climb this, Tarzan!"

And Del grinned as the umpire stepped between them. Thumped his chest and delivered a witless, magnificent Tarzan yodel that set his teammates—the famous Wade Hampton Flynn included—to snickering, faces hidden in their gloves.

Joey was laughing as well now, out loud and with innocent joy. Gabriel laughed with him, and for a moment his world seemed to speed back to August, back to the hotbox in Del's yard and the overhang of branches from the Bells'. It was a charmed place to be, as Del stretched on the mound, toed the rubber, and glared like a predator at the batter stepping back into the box.

Del rocked, kicked high in an almost cartoonish imitation of a major league pitcher, and the ball blazed out of his hand, no more than a blur as it passed the batter, as the umpire signaled strike three and the Jefferson fans rose in unison, shouting and cheering the phenomenon in their midst.

The third hitter, a lean lefthander named Burnett who had also been mentioned for the All-State team, stepped more respectfully into the batter's box now. It was the first real ballplayer in the St. David lineup, and you could tell Del knew it. He looked to his father, who shouted encouragement. Then he bent over, gathered the sign from the catcher, and unleashed a fierce fastball at the corner of the plate.

Burnett smiled and whistled, stepped out of the box. He stepped back in, a half stride deeper to adjust to Del's astonishing speed. The catcher called a pitch, and Del shook off the sign. Shook it off again.

Now the catcher, a burly senior who was not half as dumb as he looked and fully accustomed to calling the game, stood up, threw back his mask, and settled his hands on his hips. "C'mon, Smoke!" he shouted, and crouched again.

"Damn if Del's not gonna call his own game!" Gabriel whispered.

Joey rolled his eyes. "'Smoke'? Reckon they're calling him 'Smokey Robinson' now?"

The boys laughed softly as the catcher trotted out to the mound, joined by Flynn and the coach. They couldn't have a freshman pitcher calling the shots; there was something wrong in it, regardless of the heat and the talent, and they were letting him know out there. You could see something in Del struggle then bend and droop; now he was nodding, the coach's hand on his shoulder, and Flynn said something because it was Flynn's job to shape the team. All the while Mr. Robinson leaned against the fence, straining to hear, and Gabriel looked down the foul line to where Trajan stood, clutching the top of the chest-high fence, taking in the drama on the mound as if he knew every word, as if he was waiting for something important to happen.

"So that means the Polish guy shed the Tears of a Clown, then?" Joey cracked, and Gabriel's thoughts lurched away from the conference.

Gabriel laughed. "That was really funny, Joey."

Joey brushed back his longish hair, winked at his old friend. "It sure was. I Second that Emotion."

Lake Geneva, WI

11/25/92

Dear Jazz,

Looking back from the vantage of twenty-five years, I am surprised at all the things I missed that day. Joey's lame jokes and the tremor of the crowd drew me away from the serious business, when the first talent any of us showed was running straight up against something larger than talent.

Yes, I'm back on Del again. You think I've never left any of them—Del or Joey or especially Trajan. But it's memory or some kind of feeling—I wouldn't call it love, but more like setting aside all judgment—that always brings the ghosts back. They feed on it, like in all those creepy scenes out of the Odyssey—remember how the women and prophets drank blood?

At any rate, that conference on the mound—Coach Herbert and Flynn and whoever the hell that catcher was, all of them telling Del what to do. That was what punctured the magic. There's something to be said for dwelling in the moment, not stopping to interpret it or give it strategy or meaning. I know you always said so, but I know I was too much the novelist, having to plot ahead and organize and ask myself what it was all about even while it was

175

happening.

Well, that's a far too generous way of looking at myself, I suppose. I was too much the bad novelist. Dacia might have been something if I hadn't stopped to consider everything it meant. If I'd just followed the Queen of the Ghosts and let her be. And as for us, Jazz…well, I suppose we just had too many conferences on the mound.

So here's the way it happened, after that conference, after Flynn handed Del the ball and told him to get to work on Burnett.

He'd been working Burnett, bottom line. Del had a good hitter back on his pegs, and all of the Old Jeff fans in his camp. Even some of the Friar fans, I bet. Not Zefirek, because I believe that was his name, but some of the Friars, I'm sure, because St. David's wasn't one of your professional-class German Catholic schools that hauled athletic glory out of the Louisville papers. St. David's was Irish and Mexican and Polish, welders' kids and career army brats, dads who worked at "Ford's" and at Brown and Williamson. Anything shining at our end of town ended up shining on all of us.

And here was Del, with no special brilliance until this day in the full sunlight, unleashing his fastball on the world.

Well, they schooled him out there. The catcher wanted the curve ball, and Del wanted the fastball, but it was the curve after the conference, and Burnett lined it just foul down the first base line. It slapped against the base and shot up toward the spot where Trajan was standing, and he did this remarkable thing—reaching out with his bare, stubbed right hand and plucking the ball out of the air like he was some big, bushy-haired outfielder. The crowd applauded him, like they do in the majors when a spectator catches a foul ball, and Trajan bowed and tossed the ball back to the umpire, and everyone was laughing now. They had no idea how remarkable it was that he'd caught the ball that way with two fingertips missing. It seemed at that moment, for that superb half-inning, that everything tended toward wholeness, Jazzie, that everything was resonant.

Burnett got wood on the next pitch, too, but as it was a fastball he didn't get around on it, as they say. Sent an easy one-hop groundball to Flynn, who threw it to first base and got him out by two steps. And there was applause everywhere as the Jefferson team came in to bat, and Mr. Robinson pounded his fist into his hand like he was wearing a mitt himself, and Joey and I whooped and hollered as Del walked into the dugout, superstitiously hopping the foul line because he didn't want it jinxed, he wanted it all unspoiled and new and now.

And it was like everything tried to go on that way. Zefirek took the mound, still fuming over his turn at bat, and walked the first batter. He struck out the second hitter, but then Flynn stepped to the plate and lined the first pitch over the left field wall, a perfect, liquid swing, and you could tell from the sound of the bat hitting the ball that it was gone, a home run, and Old Jeff led 2-0. Then Zefirek began to fall apart, giving up a pair of singles and a smooth triple by Marcus Rowan, Clarence's big brother. It was 4-0 then, and the next batter lined a double down the first base line, and Trajan whooped and signaled the ball fair along with the first-base umpire, and the crowd was standing, cheering, already wondering what the chances were of taking District.

Del was on deck now, batting ninth in the order. He was never all that good a hitter, not even by Little League standards, but the world seemed to be opening huge and possible, and I was thinking he might even get a hit. I looked over at Trajan, who, still jubilant at his own comic performance on the foul line, waved at me and Joey, and Joey, stripped of his mocking notions of "creepiness" waved happily back along with me.

And then I saw the figure further down the line.

In the right field corner he stood, where the back wall touched against the foul line, and even the Friar's right fielder, still winded from chasing down the last double, did not seem to notice him. Wearing a long broadcloth duster, far too hot for even Kentucky April, he smoked and leisurely watched the game unfold. Perhaps it was the distance, the haze in the air, or my growing fear that something was about to go wrong, but I swear to you. Jazzie, that the coat and the man were of the same texture as the smoke, pale and translucent but solid enough to recognize that he was the same man I had seen that day when I went to retrieve the glove from Miss Vivien's back yard. And I felt the same blind, hungry presence that had come at us in the Halloween night, and that had passed through Del as he rushed for the fence and safety. Whatever it was, I was instantly afraid that it was after me, and I tugged at Joey's pant leg and pointed out to the spot where the thing stood.

But Joey saw nothing. He said I was freaking, and he laughed until I wondered if I was. So I looked to Trajan, to see if he had noticed, but Trajan had left the fence and was nowhere to be seen. It was the October Man's country now, and he leaned over the fence and stared across the broad range of the ball diamond.

I swear this is true. I also swear that, if I had left my seat and run down the right field line, run straight toward the creature in the cloudy corner, that I would have arrived to find nothing there, except a faint whiff of decay, perhaps, and a dry brown settling in the grass beyond the fence.

But Joey persisted, egging me, bringing me back to light and the field and the eighth batter, and Zefirek rattled and wild and walking the boy on only five pitches. It amazes me that I remember the particulars, given what happened and that it happened twenty-five years ago. But next was Del, and of course you know the rest.

They always say that you can tell an intentional hit batsman by the way the pitch comes in: that the pitcher throws behind the batter if he's head-hunting because your first instinct is to jump back when the ball is coming at you. That's how it happened, exactly how, and afterwards a lot of people said Zefirek was still hopping mad and was the kind of kid capable, but I've never thought that. The seconds he took on the mound after the ball struck Del's temple were shock, not triumph, and his own players dragged him away when Mr. Robinson came at him.

Coach Herbert was out there, clearing a spot to give the boy air, and he gave his keys to Flynn, who rushed into the locker room and called the ambulance that seemed forever in arriving. Because from the moment of the sound we knew he was hit bad, but how bad we had no idea until the ambulance was headed away, bound to the old General Hospital downtown with its lights and sirens flaring. Mr. Robinson had first rushed the Zefirek boy, and I know it was because he couldn't imagine Del hurt that badly, but when he climbed into the back of the ambulance with his son I could hear him sobbing before the sirens started up, and you could see Del's head drooping over the side of the ambulance cot like some twisted plant with a broken stem, and his father cradling that head in his hands, setting it gently onto the cot, his hands coming away bloody as the crewman closed the door and the truck blazed off into the shattered afternoon.

By the time Joey and I got home, Ma had received the phone call telling us Delano Robinson was dead. It was one of those freakish things, she told me, of course delighting in the moment of telling, using that hushed soliloquy voice she taught her little girls' school actresses.

It was one of those freakish things.

And there was no consolation in that, but she was right. Every district seems to lose a high school football player or two over the years—we even lost one ourselves in summer practice that year, wind-sprinting in ninety-degree weather, and the football coach explained how the boy "had lacked mental toughness"—but baseball, in that time and for us especially, had been safe ground. It was like death was in the world to stay…what was the old phrase?

Et in Arcadia ego…

I am here, even in Arcady.

I blamed the creature by the fence more than Zefirek, more than accident. But the blame spread wide, and maybe now you're guessing about why I sent you Trajan's "Guioco Piano".

Well the funeral was dismal, all Protestant and filled with shrieks and inconsolable weeping, and afterwards Ma made a casserole and had me take it over to Mr. Robinson's. I rang the bell and nobody answered, which didn't surprise me any considering the situation. I went around the far side of the house and found Mr. Robinson, still dressed in his shiny blue suit and looking unbearably old, standing up against the Bells' fence, holding his catcher's mitt like some alien thing he had retrieved from the yard. He didn't answer when I spoke to him, so I set the dish softly on the back steps and took off for home, convinced that I was at the edge of something too intimate and altogether not meant for me. And as I passed between the houses I noticed the hyacinths blooming where there had never been hyacinths before. Someone—Trajan, I am sure—had planted them new in the dried beds and left them to bloom and flourish defiantly.

It's almost Thanksgiving, and I'm listing the things I am thankful for. You and Dominic, of course, and Del and Joey. Ma, in her broken, mysterious way. And always Trajan. But you and Dominic first.

Have a wonderful holiday, Jazzie. I'll be here at work on the rest of the manuscript, if Dominic wants to call.

Gabriel

XV

On the night Neil Armstrong stepped onto the moon, a more quiet trespass took place in August Acres.

Del Robinson came to Gabriel's Dacia. Or rather, Gabriel invited him in.

Gabriel was sitting by the television, half-watching the hazy pictures coming from the moon landing with his mother and her friend Billy—or Mr. Hume, as he had to call him when they were at school.

Billy Hume had entered the picture in May, attending the production of *The Tempest*, where he met Mary Rackett after the play. Flirting had progressed to a number of dates in June and early July.

Gabriel figured that it was an OK time for his mother to start dating again, but he found himself wishing she had not settled on Billy, a cropped and sweaty science teacher from Old Jeff. Billy generally taught the slower classes—Del had been in his Earth Science class in the fall, lost interest, gave Gabriel his science notebook (soon to become the lodgings of Gabriel's Dacia), and pronounced Billy pretty much of a drag. Gabriel's opinion was still governed in ways by the impressions of his

181

friends, and so Billy was headed more or less nowhere, and maybe Mary Rackett was headed there with him. Still, the man had showed up at Del's funeral, had spoken consoling words to Mr. Robinson and joined enthusiastically in the service, and so far his treatment of Gabriel's mother had been decent enough.

Furthermore, there was always the prospect of learning some science if you watched Apollo 13 with Billy, so Gabriel had broken away from Dacia and joined his mother and her date in the living room, just as the spacecraft prepared to land and as almost all of America gathered to watch.

"It's a remarkable thing, Gabriel," his mother urged, with a strange Southern drag in her voice. Since Billy was here, Gabriel knew she hadn't been drinking, but he puzzled over where her Galway brogue had headed since she'd taken up with the science teacher. "It's remarkable because your Grandfather Conroy was your age before he seen an automobile, and now you're watchin' us land on the moon."

Gabriel nodded idly, his attention wavering between Walter Cronkite and this damp masculine presence in the room.

For Billy Hume paced nervously behind the sofa, ignoring Mary Rackett's repeated gestures that he sit and relax. "We'll know in a minute," he said finally.

"Know what?" Gabriel asked, puzzled at the strange, apprehensive climate.

"Know whether we're really landing on the moon," Billy said.

"Well, I expect since we've come so far, Billy, we'll travel the rest of the way," Mary observed, a little of the Irish creeping back into her voice.

Gabriel became suddenly attentive.

"What do you mean 'really', Mr. Hume?"

His mother shook her head, but Billy Hume was more than ready to explain.

"The Lord doesn't want us there, Gabriel. If we had been meant to be there, we'd be there already."

"Billy...." Mary Rackett soothed, but Billy raised his hand

gently.

"He should be aware of this, Mary. Part of his education. The kind of thing the government isn't allowing us to say in school any more."

Gabriel became suddenly attentive. He was drawn to things the government and school did not allow, but repelled by hearing his mother lectured.

Billy, of course, was not finished.

"The Lord doesn't want us there, Gabriel. Earth is our proper place, and we haven't been the best stewards of our own world. Why should we transgress—that means to break the rules—and seek out a place where we were not present at the first of Creation? We are not supposed to know whether heaven moves or stands still, what its shape is or whether the earth is at its center or not. It's like Galileo said: we're supposed to know how to go to heaven, not how heaven goes."

Gabriel blinked. It seemed like strange country for a science teacher. His mother was uncomfortably silent, and he wished that Trajan were there. Trajan would know how to answer this.

"Billy..." Mary soothed.

"What about cars, Mr. Hume?"

"What *about* them, Gabriel?"

Now Gabriel felt as though he was straying into dangerous ground. He couldn't out-argue a science teacher, but this surely wasn't the science he was getting at school. Perhaps Billy was right: perhaps something was being kept from him there, and he should just be quiet and listen. But nevertheless, he continued.

"Well, I was thinking about what Ma said. How my grand-da didn't see a car till he was my age. Well, do you think we were supposed to have cars? What if the priest had told my grand-da that we should study how to get to heaven rather than how to get to Dublin?"

"Gabriel..." his mother began, but Billy reddened and again waved his hand gently.

"It's not the same, Gabriel. Cars were made to improve our life right here. Trust a scientist to tell you that there's nothing to be gained from the kinds of things we'd discover out there."

Gabriel started to protest, but Billy waved at him again, this time more briskly.

"Objecting to the automobile would be something out of the Middle Ages. You know how superstitious they were back in the old days, and maybe the priests are still stuck back there. But this is different."

Gabriel's mother smiled. "Look, Gabriel. Armstrong is setting his foot down."

And theology paused for a moment, as the three of them watched the blurred screen, heard the famous misspoken words about small and giant steps.

"That settles it," Billy pronounced, stalking around the sofa and seating himself by Mary. "Has to be a hoax."

Gabriel and his mother exchanged an apprehensive glance. Mary nodded toward his room, and Gabriel stood dutifully.

"Gabriel?" Billy asked, a little too loudly and with a smile a little partial and stretched. "This Sunday I'd like for you and your mother to go somewhere with me. I think it will open your eyes, and you'll thank me for it later."

"Billy, we'll talk about that first," Mary said, with an insistence and a more Irish presence that assured her son. "It's time for Gabriel to get some sleep. It's been a surprising and historic day."

✳✳✳

Back in his room, Gabriel heard the swift, whispered exchange of words from the living room. When he was assured that Billy was getting ready to leave, he turned on his record player and placed the new album on the turntable. "Space Oddity," which he had borrowed from Joey who had stolen it from Aron after the two of them fell out. David Bowie's strange, artsy baritone growled through the room, singing about Ground Control and Major Tom. Gabriel laughed a little at the odd convergence of the music and the conversation with Billy Hume, then sat at his desk and opened the Dacia notebook.

Two pages beyond the last entries in his chronology of ghosts, Gabriel found the drawing. It was something of Del's once again—the same smudged pencil, the page scored with indentations and scratches where Del, having worn away his eraser, continued to dig and drive at his notes, trying to spell the phrase "harmonic tremor."

Gabriel would look it up later, and find that it had something to do with volcanoes. But that night he had no idea, and had he gone back to the living room and asked Billy Hume for an explanation, the adventure would have ended in science and the movement of magma. There was something musical and unsettling about the term, of course, like one object vibrating with another in the depths of things. He thought of a tuning fork, a signal, a message, and slowly drifted toward a kind of surprising peace.

Turning back to his genealogies, he scrawled Del's name among the lineage of ghosts, intending that someday, when Dacia had taken its final form, his friend would figure in the stories.

But despite that peace and despite that resolve, it was almost twenty years before Del's ghost walked through any world.

***

Four days after his birthday and four before Christmas, Joey invited Gabriel to join him downtown at a movie. *Butch Cassidy and the Sundance Kid* was still playing at what would later be called the Shangri-La, the scene of a dozen ghost stories and a huge, killer fire. The theaters downtown were giving way to a warehouse of a complex out on Bardstown Road, but sometimes a good film would find its way to Fourth Street, accessible by bus from the boys' neighborhood.

If they didn't go see it quickly, Joey warned, they'd miss it. And even if stodgy old Wade Abner had hated the movie, what did he know? Everyone said it was good, that it made fun of Westerns and buddy films. And what was more, Joey was treating: admission, Cokes and Raisinettes and popcorn were all on him. Even the bus fare. Gabriel didn't have to bring a dime.

Out of sheer and quiet rebellion, Gabriel brought exactly a dime, never thinking he'd use it. But after the movie, as the boys turned west down Broadway toward the bus station and home, still laughing over the cliff-jumping scene where Sundance admits he can't swim, Joey went suddenly serious, hands rifling his own jacket, turning, starting back to the theater, then pausing on the south side of the wide street, reeling as though he had stepped into a high wind.

"Jesus fucking Christ, Rackett," he said at last. "I must of left my wallet in the theater."

The two turned back immediately, half-jogged the three blocks to the theater. The doors were locked already, the marquee lights dimmed. Joey hugged himself, his thin jacket not much protection against the plunging temperature, as around the boys the city sank suddenly into winter.

"What'll we do, Gabey?" Joey asked. "My dad'll kill me."

It was the first time ever Gabriel had seen him like this.

"I got a dime," Gabriel said. "I can call someone."

"Not my dad," Joey said. "He'd be furious."

"Not my mom, either," Gabriel conceded. "Billy Hume's at the house, and he's pretty much a dick."

"So we're stuck, then?"

Gabriel thought before he spoke, taking off his jacket and placing it over the shivering shoulders of his friend. "There's Trajan. I know you're creeped by him, but I still don't know why. And he'd understand, and he wouldn't tell nobody."

Joey shook his head, burrowed into Gabriel's coat. "I guess beggars can't be, can they? You sure he'll come get us? It's the last money we got."

***

Trajan picked up at the second ring, whispered hello.

He told Gabriel that if they'd walk four blocks south to the library, he could park in the lot behind the Unitarian church and meet them there. It was better, he said, not to pick them up where just anyone could see.

Not in the position to parse an offer of rescue, Gabriel didn't stop to think about the strangeness of that statement. Joey, however, plied him with uncertain questions as the two followed Fourth Street to the library, past a tall bronze statue of Lincoln and around the corner to the base of a marble statue of a seated figure in front of the library steps. Beside this George Prentice—whoever he was—a young man in a leather jacket sang Elvis songs in the crisp, moonlit air.

Joey produced a joint from his shirt pocket, and the boys passed it back and forth. Gabriel couldn't and wouldn't think of declining a toke, though he'd never smoked marijuana before. He figured this new pursuit was residual from Joey's friendship with Aron, but by now he knew better than to bring up the older boy's name.

They stood beside the Prentice statue and passed the joint. The man on the library steps broke into "Suspicious Minds," a new one from the King's new album, and Gabriel listened attentively, a strange, intoxicating rush of warmth and misdirection surging from the middle of his spine over his neck and ears. It made the night warmer, made Joey's flimsy jacket sufficient, and for a moment the whole world dilated, the island on York Street where the statue sat, the amber streetlights and the first, tentative hint of snow against his face.

If Del had been around, the moment would have been perfect, but Del was nowhere now, his last notes and doodles scratched on the foundations of Gabriel's imagined empire, as though he was some Pharaoh in a fresh tomb, some half-forgotten god at the heart of the world. The tears bristled against Gabriel's eyelids, and like the young man on the steps was providing a soundtrack to the drama of memory and loss, "I Can't Stop Loving You" trailed through the icy air, and Joey, as though he knew exactly what Gabriel was thinking, rested his hand on the smaller boy's shoulder.

The man in leather pivoted by the library door, and for a moment a brightness in the night air rushed over him and his half-stoned audience, and to Gabriel the world seemed bathed in a light he would not see again until he stood in the basement of Trajan's house and opened the door to its secretive back room.

"I'm tired, Gabey," Joey murmured. "He may be creepy, but I hope Trajan gets here soon."

"I'm tired, too, Joey. It's been a shitty year. The next one's gotta be better."

***

Within an hour, Trajan was there. He slipped behind them quietly, and when he cleared his throat he startled them, so that they all laughed at the recognitions.

He was dressed in a dark trench coat like a secret agent. His frizzy, graying hair spilled out from beneath the wool toboggan he wore against the winter night, and his shadow cast halfway up the stairs where the young man was standing, ending his winter night's serenade with "Can't Help Falling in Love."

"Did you boys tip the man?" Trajan asked, his voice crackling with the cold. "He's what they call a busker. He'll buy nourishment with the money he earns."

"More like wine," Joey said sleepily.

"More like wine," Trajan agreed, handing each boy a five-dollar bill. While Joey looked at his quizzically, Gabriel, buoyed by cannabis and song, recognized what he was supposed to do and tossed the money into the singer's hat where it lay at the foot of the Prentice statue.

"Jesus, boy," the singer breathed, huddling into his jacket and picking up the hat. "You sure you can swing that amount?"

"Someday I'll get it back," Gabriel said, as Joey, realizing now what was expected of him, followed suit and handed his fiver to the singer, who pocketed it gratefully, his eyes still locked with Gabriel's.

"You sure you're all right, kid?" he asked, as Trajan draped his arm around Gabriel's shoulder.

"He's just cold and sleepy, is all," Trajan said. "I'm his uncle. I'll get him home."

The three of them crowded into the front seat of Trajan's Volvo, the back seat being filled with boxes, labeled like the ones first stacked in the Bells' garage on the day of Trajan's first arrival. Fiction, one of them said, and on two of them was Kitchen. Two were labeled Lucius, which Gabriel read in the blurry half-light before Trajan closed the car door and the dome light turned off.

Gabriel sat between Joey and Trajan, drowsing and thinking about the labels over the background of Joey's snoring, which began almost at once when the car turned onto Southern Parkway and headed southwest past Cape Cod houses and stoplights. Gabriel fell asleep himself, awakening once to the pressure of Trajan's hand on his thigh.

"You almost fell out of the seat," Trajan whispered. "I veered a little. The roads are getting slick."

Gabriel nodded and leaned to his right, resting his head on Joey's shoulders, feeling warm and adventurous between his two companions as the car moved through wooded, narrow side roads on their way home.

XVI

Dacia: A Romance was released in midsummer 1985, to a splash of mixed approval and to horrible sales. *An elaborate, eccentric book,* one reviewer called it, *splendid in some ways but maddening in its fragmentation, obscurity, and slow moving plot. Had this young novelist allowed his work to season for a while, he would be standing at the threshold of a notable career as a fantasist. As it is, he has yet to cross into genuine artistry.*

Beyond the typical sting of an ambivalent review, Gabriel understood the objections. Something of his imaginary world had never found resolution: all the parts from his own story—the wanderings of his friends, the impossible magic of those years in August Acres, the hints of Trajan in the character of a solitary wizard—had only fitfully got at the strangeness he was trying to capture. As a result, *Dacia* kept largely to his editor's old recipe of "monsters, magic, and mayhem," ending up a promising misfire that inspired Gabriel at first, beleaguered him later, and as the seventh year since its publication came and went, began to haunt him more than the families of ghosts he had created.

But back in early 1970, on the threshold of a decade heady and new, Gabriel's world had plenty of ghosts and promises. The snowy, desolate landscape of the fictional country was its only constant. Through the tenth and eleventh grades, the notebook— its cardboard cover now creased and softened with continued use and bending—had ended up being one of Gabriel's principal companions.

Trajan seemed to drop from sight after the car ride home in December. His was almost a ghostly presence, too, now and then on Miss Vivien's foliated incline, now and then with his head beneath the hood of his shambling Volvo. But these days neither Keats nor even a call over, and Gabriel began to suspect something might be ailing Miss Vivien.

Joey, too, kept a distance. He would take a bus to the university now and then, but seemed reluctant to have Gabriel join him, so Gabriel wrote it off a little sadly as a symptom of the parting of ways, the time-honored change Mary Rackett had told him was coming.

Meanwhile, he kept and made a number of friends, most particularly Toshiko Collins, whose Japanese mother was struck with her daughter's friend, his growing good looks and impeccable manners. Mrs. Collins imagined and hoped for a romance between the two teenagers, but it was never really like that. Not really.

Oh, there were times when that was a possibility. It wasn't like his old friendships—not by any means. One time, when both of them were fifteen, after a swim at the large public pool behind Jefferson High School, they returned to Toshiko's empty house (her mother worked part-time at the Kroger). During a lull in their usual conversation, Gabriel put his arm around the girl, and they kissed, their wet swimsuits dampening Mrs. Collins' sofa, where they sprawled together and began to caress one another. Gabriel slipped his hand under the soggy fabric, slid his finger into the girl and found a warmer wetness, then the spot he had read about in a smuggled *Playboy*. He rubbed until Toshiko's lips swelled, her eyes rolled, and she let out a sharp, shivering breath that assured him he was on the edge of something mysterious and new. When she rubbed him in return, her fingers closing over the fabric of his trunks and around his hardness, it was only seconds until he came, and the two of them lay together, half on the couch and half on the floor, regarding one another with astonishment. But it was 1970, and of all the revolutions that had so far avoided the American mid-South, the sexual revolution was high on the list.

Gabriel, following a vague sense of obligation, took Toshiko to a movie the next Friday: Mrs. Collins drove them, and they sat in uncomfortable silence and watched *The Sterile Cuckoo*, which had just reached their out-of-the-way suburban theater. They did not talk about the incident on the sofa, and though it recurred several times within the next year, the passion never moved farther than the petting: once, at Haller's Pharmacy, Gabriel contemplated buying rubbers, but it was all too soon and far too intimidating, and Toshiko seemed relieved as well when their friendship moved back to talk about books and music, to gossip about the kids at school, most of whom they cordially hated.

Toshiko was the first person Gabriel took to Dacia. He showed her the notebook in the dazed aftermath of their second petting session, almost as a reward or an assurance that respect and friendship were still parts of their sporadic heat and distance. Sliding the notebook from his desk and opening it to the genealogies, he explained that the stories would follow, that he had to think about the characters before he knew what adventures they might have. Toshiko was puzzled at first, but absorbed as she was with Tolkien and a new book called *A Wizard of Earthsea*, she caught on quickly, and listened to his enthusiasm with a kind of deferential silence. Gabriel liked her attentiveness, enjoyed his first brush with the fact that a lot of books are more interesting while you plan them. Then, when she offered suggestions to the maps, he backed away, nodded politely and replaced the notebook in his desk drawer.

So the companionship continued, brushing against all kinds of confidences until Toshiko, deciding pragmatically that Gabriel would always inhabit the country of friendship, began to date a senior with his own car, who took her to restaurants and a Santana concert. Soon the boy began to resent Gabriel's presence, and eventually Toshiko was around only on occasions, usually after a quarrel with this *Max* or when he was out of town for some reason.

Gabriel took the change in stride. Mrs. Collins would regard him sadly from the Kroger checkout line, sure that he was heartbroken and missing the times with her daughter. And indeed he did miss the girl, though heartbreak would never be the word he would use to describe his loss.

Right after Toshiko got her license, she dropped by the house to retrieve her brand-new copy of *The Crystal Cave*. Gabriel walked her out to the car, dutifully admired the '66 Pontiac her father had bought for a song, talked a little about Merlin to show how well he had attended to the book. He thought it was cool, he said, how Mary Stewart had made it all sound real, like the old legend was some kind of history or autobiography.

Halfway listening, tracing her finger along the windshield of the Pontiac, peeling a damp brown leaf from under the wiper, Toshiko acknowledged that she could count on him to appreciate all that fantasy and adventure, but that the book had gotten a little dull for her in the middle.

That she had expected more magic than it ended up with.

He sat on the steps and absorbed that, as she backed the car from the driveway and drove up August Street toward another date with Max. Across the street Trajan was raking the leaves from Miss Vivien's front yard. He stopped, leaned against the ramp, and waved, staring for a long, inscrutable moment at the half-hearted greeting he received in return. Then he turned, watched the Pontiac recede out of sight, and shrugged amiably before he returned to November tasks.

Not long after that, Gabriel found himself at the encyclopedia again, looking at the picture of the arch. It had been almost two years since he had folded the corner of the page, and for the first time he followed the stories carved in relief on the ancient structure. The emperor, it seemed, was priest as well as conqueror: the Dacians on the arch bore him tribute, but Trajan made offerings as well—sacrifices and ceremonies—and the gods looked over his shoulder as he performed his duties. Gabriel wondered why he had never noticed those parts of the arch before. It was like they had risen out of the stone or out of the picture to demand his attention, as Del's long-ago scribbling, still preserved on an otherwise blank page in Gabriel's notebook, had come out of nowhere to haunt his thoughts in that increasingly distant summer.

When he closed the encyclopedia, he had no thought of returning to the picture or the arch. And in the year that followed, he thought of Trajan virtually only when he saw him. You could say that Gabriel himself receded in that time, became lost in more typical high-school doings: he spent more time in books and studies than some of his classmates, but he dated, made new acquaintances, and experimented further with reefer, more cautiously with beer. So all in all, he was normal, except that Gabriel felt that normalcy as a kind of faint tremor of discontent in his daily life—something his mother dismissed as "growing pains" as she asked for more and more of his attention and help around the house.

And Mary Rackett was right, in part: all around him the growing pains ached and smarted. Joey transferred his senior year to a better school, when his parents moved out to the eastern part of the county. Toshiko had only half a senior year, when, to the disappointment of her parents, she became pregnant and married Max the day after she turned eighteen; Gabriel did not attend the wedding, despite his mother's urging. He approached his graduation with what he thought was a unique mixture of anticipation and regret: he had a scholarship to a good university in upstate New York, but no particular plans of a course of study. At the same time, as the spring of 1972 approached, he felt stripped of his past, his childhood receding into something more glorified and serene than he was entitled to imagine at seventeen.

He was honored bountifully at his graduation, receiving several awards and graduating among the top ten percent of his class, though his mother reminded him that, in a group swelled to six hundred by the baby boom, it meant that over fifty people had made better grades. He looked forward to leaving for Rochester: it was the last step in those growing pains, he figured, and he almost dozed through the ceremonies, imagining once that he saw Trajan in the bleachers of the Convention Center, and fleetingly—though he brushed the thought away almost immediately—he sensed another presence, something benign but yearning and haunted.

It was why he packed his notebook in the suitcase that fall.

He packed as well the half-mysterious gift that appeared on his doorstep in June. A scuffed volume of Keats' *Endymion*, wrapped in brown paper so that his mother suspected pornography until Gabriel showed her the contents. *For the graduate*, it was inscribed, and below, a stanza he had never read:

> *Fade far away, dissolve, and quite forget*
> *What thou among the leaves hast never known,*
> *The weariness, the fever, and the fret*
> *Here, where men sit and hear each other groan;*
> *Where palsy shakes a few, sad, last grey hairs,*
> *Where youth grows pale, and spectre-thin, and dies;*
> *Where but to think is to be full of sorrow*
> *And leaden-eyed despairs;*
> *Where beauty cannot keep her lustrous eyes,*
> *Or new Love pine at them beyond to-morrow.*

It was something from the book, he guessed. Indeed, he found it later, in an additional poem near the back of the book. And that book was from Trajan, he supposed as well, though now that he thought of it, he had never seen Trajan's handwriting. But the greater guesswork lay in why this quote was chosen. Something in it seemed so melancholy and intimate that Gabriel found it unsettling, as though his friend had reached to him in a way that was no longer indirect, but somehow a little belated.

Trajan never acknowledged that he had sent the book. Gabriel confirmed it only later, when a few scrawled notes on the cover sheet of Trajan's stories matched the handwriting that inscribed the book. When he received the gift, he thought it was a kind of farewell, but he would hear from Trajan twice more, and both times in surprising ways.

Gabriel had been at Rochester through November, and now was preparing for his first battery of university finals. Never had he been more aware of how far behind his education had left him: Philosophy 101 was a maze to him, and his Freshman Composition teacher, a smartass grad student from New York City or New Jersey—Gabriel still couldn't place accents in this part of the country—seemed to be going for a major on how bad his students' writing was. And those were the classes where Gabriel thought and hoped he would be the most talented, the most knowledgeable. Science and math were even worse, complete and utter bafflements, so that by November he was wondering whether he would be back for the next term.

And there was Jasmine for the first time, as there would be Jasmine forever after.

He met her on the first floor of the Rush Rhees Library, and it was by accident and by Keats that he got to know her.

Once again, he had Trajan to thank for something.

Gabriel saw her behind the circulation desk, so he knew she was older, but otherwise he would never have guessed she was twenty. At once he was drawn to her: another slight Eurasian girl, her silky black hair tied back in a simple ponytail, wearing jeans and a black Rolling Stones t-shirt complete with the familiar, cartoonish lips and tongue. She conjured memories of Toshiko Collins, and was all business until she saw his copy of *Steppenwolf*.

"Reading the hippie stuff, I see," she observed with a smile that he almost recognized as ironic.

Gabriel cleared his throat, handed her the book for stamping. "Yeah, I've read *Siddhartha* and *Demian*," he proclaimed. "This one...is required for English."

She looked up from the book. "Where you from?" Smiled at the answer. "We don't get many Southern boys in these here parts," she continued with the worst imitated drawl Gabriel had ever heard, and for a moment he was not sure whether he would like her or not.

"Faulkner's a Southern boy," he replied, his accent receding into his best Northeastern seamlessness. "So's Robert Penn Warren. You do get them in these here parts."

He prayed, secretly and earnestly, that Jasmine Bowers would not ask him about either novelist. Instead she snickered, and handed him the book.

"Due in thirty days, Faulkner," she announced, winking at him as she returned to her desk, the long black ponytail sweeping her narrow back.

He was hooked, simply and sweetly, and with a plan that in later years they would jokingly call "innocent stalking," arranged his trips to the library to coincide with her hours of work. She claimed that she didn't recognize what was going on at first, that she just assumed he was bookish and personality-free, but around the third time their paths crossed at the circulation desk, Gabriel struck up a longer conversation, and it was then that he was blessed with the distant magic of coincidence.

Jasmine Bowers, she said she was, and he remarked on her appearance in a Keats poem.

"*It was a jasmine bower, all bestrown / with golden moss,*'" he recited quickly, and to his surprise, she blushed when he blushed.

"You're a complicated boy, Faulkner," she said at last. "So... what happens in that bower?"

"I can show you," he replied, instantly regretting the abruptness when he saw her eyes widen, saw her back a step away from the counter. "I mean...you gonna be here for a minute? I'll just..."

And he stalked off toward the stacks, cursing under his breath as he climbed the steps to the fourth floor, certain he had blown the opportunity already, going to fetch the book instead of taking her to that bower and its prospects.

He was sounding like a bush-league Trajan, damn it.

And finding the Keats on the shelf was about as plodding and personality-free as he feared he could get.

But there the book was, recovered surprisingly easily in a Library of Congress system Gabriel had yet to figure out, and he thumbed through *Endymion* as he descended the stairs, catching his ankle as he reached the second floor landing and stumbling half a flight before he recovered, both feet throbbing. He limped to the counter, hiding the injury as Jasmine looked up.

"Here it is," he muttered, handing her the book.

She held it close to her face, squinting just a little, and for a moment she seemed less daunting, even frail, as she began to read aloud.

> *"It was a jasmine bower, all bestrown*
> *With golden moss. His every sense had grown*
> *Ethereal for pleasure; 'bove his head*
> *Flew a delight half-graspable; his tread*
> *Was Hesperean; to his capable ears*
> *Silence was music from the holy spheres;*
> *A dewy luxury was in his eyes."*

He cleared his throat and looked away. When he looked at her again, though, she was regarding him in a cagey, amused way that nobody before had ever looked at him.

"A complicated boy, Faulkner," she repeated softly.

It would become their motto for almost twenty years.

Jasmine and Gabriel never really dated. After all, it was the early '70s, and dating was a thing for sororities, fraternities, and conservative students in the business and professional schools. She was an immediate godsend, though—one of those brilliant students whose college studies were as effortless as Gabriel's were in high school—and with her guidance he salvaged his grade point average and kept a scholarship that, from that point on, he was able to keep on his own.

She was really that good.

Gabriel knew from the start that he was being kept hidden from Jasmine's friends. It made sense to both of them, somehow, and Gabriel had fully figured that, after the holiday break, she would move on to other circles, leaving him behind as another accomplishment, a kind of completed charity project. Twice over the semester break—a dim two weeks that he spent in Louisville more or less alone with his mother—he contemplated calling her, but the Boston phone book was far more filled with Bowerses than he had ever foreseen, and he took it as an omen that she had not given him the number at her parents' house.

His thoughts and doubts undermined each other, and his world narrowed to Mary Rackett and gin and pills and the television. Billy Hume was history now, set by the wayside not so much because of his abysmal politics and theology, but because his insistence on women as helpmates had not fit well with the Mary-centric universe.

There was no escape from his mother, though Gabriel combed the neighborhood. Joey had not come home for the holidays, and the Hardys were veiled about where he was and why. He dropped by to see Toshiko and Max and the new baby, but the conversation dwindled after Gabriel had offered the right praises and held the little girl under mild protest.

No sign of Trajan. Miss Vivien's house seemed abandoned, though somebody was picking up the mail and leaving the garbage cans by the curb. Gabriel's mother hinted that some change was taking place with the Bells, that she would not be surprised if Miss Vivien were back in hospital, but that the son had always kept to himself, as surely Gabriel knew, and the two of them were as close as a wick to the flame. Though he was concerned for his old friend, at least in a kind of abstract way, Gabriel's thoughts kept migrating to some indefinite Boston, where he imagined Jasmine by a window missing him, and he tried to picture that yearning as the year turned with still no sign of Trajan, as he packed his bags and took the bus to the Greyhound terminal in Louisville, the first of a complicated series of connections that brought him into Rochester after a day and night of travel.

Dirty and apprehensive, his thoughts brushing against a strangely mature acceptance, he walked across the quad on the campus, climbing onto the waist-high ridges of hard snow that lined the sidewalk. The gothic tower of the library was veiled in white, and he stood on the salted steps for a moment, realizing it was far too early, that the term had not yet begun, not even the work day, and she was no doubt in her dormitory room if she was back on campus at all.

He decided to go to Jasmine's room first. But the dorm was locked, and he sat on his suitcase in front of the main door until a returning student, thick with a parka and backpack, passed by him and labored with her key. He held the door for her and followed her in unquestioned, climbed the stairs, his suitcase growing heavier, reached the third floor, and knocked softly on Jasmine's door.

He would always remember the lack of surprise on her face when she greeted him, as though she had assumed this all along, that he would return on an early winter morning and come to her first of all things. She did not even smile as she led him into the room, into her bed, and he was astonished as the things he had read about and imagined came true for him, opened to include him, and though the first time was altogether too brief, the second time, an hour later, was longer and more luxuriant, until he knew, lying among the damp and furrowed sheets, that his suitcase would sit in the corner of her room and that he was, for the season, home.

***

Jasmine Bowers was the precocious oldest child of a Boston psychologist and a fairly prominent Taiwanese artist—the kind of family background that Gabriel knew only from books and movies, intimidating in its worldliness and its comfort with ideas. Her brother—two weeks older than Gabriel—was a high flier at Juilliard, and a young sister had redefined, to hear Jasmine tell it, the entire world of aptitude testing. Soon Gabriel began to wonder if he was not Jasmine's quiet rebellion against the good life, but for him the good life was there in her room, where studies and sex and long conversation buoyed him through the spring of his freshman year.

Jasmine was a psychology major herself, and delighted in pinning him with insights, but when Gabriel suggested naively that her own studies were somehow in the footsteps of her father, he discovered that the insights traveled one-way, that there was Bowers family terrain that he could not travel yet. She made great talk of his absent father, of a mother that she immediately discerned was addicted to so many things, but those observations were elementary, as she said, and it was far more interesting to hear him talk about his childhood, about his friends and about Trajan especially, whom she saw as a perplexing influence. By her questions he knew what she was thinking all too well, but she never spelled it out, like a good psychologist layering her answers with still more questions, with the judgments implicit in her tone of voice.

He never approached Trajan's magic—the strange things that took place when his friend was around. Nor did he mention the blossoming incline, the October Man in Miss Vivien's back yard, nor the owlish Queen of the Ghosts, nor the December night on the road back from town, though he figured they had more to do with who he had become, more than did Trajan's chosen companionship with teenaged boys.

And yet Jasmine persisted. *What should we make, Faulkner, of a man who fits so well with other peoples' sons?* And he would not give her the answer she wanted to make, but it set his memories on stories Trajan had told him about Artie, and snowy weather such as the blizzards outside. It made him remember Miss Vivien's stay at the hospital, and Trajan's mysterious guest, but something within Gabriel guarded those stories as well, and his answers were polite at first, then less polite, and when his words grew short, Jasmine stopped asking about Trajan altogether and took him to bed.

Stopped asking, that is, until the letter came. It appeared, thick and patchworked with stamps, in his mailbox at the turn of March. Gabriel glanced at the return address, saw "August Street" and assumed it was from his mother. Only when he had opened it to the typescript did he glance at the envelope again, and even then the handwriting failed to jog his memory. Later, of course, he matched it with the inscription in the book, and congratulated himself for having solved what he thought was the last mystery. But for now he burrowed deeply into the message from his old friend.

#

Louisville, Kentucky

February 20, 1973

Oh what can ail thee, knight at arms?

My apologies for missing you over your Christmas break, Gabriel. Your mother told me, in that roundabout Hibernian way she's got, that your thoughts were pretty much northeast of here through the whole vacation, that she "might as well have been whistling jigs to a milestone," whatever that might mean. She also said, in that insightful maternal way she's got, that if she didn't know better, she'd be guessing there was a girl involved up there.

Well, if I didn't know better, I'd say there wasn't a girl involved, and you are wishing there would be. I hope that, if there is, you fare well with her, bully monster, and that she has some gorgeousness about her, because the truth may make you free but beauty is the path of escape. If I were you, I might even consider summering where she summers (do they still talk about "summering" up your way?). After all there's a lot of interesting weather a boy of eighteen can get out of and into, and none of it, I fear, is around here.

Obviously, I'm not writing to you about girls and weather—you have enough of both of them where you are, and I must confess to knowing very little about either. There are changes down here, changes for sure in Castle Bell, and I thought that my chief knight errant should know the score.

There comes a time in decline, camerado, when the duties of even the most devoted son are packed up and done with. The next step is OLS. Our Lady of Serenity is what they used to call it, but it is OLS they call it these days, so that the city government can use it. Sooner or later, there will be a whole generation that won't know what the letters stand for.

"Old Lush Sanctuary" will be their best guess, though those inside OLS have given it other names. Our Lady of Thorazine and Anabuse and Perpetual Bedrest. Our Lady of Bleach and Orderlies, of Eclipse and Oblivion and the Last Good-Bye.

"Heaven's Waiting Room", some superficial smartass called it. Someone who never had to imagine heaven in a lonely place.

You've probably seen it, how it sits up on a hill like a Gothic mansion trying to hide in the sunlight. It was built right after the war—the big Confederate one that our beloved city won then lost. Back then it was the charity hospital for your Catholic Church, raised by Irish and German money in what were then the suburbs. I reckon it offered what passed for care in the days of typhus and consumption and killer influenza. Later on it became a mental hospital, then a rehab center, and finally it's a nursing home for the old and the chemically ill, a way station for old folks and drunks and addicts who have no real place on the wagon and come back to the wards, dazed and damned, all part of a long spiral that just about always ends in the potters' field in a shady corner just outside the C wing.

Heaven's waiting room, my ass. What I know of heaven could fill a whiskey bottle with room left over for the whiskey, but I can tell you that OLS has nothing to do with it, unless heaven is set up so that everything leading up to it is its opposite, so that you will be even more surprised by glory after the stained walls and acoustic ceilings.

There is a time, though, when the sunlight is just right in a room they call the Old Chapel. A room given over to vending machines now, where you can get coffee or chicken broth--both a quarter and both poured out of the same spout. The machines are set up against the wall so that if you go in there to sneak a smoke you're hard-pressed to recognize the old bricked-in door behind them, all of it blocked except for a transom that the contractor must have decided to keep, out of economy or laziness or something more...

I like to think it was something more...

There is original glass in the old transom, those melting, watery panes from the nineteenth century. And sometimes, right at sunrise, like the room was built with astronomy and changing seasons in mind, the old glass blazes with sun, and light breaks across the little formica table where the staff and the visitors and most trusted residents (among which Mother is not, at least not yet) are allowed to sit. It casts a broken shine across the table's cheap finish, and if you are there at the right time and you know where to look, it might make you believe that the world outside is trying to tell you something, that there is some kind of pattern to the light, no matter the misery of drywall and tile...

But you have to know where to look. And you have to be present, which is not the same as just being there.

I'm getting familiar with Serenity now. Mother's been a resident there for almost three months. It started when she saw ghosts in the back yard—a "man from bygone times," she kept saying, repeating it enough that I decided she needed medical attention.

So I took her pistol away, then took her straight to the hospital, where the doctors laid out my options. And I took her to OLS the next day. I'm not so sure I should be telling you this, but you're the one I thought of, and maybe it's your burden and advantage to know. I felt like I was dropping years as I sat with her in the back of the ambulance. She insisted on sitting up, and I am sure she was thinking we were headed to another specialist, another diagnosis, until we turned into the long driveway leading to the home. Mother began to wrestle and cry out for her gun back when she saw the statue of the Virgin Mary from the rear window of the ambulance. Strained against my grip until my wrists gave out, and then battered herself against the doors.

She was raised so Protestant that she was afraid they'd make her Hail Mary for a bed. But the nuns and orderlies took her into a room and off half her medication. In a few days it even reached the point where she was enjoying herself, looking forward to regular meals and afternoon television, to the drugs they gave her for the head injury and the visions. I suspect Mary herself started looking good by that time, all dressed in blue and tilting her head leftwards, her hands spread and palms out like she was saying,

You'll always find a home here, Vivien Bell. Blessed art thou among women.

I stayed two days in there with her. Could have stayed in Serenity forever, but they set loose a flock of social workers on me, who interviewed me and examined me and went on about how sensitive I was, how much potential...

Not like the other sons, they came close to saying. But they don't let themselves say things like that anymore, because the rule is that we're all sensitive, we all have potential, all that liberal song and dance...

Potential has always been the last thing I wanted to hear. Especially about myself.

It was a week until the visions recommenced, and Miss Vivien tried to escape. Next thing I know I was called back to the hospital to find her all frostbitten on face and feet, like some kind of birthmark after the fact or like she was scarring her countenance to match my own. They kept her on a liquid diet for a month—not the liquid diet of her preference, so she came close to drying out, and maybe if the visions hadn't started again, she'd have passed on through into normal old ladyhood, having passed through withdrawal and the DTs and the pukes and the late-night twirlies like they were the temptations of some desert saint....

She was right at the edge of being trustworthy and even mainstream, though respectable was never in her grasp. Almost past danger, they were starting to say, but the ghosts came into OLS, and from the end of January until today, it has been like the circle was narrowing and narrowing. I have spent more time in OLS than out, buster. It is where Mother is ending up, and for a while it seemed like the one place in my life that was reliable and eventual.

Serenity is not home. But it is a version of refuge.

Now Mother is stoked up on the tranquilizer of the

hour, asking the nuns about those people who have circled around her life in this terrible quiet place. About the man in the garden, about the dogs and the drowned boy, and always about me. All the while, the outrage and the sorrow of the world settles in the halls of Serenity, and it's like part of her doesn't notice any more, like she's given something up for good and is floating from injection to injection.

Last week, right in the room next to her, Eleanor Rigby tried to jump out the window. Yes, that's Eleanor Rigby, like in the Beatles song, and I have no idea of his real name, which he surrendered to become glittering and fabulous. Eleanor is a drag queen and a part-time prophet in a charismatic Episcopal church, of all things, on loan from a bar downtown, where she does her act with her partner, Miss Rita Meter Maid. She's a piece of work, her spike heels hoisting her up to six-three or four, her heavy five-o'clock shadow a dead giveaway under the wig and the fake pearls and the sequined gown. Made her name by seeing wheels in the air during the service, and the end of time through the spokes of the wheels, center ring in a church that loves its incense and drama.

Well, Eleanor came back to Serenity following another weekend bout with Communion wine. Predictable as the weather. All visionaries are fools or drunks or both nowadays.

Well, there she was, scanted in a dull cage, sobered up and dressed in the plain green robe that is kind of the institutional uniform. I guess she felt like her altars were stripped. So last week she decided that she had only the revelation of the wheels to glamorize her, to make her fabulous and set her apart from the rest of the patients and parishioners and drag queens. So she jumped, reaching for the wheels as they turned and burned just out of her reach outside the window, the bars were too strong and too close together. And of course when the nuns and the orderlies got there they found her all battered and cut, having hurled herself like a moth against the light of the window, glass sparkling like sequins against her green hospital robe.

I can see all of this without seeing it. I think you know what I mean.

I heard it second and third hand, but I can see Eleanor Rigby and the wheels and her leap into grace and into intensive care. The dreams of this place are lending images to my mother, who is passing them on to me in turn.

But that is too simple an explanation.

It's better to tell you early on: I know this on account of the world alongside the city. A world of invisible guests alongside Mother and the nuns and Eleanor Rigby, winding through Our Lady of Serenity and above and below the familiar world itself. It follows a changing pattern. Back and forth, like Eleanor caught between male and female and like the scales they say will measure souls on the Last Day.

You can see it beside you if you look close enough. It's why they change the maps of the city, why they rename and rebuild and redirect the streets, until the world looks nothing like it did at the last century's turn, looks like nothing that would even remember that earlier time...

And every once in a while, when the dreams blur into the waking life, I get a glimpse of that pattern.

Or I think I do. Even though it is all too big and complicated to take in, I stand in its presence, because I come out seeing new things, knowing new things, like someone has removed a dark glass from in front of my face, or like I'm standing on a tower in a thunderstorm, looking out across the geometries of this mysterious and backward city.

But Mother. We were talking about our Miss Vivien.

Sometimes at night, when the drugs wear low and she is left with her own thoughts and visions, she presses her ear against the wall of her room. Or if she is restrained by the bed rails or the tightened sheets, she simply closes her eyes, and her dreams, and the dreams of all the others, rise to meet her in the all-knowing dark.

She tells me all the dreams—wild and stinking and sometimes dirty enough to make a biker blush—but of course it is her own dreams she best remembers in the morning when the sun slips by the transom window and the whole world seems like nothing more than bed and hall, nurse and orderly, and the last legion of the damnable damned pathetic.

And her own dreams go something like this.

First, she says, is the smell of the horses. Out of the darkness it rises, a mix of silage and sweat.

It surprises her. Yes, it always surprises her, though she is a witness only, always at the edge of the dream, not a participant. It is like a movie she watches, and she tries to direct it with her thoughts but it will not comply, and this frustrates her all the more because she is convinced that, at one lost time or another, she could have controlled it, but that the story has dropped through her hands.

Please bear with me, Gabriel. I know this letter is far too long, far too unruly already, but I have to tell this, have to write down the dream, have to write it to you, even though as I place it into words it becomes my own dreaming.

After the smell of the horses, the road appears. The lantern weaving in the hand of the foremost rider, the rain spattering the dusty leather of his saddle.

There are four of them. There are always four, she says.

And even more than the rain and the other riders, it surprises her that she, of all people, is there on horseback, that somehow, even in a dream, she could straddle a horse and stay mounted.

Unsteady in the saddle, feeling the back of the beast sag, for a moment she tries to recall how she came here, what set her on this unfamiliar road. But it is always the same--no memory, no anticipation, just mud and darkness and needles of rain.

And always a mournful feeling. Like she has lost someone or something important. Like the world is ending in a stormy night.

Now a patter and pop from somewhere behind her, muffled like a distant roll of a snare drum. Then a cough from the foremost rider, and then sobbing nearby, at the margins of the road. A sound barely human, so that she cannot tell whether it comes from rider or horse. Something of loss and fear and her own mournfulness tumbling through darkness, and the rain mingling in her own tears.

That is what she says. Exactly what she says. And who would have thought the old girl had so much poetry in her, even if the poetry is bad?

Then she sees the sign. Out of nowhere at the edge of the road, given shape by a sudden flash of lightning in the hilly hot country and by the silence before and after the thunder. A white, boarded sign, framed by the broken and unbroken lines of a ruptured fencerow. It is tilted into the path of the horses--an arrow pointing downward into the dark like it is showing him a passage through the land of the dead.

It is the name of a town, a destination. And she knows that her mind should fasten on the word, should keep it in thought for remembering later.

But *Captain* she finds himself saying, repeating strange words into the rising rain...

If I forget thee, let my right hand forget her cunning...

If I do not remember thee, let my tongue cleave to the roof of my mouth...

Even as she says this, she knows she has forgotten the name on the sign, forgotten someone or something else terribly important...

Captain? she asks herself, as the horses trudge and the darkness converges, all of it leaving her with the last and only thing she will clearly remember, with that fierce and abiding sense of loss.

That is the dream that she is bound to protect herself against. According to the nuns she sleeps two hours a night at most. According to Mother, she does not sleep at all—just sits in her chair among the dreams, her pistol propped on her knees, until the darkness falls and the sweat of the horses rises out of the sudden night.

Yes, a pistol. I brought it to her on the 14th. She claims it was the perfect Valentine's present. I assured the nuns, who danced on the edge of justifiable panic, that the piece was utterly unloaded, that it had not housed a shell in my remembrance, that they don't even make shells for this kind of gun any more, and that the last time it was used was probably against the Union Army in my great-grandfather's fabled and imagined past. And still they argued against it, and I granted they were right, but when I carefully forgot to come home with the gun they carefully forgot its presence in her room, for it has ended up as a kind of peacemaker—the thing that would keep Miss Vivien from calling for the sisters at all hours.

I signed away my life so she could keep it. It's complicated, but I have a friend of a friend. Lucius, a young guy I know; I don't know if you met him or not last winter, but he helped me out around the place for a couple of weeks. Well, at any rate, he's good friends with an officer high up on the board of directors for OLS, and when I talked to this guy and mentioned that we had friends in common, he pulled some strings for me, and now my mother is as armed as an unarmed woman can be.

Like so many other times, Gabriel, this is one of those occasions when I shouldn't even be telling you such things. Your mother is doing well, all said, and this neighborhood, this town, this part of the country is something you are growing away from. Another one of those great old poets, a fellow called William Blake, said once that "we are put on earth a little space / That we may learn to bear the beams of love." You might want to remember that quote, even though people thought Blake was crazy, too. You also might want to try summering somewhere. Now that I think about it, I'm sure they still say and do summers in the great Northeast, and it might be a good time for you to discover that.

But I'm done with advice. Your part is harder still.

--Trajan

XVIII

Jasmine made a great festival of Trajan's letter.

"Nobody writes a letter that long, Faulkner," she insisted. "Not unless…well, never mind. You know where I'm headed."

Gabriel could tell she was curious, and that she wasn't about to ask the particulars, so for a while he revealed nothing of the letter's contents, his attentions tuned instead to the term's end and a chance to stay in the Northeast until the fall.

A scholarship job was there for the asking—painting university rental properties—and it would give him money for food. Fortunately, Jasmine was house-sitting for a prominent Psychology professor in a beautiful place off Monroe Avenue, and she offered Gabriel lodging to rest his head, an overflowing library to rummage through, and all the advantages (of course) that would come with being around her for the summer.

Gabriel thought it would be difficult to break the news to his mother, but Mary Rackett, it seemed, had her days full with a new suitor. He had guessed early on, when she hustled him off the telephone, that she was playing for an audience at home. But he was still unsure as to how captive that audience was until he told his mother of his summer plans. Her protests were weak, and

Gabriel knew they were formalities. He promised her she didn't need to send money, regretted the promise almost immediately, but resolved to stick by it as he hung up the phone, realizing that he had made another of the many breaks with home.

Out in the larger world, the Senate Watergate Hearings had just begun. Gabriel and Jasmine watched with fascination for the first televised sessions. Gabriel translated the statements of Southern senators to his bemused girlfriend, sent her into small ripples of laughter when he told her that Mary Rackett had called the President of the United States a gobshite and would probably do so to his face. Like so many students of their place and time, they both hungered to see Nixon's head on a platter, but like almost as many of their friends, they were too passive and preoccupied to think much farther about it. Instead, they were accustoming to each other and their surroundings.

Professor Benjamin Mountolive's house was a large mansion of many rooms, and later, when Gabriel sat down to write about the place, he found himself able to describe only two of them, the doors of the rest having shut on his memory. The first you stepped into, out of the outside light, was painted in deep and resonant reds, the bookshelves framing a narrow fireplace and rising to the heights of a twelve-foot ceiling. The furniture was scattered, eclectic, Victorian, and the single huge window was curtained in deep greens. No overhead light, but a simple arrangement of three lamps—one above a squat, stuffed chair and the other two framing a disheveled sofa, so that the room always basked in a shadowy light as though you had walked into the midst of a ghost story. It was a room that siphoned the concentration, sidetracking the mind into wanderings. Gabriel wondered how the professor could read in such a room without pulling the books from the shelves and taking them to a more illuminated and focused place. You could linger there while the pocket doors of the dining room remained wide open, showing a bright appearance, a table and eight chairs, a sideboard, and a china cabinet Mary Rackett would envy.

No sooner did you step from the shadowy parlor into the

dining room than you became intoxicated with the light and the atmosphere. You saw nothing but pleasant wonders, and there was a part of you tempted to delay forever in what you thought was delight. However, the drawings on the walls sharpened your vision: stark pen and ink drawings by a prominent Israeli artist, each presenting an appalling moment from Greek mythology— Orpheus turning toward a vanishing Eurydice, Adonis gored by the boar's tusk, Meleager bursting into flames. Jasmine told him the ancient stories that accompanied the drawings, and Gabriel was struck by the world full of misery and heartbreak, pain and oppression. The dining room seemed to lose its essential brightness in the wake of myth.

On all sides of the dining room several doors were set open— but all dark in Gabriel's memory, all leading to dark passages. In fact, it was somewhat less dramatic: they led to a kitchen, a hallway, a walk-in closet beneath the kitchen stairs, but for the life of Gabriel, he could not remember those rooms—only the dining room and the parlor, commingling shadow and light. It was on the dining room table, in the brilliance of the small glass chandeliers and surrounded by the brutal drawings, that Gabriel drew forth the Dacia notebook again, and shared it with Jasmine for the first time.

Gabriel was afraid she would belittle his imaginary world, so he started by dismissing it himself, in a way. The addiction of his childhood, he called it with a laugh. The kind of thing he kept for sentimental reasons.

But Jasmine pored over the notebook, looking over his shoulder at the maps and genealogies. Her interest flattered him, her questions sharpened and refreshed the image of Dacia in his thoughts.

"It's patterns, Gabriel," she told him, tracing designs on the maps.

Gabriel assured her he was no artist. "The last time I drew anything," he said with a laugh, "was in 8th grade Art. It was a pen and ink sketch of a house, and Miss Winn gave me a C because it was incomplete. She said it just faded into nothing, that the front upper story of the house was there, but there was nothing on the ground floor, and the perspective was lousy. She was right, because I never figured out how to do perspective: to me, it was a bunch of lines that guessed at something in the distance."

Jasmine frowned. "That's what perspective is, isn't it?"

"I don't think it is when it comes to a drawing, Jazzie. And Miss Winn didn't think so, either. I found out later she had checked with the counselor to see if I was retarded and misplaced in the class."

Jasmine snickered and rubbed the top of his hair playfully. "Well, you are retarded and misplaced in class, Faulkner. But that's not the issue here. Tell me... why would you want to make a world?"

Gabriel leaned back in his chair, resting his shoulders against her breasts. Jasmine wrapped her arms around his neck. Her cheek brushed against his as she looked more closely at the map, and Gabriel, aroused by her closeness and wanting, as always, to please her, rummaged his thoughts for whatever answer she would be expecting.

"I guess...I wanted to make things...make sense," he said, and her arms closed about him more tightly. Guiltily, he felt the approval in the weight of her body.

"Exactly," she murmured. "It's all about order for you. Making connections. It's about guessing at things from a distance, and it was a shitty art teacher that didn't understand that, no matter how bad your drawing was."

She reached over his shoulder, her finger tracing the coastline of Dacia on the page of the notebook. Gabriel breathed in the smell of her, knew she wanted to talk about psychological matters, no matter what inclination he had at the moment.

"Look, Gabe," she said. "What does the shape of your continent remind you of?"

"Amoeba?" he snorted, and she drew back and flicked his ear.

"Dumbass. It's a pool of water. Look at the ripples across

the continent—your little mountain ranges and forests. It's like when you drop something into a still pond. How the ripples spread out until they reach the shore. This whole thing is stirring waters, Faulkner. It's your way of not looking at your own reflection."

He could play, too. "Or maybe I'm stirring the waters for a better look."

Sheer contrariness had made him say that. He didn't mind Jazzie's insights, except when she tried to substitute them for his own thoughts.

And yet she liked what he said. Again he could tell in the way she leaned against him.

"Maybe you are, Gabriel. I'd love for Mountolive to have a look at these. It's kind of his bailiwick, you know. And the family trees, too: the shape they take, and the names you give the people in them."

"Those are elves, Jazzie," Gabriel corrected, turning the page. "These are the dwarves…and these…are the ghosts. There are humans among them—living humans—but sometimes they seem…so few and so small among the others."

Jasmine nodded, looked at the third genealogy. "Haven't you told me about a Del, Gabriel?"

He didn't remember having told her. Perhaps one night in her dorm room, lying in bed after sex? But he motioned her to a chair, and Jasmine sat beside him as he told her now: the barest of details, the friendship, the falling away, the accident he would describe in more detail almost twenty years later, when Del's death was more vivid to him than this moment, than the intervening time, than Jasmine Bowers herself.

She absorbed the story, placing her hand on his. And when Gabriel finished she looked at him with those black, fathomless eyes that could drown the world.

"Baby," she began. Then corrected herself, because she knew he hated that endearment. "Gabriel…you have a burden of ghosts, don't you? You're like the…like the humans in Dacia. You live with invisible guests."

"Well…yes I do, Jazzie. More than you know it."

He showed her Del's scrawled words near the back of the notebook, preserved and bordered in concentric circles. He had passed his pencil over them once, tracing the awkward sequence of letters and feeling, as he did so, a surge of something he could not put words around. And now, almost five years later, the girl he loved had seen his world's first relic, and he felt exposed and willing.

Of course they ended up in bed, and in the slow, tidal aftermath of lovemaking Jasmine talked about stories. She was surprised that it had just dawned on him: she had figured all along that the maps and genealogies meant that a novel was brewing.

He knew he couldn't do it yet. Figured that a novel was beyond his talent and experience. But as Jasmine coaxed and lectured, he lay back on the pillow and thought it through. They were all ghosts, he figured. Not only Del, who had appeared to him in a distant scrawling hidden inside an inherited notebook, but Joey as well in his long and studied absence. And his father, glimpsed briefly in phone calls and intermittent visits, and his mother abstracted by pills and drama and distance. And Trajan—especially Trajan—revealed and concealed simultaneously, who took on a strange translucency in his memory. It was as though all of the people in his life were points on a far horizon he could only guess at, only recover as the fragments of a lost and disorderly dream.

It was then he rose from the bed and retrieved Trajan's letter from the dresser. He offered it to Jasmine, who lay golden and splendid in a spill of pale blue sheets, and sitting up in the bed, her beautiful small breasts enticing him at that moment toward protection only, she began to read and make first acquaintance with the King of the Ghosts.

✳✳✳

"I can see why you like him," she said at last, handing Gabriel back the letter. "Can you see why I'm a little afraid of him?"

"I know, Jazzie. It's the thing about the boys, but—"

"Don't be a dumbass, Faulkner. That's no threat to you. You're old enough to decide about that stuff, and if the last couple of hours are any indication, you've pretty well decided already."

She laughed and pulled the sheets to her chin. Gabriel blushed, but at a depth he was grateful to her for having said what she said, brushing a last ghost out of a cobwebbed corridor.

"No," Jasmine continued, this time more soberly. "No, it's the weight of that letter, the sheer cargo he's expecting you to carry. 'Bear the beams of love', my ass. What happened to 'my yoke is easy and my burden light'?"

"Like you believe *that* one, either, Jazzie."

She lay down again, her face in the pillow, the sheet sliding to the small of her back. When she spoke again, her voice was muffled, and Gabriel had to ask her twice just what it was she had said.

She turned her head away from him now, and it was as though the temperature dropped in the room. Gabriel heard a car rush by the Mountolive house, heard Jasmine as though it was the first time.

"You want to know what happened at that school of Trajan's, Gabriel? Thracia College? You know you do. You even named your world to rhyme with it, for God's sake."

"It wasn't that at all, Jazzie. It was on the arch…it was…"

And he stopped, realizing they both had come to the same place.

"Here's what it was, Gabriel. Here's what happened up there."

And Jazzie began to spin a story—one he interrupted, deflected, and fixed as she told it. And it was not long into the telling that Gabriel realized they were making the story together.

✳✳✳

"What did he teach there, Gabriel?"

"Latin."

Jasmine stared at the ceiling. "Don't know much beyond a year in high school. *Amo amas amat.* But I know this much. It's 1973, Gabriel, and anyone teaching Latin has to have a streak of throwback in him. Deeply conservative, your Trajan is."

Gabriel lay down beside her. "I wouldn't say conservative, Jazzie," he protested.

"How about preservationist, then? You all right with preservationist?"

Gabriel supposed he was.

"There he is, then. Up in a lecture room in one of those New England three-story monstrosities. The windows thick with frost and the classroom cold enough you could see your breath—"

"Too cold, Jazzie. I don't believe it when you say the classroom is that cold."

"So how cold, Gabriel? Tell me about it."

He rested his head beside hers on the pillow. A faint smell of sweet citrus (perhaps her shampoo?) drifted in the still air of the room, and his thoughts rode with it into a watery light.

"Lemon wax," he said. "The lectern smells of lemon wax, and there is more light coming through those windows than you thought there was. The frost breaks it up, prisms it, and if you're a student sitting in this room, you can look up at the windows and see rainbows in the panes."

"Go on." She was impatient with description.

"I have to start like this, Jazzie. I have to find myself there. Make a map before I start. The next thing is Trajan behind the lectern, and he's talking about...about Ovid."

Jazzie's finger traced over his chest. He felt the widening circles of her touch.

"Not Virgil?" she asked. "Not Cicero or Caesar? *Omnia Gallia* whatever?"

"Nah. It's Ovid that Trajan would be teaching. All those stories of gods and heroes, of how one thing changes to another. Girl into trees or heifers, boys into flowers or birds—Trajan would

222

have been all about that magic, Jazz, about all those changes."

Gabriel closed his eyes and began to imagine Trajan there in the classroom, leaning heavily against the lectern, his bulbous eyes not yet red and weakened by a decade's aging, his hair more closely cropped and less confused. All about him the clean smell of lemon and of wax, and Gabriel shifted in his vision to the front of the class, his eyes skimming the rows of students, dressed preposterously in white shirts and black ties. Their notebooks were open, their pencils whirling hypnotically over conjugations. None of them were clear to his imagination's eye, and yet the longer he looked the more defined they became, like creatures breaking the surface of shallow waters.

At last he saw the boy. How he knew him, Gabriel could never guess, but the imagining singled him out in a thin black cardigan, stylish fifteen years before and bleakly elegant even now. The boy was thin like Joey, but his dark hair resembled Gabriel's own, and the olive skin and Asian eyes were Jasmine's, or Toshiko's, or someone's. When all was said and done, the boy was less and more than all of them: a countenance and bearing that seemed to absorb light, bent over his notes like he was guarding the words.

Gabriel dwelt in the scene, remembering the Queen of the Ghosts, the smoke from a winter chimney, refusing to guide the story until it told him what to say. He found no name for the boy, would settle on no name. Slowly, as the scene before him began to move and alter and evolve, he found permission to tell Jasmine about it, and she did the best of things by letting it be, by lying there and listening as he told the story—not as he *thought* it had happened, but as he imagined it.

The boy would wait after class. He would come to Trajan's office in a quandary of lessons, and listen dutifully as his teacher explained them again and again. Gabriel imagined one time in particular—it was not the winter in which the first imagining began, but springtime, you could tell by a change in light from the office windows and by the blossoming confidence with which the boy moved, as he stretched toward a high shelf for a book in a gesture that made the imagined Trajan (and even the Gabriel who imagined him) catch his breath at the glimpse of golden skin between belt and shirttail.

"What is it?" Jasmine asked.

And startled by her voice, Gabriel blurted, "not yet," although he suspected where the scene was headed. He let the scene settle in his thoughts before he continued, watched the two of them talking in a conversation that refused to rise into words, as the boy retrieved the book, sat down again, and a shadow passed over the imagined room, but not before the boy picked up a coffee mug from Trajan's desk and turned it gracefully in his hand.

"It wasn't what you think, Jasmine," Gabriel said at last. "It could have been, but it wasn't. Trajan was attracted far too much to the boy, but he knew it and pushed it aside, and it was a good thing he did because the boy was no good…"

"Why are you defending Trajan, Gabriel?"

He rolled toward her, sliding his hand under the sheet and resting it on her warm, bare shoulder. "Not *defending* him, Jazz. *Imagining* him."

Her silence was an acceptance. Gabriel tried to recover the scene and failed. At last he pulled her to him and finished the story.

"The boy *knew*, Jazzie. Whether he felt the same way about Trajan I'm not sure. I kind of doubt it. He didn't layer it over with misgivings and imaginings. He was too confident and aware. I'm more certain he told someone. Made up a story that eventually got to the powers that be. Trajan loved that place. I can tell by imagining it. Why would he want to leave it unless he was pushed out?"

"His mother?"

"No. He went somewhere in Michigan after that. If he had come straight from Thracia to Miss Vivien's—well, maybe—but he didn't."

Jasmine nestled her head against his shoulder. "Maybe you imagined it differently than it was, Gabriel," she said softly, soothingly. "Maybe Thracia wasn't such a great place after all, and you just wanted him to have that—a spell of time where he was genuinely at home somewhere."

Her hair was sleek between his fingers.

"No. I mean, probably not. I wish I knew, Jazz."

He felt her head nod against his neck. She had a way of drawing out his disquiet, soothing it and putting it to sleep.

"Where was this place again?" Jasmine asked. "New Hampshire?"

"Vermont," Gabriel murmured.

"Vermont." It was an exclamation rather than a question. "Wonder why I'd never heard of it until you talked about it? My father has a summer place on Lake Champlain, not that far from St. Albans. He's had it since my brother was a baby. They still go there on vacations and long weekends. It just seems like…"

"It's not a school any more, Jazz. Trajan told me. The place closed down a few years back."

Jasmine laughed softly.

"What? What, Jazz?"

"You want to go see it?"

"Oh, I don't know…" It seemed like there was something wrong in seeing it, in gathering evidence like spies. It seemed as well that there was something wrong in placing Trajan at the center of things, as a presence between them.

"I was planning to take you up to the lake anyway," Jasmine urged. "And now it's even more important to get you to Vermont. You need to *see* Thracia. You need to walk the grounds and map it, like you've done with the world in your notebook.

"Because once it's mapped, you can imagine it. And once you imagine it, the ghosts will come, Gabriel. And you can face 'em, embrace 'em, and tell 'em goodbye. It's a process. You imagine your way out of it.

"And one other thing. Your Trajan was right. You could stand with a little summering, Faulkner, even if it's only for a weekend."

✳✳✳

As Dacia took further shape, it began to resemble oddly the two rooms in the Mountolive house: the dark region of snows that was its first landscape was transformed in that summery time to a valley that hinted at winter and shadows, then a country of foothills rising toward bright mesas where, Gabriel imagined, a city was being built. Elves inhabited the sunlit city, dwarves the dark valleys, and on the slopes was neutral country, mottled and misty, where the living folk brought their dead and where the ghosts reigned unchallenged.

Jasmine believed it had to do with psychological matters, but Gabriel was not convinced. He did, however, believe her when she said that Dacia was a place for stories: after all, he had thought so from the start. But he was still waiting—reading widely from the books shelved in Mountolive's parlor and letting his imagined country ripen as the summer moved on.

The stories would begin, he told her, when things began to move. But now all Dacia was stable, unchanging, the maps the same as they were when he first drew them, the genealogies suggesting a slow, unruffled permanence.

Mountolive called home two weeks after Gabriel and Jasmine had mused over Trajan's letter. Jasmine answered the phone—she always took the calls at the house—and from her hushed courtesy Gabriel could tell it was neither her family nor their friends who questioned her from the other end of the line. When the call was over, she retreated to the bedroom, and he sat in the dining room a while, filling in a generation of dwarves in the most recent family tree and sensing that something was moving, headed for a change not altogether welcome.

She laughed off his fears when they emerged at dinner. Claimed there was something in Mountolive that made her feel amateur and clumsy. It was as though the professor was the keeper of mysteries, she said, and she was a novice excluded from the inner sanctum. It made him wonder how she could suspect Trajan so deeply, but he let the matter lie: he had found out already that there were times with Jasmine Bowers that it was easier to take her at face value, ignoring tone of voice, gestures, the gaps between words, and all the other shadows that outlined the depth and danger of the country between them.

"I told him I would be away this weekend," she said at last, stirring the cereal that was their Wednesday's stretch of the food budget. For a moment Gabriel was afraid that she meant *alone*; after all, she had mentioned visiting her family in Boston, and they both knew that trip would not include him.

He stared down into the soggy bowl and waited for her to continue.

But it was time for Vermont, she said. They would leave on Friday and come back Monday morning. They both needed a breather; at least she was sure *she* did, and suspected he felt the same way.

His relief diminished as he packed. He discovered he was afraid to have been that afraid, and for some reason he decided to call his mother—something he usually did on Fridays alone. Mary's voice was soothing on the line, her involved and inconsequential talk about the neighborhood gave him reassurance, and her constant focus on the new man in her life was less irritating than usual.

She said that Joey had come back into town. Had dropped by looking strange and said hello. She claimed he had left the next day after hard words with the family.

"I had wished him better," Gabriel said. "A better future. A better family."

"They're a good lot, the Hardys," Mary objected.

"Everyone's nice till the cow gets into the garden," Gabriel replied, and they both laughed and fell silent at the truth of it.

"Then there's yer boy," Mary added, almost as an afterthought. "There's Trajan Bell."

It seemed that Trajan had stopped her Sunday morning as she walked from the house toward the highway and the downtown Mass. His mother, it seemed, had become a disruption at OLS. They decided to move her to a room where they could watch her more closely, restrain her if need be, and Mary said that Trajan had been total arseways since he got the news. Gabriel knew his friend's disruption had been longer in coming, but he did not mention the letter. Instead, he asked what Mary Rackett thought would come of it.

"It won't be good, Gabie," she said. "When you figure how those two are attached."

He told his mother he'd be out of town for the weekend, and she found a way to turn the subject back to Andy Lull, joking once that, if she played her cards right, the noise in the house would move from Rackett to Lull before you knew it.

"Are you all right, Gabie?" she asked as the conversation lagged, and he assured her that he was, because with Mary Rackett, occupied with her own scenarios, a brief assurance and a cheerful voice were always enough from her son. After all, she occupied the center stage—director and producer and still the principal actress of his life, though somewhere in both of them, they knew her star was fading

And of course it wasn't until years later, until the Thanksgiving before the Christmas when it all happened, that Gabriel Rackett joined himself to that strange series of attachments—a connection he had resisted all along.

By that time there was no Miss Vivian, no Trajan, and by then others had sheared away from his life so that he felt less like he had docked in the midst of a long voyage and more like flotsam, swept ashore in the wake of shipwreck.

Perhaps the shipwreck was *Dacia* itself, the mid-shelf novel, moderate in sales and critical reception, floating with the current for just about as long as you could expect a book like that to float before it dropped over horizons and vanished from the public eye, along with quarterly royalty checks he had hoped would last forever. And all that while, he had "worked on the new one," assured his drinking buddies in Lake Geneva—a town populated by drinking buddies—that he was in the long creative process. Until one night in October, when Truman Caldwell, a hulking Fine Arts professor at the college where Gabriel worked, slammed down his beer as Gabriel announced, "Today I worked on the novel," and proclaimed in a loud voice,

"Well....*neither* did I!"

The next afternoon, the cloudy light on the table in his apartment, Gabriel opened the binder clip that contained Trajan's stories. He thumbed through them again, nodding at the shorter tale of the chess prodigy, gliding over the story of the Victorian con artist like there was something poisoned on the pages...

He was telling himself it couldn't hurt.

Couldn't hurt because it couldn't be known.

The manuscript had been sent to him for some reason. Three stories completed, more or less, and the fourth one partial, its ending not even outlined except for the words *fireworks, Ferguson...statue.* He was pretty much sure that it was left to him to complete the fourth story, though he'd be damned if he'd known what to do with the other three.

Until now.

Because it couldn't be known and it couldn't hurt.

He stopped himself. That wasn't the reason at all. Couldn't be.

If the stories had a voice.

And they had come to Gabriel for that voice, over a stretch of years...

Gabriel figured he knew Trajan well. Knew how his old friend receded before the wonder of the tale. How Trajan would have balked at attaching his name to any of these stories, simply because it would lodge them in place and time, would limit them as they drifted like clouds over the years and settled...

That was the story he told himself, and he bought into it like he bought into Dacia.

A big manila envelope held them all. He wrote Barry's address on the outside, tucked the packet under his arm, and headed for the door, hurrying before the post office closed or he changed his mind. But despite his haste, on the threshold of his little place, he stopped, re-opened the envelope, and in a gesture that would haunt him in the months to come, removed the title pages from each of the stories, and in a kind of veil sent them off to Barry Green, the natural chill of Wisconsin autumn making him shiver as he stepped from the post office into the early dusk of a northern October.

He walked past an outcropping of woods between the lake and his apartment, skirting the parking lot of a bar where the lights had just been switched on, spilling onto wet gravel and the hoods of cars. It was shadowy beneath the trees, and something in him recalled at once the *lovely, dark and deep* of the poem in Trajan's story, and he wondered what promises he was keeping or breaking.

For a moment, as he slipped his hands into the pockets of his jacket and bunched his shoulders against the cold, he thought he saw a movement on a low, berried branch of a tree at the wood's edge, at a spot just before the light failed. Something like a pale wing brushed against the edges of the darkening leaves, was there and was gone before he could put his imaginings around it, and his thoughts slipped back to the stories—the chess game and castaways that were sailing their way to Barry Green's distant New York offices.

The Isle is Fill'd With Noyses

A Story by Trajan Bell

I.

Wherein the Narrator affirms the Adventures of Mr. Crusoe, and recounts his own Connection to that ill-fated Voyage. Giving as well his own Circumstance, and the Occasions that brought him to Sea.

Mine is a Schoolmaster's wit, unsteady in the Reading of Maps and Discernment of Constellations, and my Memory, albeit still stor'd with Knowledge of Use to Scholars only, has clouded somewhat thro' the Passing of Years. Let it be known from the Start that I lack the Eloquence and, it seems, the Resourcefulness of the justly celebrated Master Robinson Crusoe. Furthermore, the sudden and recent Passing of a Wife, to whom I became at Long Last accustom'd if not altogether Loving, has made my Recollection yet more overcast. Yet vividly I recall (or, might one say, *rebuild*, for is not Recollection an imagin'd Time and Place?) the notorious Shipwrack in which Mr. Crusoe and I parted Company. That Disaster rests in the deep backward and abysm of time, near Fifty Years ago, but the subsequent and mysterious Circumstances—beyond the Straits of my Imagining, so that I might assure the Uncertain Reader that All Herein is True— have brought me Full Circle thro' Isles of Wonder back to my London Old Age and Decrepitude, where, as the Poet says, "every third Thought has been my Grave".

As a Youth of scarcely Twenty, I sign'd on board the *Emperor*, bound for Guiana. Other Ventures had brought me to Africa—Ventures that, because of my Stay on a Nameless and Notorious Island, I have come to mask, if not altogether regret. Nonetheless, it was first as a Schoolmaster I had come to the African coasts, and then, despairing of such Calling, I had sail'd betimes on a Slaver, and it was that same lamentable Trade that found me in Guinea, in the hot August of 1659, longing for Wind and Sail and the cooler Ocean Air.

Because of an Embarrassment with Authorities long standing, mine was an Assum'd Name. Ferdinando Campaihna, I call'd myself, a veil'd Jest as to my Name English'd. Such disguise, of course, is common among Sailors, the Crewes are seldom manned by Students of Divinity and a new Name oft serves as a Masque of Freedom, under which Liberty a man may fashion a newer and more comely Self.

Few Questions arose as to my History, for the Life of a Slaver springs free of the Past, abiding only in Present Conditions and the Prospect of Future Gain. Mr. Crusoe confess'd that he "obey'd blindly the dictates of his Fancy rather than his Reason" when he stepped aboard the same Ship. My motive, indeed, was its Opposite: I obey'd my Reason entirely, concluding that, as a scandalis'd French Family and an alerted Constabulary would conspire in my Undoing, sheer Sense demanded that I undertake this Voyage, and only later, after I was maroon'd and forc'd unto Hard Labour, did I begin to set aside Sense and Calculation, to acknowledge the Workings of Vision and Enchantment and larger Design.

The Crew on board the *Emperor* was an Assembly of Righteous and Ignoble, subject to all the Virtues and Vices of the Human Condition. They were, in short, a veritable

Anatomy of Mankind, and the ship lacked naught of the human condition save Women and Children—a Lack I will confess had ceas'd to trouble me in the Fortnight prior to Departure, for indeed this Dearth had seldom troubl'd me at all. Early I became acquainted with the notable Master Crusoe, but only now I can confess that, altho' a good Man, he was scarcely my preferr'd Company, having about him a Parson's Manner and the Inclination to babble on accordingly. We were not to be fast Friends, albeit I was soon to find Another.

Only a few Days into the Ill-Starr'd Passage, before the Onset of Tempest and the Calenture, while the Weather was still favourable but hot, I met the Ship's Boy sunning on the Deck. Dark-eyed, darker-hair'd, happily endow'd with the gayety of high health and a free heart, he was yet to grow into his full stature and frame. In aspect, he look'd even younger than he was in truth, owing to a lingering childlike expression in his countenance, all but feminine in purity of natural complexion. But after only a week of his seagoing, the lily was quite suppress'd and the rose had some ado visibly to flush thro' the weathering and tan.

Alexis, they call'd him, tho I doubt he had been christen'd with a name so indefinite and frivolous. For he was a boy of uncommon Gravity, a Messenger Angel fill'd with Speculation regarding the Stars and the Passage of Ocean Currents. Surely a Navigator he would have become, had not Cruel Fortune interven'd.

Of a day Alexis took the Sun and serv'd the Captain, but at Night he was left to his own Studies, and from him I learn'd the Rising Planets and the Constellations of the Southern Sky—Capricorn, and Aquarius, Equuleus and Aquila. One night, half in jest, as I watch'd him ponder the Heavens, I ask'd if he believ'd that the Stars directed our *Fates and Courses. I believe, Master Campaihna, he said, that we are Players in a Larger Pageant, tho whether it be Divine as I have been taught, or as large and Indifferent as the Stars, I have no knowing.* I thought how curious was his Answer, and whether sprung from the Wisdom of Youth or from its Thoughtlessness I could not determine. But we sat quietly on Deck that Night, observing the Water Bearer in his distant, inscrutable Passage.

And so it was for a Week upon favourable Seas, up

the Coast of Africa bearing Cargo that it now grieves me to think we carried, for below Deck, in the dark Confinement of the Hold, one hundred Negroes awaited the End of their Journey, carried Westward by more powerful Agencies, their Destination uncertain and their Say in the Crossing none at all.

Above Deck, I exchang'd both Pleasantries and Philosophies with this Boy Scholar, this Illumin'd Novice, all the while Unwitting of the Misery that dwelt beneath us, of the Secrets and Insurrections in the dark Recesses of our Vessel. Oh, perhaps on Occasion the Trouble surfac'd to fresh Air and to the Light of Thought, but swiftly I sent it Below with the Negroes, and the occasional Outcry from the Hold I sens'd, as it were, with the *Edge* of Hearing. Never did I listen, but I let the disquieting Sounds pass over me like faint Misgiving, and to my duties and to the Boy I attended, for I told myself, perhaps presciently, that he needed Protection.

Whether Divine or Indifferent as the Stars? So Alexis had ponder'd, seated with his Glass by the Bulwark, his thoughts aloft and his Eyes on Constellations. And it occurr'd to me as I stood behind him (press'd closely against him when we were unobserv'd so as to observe with him) to see with his Eyes the very Stars he studied, that if those Stars were Indifferent, did their Disregard suggest a greater Disregard behind them? 'Twas a question for Bishops and Divines, not for a humble Sailor. And this Sailor, had he train'd his Eyes to the Suttleties of Horizons and the Shifts of the Air and Waters instead of to the Constellations and to his newfound Companion, might have seen in the Wings of the Stage a Catastrophe approaching. Master Crusoe describ'd it altogether well, how the Tempest began from the South-east, came about to the North-west, and then settl'd in the North-east; from whence it blew in such a terrible Manner, that for twelve days together the ship could do nothing but drive, and, scudding away before it, let it carry the Crew whither Fate and the fury of the winds directed. Indeed, I enter Master Crusoe's Story as a kind of Afterthought or Effluvium, when he observes that "in this distress we had, besides the Terror of the Storm, one of our men die of the Calenture, and one Man and the Boy wash'd overboard."

I was that Man, Reader, and Alexis that Boy.

And on that Night the indifferent Stars themselves were

veil'd by angry Clouds, and to this Day I cannot but suppose a Vast and unfathomable Coldness behind them. Below the Deck we all huddl'd disconsolate among the Negroes, their Cries commingling with the Racket of the Storm and the Crash of Waters against the Ship, their poor Souls ignorant of the Ocean and, like ourselves, of where they were headed in the close and abiding Darkness.

I saw a Light then at the Ladder, and Alexis climbing above Deck, bound on a foolhardy boyish Adventure, I suppos'd, and when I follow'd, my own Maturity and Wisdom set aside in my Troubles for the Boy, I found him Portside on the Bulwark, training his Glass toward the Approaching Wind as it turn'd, swept the Stern, and buoyed me as I rush'd toward him from Behind. At Fifty Years remove, I understand that Curiosity alone brought him to Peril, a Desire to look into the Heart of a Power greater than his own, and tho what had brought me above Deck was part Terror, part Apprehension, I shar'd as well that Curiosity, that Desire, altho I knew at that Disastrous Instance that the Power I sought lay both within and without my Sensibility.

One Glance alone he return'd at my warning Cry, as the Wind behind me surg'd over the Deck from Starboard to Port, and failing of Purchase, the Boy tumbl'd over the Bulwark, clinging desperately to that Railing as I rush'd toward him. I grabb'd at his Wrist, and for a Moment he was safe, climbing back on Board and guided by my stronger, rescuing Hand. Then a second Wave, borne athwart by the Tempest, crash'd against us, and we fell, clutching one another then losing our Grasp, into the monstrous abysm of the Atlantic.

I shall freely admit that the Next Part of my Adventure is scatter'd and lost like Flotsam in a Deep Current. For our History is like a Pageant or Play, wherein True Circumstance doth oftentimes absent itself from the eyes of our Memory, tho when we stand witness to what comes to pass in Recollection, we know full well that for each Event we recall in its full Light and Colour there are a score of Measures yet deeper, more design'd, borne on inscrutable Currents and bearing with them the Fragments we remember. I remember indeed thrashing in the Waters, calling out for Alexis, a wave thundering over me and a glimpse of the nightstruck barren Sky, the Lights of the *Emperor* lost and recover'd and then again lost in the driving Torrent. Lightning high above the

Waters set forth haunted Illuminings, and the Emperor once more, outlin'd against a Slate Sky, strange Fire clambering up its Masts. I made many vows and resolutions that if it would please God to spare my life in this one voyage, if ever I got once my foot upon dry land again, I would go directly home to London, and never set it into a ship again while I lived; that I would swear off Behaviour Unbecoming, would return to Cambridge for Studies in Divinity, and thereby never run myself into such miseries as these any more.

How I set Ground is to this day a Mystery, tho Wiser Men than myself, both Philosophically and Nautically, set forth plausible Reason for my Survival. The Coasts of the Bermoothes, they tell me, are complex with Wonders and Anomalies. They tell of the flagship *Sea Venture*, under the command of Sir George Somers, lost in a storm and separated from the rest of the fleet, how it hit the reef to the north-east of those fabled Islands, and how, past all Reckoning and Reason, the Crew and Passengers struggl'd ashore entire, so that their garments, being, as they were, drench'd in the sea, held notwithstanding their freshness and glosses, being rather new-dyed than stain'd with salt water.

With Haste they set about building two new Boats from the Cedars native to the Isle, and from the Wreckage of the Venture. No doubt they had heard the grim Spaniard in his rash Superstitions and Accounts of the 'Islas Demonios', the Islands of the Devils, but they found Miraculous Welcome, Food plentiful, the Climate mild and temperate, and shelters easy to build from the Material at Hand. And they told me of how, despite Dissent and Insurrection (for the Devils on the Isle were, as is oft the Circumstance, most likely the Ones they brought with them) the Passengers built two Seaworthy Ships and completed their Ill-Starr'd (or strangely Starr'd) Voyage to Virginia. And so they claim'd, then, that whatever Power had set those Voyagers ashore had no Doubt guided and sustain'd me thro' my perilous Passage in stormy Water, and that despite what I remember of those dire and threat'ning Hours, my Salvation was of Nature and not of Magick.

And yet I remember these Things, my Rescue glimps'd in the Heart of the Ruinous Storm. For as the Masts of the *Emperor* flam'd Amazement as tho it Burn'd on the Water, I went under the Waves for the third Time, and, mindful of the old Superstition that the third Time under is the final, prepar'd myself for Eternity with Prayer and Lamentation, tho let it be known that Both were rais'd silently, with my Mouth closed tightly against the Intruding Waters to which I had yet not the Despair to surrender. It was then that I saw, or thought I saw—Alexis swimming toward me in a green Bedazzlement of Light, naked, his Eyes pale and lidless, as tho he had begun a Sea-Change, a strange Metamorphosis into Nix or Merman.

Laugh if you will, Good Reader, and dismiss the Vision as Rapture of the Deep, as Distraction my long Thoughts of it over a thousand Nights as the Boy swims nearer in Dream and Memory. But answer me this: if, as some say, the Kingdom of Heaven is within us and above us, who is to say where Distraction begins and where it finds Correspondence in Air and Sea, Land and Fire? Does not the Image we behold presuppose a Bringer of that Image?

Ah, but I dance on the Edge of Philosophy again, uncertain Country for one Ill-Suited to thought. Let me say that it seem'd then, as it seems in Recollection now, that the luminous Alexis beckon'd, and so I follow'd, thro' the roiling Waves and, in that aforementioned and sudden Gap of Memory, found myself next in calmer Waters, afloat on my Back, the morning Sun not yet harsh on my wakening Countenance.

II

Wherein the Narrator cometh ashore upon a wondrous Island, supposeth he sees his Alexis on the beach ahead of him, and is drawn by Vision and Music to the Innermost Parts of the Isle, where he meets its Several Inhabitants, is Impress'd into unpleasant Labour by its Sovereign, and plots his Freedom thro' the kindly, albeit not altogether witting Agency of the purported Princess of the Isle.

Master Crusoe has recounted his own Ordeal at the Mercy of the Ocean, how he walk'd about the shore, giving thanks to the Lord and marveling at his own Miraculous Deliverance. In a single Sentence he treats the Loss of his

Companions, and I have always imagin'd him gathering their cast-by Clothing along the Shore, his Contemplation shaded with the Delight that it was he whom God had chosen to survive, rather than Any of his Fellows, and it has always seem'd to me that Something about him delighted in their Drowning for the simple Testimony to his Election.

My Emergence was, I fear, less joyous. I search'd the Length and Breadth of the Beach for Sign of Alexis, and when, after a full Day's tracking, Naught had surfac'd from the terrible Surge of the Waves, and I was all but certain my young Friend was lost to the Tempest. Nor did I begin to plan my Survival at once, but sat at the tidal Edge and wept, still scanning the deep Horizon for a Movement, a Sign of my vanish'd Comrade.

It was late on the following Day before I gather'd my Self, laid hold of my Grieving and endeavour'd to look about me at the Surrounding with which I fear'd I was soon to become too accustom'd. And yet it was indeed a surprisingly hospitable Island, as it seem'd to welcome my first Search for Herbs to assuage the Pain in my Right Hand, injur'd in the Fall from the Bulwarks of the *Emperor*.

It was in this middling State, half mourning the losses of Those I would no longer meet, half scavenging the Shore for Things useful to a Survival and Sustenance of Mine Own, that I heard the Musick rising from Inland—from a Copse of Fronded Foliage the Likes of Which I had neither seen nor read of—and I resolv'd (as who would not, under similar Straits?) to follow that Musick to its Source.

This Resolution carried me into Shadow, wherein a Tangle of green Light illumin'd the Vine-choak'd Paths ahead of me. It was altogether like Walking Underwater, the Musick ambient in the dense Groves, and for a Spell I despair'd of finding the Source of the Music or my Way back out of the Tangle.

It was then, at the Edge of my Sight, I saw the comely Form of a Youth or Girl—it was Shadowy, and blinded by Frond and Branch, so I could discern no more of my Visitor than that he (or she) was young, luminous, and circling me at great Distance. I follow'd, my Thoughts equidistant from the Joy of Reunion with Alexis and the Fear of some terrible and mortal Deception.

That Source of the Musick was, indeed, a Clearing but Half a Mile from the Shore. A Brook ran into the Midst of it, settling in a Pool more devised than Natural, for the Waters were still'd in the Midst of it, as though defiant of Current and Flow. Little did I know that I had travel'd to the Midpoint and Heart of the Isle, and there would find its Spirit and Eminence in the figures of Master Abaddon Maze and his Daughter Mirandelle, who would figure from that Moment forth in the Shape and Meaning of my Days.

But at that Time, there were more immediate Needs before me. My Foreboding gave way to Weariness, then Weariness to Sleep, so that when I awakened, Night had befallen the Clearing, and though the Moon shone unperturbed on the Face of the little Pool, the Shadows encircling me were fill'd with Noyse, and Movement, and the Glittering of feral Eyes. Unarm'd, scarcely clad, and weakened beyond Endurance, I despaired of my Survival. And yet neither Despair nor Apprehension could fend off Sleep, and I drows'd again, as tho' drugg'd or enchaunted.

I awakened in Shackles. Or so I believe I awakened. Nonetheless, the Imagining of Manacles is oft as constraining as the Chains themselves, and chain'd I seem'd, in the very Clearing and beneath the same large, Oceanic Moon.

A Man stood above me, robed and ominous in the Apparel of a Stage-Conjuror, to the Conical Hat and its Arrangement of Stars. Had I been certain of Dreaming, I would have laugh'd at the Appearance. But as you will come to see, Reader, the Line between Waking and Dream can be porous and unstable, a Border we cross not only in Sleep, but also in Times contemplative and inebriant.

My first Prompting was to Laughter at this Tailor's Mage, this Assemblage of Robes and Arcane Stitchery. But you would not believe how much Shackles and Manacles can curtail a man's Merriment, so instead I lay attentive, awaiting whatever Circumstance might arise in this strange Encounter.

He spoke to me then, in curious Cadence, and as he spoke the Musick I had followed to this Clearing swell'd again, as Score and Setting to his firm Pronouncements. He first ask'd my name, and grew quietly wroth at the reply. It was as tho' he saw thro' the Maske at once, as tho' his Magick or his Insight told him that the Name I presented was not truly my own. "I charge thee," he commanded, "that thou attend me: thou dost here usurp the Name thou ownest not; and hast put thyself upon this Island as a Spy, to win it from me, the Lord on't."

It was a Charge I was unprepar'd to answer. For a Spy's Denial is remarkably close to Confession, and neither Yea nor Nay could avail me in this Difficulty. But as often is the Case when Governance is swept from the hands of the Beleaguered, yet another Person entered the Clearing— another Character in our dire and developing Drama. It was a Girl, no more than Sixteen and less than comely at my best Estimate, her Gaze fixed upon me in a Kind of giddy Admiration, and in those Eyes I saw at once my Deliverance, the Key to my confining Bonds. Drab-hair'd and watery of Eye, she drew back until the old Man (who was no Doubt her Father) beckoned her forth from her Remove and Timidity.

"Make not too rash a Trial of him," the young Thing urg'd her Father, clutching at his Robes in her pathetic Entreaty, "for he's gentle and not fearful." And I smil'd in Response to such Bravery, attempting to forge a firm Alliance to match the forging of my Chains.

"Hang not on my Garments!" the old Man thunder'd. "One Word more shall make me chide thee, if not hate thee. What! An advocate for an imposter! hush! Thou think'st there is no more such shapes as he, having seen but him and the shipwrack'd Bodies wash'd ashore this Isle. Foolish wench! To the most of men this is but Flotsam, and they to him are Angels."

I was mov'd to protest, for I was young and hardly monstrous, but I counsell'd myself to a Kind of quiet Compliance, knowing that my Appearance was scarcely my best, entangled as I was with Seaweed and Restraints. I made it be known that I had not always been as humble as he saw me now, that I yearned to depart the Island if only to see to the holdings in my duchy north of Lisbon (for remember, I had sign'd on to the *Emperor* under an assumed and Portuguese name, and under such Circumstances, claiming Residence in London seem'd almost deceitful). Upon hearing this, the Daughter, in the First of her many Rescues, sooth'd the old Man with the Argument that her Ambitions were humble, that to her Eyes I was goodly enough.

I strove to express my Gratitude, to proclaim (tho' I

scarcely meant it) that if, in my Imprisonment, I might behold such a Maid, that 'twould be Freedom enough. But those Words were lost in the Clamour and Swell of the Musick, and Years later she would assure me that she heard them not, albeit her Father gazed at me with a kind of wary Speculation.

I knew by now where the Game was headed, here amidst the enchaunted Desolation, nor was it a Masque nor a Role that I was unaccustomed playing. For years as Schoolmaster and Sailor and erstwhile Slaver, I had known my Part on Stage, and I knew the Plot and Story of the Lady Mirandelle's Attentions (for indeed she had revealed her Name on Short Acquaintance). Off before the Prospect had risen into Possibility, like a drowned Sailor afloat on a crested Wave, but this time it would wash ashore, it would return to Life and breathe and spout forth Water, and I would spend my Days either here in Captivity or elsewhere in the Prison of a Manly Role.

My captor had me chop Wood as the first of my Prisoner's Duties, and Lady Mirandelle appointed herself as Overseer to my Labours. We were a Kind of Spectacle, unbeknownst to Mirandelle: as we talked over my Labours, as she prattled on about Constellations and Winds from the Sea, I spied on Occasion her Father peering at us thro' the Foliage like a nervous Playwright watching the Course of his Drama. Indeed, in another Life far away in London, Doctor Abaddon Maze (as he was known to Friends and sometime Rivals) had been a Playwright of minor Stature, vanishing inexplicably some Years before, and presumed dead under Circumstances mysterious. Accordingly, it was my great Fortune that I gave my Part new Passion, turning the Matter constantly to my sympathetic Companion, feigning Interest in her Babble of Zephyrs and Horse Latitudes, in her constant Singling Out of Virgo in the Evening Sky.

It was Mirandelle who told me of the Vagaries that had beset her little Family, from the Time of the Closing of Theatre and the Eight Years that ensued. How she and her Father had fled to the Continent, where he practiced his Art less and less successfully, and then, Five Years ago, set Sail for new Prospects in Virginia. How they had never made Landfall in that Promis'd Region, but instead were set adrift by a Sea Captain of Puritan Sympathies, only to find Refuge on this Strange and Wonderful Island. How they, too, held Lands in the South of Scotland, and how they yearned for comfortable Return to their Seiz'd and Ancestral Legacy. All the While the Old Man watched attentively, as I coo'd and courted the Lady Mirandelle with soft Words made softer by the Prospect of Lowland Property.

Soon I allow'd her to carry the least Bundles of Wood (after assuring her that I would rather break my Back than let her lift a Plank), and then, under protest, allowing her to wield the axe a little, for in fact she was a rather large Girl, fully rivaling me in Height and scarcely my Inferior in Weight. But despite her daunting Stature, in my Kindness and Courtesy I took on altogether the Role of a Hero in some Novel of Sensibility she would surely lack the Wit to read.

I told her, then, of the numerous and sundry Ladies who had drawn my Eye over the Years, how some display'd one Virtue, others Another, while she combin'd the Best of all in Arrangement so flawless as to be fated or design'd. And but once did I regret this Fiction, for I play'd for my Freedom and Life; and that one Occasion was, when glancing sidelong at the Architect of this Drama, I thought I saw beside him a willowy figure, shrouded by Leaf and Mist and perhaps even Magick, but clear enough in Form to suggest at serene Nights on the *Emperor*, and the Brilliance of innumerable Stars.

For I assure you we were not alone on the Isle. Not only did I glimpse the boyish Apparition at the Edge of Sight, but there were Others as well: Sailors, it seemed, and those in more regal Costume, and Things Celestial and Profane, descended on the Island or rising from the Conjuries of Earth and Fire. A Pyrate in a Coracle I spy'd, clothed with Tatters of old Ship's Canvas and old Sea-cloth, the Patchwork all held together by a System of the most various and incongruous Fastenings, Brass Buttons, Bits of Stick, and Loops of Tarry Gaskin. A straggling Line of Schoolboys, I believe I saw, and a yearning, red-hayred Warrior of the Grecian Style. And perhaps there were Others, bedraggled and Oriental, helmeted and wearing the Red Sun of the Japannes.

But as to this, I cannot be certain, for the Figures flitted between Seeming and Belief. 'Twas a Pageant that took place just beyond my Knowing, so that I could discern the Actors but not the Act, the Players but not the Play. Days on end I labored with Lumber and the Lady, assured and indeed hoping that some Other would enter the Scene, but it never came to pass, and wearied of the Waiting, at last I followed my Role where it led me, asking young Mirandelle for her hand, and in turn, asking the Blessing of her stern and unnatural Father.

The Joy of the old Man rivaled that of his Daughter. At the time I marvell'd that I was received with such Favour, having only lately been in his brutal and demanding Service. Perhaps it was a Greater Power that had brought the Three of us together, for though I had discarded my Promise of Divine Studies when I lay on dry Land, it seems that Doctor Maze had continued his own obscure Speculations, conjuring from stormy Waters a Suitor for his unfortunate Daughter. All that remained, he assured me, was discovering safe Transport from this forsaken Island, and when I despair'd at such Assurances, he encourag'd me to believe that they were possible, that indeed his Art had brought them Close at Hand.

III

Wherein the Art of Doctor Abaddon Maze bears sometime Fruit, and the Narrator is left wondering at the Dream to which he was Witness. With a Digression upon the Elements of Belief, and Speculation upon the Wedding of Life and Art.

Some allow that the World itself is a Dark Conceit, sometimes an Allegory in which we all troop over the Stage, each portraying a Virtue or Vice that the Divine Poet finds Suitable or Fit. To me that World is Cloudier than that; the Story precedes us, but as Story, not as Idea. Somewhere in the Recesses of the Tale, I believe, lie the Principles of Love and Pride, of Faith and Avarice and of all their attendant Opposites, but in the World there is Nothing Pure of that Kind, and we labour in a Vale of Alliances and Corruptions, where though we say afterward that we were cheated or cozen'd, yet we can never say who or what has cheated us— only that we have stepped into a Story that is larger than all Deceptions and Misgiving.

Surely the Isle was full of Noyses, and the Three of us added to the swelling sound. For I have come to believe, at this improbable Remove, that if we are indeed the Stuff of Dreams, what we know as Dreaming is but the greater Purchase of who we are, and that Reveries may indeed slip their Confinements and wander, finding their Homes within and beside us untill we Dream the Dreams of Others past and future, opening the Doors of our Imaginings ajar to admit new Visitors recently Estraunged.

Much of this Vagary was due no Doubt to Desire, as it was through Yearning that Doctor Maze held on to my Portuguese Nobility, his Daughter to my feign'd Devotion, and I found myself clinging to the Promise of Freedom with their same Desperation, as though if All of us grasp'd at our Hopes with Passion and Ardency, those Hopes would find Substance and Name thro' our simple Wish that they be.

But it would take more than Desiring, and it was Something in the Design of the good Doctor that made this clear to us soon after Mirandelle consented to be my Wife. In Celebration, Abaddon Maze offered a Betrothal Show—a Masque, as it were, which he claimed would be a bit shabby and awkward for display in my Ducal Palace, but serviceable for this rustic Isle.

I encouraged him with the Promise that in my Place of Abode a humble Show was less than unusual, that I had seen rude Masques and Dramas for most of my Days. He considered these Words, and urged that I seat myself, along with the ordinary Mirandelle, in a curtained Box he had devised on the Edge of the Clearing in which he had first discovered me only Days before. For a Moment my Apprehension rose in the False Belief that he intended the Marriage be consummated before the Vows—a Tradition to which, I had heard, some Islanders adhere. But my Fears subsided at the Sight of the Place, which was furnished with no Bed, but with only two Chairs and a little Table, upon which he had placed a curious Chessboard, its Pieces the Figures of the Ancient Gods, Juppiter and Juno, Venus and Apollo and the Rest.

I begg'd Ignorance of Chess, sensing an Ambush to my Masquerade, to which my Companion express'd her Surprise that a Portuguese Duke knew Nothing of the Game of Kings. I explained that in my less mannerly Region of Portugal the Game of Kings involved the Torment and Killing of large Animals, and she flourished an equine Grin, drawing her Chair even closer to my fancied Masculine Brutality.

The Clearing fell hushed at last, and Mirandelle and I peered thro' the Curtain at the entering Players. Among them I recognized the Sailors I had seen at the Edge of my Vision. Once elusive in the Groves of the Island, they stood before me in new Illusion, dressed in the Robes of Gods and Goddesses, their Figures the Likeness of the Chessmen on the Table between us.

Something was winding its Way thro' the devisings of Abaddon Maze: this much I knew. I look'd at the Table before me, at the Players array'd upon the Stage of our Clearing, at the Doctor's dim Daughter, the Bride of my Pretext, who regarded me from her Station behind the White Pieces and slowly moved one of them—she would teach me later that it was called a Pawn—to a new Space on the Board.

Much later, the good Doctor would recount the Subject of this Masque as a Celebration of Wedlock and Fertility, but perhaps his Memory clouds as well, for as I remember, it was the Story of Echo and Narcissus.

Under his Words (for the Good Doctor performed as Prologue to his own Masque), the Clearing took on a Clean and Ethereal Light, its Source the reflected Moon in the still Waters of the Pool. His was not the immortal Verse some would claim for him in ensuing Years, but a Kind of Doggerel that gathered Power thro' Command rather than Suggestion; I daresay it was more Incantation than Poetry. What I recall of it is fitful and scant, but nonetheless the Prologue hangs in my fading Recollection, not for its Beauty but for the Events it conjured.

> Our eyes behold the beauteous Youth,
> Borne on the Waters of desire,
> His blue eyes summoning the Truth
> Out of the gathering Sea and Fire,
> But where is it that Beauty lies,
> In Forms apparent or conceal'd?
> In ev'ry evidence of Eyes
> Or what Imaginations yield?
> As Life below, so Life above,
> As Life in Nature, so in Art,
> The Gods have curs'd each Boy to love
> The cover'd mirror in his Heart.

As if summoned Narcissus made Entrance, wading through the slow-moving Brook, and my Suspicions were at last confirmed that we Three were not sole Inhabitants of the Isle.

It was a Boy who approached the Pool in the bedazzled Moonlight, brilliant and watery as tho' he had been fashioned of Spindrift. For a Moment I thought it was Alexis, but his Form was altogether fluid and flick'ring, and as he knelt by the still Pool my own Sensibility launch'd itself in his Direction, and were it not for my Companion at the Table, her Eyes intent on my Demeanor and Reaction, I should have risen, parted the Curtain, and entered the Masque to sit at his Side.

But that was Echo's Role, of course, and a Young Man, no Doubt one of the drunken Sailors I had glimpsed in the Margins of the Grove, came forth sober at last, transformed by the Play and clad in dried Leaves, in Bramble and the other Weeds of Mourning. I settled on him (or her, as the Masque would have it) and Imagined the Sorrow of the Girl, wasting away with Love unrequited for the simple Offense of having kept her Father's Secrets from the Eyes of the jealous Gods. Clean-shaven and intoning her Lines in an ungainly Falsetto, she knelt within Sight of the Boy, within our Sight as well, as the Story in the Clearing inveigled itself into our Desires and Fancies.

We watch'd as Echo called out to the Youth, waiting in enforc'd Silence for his Sighs and passionate Entreaties to the resplendent and reflected Form of his Admiring. He would declare his Love, and she would follow, constrain'd by the same words and the same Voice, until when the Boy lifted his Head as tho' he were listening, we were rapt with the Understanding that he listened only to Himself.

Mirandelle gestured at the Board that lay before us. Again I protested Ignorance of the Game, but she told me softly that I should follow her moves a While, should mirror them exactly, and that from that simple Tactic I might assure a long and spirited Contest. I obeyed in Distraction, my Eyes and Thoughts yet fix'd to the Tragedy we glimpsed through filmy Curtains.

Now the Words of the good Doctor set the Scene, this time Intonation rising into Song, for around us recommenc'd that unearthly Music:

Kneeling there to quench his thirst,
The Voice of Echo brushed aside,
He drowned the Blessed in the Curs'd
And drank the shadows as his bride.

We both sat chasten'd by the Show. I answer'd the Movement of Mirandelle's most solitary Pawn with a corresponding Movement of my own. The Game had commenced, tho' I knew neither its Strategy nor Rules, and so I mov'd my Pieces at her Instruction, knowing thereby I had conceded the Match.

But her Father intervened, and open'd the Curtain. Astonished, Narcissus and Echo look'd up from their Masquerade, and the Worlds met in the Convergence of Eyes. Then out of the Forest they came—other Sailors along with outlandish Island folk that I scarce might recognize as Human were it not for their upright Stance and their Confusion of Tongues.

Two Men among these outlandish Denizens, carrying Musketry and Ramrod, stood green as Verdigris, as though wrought of Bronze or Copper in a far-off country where the Statues come to Life. They stood guard over a squat, uncommonly ugly Child, who drooled and stroak'd her batter'd, translucent Wings like a fallen angel. Behind them milled a Multitude of Sailors, some from our Crew and Others yet Pale and Swolln like the Drown'd Men in the Song. You could glimpse them, as it were thro Veiles, one arrayed behind the Next. And behind them all, the good Doctor Maze, arraunging like a Wizard Earl the Trappings and Entrapments of his Drama, dress'd in a long pale Robe the colour of flat and autumnal Horizons.

But nowhere among them was I to see Alexis, tho I looked for him in the long passage back.

Some would tell me, when we boarded the ship to the Bermoothes, to Safety and to England and to our relinquished Homes, that they too had been adrift in the Woods of Master Abaddon Maze. However, there was a Moment in that Glade, when from the Chess Board I arose and gaz'd across the Clearing, that it seemed all of them had been rapt into Timelessness like at the Last Trump, though they waited less for Judgment than for my attentive Eye and Thoughts.

It was this Apprehension that set me thinking, as we

rode toward Britain over Seas surprisingly calm'd. For could the Nature of Story be far different than we foresee? Could it be that neither our Thoughts, nor Passions, nor Ideas formed by the Imagination, exist without the Mind? And if so, does it seem no less evident that the various Sensations or Ideas imprinted on the Sense, however blended or combined together (that is, whatever Objects they compose) cannot exist otherwise than in a Mind perceiving them? The Idea staggers the thought, for I am a mere Schoolmaster and a Writer of Sailing Memoirs, scarcely a Philosopher able to trail down such Thoughts to their Lairs, but if Sense and Object, Mind and Body conspire in the Way I have expounded, then is it not possible that every Story waits for its Beholder, that every Character and Sceane stands ready like a Ghost in a Mansion, awaiting Eye and Imagination to embue it with Life? And wanting that, could it be that then they wander from their Story into what we have so complacently call'd the Real World, seeking to continue their Tale howsoe'er they can amidst the Shards and Fragments of our Daily Lives?

For my Daily Life went on, indeed, after we arriv'd in London, though never again was I swept up and away in the great Story. Instead, I set up House with my new Bride, the former Miss Mirandelle Maze, in lodgings not far from St. Bartholomew's, and from there passed my Days as Tutor to the Daughters of a Number of wealthy Merchants until, my Eyes and perhaps even the far Borders of my Mind failing, I took lodging in more humble surroundings, nurs'd into Old Age by that same devoted Mirandelle.

Now sometimes thru my Window, when the Sunne is placed just right above the Roof-Tops and in those Rarities of London Days that are cloudless, I still glimpse a Movement amid the Cherubim who top the Façade of the Building opposite my Rooms. One of them, caught in that especial Slant of Light, takes on a ruddy and supple Colour, its hair darkened and, though I am too far away to see its Eyes, I am not too far to imagine them as dark and speculative, agaze on undiscovered Country, and in the very Act of Gazing, drawing my own diminish'd Sight with them into the deep Celestial. And when my Attentions turn again to my Rooms, my Desk and the spilled, awaiting Papers, the Ayre itself has switched, there is a Depth and Consequence to Breathing, and the humble Furnishings, the worn Rug and even the ashen Andirons before the Fire have assumed a Cast of Wonder and of Promise, and in this Enchauntment I hope for a Moment that it might be true, that Alexis will descend from Frieze or Façade or Battlement, breaking at last from his carved and foreordained role, bringing with him at last a final Array of Stars.

"So, the first two I like," Jasmine said, reaching to the cup holder for her sunglasses as the car sped east along the New York State Thruway. "But not the *Tempest* one so much. Forced marriage by Jacobean drama? That's a misdemeanor in any jurisdiction."

She laughed, evidently amused at her own inventions. Gabriel wasn't in the mood for it, but he wasn't in the mood to be irritated with her, either. "But it's not really *The Tempest*," he objected, fumbling for change as the Saab approached the toll booth outside Syracuse. "Those verses are Trajan's own."

"Obviously, Faulkner." Jasmine pitched the coins and sped through, the morning sun bright on the windshield. "Your friend's short stories were decent, I guess. The poetry nowhere near. But I'll admit there was something about the boy on shipboard..."

Gabriel peered dramatically into his Robertson Davies novel. Davies was a friend of Ben Mountolive, to hear Jasmine tell the story, and Gabriel had picked up *Fifth Business* at a used book sale, reading at first out of a sense of faint and unmoored jealousy, then with increasing interest, drawn into the novel's play between realism and myth.

Right now, though, he could barely focus on the words, the book cover a shield against his girlfriend's intermittent gaze. She had read the shipwreck story and she was fishing for insight.

He had nothing to offer but change for the booths. From the distance of miles and years, Trajan was cloudier than ever, like the side of the road glimpsed in the depth of snowy night.

By late afternoon they were thoroughly into Vermont, having left Route 9 and taken a ferry over the southernmost tip of Lake Champlain. Gabriel remained in the passenger seat, roadmap in hand, and watched the trees rise ahead of them as Jasmine negotiated the winding inclines of county roads.

As they crossed the state line something had eased in his breathing. For the first time that day he had felt beyond recall, out of range of business or encumbering need. Now it was the two of them, like on the threshold of some solitary, small adventure—Jasmine mantled over the steering wheel, peering out at the road over what she claimed were her driving glasses, Gabriel along for the ride, clutching the map and drinking a generic soda that he called "a coke" and his girlfriend "a tonic".

The woods on either side of the road were dense and almost exotically green; none of the red mud of the South, and the undergrowth trailing away in layer after layer of thick foliage. It felt like they were traveling back in time, and though Jasmine assured him that there was nothing primeval about the Vermont woods, it still seemed as though they were headed for something veiled but recoverable if they looked long and hard enough.

They passed through the small town of West Pawlet, headed for the even smaller East Pawlet, site of Trajan's old college. Gabriel had found the village on the map with little difficulty, but as they approached the outskirts he expected to see signs for the college, or perhaps a spire or dome or cluster of buildings at the crest of a hill. As they entered the town, nearly passing the inn that seemed to offer its only accommodation, for the first time Gabriel raised the question that had been nagging him for almost half an hour.

"Jazzie?" he asked, taking a long draw from the soda bottle

and setting it empty on the floorboard of the car. "You think there's a chance that the college *isn't* here after all?"

Jasmine smiled, steered onto the roadside next to the inn. "What are you asking, Faulkner? Whether there's no longer a college? Or whether there ever was?"

"You're thinking it, too, then," he said.

She nodded. "But we still have two hours to go. We can always ask directions at the inn."

To Gabriel's relief, the innkeeper assured them that Thracia College had indeed been there. Upon Jasmine's insistent questioning, the old man revealed more: the school had closed down in '65, and the buildings had burned in a dry summer two years past. He wondered what two young people found of interest in a dead school. Did they have people who went there or something?

In the midst of the tentative conversation, Gabriel examined the walls behind the inn's desk. Photographs, only the last two in color, were arrayed in a kind of catch-as-catch-can pattern. Each was a group portrait of boys roughly high school aged, dressed in white shirts and ties, their features unclear from where he stood. They were obviously class pictures, and he leaned over the counter for a closer look, despite himself scanning each photograph for the smaller, darker boy he and Jasmine had conjured out of memory and fancy and conjecture.

The color pictures, the last two on the wall, were a disappointment. It seemed that all of the boys were tall and unfailingly white. Still, in one of the more recent black-and-white photographs, a dark-haired figure knelt at the left end of the front row, his arm draped over his knee in striking contrast to the background white of his shirt. Eagerly, Gabriel squinted at the photos on either side, but the same figure was nowhere to be found, and crossing the boundary of the desk for a closer look seemed like a bold and intrusive act.

Meanwhile, Jasmine was losing interest as well. Thumbing through a brochure at the desk, groping for conversation, she asked if the school was any good.

"It would depend on what you called 'good'," the innkeeper replied. Gabriel listened closely: the man was sounding more and more like a stereotypical Vermonter, all dodge and short answers.

"Well, like Middlebury or Bennington are good," Jasmine said. "Or Goddard."

"Goddard's a hippie school," the innkeeper pronounced.

"I reckon that's good for some," Jasmine said, setting down the brochure and regarding the man directly.

"You're not from around here, are you?" the innkeeper asked, and Jasmine allowed she wasn't, but that she would have thought he would like outsiders because they were more likely to stay at his inn than the natives.

"Thracia was a school for rich kids," the innkeeper blurted out of nowhere. It was obvious he was not warming to the new arrivals.

"So is Middlebury," Jasmine said, not willing to let him go. "And Bennington."

"And Goddard," the innkeeper added.

"Rich hippies, you're saying?"

"They've been heard of, ma'am."

Now Gabriel intervened, asking the man where the site of the old campus lay. He pointed them to a gentle hill on the far end of the village, and they followed his directions to where the fire-blackened stone foundations of the old college lay. You could make out the ruin of at least four definite buildings amid the high grass—perhaps there were more somewhere nearby, or perhaps the two closest were actually part of the same structure. It was really too damaged and remote to tell.

Gabriel sat among the stones and watched the dry weeds shudder in a summer breeze. One adventure was over, and when he looked at it closely, it didn't seem much of an adventure at all: he had simply imagined a boy in a far-off place, and when the place came nearer, the boy wasn't there. Nothing more than that, he decided, and wondered why it discouraged and saddened him so.

Jasmine stepped over the smutted skeleton of stones to sit

down by him, to put her hand on his shoulder.

"You weren't really expecting anything, were you, Gabriel?" she asked, offering him the bottle of red wine she had packed in the Saab, that they had saved for an indefinite celebration in the summer house on the lake.

"Yes, I was, Jazzie, but I'll be danged if I'm sure just what it was. I thought I saw this boy in one of the photos. You know the one."

Jasmine nodded, regarding him skeptically as he took a long pull from the wine bottle.

"Damn, this stuff is warm!" he exclaimed, and she burst forth in a brief and necessary laugh.

"Red wine, Faulkner. You don't chill it, remember? And you serve it with red meat, or in our case, peanut butter and Ritz crackers."

"You've always been a hell of a cook, Ms. Bowers," he replied with a smile, and prepared to be out-bantered as usual. But then, in a line of trees shadowed by the descending sun, he saw something white move quickly in and out of sight.

And for a moment he thought it was a human form.

Later on, as he drove the car north along Route 7 toward the summerhouse, struggling with the standard transmission to Jasmine's alternating irritation and amusement, Gabriel tried to settle his thoughts on what it might have been. One deep swallow of wine did not make for apparitions, so it was either a sudden trick of light or it was someone. In his deeper inclinations he had wanted to see the boy in the picture, returning to a crime scene of false accusations, but then he remembered that the story in which such things had happened was one he had spun out of nowhere, lying in bed with Jasmine at the house of Benjamin Mountolive. And at any rate, the white form was larger, almost hulking, but swift and silent like the swoop of a bird or the retreat of a deer into safer forest. His thoughts jostling back to the road as the car lurched into gear and gathered traction, he soon reached that state of floating inattention in which auto accidents are bound to happen but almost never do.

And now he thought of all the appearances: the kneeling boy in the photograph, Del's smudged scrawlings in the Dacia notebook, the October man and the Queen of the Ghosts, and they all kept converging on Trajan himself, on that first glimpse of his friend in Miss Vivien's window on a receding August night. For even those things that had nothing to do with Trajan Bell had something to do with him when memory took them up, and Gabriel thought on those things even more after Jasmine ordered him to pull over and took the wheel back in exasperation, guiding the two of them along the increasingly narrow roads and finally onto a gravel drive, winding for over a mile through tamed and supple woods to the steps of the summer house where they would spend a weekend as the world shifted.

∗∗∗

"What have you heard about the Champlain Monster?" Jasmine asked, as she set two bowls of lukewarm Spanish rice on the table.

Gabriel looked up, closed the notebook. "Not a thing. Are we expecting a visit from him?"

"Sitting there making family trees for elves and ghosts while you make fun of the Champlain Monster? You are a paradox, Faulkner. The Monster is right up your alley. A local legend that has been around through three centuries."

"I prefer my own monsters," Gabriel said. Then wondered why he said it, as the briefest tremor of a chill passed over him. "No. Tell me about it, Jasmine."

"It's quite famous around here. Kind of like the Loch Ness Monster—at least you've heard of that one, right? And the locals have tamed it as well, calling it 'Champ' like the Scots call their monster 'Nessie'. Makes it more friendly somehow, if you have a first name for it."

Gabriel was suddenly less interested. "So it's a sea serpent?" he asked, imagining the tourism and the souvenirs, but Jasmine kept at it, telling him how the old explorer Champlain had apparently sighted a large creature in the lake, "twenty feet long with a neck like a barrel," if you believed the accounts in Vermont and Canada, but that her father maintained that the whole thing was a misreading of Champlain's journals, that he talked about huge gar—*chaousarou,* the Iroquois had called them—and even drawn one on the western shores of his map of the lake.

Gabriel ate the rice as he mused. Leave it to Doctor Bowers to take the mystery out of things, he thought, and immediately he wanted Champ to *be*, even though his own good sense told him the map and Jasmine's father were no doubt right. And there was something in Jasmine's letting the creature rise from dark waters only to dismiss it right off; that bothered him. Though when he looked at her in the brightly lit kitchen of the summer house, the soft curve of her body still evident through the large, ill-fitting t-shirt of his she had slipped into for comfort, he was liable to forgive her anything, especially a typical bout of teasing.

But he would call her bluff on this. That much was certain.

"Let's go find Champ tomorrow morning," he said, pouring the last of the wine into her glass.

"I beg your pardon?"

He gestured at the wine glass, and she drank.

"If he's the gar you promised," Gabriel said, "then we'll have a fish dinner tomorrow night. Fresh from the lake."

"But what if he's the monster?" she asked, taking up the challenge.

"Then you've underestimated him, haven't you, Jazzie?"

"I underestimate all the time, Faulkner," she teased. "Who'd have thought *you* were so adventurous?"

He emptied her glass with a swallow. He knew she'd be the first into her father's rowboat the next morning, and that—along with everything else, his senses told him—was going even better than he had planned. He rose from the table, took her hand and led her from the kitchen down the hall, the rice in the bowls left to dry overnight, and Jasmine compliant and following him toward the shadowy bedroom.

"Just one thing, Gabriel," she said, stopping for a moment at the threshold of the room. "The gar is probably the nastiest eating fish in North America."

"Well, I don't think we need to worry about that," he murmured. "It'll be a monster after all."

***

"There's a story my father tells," Jasmine said, as Gabriel rowed unsteadily along the coast of the lake. "He was at a conference in Burlington, back in the 'Sixties, and stopped at a doughnut shop for coffee. There was this drunk down the counter from him—it was way in the morning—and the man was asking how far he was from New York State. Some helpful kid, according to my dad, told him, 'It's right across the lake from here,' and the drunk says, 'You don't expect me to drive my car over *that* much water, do you?'"

"I don't blame him," Gabriel said. "Hard enough in a boat."

The lake was narrow by the summerhouse. Tall trees lined its bank on the New York side, and Gabriel remembered something from his American history about the French and Indian War— that this had been disputed ground over two hundred years ago. They were seeing the monster even then, according to Jasmine, and though he was totally wrong in his guess that here the water was deeper than it was wide, the southern finger of the lake darkened swiftly and considerably, from blue to purple to black not fifty yards from where he rowed.

His own stories of growing up near a river—of sandbagging streets against flood and of Del's spotting a television afloat in the clubhouse of the drowned golf course—had led Jazzie to believe he had more experience on the water. But Gabriel stuck to the shorelines of everything except those swimming pools where the depths were fathomable and striped with racing lanes, and now he regretted last night's challenge, thrown down in a mixture of contrariness and lust. When she urged him out toward the middle of the lake and the dark currents, it was masculine ego that got him there more than his rowing, and soon the little boat was barely swimming distance from the banks.

"Put on your life jacket, Jazz," he said.

"Not until you put on yours, Faulkner."

The boat rocked a little as they dressed for disaster, and Gabriel felt a turn in his stomach. Surely Jasmine wouldn't want to stay out here long, but he would have to wait until she wanted dry land, have to make a show of being persuaded.

Out in mid-lake he was grateful for the day's incredible calm. There was a silence here that softened his fears, and from both banks he heard the summer ratcheting of insects. He caught a feel of the old Kentucky sun and humidity, and perhaps that was what set his thoughts adrift.

He never wanted to return there. Nor did he have an easy and definite reason. Part of it was a love for Jazz, who would not take to his mired and backward region, and part of it, if he owned up, was an ever-increasing feeling that he had outgrown his roots—that if he went back to Kentucky he would end up fixed in his mother's house, trapped in red dirt and fending off ghosts.

But it was more. It brushed against mythology. Though its history ran deep, though it was the oldest region of America, there was something still possible in northern country: you could see it even in the wilds, even in the lakes and woods up here, in the tight-lipped locals with their reverence for silences, in the loud cities with their convergence of languages and libraries and music. He could already understand why Trajan had yearned for it, perhaps why the Bells' back yard was shadowy, overgrown, green to the doorstep and filled with the sounds of blue jays and Bach.

"What are you thinking?" Jasmine asked, and he was hard pressed to answer. To tell her the truth would be a kind of betrayal of home, and perhaps of the truth itself: because he was not sure what he thought and why he thought it.

"Back in the Confederacy, I guess," she concluded, and the smugness of it irritated him, especially since she was right. It was all right for him to think those things, but an encroachment for her to say them. He forced a smile, shook his head, and set off for even deeper waters.

There was a place north of the summerhouse where the lake widened, promised a broader stretch of water. Now there were sailboats ahead of them, flying colors like a bright scattering of confetti, and Gabriel realized how remote the summerhouse was, that perhaps the draw of this place was not the region but the solitude. He lifted the oars and let the boat drift, as Jasmine opened the picnic basket and promised she'd lend a hand in rowing back.

It was a relief to hear the excursion was half-over. Jasmine had given in first, and Gabriel decided not to seem reluctant, to cooperate cheerfully but let her know that returning was her idea after all. Quietly victorious, he bit into a yellow apple, lay back in what he had been told was the stern, and surveyed the high, shredded clouds, the circling of two birds oblivious to the sun and breezes, caught up in an instinctual dance.

It took him a moment to notice that the clouds were rocking. That of course it was not the clouds on the move, but the rowboat tilting gently, then with a more emphatic shudder, as water spilled over the gunwales. Gabriel sat up, clutched the oars with absolutely no idea what to do with them or how it would help…

And saw a furrowing of dark water to the port side, wavelets tumbling over an even darker, surging form. He looked to Jasmine in alarm. She was watching the sails in the distance. He started to shout, to point, to warn her…

And the thing vanished, whatever it was, diving into the water with a sleek and powerful twist, its back surfacing for a second, the white water spilling over a black, slick column before it vanished and the lake shuddered and stilled.

And now his girl looked up, a strange, unsettled attention washing over her face. "What was that?" she asked, before her good sense recovered, and she scanned the surface of the lake where nothing more than distant sailboats ruffled the surface.

"Mighty big gar I guess," she concluded dismissively. Then frowned at Gabriel.

"Why so pale and wan, my love?" she asked.

And he had no answer, joked back about rapture of the deep. Was relieved when she took the oars, rowed steadily toward the summerhouse with the experience and skill he had expected her to hide all along. Behind them the lake shimmered and beckoned, but they were past the invitation now, and he slept restlessly that evening, awakening to find her snoring lightly, her cheek pressed against his bare chest, over his racing heart, which remembered something too deep and too powerful to surface.

✳✳✳

They returned to Rochester on Monday afternoon, home to that strange, smothered stillness that a house takes on after a brief vacancy, before it slides into the cold clarity of being abandoned. Mountolive's mail stuffed the box, the Sunday *Democrat and Chronicle* lay on the front steps, and as Jasmine gathered it all together, Gabriel unlocked the house and stepped into the parlor.

The room seemed closer now, almost surprised at his arrival. The shadows had retreated, driven back by the high sun at the rooftops on the other side of the street. In the dining room he waited, opening a can of beer while Jasmine made some calls to friends, announced their presence, and promised a full account later.

"There," she said, hanging up the phone. "We're caught up on this end. Now call your mother, Faulkner."

He didn't want to. He wanted to rest and put his feet up, wanted a reprieve from Mary Rackett's non-stop dramas and gossip. But Jazz was right, and again he considered what a great daughter she must be, and how sad and hyper-attentive a son she might have been.

Mary picked up the phone with a "hello" that predicted disaster. At once Gabriel was certain that something had happened, probably a falling out with Andy Lull. He said hello, mentally preparing the right speech, the assurances of wrong man at the wrong time and that of course she would find the right one down the road.

"Oh, Gabie," she said at once, and he knew it was something different, knew at some deep level what it was.

"Oh, Gabie, Trajan Bell's been killed."

He leaned against the wall, took in the awful details. At some time during Mary Rackett's involved and dramatized account, Gabriel felt Jasmine's hand on his shoulder. He reached behind him, pulled her close, and slowly absorbed the story of Our Lady of Serenity, of Trajan's midnight rescue and Miss Vivien's terrible mistake.

XXI

He pieced together part of it that Christmas, in a talk with Lieutenant Hardy. Gabriel had visited the old detective's house, in part to find out about Joey, but there was a veiled intention at the heart of his dropping in. The detective, long a heroic figure in the neighborhood, was famous for his intuitions, having solved a famous murder case back in the late '50s, and still, when a high-profile crime occurred in the city, Dave Hardy was your go-to guy, the man whose guesses gave the authorities direction, established the what and why that got them where they needed to go.

But now he seemed drawn and a little tattered; Gabriel's questions about Joey and his whereabouts were met by half-answers, and the pictures of Joey had been taken off Mrs. Hardy's upright piano. Joey's mom was a specter in the house, slipping in to hand Gabriel a glass of lemonade, then vanishing into the kitchen, emerging only to say goodbye when he left.

Stepping into the brisk humid air, Gabriel struggled to make sense of it. He thought he knew the facts about his friend, but the Joey he remembered was scattered by the years and by hidden evidence. It had felt like a crime scene in there, that

Louisville's best detective did not know or was not telling.

The whole business of Trajan was not much better. For the first time, at least, someone had confirmed that it was the gun all along—the pistol Trajan had left with Miss Vivien in a fit of foolish sympathy—and that Miss Vivien herself was involved in the shooting. But Lieutenant Hardy insisted he was not studying Trajan Bell, and Gabriel caught a tremor of disgust in his voice. The detective's last words on the matter were peculiar as well, as hidden as his wife or the pictures of his son.

I guess that shouldn't happen to anyone, Lieutenant Hardy said, as he shook Gabriel's hand and ushered him toward the door.

Back in his room, Gabriel put in a call to Jasmine. As usual, there was the cool reluctance at the other end of the line when her father answered, and Jasmine herself started out in a whisper, gaining warmth and liveliness as they talked. He knew things were hard for her in Boston; that somehow and at some level her family disapproved of him, but he had decided not to bother with it, to trust her strength and cleverness. By the time he got to the conversation with Lieutenant Hardy, she was the old Jazzie: strangely enough, she had become more interested in Trajan since his death, and now she wanted the particulars. Gabriel had changed as well: the long silences on the other end of the call no longer unsettled him. He knew she was concentrating, was listening.

"I know the lieutenant was kind of your outside hope, Faulkner," she said at last. "But forensics don't tell *your* story."

"But I was hoping..." he began, and she interrupted.

"Remember when you told me about the school? When we visited it last summer, and all we found was the ruins?"

"That may be all *you* found, Jazzie, but..."

"I know, I know. It was haunted, right? Monsters in the water. Southern gothic on the march."

He couldn't say yes or no to that. He kept silent, waited for her to continue.

"Well, Gabriel, everything is ruins. The detective…he looked crappy, right?"

"He looks like shit, Jazzie. Twenty-five pounds heavier and alcohol eyes. His wife is a ghost, and they've taken all Joey's pictures down."

"They have a son who disappointed them."

"We don't know that, Jazz."

"Yes we do. If you own up to it, you know it. Remember that night the two of you went to see the band? You and Joey? Gabriel? Gabriel?"

"I'm here. And you're right. But what's your point, Jasmine?"

"My point is…that Lieutenant Hardy is a ruin. The signs are there with his son. What he told you about Trajan…well, that's a ruin, too. Remember what you did about Thracia? How you imagined it? And what went on with Trajan there?"

"But we don't know about *that*, either. I looked at the photos. There might have been a boy—"

"That isn't what matters. That's forensics. We both found the ruins, but you found something else. So you take the ruins and you dwell in them. You settle there—do you understand me?—and you don't leave until they tell you the truth. And the truth is not a diagnosis. The truth is the story."

"Hold on a minute, Doctor Bowers. Let me lie down on the couch here and tell you sad tales of my childhood."

A long pause on the phone erupted into Jasmine's exquisite laugh. "All right, all right, Faulkner. Just remember how right I am when you lie down tonight and start to imagine things."

"Every time I imagine things, I remember how right you are, Jazzie."

"Do I detect flirtation? Or is it out and out lust?"

"You're the one who makes stories of signs, Doctor Bowers. Choose your weapon."

"I was hoping for lust," she said, never one to give him the last word. "It's dinner time here. Get to the couch and the story, Faulkner. You can tell me about it when the year turns."

***

Lying on his bed that night, Gabriel looked up at the map of Middle Earth he had taped to the room's low ceiling six years ago. He had not outgrown that world, he knew, but now he had set out from it. Now there was Dacia, and New England, and Jasmine at the heart of everything. She was right: he would imagine it all, would discover its truth rather than squaring it with the facts, and tonight was his point of departure.

He smoked a joint and stared at the streetlight trickling through the closed Venetian blinds, his thoughts retreating into summer. For a moment he felt himself drop, the room around him receding, the posters and maps vanishing, the rush of the cars on August Street fading into a murmur at the borders of his hearing. Now he was like a cork bobbing on a huge dark sea, and things swam beneath him, but he refused to notice them, to give them space, his thoughts settling instead on the lonely neighborhood and Trajan Bell.

Now he was standing outside, dressed in the same green robe he had worn when he imagined the Tarot fields and the high, sunny rooms of Thracia College. By his clothing he knew he had entered the dreaming space, and at once he looked for a place to settle, for a green point in this wintry landscape. The asphalt of the street was crusted with frost, but the incline leading to the Bells' front door was dark in a flourish of leaves, and he knew at once that it was the spot he would go to, though he did not force the journey, waiting instead to find himself there, for the place to come to him in the strange, lurching movement of dream.

Now he was there, and it was suddenly summer and the leaves were waxy and firm between his fingers, and for the first time he recognized them as laurel. Clouds settled on the street lamps, and the light smoldered in gray and silver. Gabriel sat on the ramp and waited, plucking a hard, black berry from a sprouting branch and breaking it with his fingers as a warm wind swept over the landing.

Trajan opened the front door and stepped outside. It was

more like remembering him than meeting him, so there was little surprise in the encounter. He sat beside Gabriel, white shirt glowing in the muted light, and placed his hand on the railing.

Now the last of Gabriel's alarm and wonder faded into waiting. He expected a revelation, pushed his expecting aside, and Trajan sat with him in a long silence, and then spoke at last.

"I cannot see what flowers are at my feet, nor what soft incense hangs upon the boughs."

Gabriel smiled. "Keats again?"

He received no answer.

"You can't be Trajan," Gabriel said at last. "I can't have you be Trajan. Who are you? What do you want?"

He looked beside him at the white-robed and bearded figure, whose features had softened into something beautiful and majestic that had slipped entirely away from the image of his old friend into something abstract, almost geometric in the transformed lamplight. It was the same creature he had seen in the high-roomed Thracia of his imagining, but less forbidding, more stunned and sorrowful, as though it had fallen into a shady country.

Indeed, something rippled beneath the whiteness of the robes, like a pale current under a still and featureless pool. *What is the color of pale?* he wondered, before his thoughts bucked and settled on the house, the smells and shadows inside.

"I want you to step inside," the figure said.

Through the house they passed, Gabriel reassembling it from memory—the cluttered table, the grease-encrusted kitchen rife with the smell of Chesterfields, the head of the basement stairs caught in a glint of light from the moonstruck backyard grove. Then Trajan led him down the stairs to the cellar, lantern tilting across his white robe in a drift of geometric shadows.

When they had reached the foot of the stairs, Trajan extinguished the lantern, and for a moment the world vanished, devoured in darkness. Gabriel heard footsteps trailing away to his right and followed, headed toward an even more abject pocket of blackness, a whirl of dark inside the dark. At the edge of an absolute, cavernous blindness—the kind that, given a generation or a span of years, would make creatures evolve away from eyes, he was thinking—Gabriel paused and inhaled the cellar air. Again the steps echoed ahead, and he heard a voice; Trajan's, to be sure, but changed by night and memory, muted, the vowels broadened and the words stretched, saying,

Close your eyes here, Gabriel, 'twill make it easier to follow…

And compliant, following the poetry of dreams though he knew it was no substitute for logic, though he knew he wasn't even dreaming, Gabriel closed his eyes and, in the dodging false light beneath his lids, followed Trajan through the ever-expanding cellar until water licked as his ankles. He imagined for a moment the flood of a ruined basement on August Street until the thought receded into the wash of tides, the plash of oars on a forbidden lake.

Imagining monsters now, Gabriel climbed into the boat, and guided by a figure who was less and less Trajan, more a column of light, he drifted across still water toward a luminous shore, a seascape like some old painting, some voyage to an Isle of the Dead.

Now, as the keel of the boat scraped sand and lodged ashore, as his guide disembarked and motioned him, Gabriel held back. He wanted to refuse. But the smell of summer and bruised leaves gave way to ammonia and must and the salty odor of overcooked meat, and he knew that refusal was out of the question. The figure rose and drifted into Miss Vivien's house, and Gabriel followed, the warm breezes of the air outside battering vainly against a close, humid stillness as he abandoned expectation and hope, entering a region of brazen light.

Now he understood the letter, knew why Trajan had spent so much time describing Our Lady of Serenity.

It was to bring him here. To take him below the stories.

He followed the glowing, abstract figure down a narrow corridor, cries and mutterings and curses erupting behind the doors on either side of him—doors he did not think of opening until much later.

"It's night outside," the specter in front of him announced for no apparent reason, and beckoned him on. "It's night outside, but this is unending day, and there is something fearsome in all this light, isn't there, Gabriel? Do you understand why the scavenger flies from the light? Do you understand it now?"

"No, I don't. Unless it is a fear of..."

"Being found out," the creature said. "Did I complete your sentence? It's good if I did. You'll complete enough of mine. But it is midnight here, indistinguishable from noon and a long day of waiting. But don't *you* wait: I have things to show you."

They reached an intersection of halls, and the figure turned left, gathering substance and forming a body that was not Trajan's—more slender, younger, long hair flowing in impossible reds and golds like a field of daylilies. Gabriel followed still: a question rose in his thoughts, but he pushed it aside before it took shape in words.

"They are all Lotus Eaters here," the creature said. "You know that by now. Stoked on the pill of the moment, immobilized, their sentences, like yours, left unfinished, trailing off into darkness. But you know that as well. What you don't know is that she's at the end of this hall. Spent Valentine's Day here, and May Day, and the Fourth of July."

Gabriel stopped. "Where are we going?"

"Oh, you'll see." The creature, now translated into a young man Gabriel's age, leaned provocatively against the wall of the corridor. "You're not being seduced, Gabriel. Just summoned. Do you want to see Vivien now?"

"No," Gabriel replied, preparing for the sight, because he had come this far and it had to happen. The creature opened the door into shadow, and Gabriel peered into Miss Vivien's room.

She sat in the wheelchair, facing the door. Her limbs and hair were sprouting dried leaves, the pistol nestled like a child in her lap, her face in shadow. The room swam with the smell of urine and rubbing alcohol.

"Is that you, Marcus?" she whined, raising the gun as her eyes met Gabriel's. Her eyes were as dead as a shark's, as a subterranean creature's.

Gabriel wanted to say *No, but Trajan is always beside me.* But it was too much; it was explaining the moment away. Then he wanted to say *yes*, just to see what would happen. But he knew it would be *no*, definitive and lonely, because he had been guided there to say it.

So *no* he said, and Miss Vivien stared at him with those glittering little brown eyes. "You never were Marcus," she declared, and the words balked and settled in the stifling room. "I wanted you to be Marcus, but you weren't. You have survived on that lake out there, and so far you're still intact. Come into the music, and where the old folks shake their heads in violence, where we rouse old secrets with forgetful cries and the gurneys rumble over halls we should walk on swift and dancing feet."

Gabriel shuddered, as Miss Vivien—or his dream of Miss Vivien—lifted and leveled the pistol. "You wanted me to do the right thing. That's what you said when you give it to me, and the shells that you never told them you was giving. Now turn yourself around and get out of here. And don't look back."

Gabriel turned toward the door, and the dry leaves rustled. *Joey was always right,* he told himself. *She is turning back into a tree.*

The absurdity of the thought struck him. He had to look. He spun around, stared into the endless barrel of the pistol.

The white flash out of the shadows rushed over him, and he felt a heavy blow at his groin that sharpened and burned as he absorbed it. He fell back through the doorway, and the dream went dark in the smell of cordite and ash.

✳✳✳

Gabriel awoke with a desolate gray sky above him. He was in a bare field, littered with construction equipment. Concrete foundations circled him like squat rows of tombstones, and to his side, seated on a line of cinder blocks, Trajan sat in a white robe.

It was Trajan again. The glory and abstraction had fled

from his figure, and he was the stocky, rumpled man that Gabriel remembered, but pale, sadly pale, his thick arms folded over his knees and his hair a curly chaos, glittering in the baffled moonlight. Mandalas on his chest looped and circled into a huge, spreading spiral of blood between his legs, and his hands were stained black as the crushed berries on the wooden incline.

"Half in love with easeful Death, Faulkner?" he asked.

Gabriel flinched at the poetry and the intimate name. He ran his fingers over his lap, expecting moisture, an open wound.

"You survived untouched," Trajan assured him. "Or at least untouched in that way. It's our old country here, Gabriel. Look at it now. The country that bore me and shaped me, that I left like I was running away from bondage. I have come back here, making forests in back yards, haunted by snows and memories and owls…"

It was unsettling. It was Trajan and not Trajan, Gabriel kept telling himself: figures layered under figures, ghosts trying to rise through surfaces of white light.

"Where is it, though?" Trajan asked. "Where's my home? The school? Where's the old woods south of here? All those places I've been? Look at it, Gabriel! It doesn't stay the same. You think it's solid, then it shifts under your feet like melting ice on a wide lake, and you're looking toward the shore, and you want it stable, you want a landmark, a still point, but it isn't there.

"Nor am I the still point. I look at who I've been, two dozen people in a handful of stories—man, woman, youth, boy, child—and when I see myself in every one of them, in every character in every story I've written, well, my edges and surfaces start to get away from me. They blur and fade, like currents in the water. I don't know where or whether they leave off."

Gabriel thought about Miss Vivien's accusations. *You wanted me to do the right thing. That's what you said when you give it to me.*

What was *the right thing?* Where did it leave off?

It was too much. Gabriel buried his face in his hands. "I would have taken that gunshot for you," he said, his voice

271

breaking. He tried to sit up and failed.

"No you wouldn't," Trajan said. There was no accusation in his voice. "People like us don't die for our friends."

"I'm not you, Trajan. I'm not even *like* you."

Trajan leaned back and smiled. "Well, then," he replied, the words tunneling into loneliness.

And he was gone.

Someone was calling from a distance. Gabriel lay back, and the gray sky began to change, to darken then transfix in slanted light, to resolve into shapes. It was like he was reading the clouds, as slowly the map of Middle Earth took form, and the Barbara Remington poster taped to the door of his old room, the lizard climbing up the gnarled tree and caught in the fragmented streetlight.

His mother was calling him. He jumped out of bed, spraying the room with aerosol to get rid of the thick, sweet fog of marijuana smoke. He tried to hang on to the story as he answered the door, explained that, yes, he had been burning a rather foul candle and yes, he would stop burning it, that yes, he had spent far too little time in her company over the holiday, and that the rest of the time until New Year's was hers.

Yes, he would pay for his long-distance calls. No, she was not Japanese, but half-Chinese, and no, she was not a Maoist, but more like a psychologist.

And all the while, the story trailing away from him like receding mist, as he retreated to his room under Mary Rackett's questioning, lay back down on the bed, and let her words drift off as he stared into Tolkien's imagined countries, mapped and glossy on his shadowy ceiling, all the while remembering his last words to Trajan in a dream that was not a dream…

I am not you, Trajan. I am not even like you.

THREE

And we are put on earth a little space,
That we may learn to bear the beams of Love
--Blake

XXII

Schooled by that winter night of dreams, Gabriel rarely looked back. But looking ahead was an art he found impossible to master.

He rushed to Rochester when the holidays ended, waited at the dormitory for Jasmine's arrival. Through that winter she could not account for his fierce attentions: overwhelmed and aroused at first, she soon became frightened at his insistence: when he was not guiding her to bed four, five times a day, he was neglecting classes and smothering the room with the smoke of marijuana and hashish.

In February she had enough. Returning from her eleven o'clock class to find him face down and drowsing in the bed, she nudged him awake until he rolled over, reached for her, and started to pull her close.

"Hold your horses, Faulkner," she said, wrestling out of his grasp. "We have to talk."

She drew it out of him then. Summoned the phantoms and put them to rest for a while with questions. No, he was not like Trajan, she assured him, the bed a makeshift psychologist's couch, straight out of cartoons were it not for the patient's head resting in the analyst's lap as she stroked his ragged brown hair with her thin fingers.

No he was not like Trajan. But then again...

"'Then again', what?" Gabriel asked, reaching up and stroking her breast.

She brushed his hand away. "Then again, it wasn't Trajan that you talked to, now was it?"

"If it walks like a duck..." Gabriel answered, reaching for her again as she slid from under him and settled on the chair at her desk.

"For a boy who sees ghosts, you're surprisingly literal, Gabriel," she said, and he caught the hint of anger in her voice. "It's time for you to talk to someone."

"Mountolive, right?"

"You know he's amazing, Gabriel. He's not at all like a high school counselor, which seems to be the image you have in your head."

"Like Trajan is an image in my head, Jazz? Is that what you're after?"

She looked away, thumbed the pages of a textbook on the desk.

"Look, Gabriel, the Mountolives invited us to dinner. I think we should go."

"Invited *us*?" He propped himself on his elbow, tried to catch her gaze.

But Jasmine wasn't looking. "He invited me," she said. "Told me to bring a guest—a 'significant other', was the way he put it."

"Just loads of warmth in that term, Jazzie."

"But you're the significant other, Faulkner. There's loads of warmth in that."

He allowed there was, pushed the jealousy down into a dark place. "Set the day and the time, Jazzie," he said at last. "I haven't been going anywhere lately. I guess it's reached the Wise Old Man part of the story, then."

Jasmine glared at him. "Professor Mountolive is not that

276

old, Gabriel."

"I see."

She softened immediately, met his eyes and smiled. "As to the wisdom…well, we'll let you be the judge."

***

The dining room was just as he remembered it. Mrs. Mountolive, it seemed, was not a slave to interior decoration.

But when he looked at the room that Friday night, Gabriel concluded that she probably didn't have a say in those matters to begin with. Rumpled and distracted, deferring to her husband in almost every matter, she was a striking contrast to Mountolive's slick and manicured brilliance. Indeed, it occurred to Gabriel that through the months he and Jasmine had stayed in this house, he had always thought of it as the dwelling of a single man, had been surprised whenever Jazz had mentioned that Mountolive had a wife, and yet he felt as if he knew Brenda Mountolive, that he had known her all along.

The professor was, he had to confess, not that old. Gabriel guessed Mountolive in his mid-thirties, which made the books and the trips to Switzerland all that more impressive. He had little to say to Gabriel through the early part of the evening, talking shop to Jasmine before and during dinner, and on the few occasions when Gabriel tried to enter the conversation, he found himself regarded politely but almost indulgently, and he began to wonder if the invitation had been extended to a 'significant other' in the first place.

After dinner they settled in the parlor for more drinks. Mountolive took the large, comfortable chair next to the entry to the dining room, so Gabriel was forced to sit in the decorative, straight-backed rocker by the front window. Nursing Irish coffee ("In honor of your particular Irishness, Mr. Rackett, but with only half the accustomed whiskey," the professor had said), he rocked and listened while Jasmine drew Mountolive around, mentioning Gabriel at every quiet and juncture of the conversation. She was his girl, and he was glad of her attentions, but he wished the evening would come to a close before he became the focus of Benjamin Mountolive.

"Gabriel is going to be a writer," Jasmine announced at last.

Dismayed, he looked down into his cup, where the whiskey shimmered like oil in the black coffee. He wished she would stop insisting on that.

Mountolive turned to him and raised an eyebrow—an expression that Gabriel instantly disliked.

"Well, I don't know about that," Gabriel said, looking away. "I've been working on a story or two, but it's not like I'm building a career or anything."

He looked back. All the eyes in the room were on him.

Jasmine cleared her throat. "He has this incredible imaginary world. Kind of like Tolkien's. And we've been talking about how many stories are there, and just lately he's been starting to tell them."

Mountolive nodded. "A lot of my students read Tolkien," he said. "Especially the in-coming freshmen. They seem to be taken with that kind of thing. Probably some money in that, Mr. Rackett, if you keep at it."

Gabriel liked Mountolive even less. "Maybe so, Professor," he replied. "But I don't know if it's money I will make. Most of the people around here who are going to be writers…well, they write the same old stream of consciousness story and they drag it from workshop to workshop, like it's some foreign car they take from garage to garage to get tuned just right."

Mountolive leaned forward. "And…?"

Gabriel frowned. "*And* it just doesn't seem like that's the way to prepare for a career, sir. Writing and rewriting the same short story for four years of college and a couple more in a grad program."

"Maybe so. But there's always your craft, isn't there? I expect your Tolkien spent a number of years on his tome."

The word "tome" dropped silence into the conversation. The phone rang in the parlor, and Brenda Mountolive leapt up to answer it. Gabriel wanted out of the room, out of the house. "My Tolkien is everyone's Tolkien, Professor," he said quietly, and Mountolive smiled indulgently, rising from his seat.

"Of course he is, Mr. Rackett. No offense meant."

Mrs. Mountolive returned to the room. "It's for you, Benjamin."

He was already to his feet. He knew it was for him. Gabriel guessed that, in this household, all of the calls were.

Mountolive slipped from the room. "Maybe it's Freud calling," Gabriel muttered, earning a glare from Jasmine and a stifled laugh from Brenda Mountolive. In the professor's absence, his wife blossomed a little: she dispensed more coffee and whiskey, and told Gabriel not to mind, that sometimes experts in one field fancy themselves experts in another. It wasn't that great of an insight. But it *was* the kind of thing you needed to be reminded of if you spent any amount of time at a university. Gabriel was glad she said it, grateful for friendly words on indifferent terrain.

All the while Mountolive's voice droned from the dining room. He appeared at the entrance once, still attached to the telephone by the long cord, to wave at Jasmine and vanish again. When he finally emerged, he sat down and resumed the conversation as though there had been no interruption, as though all of them had waited for his return.

"So...I hear that you've been seeing ghosts, Mr. Rackett," he said.

Jasmine rose quickly and followed Brenda Mountolive into the dining room. Gabriel watched her go, waited for her to look back, to see in her face just what she thought she had managed, but her retreat was steady and swift.

"This Hadrian fellow," Mountolive began.

"Trajan."

He brushed away the correction. "Trajan, of course. I remembered it was one of the better emperors. This...Trajan. Killed in a sporting accident last summer, if I'm not mistaken."

"But you are mistaken, Professor," Gabriel replied, shocked at the depth of betrayal. "He was shot."

"My apologies again. And call me 'Benjamin,' Mr. Rackett."

"Well…he was shot. Benjamin."

"He was a teacher, right? And his is the ghost you claim to have…sighted?"

"The ghost I imagined. I'm not so sure I *sighted* anything."

Mountolive nodded. He gestured toward the whiskey, which Gabriel declined.

"Ever seen anything like that before?"

Gabriel closed his eyes. For a second he felt himself tilted, glimpsed a white broadcloth coat at the back of his eyelids.

"No," he answered, and opened his eyes again, to the sight of Mountolive pouring whiskey into a cup.

"You know, it's not altogether an alarming thing, Mr. Rackett."

He's fishing to use my first name, Gabriel thought. *I'll leave the bastard hanging.*

"I'm not alarmed, Benjamin."

"I thought you were. I thought it was part of what brought you here tonight."

"Jasmine brought me here, Benjamin. We do those kinds of things for each other."

"Very nice. Very… reciprocal. Would you like to know what I think of your ghost?"

"I'm all ears," Gabriel answered curtly. The clatter of dishes reached them from somewhere back in the house, and he tried to imagine Jasmine, domestically washing dishes with Brenda Mountolive.

Mountolive laughed. "Seriously…Gabriel…this ghost is nothing but a shadow. Simple Jungian stuff, actually. The bottom line is that not a one of us is, on the whole, as good as he imagines himself to be, as he wants to be. The shadow is that part of us that we can't fit into the best image of ourselves. A sort of dark side, if you will. Everyone carries a shadow, and the less you fit it into your conscious life, the deeper and darker it is. It's what you fear about yourself, in ways: about what you are, about what you might become."

Gabriel glanced into the dining room. No sign of Jasmine.

"And it's a good thing you're imagining this ghost…this Trajan. When your failings and weaknesses are conscious, you always have a chance to correct them. The ghost is close to your surfaces, too, and constantly in contact with other interests, so there is a way that it becomes 'civilized' by continually being subjected to modifications. That's a good thing, because if it is repressed and isolated from consciousness, it never gets corrected."

"I didn't know I was trying to correct anything," Gabriel said.

"Probably not. It's healthy that you are, whether you're aware of it or…not so aware. Just look at this Trajan: he was middle-aged, and you're not, homosexual where you aren't…"

"I'm not sure that he is," Gabriel interrupted, but Mountolive shrugged away the correction.

"Whether he is or not, you've imagined him so. More importantly, he spent his last days in failure and in confinement. Almost in imprisonment. If *that's* not a young man's nightmare, I don't know what is. You're afraid that will happen to you. That you'll be pushing forty *without* the pretty house or the pretty girl, with no fine whiskey and no good cigars—and, by the way, wouldn't you like a cigar?"

He reached into a small humidor on the table by his chair—everything, it seemed, was arranged to be within the reach of Benjamin Mountolive.

"I suppose I should have one," Gabriel said. "Seeing as it might be my last chance."

Mountolive chuckled. "I'm saying nothing of the kind, Gabriel. Just that your depths have yet to be sounded. The stories aren't a novel, your personal life is…well, a student's life, I would guess. And speaking of student matters…why, you've yet to negotiate your college years. What are you—a year behind Jasmine in school? Two years?"

"Oh, she has a fellowship," Gabriel answered lamely. "She'll be here for graduate work."

Mountolive smiled. "And you think I don't know that?"

"I think," Gabriel replied slowly, "there's an awful lot you don't know. Benjamin."

They sat in silence for a moment. Mountolive started to say something, drew back his words. Jasmine stepped back into the room, followed by Brenda Mountolive. Drying her hands, she looked apologetically at Gabriel and nodded, almost imperceptibly, toward the front door and escape into the night. Gabriel rose from the chair as she made hurried goodbyes, pleading an early morning though they all knew it was a Saturday.

"Think about what I've said, Gabriel," Mountolive urged, shaking his hand far too warmly.

"I appreciate your interest, Professor," Gabriel replied, doing his best to push all irony out of his voice.

✳✳✳

Jasmine caught up with him halfway to the car.

"I can't tell you how sorry I am, Faulkner," she whispered. "He has a way of extracting things. I told him that I wanted you two to meet, to bring you along, and he seemed to be asking why, so it just seemed like..."

Her words trailed away, as her hand brushed over the back of his head.

Gabriel nodded, placed his arm around her waist, and pulled her close to him. "I can't tell you how sorry *I* am, either, Jazzie," he confessed, and it appeared to soothe her as she let herself slide above the depth of words.

He slipped into the passenger seat and rolled the unlit cigar between his fingers as Jasmine drove west toward the campus and home. He would smoke it outside the dormitory while she prepared for bed, his thoughts on desolate fields and red mud, savoring the thick fragrance, the burning at the back of his throat, as he took in a bright, constelled sky where he recognized none of the stars.

XXIII

As her graduate work began, Jasmine moved into a tall, ugly tower off Mt. Hope Avenue. The move took place on the very day that the gobshite Nixon resigned, and the two of them celebrated new surroundings and new life before a crackling television with terrible reception. By this point, they had dropped the masquerade of separate residences, and Gabriel began his third year at the university, anchored and domestic.

The tower, known antiseptically as the Graduate Living Unit, was good for nothing more than a bed at night. It rose fifteen floors above a desolate little lot (Gabriel and Jasmine were on the eighth floor), and was ill-equipped for comfort— no air conditioning and only sporadic hot water. Gabriel was surprised that Jasmine's family would let her live in such tattered accommodations, but suspected it had something to do with him.

For the most part, the GLU housed foreign grad students, and Gabriel often felt as though he had been launched into a wider, shabbier world. The stifling hall reeked of curry and the more pleasant, nutty smell of ghee, and on occasion, the Taiwanese students two floors down would greet Jasmine in

Chinese, unconvinced when she answered back in English.

Jasmine took to calling him Nimrod, and it was a week or two before he got the joke.

Mary Rackett, of course, did not approve of her son's decision. She urged Gabriel to go to confession, and he promised he would, forgetting the vow immediately. Confession, of course, would involve repentance, and he was not prepared to repent anything. It was not long until she forgot the conversation as well, settling back into layers of denial and the assumption that Gabriel and Jasmine must have separate bedrooms in a large and comfortable high-rise.

Mary Rackett was not the only one to masquerade truths. Gabriel had not quite forgotten the night at Benjamin Mountolive's, how Jasmine had said too much in her great enthusiasms. Or so he told himself, pushing back the word *betrayal* and all the injury it conjured. There was one night, however, late in November, when he sat by the clanking radiator, reading for an Age of Shakespeare class taught by a dwarfish, brilliant scholar whom he feared remotely.

It was like that at the university. His professors all seemed inspired and damaged, from the drunk who taught him Keats to the vicious Religion professor who lent belief to everything from the credible to the preposterous except, of course, for Catholicism. He wondered what had brought them here, imagining a huge sack shaking them out over Rochester, where they tumbled into classrooms shut off from the world outside. But he knew it was more complex than that. They stood on bridges, he guessed, from the mind to the heart, and it was a dangerous, lonely passage where sometimes the madness helped you stand.

At any rate, it was the Age of Shakespeare that plagued him this term and that evening. He was in grade trouble to begin with, having submitted an essay on Hamlet that had sent the scholarly professor into apoplexy. Gabriel, of course, had thought he had a good idea: after all, Hamlet had staged a play to trap his bastard of an uncle, and before the play was performed, had intended to add a "speech of some dozen or sixteen lines."

Gabriel thought he had it figured, thought it made a great play somehow greater that a fictional character was supposed to have written part of it.

The professor did not think such figuring added to his knowledge.

The D+ (a particularly insulting grade) smirked at him above a lengthy penciled commentary about *woolgathering*. At that time, Gabriel shrugged it off, thinking he had an entire term to compensate, but the end of the term was coming fast.

Settling again into *The Tempest*, he read the famous lines, when Prospero, the old enchanter, calls off the magic that has run through most of the play...

> *These our actors,*
> *As I foretold you, were all spirits and*
> *Are melted into air, into thin air:*
> *And, like the baseless fabric of this vision,*
> *The cloud-capp'd towers, the gorgeous palaces,*
> *The solemn temples, the great globe itself,*
> *Yea all which it inherit, shall dissolve*
> *And, like this insubstantial pageant faded,*
> *Leave not a rack behind. We are such stuff*
> *As dreams are made on, and our little life*
> *Is rounded with a sleep.*

He closed the book and rubbed his eyes. There was something inexpressively sad about the whole farewell.

"Done with *The Tempest*, Faulkner?" Jasmine asked gently, startling him from across the room.

Gabriel looked up. She sat at her desk, three books open before her amid a reef of papers.

"Are we the stuff that dreams are made of?" she asked, and he blinked stupidly, for a moment believing she had read his thoughts.

"We are indeed, Jasmine," he muttered at last, wrestling on dark currents, sailing past a sudden storm of tears.

***

Trajan as well slipped to the back of Gabriel's thoughts during these times. When his old friend emerged—generally in an association of images, sometimes in dreams—Gabriel would feel a similar sadness, rising out of nowhere, as though the ghostly memory had wrapped itself in a kind of abandonment.

He heard from his mother that Miss Vivien's house remained empty. To his surprise, he discovered there was another child—a daughter, older than Trajan—and Mary Rackett claimed to have seen her around the house, once in April after a devastating tornado hit the Louisville area, then again in December. The best guess was that Trajan's mysterious sister was getting the estate in order, and during the holidays, which he spent this time in Rochester, Gabriel decided on ordering his own business as well.

He went back to the notebook on New Year's Day. With a soft lead pencil he nudged around the borders of the map. Jasmine was in Boston for much of the break, and though Gabriel missed her, he welcomed the solitude. As usual, she had asked him to join her, fully aware he would not: they had established he was no favorite among the Bowers family he had yet to meet, and Gabriel liked to imagine her defending him, justifying his Southernness and bad Catholicism to an array of disapproving, intellectual stares.

Odds were she did nothing of the kind. That the stares were not that disapproving, and that perhaps his name never even came up. But the simple imagination calmed him in her weeklong absences, settled him enough to do the work he was planning to do until Jasmine returned.

It was a ghost story rising out of his mapped terrain. Mountolive would laugh, to be sure, at the boy who continued to see specters, but as Gabriel remembered his father saying, "Smoke 'em if you got 'em," and he *had* the ghosts, had them thoroughly, and the best exorcism might be the writing.

Or so he told himself as the story took shape in his mind.

He looked first to the map of Dacia, and settled his thoughts.

As the map had grown, Gabriel's pencil smudgings had shadowed an area between the weed-entangled lowlands and a city on mountainous heights. He imagined all of Dacia as sloping country, foothills and inclines, and by now it reminded him of the steep inclines of the cemetery in his father's small-town Appalachian home. It had been a land of ghosts for some time, but Gabriel was still unsure as to the kind of ghosts that peopled it.

Now, in the depth of a New York State winter, he closed his eyes and loosed his thoughts on a bleak, sloping landscape, littered with crumbled stones. He thought of Thracia, of the burnt foundations of the school protruding like broken teeth, merging with the high whirring sound of cicadas—what Tom Rackett called "jar flies"—as Gabriel's summer thoughts blended uncannily with winter and the landscape of his book glazed over with a thick layer of ice.

Now Gabriel imagined the ghosts, bent in their graves (why bent?) as they sloughed off the shells of their bodies and rose painfully (why painfully?) into the frigid, damp air. *It is painful to leave the body*, he told himself, remembering the dull, hot impact of the pistol blast in the small room at OLS, and wondering what Trajan felt as the shot entered him, as he rocked back on his ankles and fell.

All these thoughts passed through him, and he set them aside, scanning the air above the desolate landscape, where white tendrils of mist hovered and quivered like flames, then circled like white owls over the ruins.

Not yet, Gabriel. Don't let her rise into words just yet, Trajan's voice reminded him, echoing in a place below hearing.

Again he asked, *What do you mean?*

Keep her in thought. Keep her image there. Do not even name her parts, or call her what you think she is.

But then... he began, and felt a hand brace his shoulder, so firmly that he was tempted to turn, to look around him, to dissolve the dream.

No. Not even that.

And Gabriel watched as one of the threads of mist took more solid shape, the pointed tip of the tendril of vapor transforming to a bishop's glowing miter. Now it was a young man before him, as something in him had always known it would be, though he had neither forced nor guided the image. And suddenly the faint light of the figure pooled around Gabriel Rackett, and he saw the desolate world through the eyes of the imagined and ghostly young man he called simply Jack, after the same kind of figure in a host of folk tales. And in this world the slope led down to a greater darkness and rose toward a brilliant, indeterminate radiance, both of which scattered at the edges of Jack's vision.

Gabriel felt the boy's thoughts jump and stir. He was becoming what he imagined, and it was no joyous thing, but a feverish, anxious uncertainty.

Now Jack headed up the slope, the rough stones at his feet giving way to an ice-encrusted dirt path winding between squat marble mausoleums, some of them sealed against the humid twilight, others broken open, bones and rotting cloth spilled around their thresholds. His first impulse was to get going, to leave this benighted place, but something in it lured him to stay, and the bright horizon kept receding. A nervous, skittering sound behind him grew louder as he moved, a rustling over dried grass, and the sour, metallic smell of rats reached him on a breeze.

Again, he was tempted to look back—down in that dark valley where something fearful was stalking. But instead he raised his eyes to the retreating light, now only a faint glow on the hilltop.

Now Gabriel knew the first thread of the story. This imagined man, this Jack on a journey toward an ever-receding light, the darkness approaching from behind as he trudged up the frozen incline, hounded by smells and noises. Both of them followed the thread, the trail ahead of them widening as they left the stones and mausoleums behind, no closer to the light but farther from something, the noises behind them louder, more insistent.

Do not look back, Gabriel told himself. But despite his own warnings, Jack turned, and Gabriel looked.

Down in the shadowy vale, a form in white broadcloth lurched from crypt to crypt with surprising speed—a tall, translucent, gangling figure, bent to a crouch. The figure passed between stones, clouding the markers and the buildings with a faint, glittering trail of steam. Then, before the dream faded and Gabriel found himself again in the spare little apartment at the edge of a snowstruck city, the thing peered at him from behind a dilapidated stone angel.

The glittering eyes were black and depthless as onyx.

The thing grinned at Gabriel, sliding its pale hand slowly over its throat in an ancient gesture of menace and murder.

It was still far from a novel.

At only twenty, Gabriel had no way of knowing where to take his imagining. At first he thought everything was threatened by the intrusion of the October Man into his inner thoughts. For days, schooled in the horror movies of his childhood, he was afraid to look in the mirror, afraid he would greet the spectral face from his past. When Jasmine returned it became easier: she deflected the undercurrents, so that the two of them lived on bright surfaces, where even the darkest tides could be brought to light and explained into a kind of health

The spring of his third year passed into the fall of his fourth without disruption. At home, his mother's romance with Andy Lull deepened toward a planned marriage: obediently she had started the steps toward annulment, and to hear her side of the story, Tom Rackett was kind, almost encouraging in the process. For Gabriel, though, it was a ripple in what he thought he knew, like something in his own past was being erased. Here Jasmine was of no help: she saw his troubles as psychological. *You were used to being the man in the family, Faulkner,* she would tell him, *and the only one who could take your place would be Tom Rackett.*

Part of you is still that kid, waiting for Mother and Father to get back together.

But he tried to explain how his mother and the Church were already at the job of making part of him vanish, that the *annulment* she sought was a kind of canceling out. And yet he knew that was not it, either. There were regions, he knew, where neither knowing nor believing covered the ground; there was a country like the littered slopes he had shaded in his maps of Dacia, where the pathways rose into light or slid down into darkness, and you could take those trails both ways, in either direction.

The subject came up again and again in the fall of '75, as the former Georgia governor mounted his surprising campaign for the Presidency. Gabriel was surprised to see Jazzie's mistrust of the whole enterprise, how she was torn between her contempt for the Republican Party and her fears of a new Confederacy. She saw the family of evangelists and rednecks, noted the toothsome Carter children and the broadened vowels of the accent, but she did not hear the *insides* of the candidate, he guessed—things you always felt you'd have to go north to find, but when you got to the North, those things weren't there, at least not in the way you had imagined or hoped. Jazz and Gabriel argued the Carter campaign lightly and playfully, until the holidays approached again, when inexplicably she became more distant, less political, as though she was taking the whole thing personally now. Longing for the old sunlit face of the waters, Gabriel let the matter drop into events they refused to notice.

Something had shifted between them. It was a secret Jazzie was carrying, and this time when she asked Gabriel to join her for the holidays he consented, knowing that this year was different, this year he was expected to agree to it all.

They drove into Boston on the 23rd. The narrow, winding streets of the old part of town reminded Gabriel of the Galway he remembered faintly, and the weather matched perfectly—an icy drizzle and forbidding wind from off the shore that took him right to the edge of Dacia, back to the boy Jack and his climb out of the shadows.

The Bowers' Beacon Hill townhouse was as close to downright opulence as Gabriel had ever ventured. Jasmine had assured him that the family was not rich; he wondered about that as he bunked down with Danny Bowers in a room as large as the Racketts' living room at home, where from the window you could glimpse the Esplanade and the Charles River. Two burnished (and, Gabriel guessed, expensive) cellos leaned in the corner, a stereo system that looked like something you'd set up at a rock concert, and more classical albums than Gabriel had seen, even in the big record stores in Louisville.

If this wasn't rich, Gabriel was hard pressed to imagine what was.

Danny himself was pleasant enough. He played his instrument for Gabriel, who feigned a mild interest into a greater one. Then Danny revealed his "rather limited rock music collection"—a shelf of about thirty albums that was largely experimental, it seemed, filled with odd, exotic percussions and electronic instruments, names like Roxy Music and Brian Eno and Frank Zappa. Gabriel knew Zappa only for the jokes: the more abstract compositions were beyond him, and he longed for the melodic lines of the Beatles and the bluesy strut of the Rolling Stones. Still, Danny was his age, and in some ways a natural ally. Cyrus and May Bowers were tougher to figure, though Gabriel thought it might be time to do so.

Cyrus Bowers was textbook rumpled, down to a matted forelock that draped over his left eye, giving him a look that crossed Mad Scientist with Buccaneer. It was a marvel how a girl as glorious as Jasmine could spring from that bloodline, until you looked at May and saw a quiet, surpassing beauty that somehow had filtered down to each of her children—not only Jasmine, but young Lily and even to Danny in a way. The parents were a study in opposites, in appearance and in temperament— May was gracious and conversational, while Cyrus was elusive and bluff—but Jasmine's parents united in their distance from Gabriel that Christmas. His contact with Lily was fleeting and almost stealthy; she spied on him as he talked with Daniel in his room, and fled from him when he came across her on the landing or in the parlor. Gabriel could not imagine this doll-like girl, scarcely into her teens, as the prodigy she was supposed to be. She was all intrigue and giggles, but ultimately the most normal of the Bowers family.

Christmas arrived, and Gabriel received no gifts at first, except a pendant from Jasmine, upon which hung a Roman coin from the reign of Trajan—by this time a kind of inside joke between them. May Bowers thanked him warmly for the bottle of expensive wine he had bought them with the last of his December scholarship, but for the most part he felt tolerated: with Jasmine's attentions frazzled by something in the air with her parents, Gabriel was thrown back on Daniel and felt as though he was a friend the brother had brought home.

"I think it sucks how they've done you," Daniel announced on the last night in Boston.

Gabriel replied carefully. "No, they're cool. It's a family holiday, after all. They've really been quite...polite."

Daniel laughed. "Oh, they're polite, all right. Think you could stand them in the long run?"

It seemed like an odd question. But Daniel gave him little time to answer.

"Got something for you," he said, reaching into the drawer of his desk and producing a cassette tape. It was still a relatively new thing to Gabriel, whose music collection was all on record and turntable; in fact, he didn't know too many people who had either a recorder or a player. Quietly he listened while Daniel explained that he had recorded a number of his own compositions. That, no, the quality of the recording was not nearly as good as reel to reel, but he had yet to take his work to a studio, and he just wanted Gabriel to have one.

"You don't even have to listen to it, Gabriel," he said, looking out the window over the gray river. "Just don't tell me you hate it if you do, and don't pass it off as your own."

Gabriel started to object, but Daniel waved away the words.

292

"Just kidding," he said, "and really I don't know why I want to give you a copy of this. Maybe because you seem like a nice guy and I might or might not see you again..."

The sentence struck Gabriel like a blow from behind. He started to ask what Daniel meant, what he had heard, but instead he took the cassette, turned it over in his hand, and looked up at Daniel, who was still staring out the window, his face unreadable in the reflected winter light.

All the way home Jasmine kept silent. Her answers to Gabriel's questions were brief, mechanical at best, and eight hours of driving seemed interminable as the road swept quietly by, as he closed his eyes to try to relax, to calm his rising worry, but he kept seeing the green markers rushing toward them on the road ahead—the signs for Albany, then Troy and Syracuse passing by as he slipped in and out of an unsettled sleep. By the time they pulled into the lot of the GLU, Gabriel was prepared to leave his duffel in the car. He did not want to be without Jasmine, and his senses were settling him at the edge of a rift, the ground unsteady beneath his imagining. He tried to be sensible, wondering where he could find January lodgings on such short notice, but his thoughts spiraled deeper into a fear that, just the night before, he had never seriously entertained.

As Jasmine touched the handle of the car door, he reached across her and locked it. She glared at him, and he spoke quickly, gently, his hand resting on her shoulder.

"OK, if I've done something, Jazz, tell me what it is and I won't do it any more."

Her anger melted in front of him. She managed a weak smile.

"You're damned right, you won't, Faulkner. Not even possible, at least not for about six months. And even then, if you think you'll knock me up again, you're even more stupid than I thought you were."

***

Hirsch & Green, Ltd.

_____ Avenue of the Americas

New York, NY

1 Dec 1992

OK, Gabriel. This is something, at least.

Must admit I don't know where you're headed with the stories. I like the whole idea of "the tale," don't get me wrong, and I do like the turn-of-the-century ones, especially the partial one about the Civil War veteran. At the bottom line, it's great to see you putting words on the page at last, but the next steps are the hard ones.

It's very hard to market a string of short stories as a book. If you were King or John Grisham, it might be done, but you're Gabriel Rackett, who is talented but who has only DACIA under his belt, so unless this is going to tie together as one continuous narrative, I don't know where I can go with it.

Could you tie the late 19th century stories together? Looks like they could fit somehow, and I could place a novella in an alternate history anthology that Speculative Visions, a new press out of Los Angeles, is planning for mid-1993. You'd be sandwiched between a space opera and a Tolkien-King Arthur heroic fantasy. The kid who's running S.V. insists on a 3-way split of 6% royalties with a $3000 advance—not much, but a way to get your name back in sight.

Even better...have you thought of a sequel to DACIA? You know how it is in this business. One book cries out for another. It was funny five years ago, when you said you didn't want to "commit trilogy," but maybe the time has come? This stuff you've sent me, though it has some good things in it, is at double disadvantage: the length, and the simple fact that parts of it don't sound much like you.

It's not the time for departures. I can't wait for BROTHERS KARAMAZOV or MADAME BOVARY, not to mention that I don't think you can wait for them either, much less do them. I may have broken confidence a little, because I called Jazzie last week, and she says things are not well with you. She suspects that whiskey is at the bottom of it, and none of us can ride that out with you any more.

You can go back to DACIA. Honest you can. You never did much with the dwarves in the valley—we talked about that, remember? Your hero took 17 years on LORD OF THE RINGS— he just published them all at once. The trick will be getting your old publisher to re-issue the first book, but I have to have the second one in hand to get started.

Call me. Call me. You're occupying too much valuable space in my worries. I'm not crazy about things that take up space.

Sincerely,
Barry

XXIV

Later, when Gabriel remembered the time of awaiting his son, he thought of all the Greek myths—of the heroic children born to beautiful mortals, abandoned by supernatural parents. Children conceived in a flash of light or a sudden rush of water, bursting from the trunks of trees or set afloat in a small and perilous boat, reared on forgotten islands, waiting for the time and place to come into their own.

It was far too flattering, he guessed. And yet he watched Jasmine's pregnancy helplessly from a distant height, as though it had little or nothing to do with him. The morning sickness gave way to a low-grade, constant irritability, and the once-perfect, concave stomach started to swell, an array of biological mixed signals that drew him closer to her while simultaneously pushing him out of the apartment at any opportunity, back to the library where they had first met, where he settled on the fourth floor and studied seriously for the first time in a year, wrestling with a dread that wrenched him away from his books, into the prospect of a long and settled future.

The greatest drama had come from breaking the news to the parents. May Bowers was kind and distant (Jasmine had told her in the last visit to Boston), and Tom Rackett was perplexed as always, remembering his son as seven years old and wondering how it had all happened. But Cyrus Bowers refused to speak to Gabriel, and Mary was furious, convinced that Jasmine had conceived on purpose to steal fire from her own upcoming wedding.

But in March the young couple made it official anyway, in a quick ceremony before a justice of the peace that felt like elopement and brought no change beyond hyphenating their last name: Gabriel remarked that, if the name changes continued over generations, their grandchildren would be mistaken for Spanish aristocrats, but Jasmine didn't think it was all that funny—in fact, humor had passed her by when the morning sickness had arrived.

Names were shifting wherever Gabriel turned. On a Saturday in early June, he and Jasmine returned to Louisville to watch Mary Rackett become Mary Conroy Lull, and it was there that Jasmine went into labor an hour into the reception. Still abuzz with wedding champagne, Gabriel steered the Saab into General Hospital, and Dominic Cyrus Bowers-Rackett, his name already seeming to promise an estate north of Barcelona, came into the world soon after midnight on a Sunday.

The Lulls went ahead with their honeymoon, promising vaguely to see the baby when they returned. But for Gabriel and for a while, Dom's arrival seemed to change everything. In the first weeks of his infancy the baby slept soundly in his father's arms, the warm, souring smell of milk on his breath a kind of reassurance, a thing that erased the world if you placed your nose on his soft skin. At first he was dark—more Asian than Jasmine and almost as Asian as May—but in his first several months you could see the Irish intrude and his hair begin to lighten, and from day to day Gabriel was surprised by his transformations, as though each night strange powers would slip into the apartment and substitute one baby for another.

By his sixth month, Dominic almost seemed to prefer his father. Gabriel had continued at the university, returning each afternoon laden with books Jasmine had requested from the library so that, even if she had taken a year's leave from her courses, the research for her degree could continue. Dominic would squawk a greeting from the moment he entered the apartment, and until bedtime in the evening he was the center of his father's attention, his flea-market cradle rocked with one rhythmic foot as Gabriel read, or studied, or worked on his story of the Dacian brothers. Years later, when the feminists celebrated women's ability to "multi-task," Gabriel instinctively understood the talent, and wondered why the women around him continued to deny he had mastered it.

Perhaps it was because of his focus. Though he could do several things at once, there was a way in which he could be present to them only in sequence. Back and forth his thoughts would go, from Dominic to the page in front of him, and on a number of occasions, looking down into the rocking cradle, he would be surprised to see a child in it, peacefully still and so pale that for a moment he would be alarmed, would jostle Dominic awake and endure the crying until the steady movement lulled the child back to sleep and he could continue with his reading.

It was a tender and domestic scene when he looked back on it later, missing his son from yet another apartment, this time north of Chicago. But to be honest, his thoughts were drifting away from Dominic even as the cradle rocked—drifting to Dacia, to the new world and the story he was inventing.

✲✲✲

The names of the Dacian brothers, he discovered, were Orlando, Valentine, and Jack: the journey of their story was, in fact, a quest. Born in the cemeteries of the Dacian Slopes, the brothers had grown to maturity amid the monuments and cenotaphs of a vanished culture. Statues of angels hovered over them, and sometimes the statues would move, would whisper, would urge or demand secret things.

It was apparently only Jack, however, who heard the statues' voices. His father and brothers dismissed the whispers as a kind of unmoored sadness or the persistence of family memory. But as none of them—not his family, not Jack himself (and at this stage of the story, not even Gabriel)—understood that persistence, they seemed to agree that it was not important, that the memories nagged at the boy because they had yet to be replaced by something else. It was this melancholy, not necessarily that he was the third-born brother, that made Jack the least likely choice when the King of Dacia sought a consort for his only child, the Princess Anamchara, sending out a challenge to all likely suitors that the object of their quest awaited them, somewhere at the top of the slopes, among curtained walls and unbearable light. Everything, the statues whispered, from the sparse plants on the Dacian slopes to the stones and cenotaphs and even the carved and guardian angels, faced toward the light. Therefore, it was the way things tended, the way they all were headed, and if Jack was stirred by murmurs and desires, why, it was because something missing in the bleak landscape of his birth was provided for him in the castle atop the mountainous heights…

That, according to Jack's brothers, settled the matter. It was the way things were in a land of shadows and cloudy longings. It was, in a phrase of his own that Gabriel came to admire, a "ghostly yearning."

Well, Gabriel knew that no worthy story would leave a ghostly yearning unsatisfied, or at least unpursued. So the brothers prepared for a quest into the bright lofts of Dacia, impelled by a beautiful figure they had seen sometimes at dusk, when the cemetery shadows deepened even further. She was framed in the glow of the twin moons and attended by small companies of shades—ghostly creatures, but none the young men could recognize.

Rocking a cradle, seated at his desk beneath the minimal light of a Tensor lamp, Gabriel himself strained to name or identify the courtiers, but he knew that to rush them was to force the story, so he waited. He did not let them rise into words—not yet. So the story revealed itself to him slowly and gradually as the winter passed into spring.

Meanwhile, Jasmine worked for her doctorate and Dominic's cradle rocked in the shadowy hours, as Gabriel finished the last of his coursework and looked unsuccessfully toward graduate school in the area. In short, they both had settled into a life of quiet exteriors, while their imaginations branched into wide and separate ways.

Often, as he began to write the story, Gabriel would feel himself vanishing into the world of Dacia. It was a process he had gone through before—that sense of dropping and momentary, dislocated fear that soon settled into icy grass and the slopes of the imagined mountain, growing so suddenly vivid that, when Gabriel emerged hours later, sometimes having written a page and sometimes nothing at all, he would feel the same estrangement, the same nervous struggle for purchase, until he recognized the apartment, the light at Jasmine's desk, and Dominic rocking at his feet. Even the baby, whose dark hair and eyes seemed uncommonly beautiful at those moments of return—more beautiful for the shimmering contrast with its smooth and vulnerable skin—seemed somehow alien, so that Gabriel shivered at the prospect of having had a part in its making.

Lakes College accepted Gabriel at last, after rejections from Cornell and Syracuse and Buffalo and, finally, his own school, where he had thought at least to have an advocate to the committees who admitted questionable students. Indeed, he *was* questionable: his standardized examinations showed he knew something and had read something, but the grades were erratic, typical of someone trying to travel more worlds than one. Lakes had been his safety school—a small liberal arts college that had a new, "experimental" Masters in Myth and Art. It sounded like a '60s kind of place, and the fact that the program took place over four summers, and only in the summer, made it seem even more flaky to a couple so traditionally schooled. The only problem was that the school was in Vermont.

"It might be fun for you," Jasmine suggested, as they looked at the Xeroxed brochures, headed with the irregular, inflated letters of a Fillmore West poster. "Worst case, you'll know by the end of the summer and can apply for a legitimate degree somewhere else."

She said she'd go with him.

He was surprised that she felt she had to say it.

But of course she wasn't done.

"I could join you about midway through the term," she suggested. "Dominic and I could hole up in the summer house—they'll be out of there in July. You could commute. It's only forty miles or so."

Gabriel pointed to the brochure. "Look, Jazzie. They have family housing. Why not stay with me, stay for the whole term? We'd be the most traditional family there, I guess: one man, one woman, one baby. You could have a vacation there. Or take a lot of reading, if you want to."

"It's three hundred more, Gabriel. We can't afford that."

They both knew that Cyrus Bowers' generosity extended only to daughter and grandson. He would say the right things, offer words of encouragement in Gabriel's "quest to better himself," but it would be words only, and they could not lodge with words.

"It's not like it was, Gabriel," Jasmine said. "Vermont's not Trajan country any more."

It was a remark that would have amused him two years earlier.

✱✱✱

And Lakes College, too, would amuse him years later. A renovated Vermont farm, complete with a central house, barn, stable, and a half-dozen ramshackle cabins that housed its fifty-or-so students. Again, like years before at Old Jeff, he was attending classes in the barns, braving unseasonable heat, and nodding through lectures, wondering if the place could float financially long enough to confer his degree.

Wondering, for that matter, what such a degree would be worth in a tightening job market.

For Gabriel was trying to make peace with the idea of settling down.

It was high time, most anyone would have told him. Wife and child, no job prospects without a degree. Jazzie and Dominic were entitled to more than an eighth floor apartment in a GLU somewhere. But Gabriel was not yet twenty-two, and all around him studied the unsettled masses—hippies beginning to age, housewives recently divorced, and several foreign students, their white linens and incomprehensible accents further indication that Lakes was not altogether the most exclusive of schools.

He was writing short stories now. His teacher, a preoccupied woman named Athena Bumpas, was the author of an award-winning collection of stories called *Late Night Thoughts on the Eroica*. The title intrigued Gabriel at first: he thought of eavesdropping, of an ear pressed to the door as two people made love in a secret room. He was disappointed to discover that it was "eroica", not "erotica", and that Doctor Bumpas had, it seemed, a more lofty and spiritual desire that had something to do with Beethoven's symphonies.

He laughed, and thought of "Esoterica" on a box in Miss Vivien's garage. At least until Doctor Bumpas characterized his first submitted story, a segment from *Dacia* called "How Jack Received His Calling," as "sensational." Gabriel was encouraged by the word, thought it meant "great" or "marvelous," but discovered on reading a page of comments that sensationalism was a bad thing. He thought as well that a graduate "B" was like those he had received in college, but when he discovered otherwise, he settled down and began to write more realistic stories, assured that the magic and the ghosts were the things that Doctor Bumpas did not want.

So he wrote about his excursion with Trajan into the construction site, about Del's death on the baseball field. And when those two stories came back with sensational "B"s, Gabriel decided to endure, to live in the professor's diminishing realism, to practice Dacia in secret like a clandestine bad habit or a smuggled drug.

He received only one note from Jasmine in his first three weeks of classes—a post card, telling him that Dominic had begun to crawl and call her "dada". In the meantime he wrote her daily, long complaining letters that spelled out the trials and urged her to come early. There was only one phone available to the students, and twice in the first week Gabriel tried to call her and failed to find her at home. He knew from the silences that something was shifting on the horizon, and he resolved not to think about it, to dwell in daily things. And so he would have passed the term, had it not been for two events—one that thrust him into the past, into the shadows of cemeteries and angels, and one that showed him that the bright world ahead of him was receding.

✳✳✳

The Introduction to Myth class was held in a stable, its loft converted to a pair of professorial offices, beneath which lay a windowless classroom, lit by two bare bulbs. Doctor Petasos, a gaunt, tattooed Greek presence, wore a floppy, Haight-Ashbury felt hat and gave Gabriel immediate nightmares of his undergraduate years. Barely thirty from Gabriel's best guess, the professor showed all the signs of 'Sixties burnout. He lectured from a yellow legal pad on which the edges of the paper had buckled and crumbled, and his eyes would drift from the page and settle on an indefinable point somewhere in the rafters, as though his words could summon the gods into a hot Vermont classroom.

It was indeed hot in there on the second day, the students bunched closely together because Petasos was reputed to grade easily and lecture dramatically, adopting strange voices and comic impressions, so he consequently drew a crowd every summer. He was reading a lecture about myth as *the stage for a huge interior drama*, and Gabriel was already nodding, drowsy from the morning heat, the whirr and pop of a malfunctioning air conditioner.

Petasos sounded like Ben Mountolive, and minus the tattoos and shoulder-length hair, could have passed for the psych professor's cousin. Gabriel thought of the drawings on the wall of Mountolive's dining room, how at night they seemed to move when you glimpsed them from the parlor, but as you approached them they settled into black ink. The closer you got, the more defined they were, but Gabriel believed that they were best viewed from a long step away.

For they both were wrong: Mountolive and now Petasos. The gods were not merely complexes, syndromes, and guilts. They stood on thresholds everywhere you looked, and you could let them in or let them out, and the fact that you could let them in was important, because it meant they were outside your head to begin with—at least outside some of the time. The thought struck him like his glimpse of the Queen of the Ghosts, like the sight of the October Man leaning against the baseball fence. It was as though he had suspected this all along, so that when he came to the thought, he uncovered it like an artifact rather than spinning it out of the air.

And the insight was like a cue in a play.

Because the young man entered the room as Gabriel was thinking it, and the eyes of the class shifted toward him, as you always do a late arrival.

Dark hair, dark complexion. In his mid-twenties, from Gabriel's best guess later. But at the moment Gabriel was struck by something familiar in the slight, lean figure, by how he took in the stares as somehow his due, how he settled into the attention more readily than into the desk at the back of the room, his black brilliant eyes taking it all in—the professor, the terrain, the intrigued students.

"You must be Reynaldo Rosa," Petasos said. "Glad you could make it." And then, as if nothing momentous had happened, he resumed his talk in mid-sentence, and all eyes but Gabriel's fixed on the podium. Half-listening to Petasos' lecture, Gabriel stole glances over his shoulder at the new arrival, like you would at someone who pursues you from a great but visible distance.

Petasos was going on about the gods now. Something about them was universal, he said, and they were still with us, in dreams, religious beliefs, myths, and fairytales. In dreams they were at their most primitive, but when they came out of the shadows, like all of those figures who traveled in the underworld, we made them conscious, he said, and we dressed them up in more complex forms.

"And it's not just the Greek gods, brothers and sisters," Petasos said, adopting the faked drawl of a Southern evangelist. "They come out in all your religious dogma, and when they become *structures*, that's when you gotta beware! They still do their job, but they take the long way home, as the man says, by a path so roundabout that they're hard to recognize. Which is why you don't think they are here anymore."

From his perch in the back of the room, Mr. Rosa frowned and shook his head, and continued to take notes.

"Since the Protestant Reformation rejected nearly all of the carefully constructed symbol structures," Petasos said, shaking a melodramatic warning finger at the class, "you've been forced underground—every last one of you. You feel isolated and alone without your gods, without your symbols. So you look inside yourself. And that's the quest, people. It's down in your souls where the action is, where they all wait for you. The shadow is there—your hidden nature—and like the old radio show used to say, 'the Shadow knows'. There's the anima, too, or the animus for you ladies, and what that is, quite simply, is your hidden opposite gender: the girl in every boy, or the boy in every girl."

Rosa looked up, caught Gabriel's glance, and burrowed back into his notes.

"And somewhere under that," Petasos said, intoning like the voice-over in a science fiction movie, "or beyond that, because when you get down there, the only 'below' is 'beyond'… somewhere down there is meaning. Meaning, pure and simple. The thing that gives you a purpose.

"Those are the folks in your cellars. They pop up all around you if you pay attention. But there are stories down there, too—

stories already made, even though you didn't make them yourself, so that it's more like someone has slid a manuscript under your door."

Now Gabriel focused more intently on the tall man at the podium, whose swirl of tattoos was dizzying, almost hypnotic, as he waved his arms. "Those stories are still your stories, people. The Odyssey and the stories of Orpheus, Moses, and Jesus. Krishna, too…and I'm not just talking to the Indian students when I say that. They are everyone's stories, stories from way back. They have to do with you becoming who you are, and the cast of characters—anima, shadow, wise old man—keep popping up in all the stories, all *your* stories. You live by them and sometimes die by them. You get sick and well by them. And to be healthy and whole, you do one of two things. You let them out on your own, know them for who they are, and accept them—that's one way. Or if you're like most people these days, you find someone who can help you get to know them."

Someone to help you get to know them, Gabriel thought, writing the phrase down in the margin of his notes.

Someone like Trajan.

He looked back at Reynaldo Rosa. And knew, at a depth below and beyond knowing, who it was.

Somehow Reynaldo seemed to recognize him as well. The thought struck Gabriel as bizarre, passing from implausible to impossible, but several encounters over the next week (it was a small campus, you could avoid nobody) seemed to strengthen his intuitions.

He saw Reynaldo by the pond bordering the campus, white dress shirt brilliant through a tangle of leaf and branch. Gabriel thought of approaching him, but he was sure that Reynaldo had already noticed his attentions, and it was the last thing Gabriel had in mind, to come off as a pursuer or stalker. But in a way, he was just that. Everywhere he turned, it seemed Reynaldo was in sight: whether crouched over the herb garden Petasos kept by the side of the main house, or seated on a green Adirondack chair playing chess with several of the other students, Reynaldo was all around him, haunting his wanderings.

Reynaldo seemed to be quite good at chess, though Gabriel, barely knowing the names of the pieces, had no real way of knowing. It seemed that Reynaldo never had the same opponent, and that all who tried to go up against him were reluctant for a second chance. It was like a quest that each chess player among the students—all of them male, Gabriel noticed—had to undertake if only to wear a badge of noble defeat, to rise from the chair shaking his head in admiration or frustration while Reynaldo, never smiling, simply shrugged and returned to what he had been doing before the game began.

They took to calling him "Fischer," after the chess master, the tournament in Iceland still clearly lodged in their memories. For a while Gabriel considered approaching him, asking to be taught the game. But he figured it would be pointless, that Reynaldo's indifference to his opponents would spill over into contempt for initiates. It was bound to be embarking on the wrong foot, especially since Gabriel had come to realize that Reynaldo occupied far too much of his thoughts, that by now even trying to speak to him would be freighted with heavy imaginings.

It took Petasos, that strange conductor of souls, to bring the two young men together. In the third week of class, the professor announced that he would pair his students for a presentation on one of the myths. That, having closely examined their interests and psychologies, he had discovered it was best to assign them alphabetically.

"For what is alphabetical order," he asked, in the mock Germanic accent he adopted whenever the subject turned toward psychology and he wanted you to wonder whether he was kidding, "but an arbitrary pattern that encourages synchronicity—by which term I mean a significant convergence."

Gabriel thought it was Petasos' customary bullshit, until he realized that no names fell between "Rackett" and "Rosa" on the roster.

Gabriel met Reynaldo Rosa, then, by the Adirondack chairs, on a Friday before he was to meet Jasmine and Dominic at the summerhouse. Reynaldo was gathering the chess pieces after what seemed to be yet another effortless victory. Placing the white horse neatly in the box amid the pawns rowed like a pointed set of teeth, he looked up at Gabriel and smiled, far more gently and amiably than the jagged, canine white of the arrayed pieces.

"Rackett, isn't it?" he asked.

And when Gabriel nodded, sprang right to business.

"And its Orpheus we're after, am I right?"

Of course he was right, and the pretended uncertainty irritated Gabriel, who had awaited and planned this encounter for two days. Reynaldo rose and motioned him to walk, and Gabriel followed reluctantly, his eyes still on the box of chessmen lying athwart the seat of the green chair. For a moment he thought he caught the faint whiff of tobacco, but the odor vanished at once into the brilliant green smell of Vermont juniper and pine.

The woods toward which Reynaldo headed floated in that summer haze so rare in Vermont, but familiar to Gabriel from the hot Augusts of Kentucky. He caught up to Reynaldo when they reached the edge of the woods, and for a moment his eyesight baffled him, refusing to take in the bottled green light that filtered through the leaves.

Resting a hand on Gabriel's shoulder, Reynaldo guided him onto a forest path, where dried evergreen needles rustled beneath their footfall. "So what have you been thinking, Rackett?" he asked. "Any ideas on how we talk about Orpheus?"

Gabriel cleared his throat. "I think it's kind of easy," he began. "The poet loses his wife, goes into the land of the dead to recover her. Gets instruction that he can have her back, providing he doesn't turn around as he guides her out of the Underworld. But he does, and she dissolves into mist. It's pretty easy instruction about not looking back. You know, when you undertake an adventure."

The footsteps stopped on the path behind him. For a step or two, Gabriel went on. Then he turned. Reynaldo stood on the path behind him, one hand on his hip, the other clutching an evergreen branch, waving it mockingly.

"Not so easy, is it, Orpheus?" Reynaldo asked mockingly.

"But that's different...that's..."

The green branch swept the air dismissively. "That's the problem with heroes like you, Rackett. You're so sure of the words behind the story that you get the whole thing wrong."

"Oh, please," Gabriel began. "Like I need a lecture on—"

Reynaldo raised his hand. "A lecture's the last thing you need." Passing by Gabriel on the trail, he took the lead, and, his curiosity outweighing his irritation, Gabriel stepped in line and followed. Like a slow breeze the two of them passed between the boles of the trees. The slanted sun cast bloody shadows on the tree roots, and it looked marble-hard in the darkness.

They passed a squat cliff, a heap of felled maple, the dried branches spanning a void and plunging into a pond, so still and reflective that the descending branches seemed to go on underwater, down into a rain-filled sky both above and below a wooded country.

Then up out of the shadows, soft and full of patience, a

solitary, pale path appeared, like a long bleached filament. And up this path they went, in front the slim, dark man in the brilliant white shirt, spilling words behind him as he vaulted up the trail toward the light.

Gabriel followed, no longer aware of his notebook, of his thumbed copy of Ovid. But something in his thoughts kept telling him these things were there, in his possession, like he was in two places at once—housed in his own body, following the white of Reynaldo's shirt, and at the same time somewhere behind himself, his sight loping ahead to where he labored in a green shirt and jeans, something clutched in his hand that he recognized, lost, and recognized again. It was like his senses were split, his sight rushing ahead and settling, his hearing falling behind like a scent.

Someone was behind him, he suspected. Someone who ought to be following him, just as he followed Reynaldo Rosa. He heard the insects drop into silence far behind him, and the quiet they left was brushed by the sound of more footsteps on dried needles. If only he might turn once more, but he had taken up Reynaldo's challenge, and looking back would ruin the moment, would be a betrayal of his best self.

At first he was afraid, his thoughts settling into that floating apprehension that you feel when you suspect someone is pursuing you. But then he calmed, and for reasons that made sense to him later, he thought of Jazzie. Ahead of him Reynaldo reached the lighted meadow, gestured back to him, still without looking, the sunlight blurred on the white of his shirt and tennis shoes, and as Gabriel followed, something sighed in the shadows behind him, something more grieving than he could imagine, and the whole world—the woods and the meadow, the cropped hills of the campus and the Green Mountains rising in the distance, the sky and the hooded stars, all of it—spun mournfully around that desolate sound.

He paused there, at the lip of the light, Reynaldo standing in mid-meadow, his arms lifted in sunlight, and the sound from the woods behind them rising from rustle to murmur. And Gabriel imagined Jazzie at the source and heart of that sound, following, rising out of the wooded shadows and taking form in the gabled light, her steps shortened now by gray-green cerements, her long hair matted and cobwebbed, her stomach swelled and heavy, like in the time she was carrying Dominic.

He pushed back the imagining. If he turned, he knew that it was Jazzie he would see, so he did not turn, he waited until the image trailed from his mind's eye in tendrils of green mist.

Now ahead of him, Reynaldo stood in the sunlight, almost unrecognizable in the reflected blaze of his white shirt. His arms stiffened at his sides and his fists clenched, as though he was preparing to scream across the meadow. Gabriel approached him, stopped a few steps away, and in the silence that followed, he heard the rustle of dried leaves in the shadows behind him, and the wind snickered with a low, masculine wheeze.

"So you know now?" Reynaldo asked. "Now you know what it means to follow him?"

Stupidly, Gabriel shook his head. Then realized that Reynaldo had not turned around, was facing the long ascent of the meadow and the line of trees beyond it.

"What do you mean, Reynaldo?" he asked. "What am I supposed to know?"

"That there are others in the story, Gabriel. That Eurydice is there as well."

It startled Gabriel when Reynaldo used his first name. Somehow it seemed, intrusive, almost intimate.

"Of course. She's there…there to be rescued. And his song does that…Reynaldo. Or almost."

Still, Reynaldo did not look at him.

"It's not about words," he said, so softly that Gabriel could barely hear him over the soft summons of the wind. "But about the things under the words. Because Eurydice is back there all along, and not just *there to be rescued*—God, that's so like a man to say it!—but consider this, Gabriel, consider that she might *not* have thought of the man, going on ahead, or the path, climbing upwards towards the light and the life. Imagine her there in herself, Gabriel. Imagine her death filling her with completeness, with abundance, like ripened fruit fallen from the branch."

The words invaded Gabriel's thoughts. He imagined Jasmine swelling with sweetness and darkness, succulent, eaten away by death. It was too much to imagine; he tried pushing it back into shadow, but Jasmine kept emerging, full and untouchable, her gray hands weaned so far from marriage that when she lifted them toward the light, it was a vague gesture, completely indecipherable, and briefly he hated Reynaldo Rosa for having summoned her forth.

For he had, hadn't he? Wasn't it Reynaldo's doing that the strange apparition of Gabriel's wife had come unquiet from a nest of memories?

"Now she is no longer that blonde woman, sometimes touched on in your dreams and songs…"

"Not blonde," Gabriel objected weakly, thinking not of the Jasmine he imagined behind him, but the one miles away, waiting for him at the summerhouse with what he hoped was eagerness and impatience.

"Not blonde is better," Reynaldo said, an observation out of nowhere as a cool breeze smelling of secluded water rushed out of the woods at their back, brushing the high grass in the sunny meadow. "But she is no longer the wide bed's scent and island, and your possession no longer. She is already loosened like long hair, spent like fallen rain. She is already root. So, when you turn and, with anguish see her dissolve into mist, recede into shadows, she is looking at your silhouette caught in the act of turning, wondering who or what you are…why it is, in the fulfillment of deep rest, she should concern herself with you at all."

***

And so he promised Reynaldo he would think on these things. He marked them down in his notebook—an indecipherable, scratched series of notes that it embarrassed him to be writing after that moment of emerging into the woods, when the sunlight had dazzled them and Reynaldo had turned an old story into mystery.

As he wrote, he felt like the stupid one, the one who could not catch up. The one who turned mystery back to an old story.

Even as Gabriel drove the bulky rental north toward the lake and the Bowers summerhouse, the myth—and the way Reynaldo had talked about it—still settled on his thoughts. Pulling behind a pickup truck, following a driver who passed slowly through shadow and light on Route 7, Gabriel felt a kind of peace, turning the radio to one of Vermont's many country stations and listening to the mournful slide of George Jones' baritone, to the end of love and the emptiness of taverns and houses. Slowly Gabriel's thoughts receded to Dacia, to how the sloping funereal landscape of his imagined kingdom was, when you thought about it, a path between underworld and the innocent land of the living. No wonder that Jack did not look back as he ascended from darkness to light.

Gabriel wondered who or what was following Jack, and as the road wound up past Rutland, never looked into the rear-view mirror of the big, cumbersome automobile he was driving.

Now, as the road took him toward a meeting with Jasmine, it amazed Gabriel that, months before he had taken up the myth with Reynaldo Rosa, he had been writing a version of the same story, one set in his magical kingdom. There was something heartening about that. Something that told him that all of this had a pattern. A plan.

But then there was Reynaldo, who had swept into the dark of the story, making it about the girl left behind.

The truck darted up the road toward Burlington, and Gabriel took the gravel trail that wound sinuously to the summerhouse and his wife and child.

✳✳✳

He could not say that Jasmine was delighted to see him.

A smile at the door, a peck of a kiss, and a hug when he insisted—she seemed like she was greeting him after a day at school rather than two weeks of absence. Immediately, she began to major on some ailment that Dominic had just weathered, and he wanted to ask *why bring it up since it's over?* But he knew he couldn't and shouldn't, and he was grateful he had remembered his child long enough to pick up an amorphous stuffed animal—some unnatural cross between a squirrel and a bean, he had told himself—at a country store south of Brandon. The baby was fascinated with the gift; Gabriel pointed this out several times to Jasmine, who, he guessed, had the toy figured out as an afterthought.

Over a thrown-together meal interrupted by an increasingly irritable Dominic, Gabriel tried to tell Jazzie about the classes at Lakes, the teachers. He even thought about mentioning Reynaldo Rosa, but held back, knowing that she had pretty much wearied of any story that might have something to do with Trajan. He did mention the Orpheus presentation, and she agreed that it was a good myth to study, in that absent way she had when she was half-listening, half-attending to their son.

The distances widened when Dominic was asleep and they approached the bedroom. For a while Jasmine delayed in the kitchen, drinking a glass of wine and smoking one of her rare cigarettes, then when she came to bed, lay above the sheets in a nightshirt and shorts, insisting that the room was warmer than she'd remembered it. Later, when Gabriel moved toward her, she offered a little resistance that he took for drowsiness, but eventually he removed her clothes and, guiding her onto hands and knees in the center of the narrow bed, covered and entered her, his chest pressed against her smooth and surprisingly cool back.

Only near the end did she seem to respond, pushing back to meet him a minute before he spent himself inside her. She flinched as he clutched her shoulders, and he bent over her, apologizing softly and gently, thinking that indeed it had been a while since he had her, indeed he had been a bit rough.

As he whispered to her soothingly, as he kissed her ear amid the whispers, he noticed the small brown bruise on the back of her neck, the tooth's indention above the little mark. Rolling off of her, Gabriel looked at the ceiling now, his confusion seizing on an old water stain that he told himself Doctor Bowers should attend to. Because where you found a stain, he told himself as his pulse raced and a low terror knocked at his chest, when you found a stain, it was a sign of other damage. He told himself repeatedly, wrenching his thoughts back, again and again, to the insistence that it was ceilings he was thinking about in spite of everything, that it was a roof leaking in an out-of-the-way cottage, and that was all it was and all it could be, as Jasmine breathed slowly into sleep beside him.

***

November 23, 1992

Dear Dominic,

There are some things you will need to know, though you will probably receive this letter long after I write it. It will come to you like a visitor from the past, and you will be a man when it comes, and pondering the mysteries of how and when and why it reached you.

By the time you receive this, perhaps your mother will have told you some of the story that led up to that winter day in 1982 when she packed you in the back of the old Saab and headed east on the Thruway. I'm not saying that her version is the wrong one. I'm not even saying her version isn't the same one I have. All I'm saying is this: that the shape of the things that happened changes a little depending on which way you turn it, even if the people involved all agree, more or less.

So I can tell you more than most divorced parents tell their children: not only that what was wrong between your mother and me

316

was not your fault, which is what they all say. But even more than that, you need to know that not much of the sorrow was her doing, either. What she has told you about your scattered, irresponsible father is, at the end of the day, entirely right.

And I was never more scattered than that day you left. Because I mourned only an hour, when something else arrived, and my thoughts rushed away from you and from your own proper sorrow, landing in a world where thoughts and sorrows did not belong.

But more of that in a moment. For now, I have things to tell you.

Remember that Benjamin Mountolive has been good to you. It is a noble thing to take in another man's child and raise it as your own. There are all kinds of temptations to do wrong by a stepchild: you can neglect him and focus only on his mother, or you can try to shape him into something that he isn't.

Or you can try to claim him as yours—the worst temptation, because of all of them, this one makes you feel noble and generous and right.

But do not forget, Dominic, that you are not "mine." And you are not Ben Mountolive's, for God's sake. Nor—and this is important, more important than you might imagine now—nor are you your mother's. She may have given birth to you and raised you, and in some way she may be accountable for you, but by now you are not hers, Dominic.

By now you are becoming entirely your own.

You could not choose us when you were born. That's what they'll tell you as well, on the psychologist's couches and the television talk shows, in the self-help books and everywhere wounded children cry out in torment. What they won't tell you about are all the guilts that fall away when you really know this. Let's start with a big one: my best guess is that, given an option in the here and now, you would not choose me as your father. But you wouldn't choose Ben, either— or at least that's what I figure.

Your mom, now, you might choose. Because we all choose her.

I have always thought that. Even on the day when she packed you in the Saab and drove off to Boston to be with her family and, it

turned out, with Ben Mountolive…even on that day, I was thinking
that, given an option, I would choose her again gladly.

Because your stuff took up all her suitcase, Dom. If for no
other reason, I would still choose your mother for that.

I know there were clothes waiting for her at your grandparents'.
We both knew she traveled into a safe harbor, and that it was like
some movement from darkness into light. I found out later that
Ben had accepted a job at Boston University, but by that time I was
almost relieved to hear it, because your mother always believed it
would be good for me to keep in touch with you, and Ben was the
kind of man she was able to persuade.

But about that day.

There was this gesture you made with your hand as a baby,
Dominic. When you waved, you would roll your fingers, so that they
looked like they were racing over a keyboard rather than saying hello
or goodbye. You were somewhere in yourself as you waved, watching
your hand move rather than whoever it was you were greeting, and
you still waved that way even at five, so when you looked out the
back window of that tumbledown Saab and waved at me, it was as
though the summer's heart was breaking, and it was all I could do to
look at you and wave back.

Yes, I was sorry to see you go, and yes, I knew I would miss you.
Keep that in mind as the hard part of this letter comes.

And it's coming now.

First of all, I suspected then that the ways I would miss you were
self-centered and the kind of things I'd read about in novels rather
than felt in my heart and behind my eyes and along the surface of
my skin, where I wanted to feel them and wanted to mourn. So
since I was not sure I was grieving like I should, I tried to think of
you in the process, of being a small child transplanted, in the care of
his mother with his father half a country away, and I was astounded
that I could barely imagine it, even though something very much like
that had happened to me.

And so it became about me, Dominic. I went back to the
apartment and poured a long whiskey, knowing this was something
I could do freely now, without your mother cautioning me or at

least disapproving. *I figured I'd settle in; there was enough George Dickel in the bottle to keep me company till bedtime. He's a friend I promised your mother I'd set aside when you visit, and as far as I know, you've never met him.*

But there I was, Dominic, in a horrible 1970s-yellow easy chair, a glass of bourbon riding shotgun, and unprepared for the arrival that would follow. Because this was a day of magic. Most people mean something wonderful when they say that, because to them "enchantment" means the high road, something that makes you happy and better. But you've seen the movies. There's good enchantment and darker enchantment.

I received a manuscript in the mail that day. When I saw it, rolled like a newspaper in my mailbox, I was figuring it was a returned copy of Dacia—you know, the novel your old da wrote and dedicated to your ma—because I was already sending out chapters with no real end of the project in sight, but imagine my surprise when I saw the return address and, for the first and only time, the handwriting of an old friend's sister.

You are probably wondering what this has to do with you and me. And perhaps it is nothing more than things coming together in time—synchronicity, by which term I mean a significant convergence--one of those moments when an accident seems more important because of the whiskey and sorrow. But I opened the package as you and your mother drove down the Thruway toward Boston, and it took me a few seconds to realize that it wasn't mine, either.

It was all stories that belonged to this friend of mine, a man named Trajan Bell, who had passed away almost ten years earlier. I never even knew he did that kind of thing—wrote stories, I mean— so the whole manuscript came as a kind of surprise for me, and I was wondering why I'd received it. I had looked up to him a little for a while, back when I was a kid, younger that you'll be when you read this letter, but time had passed and I suppose I hadn't even thought of him in a while.

And now I was thinking of him again, brushing the condensation from the bourbon glass on the arm of my chair so I'd

have a place to prop the manuscript as I looked at it. I wasn't sure
how I felt about being singled out to receive his stories. It wasn't
like we were related and, when it came down to it, we really hadn't
been friends that long. But I sat down with the first one, and it was
like I knew the story already because I thought I knew one of the
characters.

I'm still not sure why I'm telling you this.

I found myself wondering what part of the story was fact and
what part biography, what part of it was all Trajan's imagining. I
mean, at the end of the story the boy flies away, for God's sake, but
I'm still wondering if it was the boy I knew, or based on the boy I
knew. And if it was…well, flying away doesn't seem that far out of
the question.

I set the story down, deciding not to start the next one because
it seemed too long. And for a moment the whiskeyed walls seemed
unbearably bright and close, as though the room had contracted.
They looked softer, too—the walls, that is—fleshy and supple, like
you could stick your hand through them—not that you'd want to,
because there was something smothering and yellowed in the rose
paper of the living room.

It felt like something had lodged in my throat and become
solid. For a moment I struggled for air.

And then my eyes shifted, and the room had settled back to
normal. Outside the sky was that flat gray I had come to expect
from a winter in upstate New York, and it's the gray I have seen in
Wisconsin ever since. There was a comfort in that dullness, and I
set the stories aside, not to pick them up until a couple of years later,
after the novel came out, and after a number of losses.

It's funny how people come back for you, Dominic. Sometimes
they've never left after all, but sometimes they've almost left, and
sometimes they've left entirely, but something in time or in your
thought calls them back. Maybe that's why some people call memory
"recall"—you think? Anyway, it didn't just happen with my Trajan
after all. Trajan Bell was named for the Roman emperor—one of
the good emperors in a sorry lot—and the story goes that a Pope (I
think it was Gregory the Great, but I'm not sure) admired the old

pagan, and wished that he could help him into Heaven.

Problem was that Trajan had been dead for years. He was probably somewhere down in Limbo, because that's where the good pagans were supposed to end up, according to what they thought in the Middle Ages. But at any rate, this Pope prayed long and hard for his rescue, Dominic, and even though your mother and Ben don't hold much stock in praying, remember that your Grandma does and as for your old Da, well, he's seen some strange things in his time, like apparitions and stories arriving on the day his son leaves him, and apparitions inside the stories themselves. It all makes him think that there's another whole world covered by the world we see and hear and feel, so that prayer may just be better than not praying.

And it was for this Pope and this Emperor. According to the story, Trajan did this one good deed that caught the eye of Gregory (I think it was). There was a poor widow whose innocent son had been murdered, and the Emperor stopped a military campaign in order to find and punish the killers. But it was the prayer, it was the words launched out into what you might think was nothing or nowhere, that was answered. Answered for Trajan, who like a soul at the Trump of Doom, came back to life, converted to the Christian faith, and started the long march through Purgatory toward Paradise.

I want you to forgive me, Dommie. Forgive me in the long march of my own. And all the Trajans in this story—forgive them as well.

Love,
Da

XXVI

The novel came out in 1985, not long before Gabriel's thirtieth birthday.

He sent the first copy to Jasmine in Boston. After all, he had dedicated *Dacia* to her. And though now the dedication might seem like a barb or at best an intrusion, she had been there when the world began to take shape, and Gabriel still felt that he owed it to her.

He called her to see if she'd received the author's copy. Ben answered the phone, and there was an uncomfortable territory of mutual congratulations, both of them wanting to mean their best wishes, while neither meant them altogether. Twice he asked to speak to Jasmine, but Ben had already read the book, evidently, and was prepared to comment.

History is written by the victors, someone said, and Ben Mountolive had won the girl. His observations, then, were mockery masked in kindness. Or that was the way Gabriel was hearing them. It was his first book, after all, Ben assured him, and first books are a testing ground for things that you might attempt later—why, even Ben himself had tested a number of things in his first book (which, of course, the implication went, was altogether different, being more an intellectual than a, shall we say, *popular* effort). Who knew? Perhaps there were things Gabriel had learned in writing *Dacia* that he could use later on, perhaps in something more literary. And, at any rate, Dominic would probably like the book, since after all, it was geared more to a reader his age, and even more since his father had written it.

Jasmine's voice was hushed when she took the phone at last. Gabriel missed the music of her laughter, and was surprised that he recalled it enough to miss it since he had not heard it in so long.

I don't really understand, she insisted. *I really don't know what to do with this.*

He suggested she should read it, but at once regretted the sly answer.

Who better, he asked her, to receive the dedication? Who was with him when it took shape?

I can think of a better one, she replied. *One who never left your side as you wrote the novel.*

Instantly the guilt crept over him. He recalled the nights at the desk, the tensor lamp trained over the bed, Jasmine asleep or studying in the adjoining bedroom, his foot rocking Dominic's cradle.

He told her she was right. That the next book would be Dominic's. That he would promise it.

There was a long pause on the other end of the phone. The line crackled, and he could hear faint music drift through the static, whether from Jasmine's house or from another call, momentarily brushing the edge of the silence.

Did you think I meant Dom? she asked, and it would be hours before he knew for sure what she meant.

***

Like any beginning novelist, he clipped the reviews. His agent, Barry Green, reassured him that any attention was good attention, that there was enough praise to make readers want to read him again. But the reception was a time to go into hiding, to lick his wounds: the sales indicated that no book tour was in the offing, and what was left for Gabriel was the simple question that everyone asks of a novelist in a commercial field: "What will you do for me next?"

***

From Nexus Magazine: Spring 1985

Reviewed In Short: *Dacia*, by Gabriel Rackett

Gabriel Rackett has to bear the most apocalyptic name of any young writer in the field of speculative fiction. And his first novel, *Dacia*, released in February by Wizardry Press, lives up to the name.

At least partially.

Dacia is the story of Jack Maze, a typical "likely lad" of heroic fantasy, a young man who inhabits a gloomy funereal land reminiscent of Gene Wolfe's Necropolis in Book of the New Sun. And indeed, the first section of the novel, in which Jack begins to receive hints, in bits and snatches, of his former life, is suitably strange and evocative, as Rackett paints a desperately gothic landscape, complete with mysterious epitaphs, crumbled angels, and the rustle of rats in opened cenotaphs. Intermingled with these scenes straight out of the 18th century Novel of Terror, there are striking descriptions of abandoned machinery, apparently left from a more technologically advanced civilization, tantalizing to any reader of "end-of-the-world" fantasy and just as unreadable as the worn inscriptions on the graves.

Jack is, it seems, a reader of fragments. Wading through the evidence, he comes to understand that somewhere, in the sunlit high ground of the island of Dacia—which seems to be a kind of icy mountain rising out of the sea—lies a plateau of ruins, wherein lies the castle of the King of Dacia, long thought to be a mythical or fanciful figure. The King's daughter, apparently, has come of marriageable age, and her father has sent out a call for suitors. Jack, along with his brothers Orlando and Valentine, take up the call, and we have a story that follows the simple, evocative patterns of fairy tale, as Rackett brings changes to the princess who waits atop a slippery, glassy mountain.

Two ruinous landscapes—the necropolis at the foot of the mountain and the capital city atop it-- seem a little excessive, even if the second one is sunny and beautiful to contrast with the gloom of the first. But Rackett is a kind of phantasmal poet, and even though the poetry gets a little overgrown at times, it is good enough to earn our trust and forgiveness, and by the second part of the book, we are ready for that moment in the narrative where things begin to move with purpose and speed, where we are drawn not only by the characters and the setting but by the story.

Unfortunately, it doesn't happen. Jack himself says to his brother Orlando (a hugely entertaining character of Rackett's, whose talent at throwing objects is used for comic and even heroic effects) that "everyone's story is a quest." Well, Orlando is not satisfied in this, and neither are we: do we have to read another quest story, when Tolkien, Leguin, and Terry Brooks have done it well and often? Is this going to be another Arthurian romance, exchanging armor for the tattered cloaks and monk's cowls of the Gothic?

It's true enough that Rackett's Jack discovers what he wants to discover (are we in any way surprised?) and then returns to his gloomy home to complete his journey. The return could have been a nice touch, a kind of "Orpheus in the Underworld" conclusion, were it not for the fact that Rackett doesn't seem to know how to resolve the quest— the courtship of the girl is resolved as you would think it would be, but the middle of the novel spans five years in a paragraph, and Rackett sets us off on another, apparently more important quest involving larger and darker questions about the ghosts who inhabit the foothills of the mountain. In short, the book leaves so many things hanging that you begin to wonder if Rackett doesn't have a sequel in mind.

But ultimately, a good fantasy novel sets us off on a gripping story, with a beginning, middle, and end; Rackett's first effort, though promising (I understand he's barely thirty, so he should have other books in him), leaves us somewhere in a gloomy middle ground, between the sunlit heights and the darkened shores. And is this any place to leave us?

All in all, that is *Dacia* in a nutshell: An elaborate, eccentric book, splendid in some ways but maddening in its fragmentation, obscurity, and slow-moving plot. Had this young novelist allowed his work to season for a while, he would be standing at the threshold of a notable career as a fantasist. As it is, he has yet to cross into genuine artistry.

∗∗∗

From Fantasy Now: Summer 1985
Dacia: Raising a Rackett

My gaming group was looking for a new world we could set our campaign in, and when I saw a copy of *Dacia*, by Gabriel Rackett, on the shelf at Walden's, it looked like a plan. Cool cover, cool copy on the back—everything that would lead you to believe that here was a source for the long-suffering gamer, tired of Tolkien and the traditional dungeon crawl.

Let's face it, fans: those kinds of books are few and far between, when all is said and done. Some of the ideas in *Dacia* were really good—the whole sloping world and the home country between shadow and light, well I liked all that. But so many things bothered me that, even though Dacia would be an OK place to set a campaign, it isn't so hot to read about.

Dacia is the story of Jack Maze, who lives in some kind of tiered island cemetery (I suppose that's how you could characterize it, because for all his love of description, Rackett is cloudy on the details). We get a kind of Boris Karloff setting, but somehow a little more sad than frightening. It's like it's trying to be *Blade Runner* but without the cool menace.

Well, things move slowly in *Dacia*, almost at a glacial pace (no pun intended—after all, a mountain of ice figures strongly in the story). The description is really lush but really loose, and Rackett goes on and on about shadows and things following the central character, Jack Maze, and his brothers Orlando and Valentine as they leave their cemetery and head up toward a princess in a sunlit kingdom that Valentine seems to sense by visions, as he hoods his eyes to suppress his earthly sight. How he does this exactly was never too clear, so how it could translate into gaming terms becomes pretty near impossible.

XXVII

Joey Hardy died in October of '90, not far from Gabriel, in Chicago. Gabriel was the last of Joey's friends to see him, because the partner nobody really knew was dead already, and the Hardys were still estranged and down in Louisville. On that last visit, Joey gave Gabriel a trust—an envelope that rattled mysteriously as Gabriel took it from his friend's hands, promising to bring it to the Hardys.

He never delivered the letter. It was Christmas of '92 before he even tried to return it, carrying it heavy back to August Acres, because now Gabriel Rackett was the only one to have survived his past.

It was early '89 when the tests came back positive. Gabriel hadn't heard from Joey in five years, and in the reunion phone call, he found out first that someone named Nathan had passed away. Nathan, it seemed, was the lover or the partner that Gabriel never met, fashioned out of smoke and air in a single conversation, so that Gabriel wondered what the man was really like, was mildly glad he had never met Nathan. Joey's description conjured some country of mature sex and of all the stereotyped leather bars and outlandish parades that Gabriel had come to associate, however wrongly, with preferences like those of his friend.

But it wasn't like that. Joey said they had met in a bookstore, both reaching for what he told me was "the remaining copy of *Dacia.*" Gabriel said that he figured most of them were remaining or remaindered, and when Joey snickered, it was the old Joey laugh, and twenty-five years dropped away in the pauses on the phone line, and with them the new and menacing images. It was like for a moment they were back together in the fields north of Gethsemane Lane, and the summer and the smell of blacktop poured over the rattle of locusts.

"Gabey," he said, and Gabriel wondered if anyone had ever called him that, and let it slide because it was old times again, because Joey was wounded and mournful. "Gabey, Nathan was a fan of your kind of books—"

It was another thing Gabriel let slide.

And Joey told him he had gone there to buy *Dacia* just because Gabriel had written it, and Gabriel let that slide, too, as Joey went on about this invisible man who had been so important to him, someone Gabriel had not known nor known about, but only guessed at because he imagined he must be…

Nathan, it seemed, was amazed that the second brother, archer nonpareil and wit and perhaps the most conventional fantasy character in the book, was based upon his new acquaintance. Joey asked Gabriel in that phone call to come clean: "Am I really Valentine?" and since it seemed so important to Joey, Gabriel had to say that yes he was. It struck him then what one of his writing instructors—perhaps even Athena Bumpas, for God's sake—had said about making friends and relatives into characters in your fiction. That they recognize themselves in characters you'd never intended would resemble them, while they miss themselves in the ones you'd drawn from their example.

Well, all along Nathan and Joey had been in Chicago, it seems, on the North Side near the Art Institute and the Brentano's where they met, and Joey said that, a few months after this meeting in the fantasy shelves, they had moved in together.

Nathan had found out he was HIV positive about a year after that, so Joey watched a long disease and dying and death for four years, before something told him to pick up the phone and he called. It seems that pasts catch up with presents no matter how and where you turn, and Nathan was a few years older than Gabriel and Joey, and had spent the seventies and early eighties in the ways a lot of people his age had spent them. It just never occurred to Gabriel that Joey was telling him more than his mourning for his companion.

Never occurred, that is, until Joey told him about his own tests, and suggested that Gabriel might like to visit sometime.

Sometime maybe really soon.

It did not turn out like they both feared, and yet Gabriel was glad he went to see Joey when he did, at a time when the drugs could let him resemble the old Joey for a while, and he hadn't reached that point where the talk was all of AZT and T-cells, where he had become named by the disease rather than someone who happened to suffer from it.

The hospice was a renovated motel north of Chicago and not far off I-94. Joey's directions to the place were perfect. It was a squat series of out buildings, something from the more dismal end of the 1950s. Joey had his own room there, and an earnest little attendant who was there in the room when Gabriel arrived, and reluctant to leave off spreading cheer even when he motioned her, with some impatience, out of the room.

He had not thought Gabriel would come, he said.

And Gabriel caught himself thinking that he was surprised as well. But then there was no reason he should stay away.

Joey's blinds were half-closed against the sun, and dust motes hovered in the slatted light. The friends talked about old times, each of them dreading that moment when all recollections arrived in this narrow, airless room, and reminiscence came back to the here and now. Both wondered if they would have anything to say then.

Joey brought up that night when they passed through desolate fields on our way to the Country Ball Room. He made clear what Gabriel had suspected for years, that their trip to the dance had followed in the wake of heartbreak.

Aron, it seemed, had been experimental with more than his music.

It wasn't long, of course, before Joey's parents found out. Or they found out enough to float their son off to a private Baptist school several miles from Jeff, a new one tacked on to the old Gethsemane Church. There he would study the basics that students were supposed to be getting back to at that time in the 1970s. He would study the Bible as well. He would turn out right.

But Joey remembered little beyond the windows in Cedron Academy. How, by late autumn when the trees were bare you could see not only Gethsemane Lane, but also the field beyond it, the construction equipment and the creek and the golf course. By Joey's second year, Billy Hume—the one Gabriel's mother betrayed her son for—was teaching science there, or what resembled science in that strapped and fundamentalist place. He was typical for what passed for instruction there, and Joey and Gabriel had a laugh over him until Joey began coughing and wheezing, and Gabriel stepped to the door to call the attendant over his old friend's protests.

The girl came back with nothing more than a blanket to place over Joey's hunched shoulders. Gabriel could have done that much himself: the fact that Joey's care was not so special felt like a kind of surrender.

On the other hand, Joey was oblivious to the whole transaction. His thoughts skimmed hungrily over a fragmentary past, as though if he looked long enough, he would find a cure.

Cedron Bible Academy, Joey said, was the slow death of him. He said you could tell when a place was designed to clamp down on you by its colors, the grays and browns that define its contours and its limits. Through that window, he said, the whole world contracted and entered a still, climate-controlled room, and your thoughts beat against the glass like a trapped fly struggling for sunlight and air.

He brushed over the image lightly.

"Sometimes, Gabey," he murmured. "You could see things down in that field. You of all people know what I mean."

Gabriel didn't know. At least not for sure. And it was always disconcerting to be singled out as *the one who knew,* of all people. But he knew that field, remembered his journeys over it on winter days and summer nights. He nodded, encouraged the story.

"One afternoon," Joey said, "It was overcast." He looked over his shoulder at the attendant, who noticed, smiled and left the room.

"One afternoon, Gabriel," he continued. "Must have been that winter when you took up with Toshiko Collins."

"I didn't know you knew her, Joey."

Joey wrapped the blanket tightly around himself. He looked out the window of his room. From where Gabriel sat, a gray and baffled light filled the frame.

"Knew her to see her. To say hello. And yeah, I could see what you saw in her." He winked, and for a moment it felt like August Acres, and 1968, and looking forward to prodigies, to autumns that had already passed and led into decades that, in turn, led them to this room. It was like they were waiting for Del again, or for Trajan, and for a world that was a maze and abundance of prospects.

"But this is about that winter, Gabriel. And one overcast morning. And looking out a window onto the construction site."

Gabriel leaned forward in his chair. "Go on."

"You know how it gets by the creek. How the fog comes in and settles. How it all seems to make a place between your mind and body, between what you see and what you hear as well."

"I know what you mean, Joey. Or I think I do."

"Fog can be a stopping-off place, Gabey. The halfway house where things come to call."

Gabriel shifted uncomfortably. "How do you mean?"

"I mean there was this time, Gabey. I was looking out the window, and there was a fog settled on that field."

Gabriel nodded. Something in him knew where this was headed.

Joey's fingers, pale and netted with blue, kneaded the hem of the blanket. "It was one of those times, you know, when the world outside of the window makes you miss the childhood you are barely out of. It's a kind of nostalgia you shouldn't be having so young.

"But there you are. You know that a time has passed, and you know that Cedron Bible Academy is closer to the way things are going to be, so you miss things already...."

"The fog, Joey. About the fog."

"Well, it isn't the fog, Gabey. It's about what I seen in the fog, you know. It's all about your buddy Trajan."

Gabriel turned to his old friend, his attentions suddenly re-arranged. On the chair, swallowed by a baby-blue blanket, Joey looked diminished, almost papery, the hint of a bruise on the bridge of his nose.

Gabriel knew his old friend hadn't much time.

"Did you ever wonder, Gabey...why Trajan took up with you? I mean, instead of trying to take up with me?"

"You were involved with Zuice, Joey. And with music that he didn't understand or even like very much. You were..."

Joey hunched into the blanket, hooded himself against the light. "Oh, you know what I mean, Gabriel. Haven't you ever wondered?"

Gabriel looked out the window. "I know what you mean. And, no, I've never wondered. You just weren't interested in the things that Trajan knew about. And it was about nothing more than that. Really, it wasn't.

"But why do you ask, Joey? Why did you bring him up, after all this time?"

"Because that fog on the field was about him, Gabriel. And I didn't warn you then. And now...well, it's been years, and here you are sitting by me, alive and well and, as far as I can tell, not damaged. Are you, Gabey? Are you?"

Gabriel blinked. "No, Joey. Not at all. At...at least not in the way you're thinking."

'Are you sure? Well, then. That's good. That's good, Gabey. I only knew him through you, mind you. But the fog on the field. It had everything to do with him."

It was as though the noise outside condensed into silence. Joey worried the edge of the blanket between two pale fingers.

"You know," he said, "how shapes come at you in the fog. How the center of them is solid and dark and…and defined, Gabey. But how the borders of them aren't? Well, there was something I saw, out in that field in the middle of the fog. And it was just the opposite. Like a dark border circling around light. So unexpected. When that happens, you pay attention.

"It was foggy that night you and I sneaked out to the Center to hear Aron play, remember? But this was different, Gabriel. That kind of sunstruck fog that dazzles you, you know?"

Gabriel nodded. He didn't expect Joey to have the poet in him, but there was something in the anguish of this room that lent itself to a dark imagining, the whiff of poetry mingling with the alcohol, the chlorine, the bleak amazement. "Yes, I know, Joey," he replied, aware that his friend was edging to the brink of telling him something.

"Are you *sure*, Gabey? Are you *sure* you came out of those years all right? Because…I should have told you what I saw in that field, on that day. The not telling might have put you in danger, Gabey. But you would have thought I was crazy, I figured, like you thought that night when we peeked in the Community Center, so I held my words."

"It's all right, Joey. Whatever it is, I was undamaged. So tell me"

It was like coaxing a barb from a wound. Something in Joey balked at the telling, even now, when the cramped quarters of a renovated motel, the closeness of the air, the still slant of light through the blinds—all were saying, *this is your last place, Joey Hardy, the place where you'll make your peace with the receding world*. And Joey knew it, and he knew Gabriel knew it as well, and still he was reluctant.

"Why not, Joey?"

The sunken eyes looked toward the light. "Because if you don't believe me, I'll know it. And it will raise the question whether I remember it at all, or whether it's a memory I'm making out of this place and medicine and…"

"Tell me," Gabriel urged. "You may be surprised at what I'll believe."

It was like that day years ago, when he stopped to listen to secrets, to hear of snowstorms and a vanished love he understood at last. But Joey's story was altogether different, and the slow drip of a faucet in the bathroom marked the only sound other than Joey's voice, as recollection built on recollection, and the room seemed to fade into dazzlement and mist.

***

What Joey had seen was the Queen of the Ghosts at first.

A moment when the fog solidified, the light became movement and substance and wing, and even in retelling the story, Joey marveled that it was the first time he had seen an owl—bright wings of mist over the more solid wings of the bird, and below them a third pair in shadows. Six wings, like in the hymn.

"And then it swooped, Gabey," he continued. "A long dive, like it had seen its prey somewhere in the high dry grass and the fog. It skimmed the ground, skidded and staggered, and then it was like it began to run, Gabey. It lurched along and it staggered like a wounded thing, and it seemed to grow as it ran. It looked like a man, then, like a man in a long pale coat, hobbling across the field, crouching and weaving through the still machinery so that you would have thought it was looking for cover from something—from my eyes, perhaps, or simply from the sun.

"Gabey. The owl looked like a man now. Like a fugitive in a long duster coat. And I had to own up that I had seen him before. In the Bell's back yard."

Gabriel drew in his breath sharply. "Yes. On Halloween."

"Yes, and not only then and there. On that day at the ball field, when Del…"

Their eyes met. For a moment the two old friends stared at each other, struck by the secret that each had guarded from the other for years. Gabriel thought to tell him about it all then—how he had glimpsed the man himself on the vine-covered incline in front of the Bell house, in a window once on the way back from Toshiko Collins' house, in a strange dark convergence of pylons near an overgrown path from the Rochester River Campus to the housing where he and Jazz had spent one unhappy year. And finally, perhaps most menacingly, in the pages of the manuscript lying back in his Lake Geneva apartment, as a character in a story that Trajan had written but never completed, an ominous presence that his old friend had dwelt with and somehow understood.

But there was more. Joey looked at him insistently, drawing the blanket to his chin.

"Yes? Yes, Joey?"

"And then it became Trajan, Gabey. I saw the man go down into the creek bed, and for a moment I lost sight of him in the fog and the dried branches. Then he climbed back up the far side of the bank, and I knew him by that shock of hair, by the way he stood up against the brush."

The room was completely still. Out by the road, the cars had vanished, and the dripping faucet had lost its water for good.

"What do you mean 'it became Trajan'? You mean the October—the man in the pale coat—he became Trajan Bell?"

"I think it was more, Gabey. I think he was Trajan all along."

✳✳✳

He could have argued it with Joey. Argued that the pale man, the October revenant, was in no way and in no fashion the same as the man who had baptized him into small mysteries and left him a book of poems, a brace of letters, and finally, a manuscript sitting like a specter in his rooms.

But it all seemed past argument now, as Gabriel backed the car out of the parking spot and Joey watched him from the door. *I'll see ya soon*, Gabriel had offered, and his old friend nodded, and the truth was another specter between them, a shadow lodged in the bright foreboding of an Illinois autumn afternoon.

XXVIII

"Honestly, this was not my idea."

Jasmine sounded strained, her voice thin and intermittent on the phone, as though she was turning from the receiver and back again.

Mountolive, it seemed, had decided at the last moment to attend a convention in Washington. Gabriel made a lame joke about the event—something about when you got that many Jungians together, you couldn't avoid a collective unconscious—but Jazzie wasn't laughing. He could tell from the pauses and distances there was stress at home, and the kinder part of him warred with the smaller, meaner part that delighted in the Mountolives' discord.

Dominic, it seemed, had been in the pits of sulking, his holiday wasting toward a handful of days in a Washington hotel. At the last moment the boy had thrown an Irish tantrum, and Gabriel could hear him at it in the background, his voice cracking, wrapping around Ben's lower, insistent tones, the counselor and his hysteric at a baffled distance. Suddenly Gabriel caught a glimpse of what daily life might be like for Dominic, and he wished he had seen more attentively to things.

"Of course, Jazz," he replied. He could hear her sigh, and knew that even through divorce and distance, he could lift her burdens. "I wanted Dom for the holidays to begin with, remember? His gramma will enjoy seeing him…"

That last was a kindly lie. They both knew Mary Lull was perplexed by any child who did not give her center stage.

Gabriel and Jasmine determined that he would meet the boy at O'Hare airport, would shepherd his son between connecting flights. But as it turned out, no seats were available on Gabriel's flight from Chicago to Louisville, so Gabriel decided to drive to the airport, meet Dominic, and drive the rest of the way. It was a chance to re-acquaint, he supposed, but the drive gave him time to think.

There was a mystery back home, and he was headed for it. At first he had thought it was good to face it all down—August Acres, the apparitions, Trajan and the losses—and that to face it down he had to fly solo, to be John Wayne in the midst of shadows. Then, when it turned out Dominic would accompany him, Gabriel's first thoughts were those of a kind of relief and circularity; that his boy would be there to pick up the story, that he would have a sidekick and companion in the dark.

But soon he called those thoughts into question, unnerved by the possible danger.

So he decided on a holiday, instead, and on transactions. His mother would have him sign some papers for her—why it had been necessary to have him present at the signing, like some feudal vassal, he had yet to figure out, but the visit seemed safe enough now that the ghosts were no longer part of their destination. He would pretend they weren't there, and yet even this prospect seemed unfair to his son, for bringing the boy into unfamiliar territory—to a landscape as alien as the barren face of the moon—seemed like a violation of a bond father and son had yet to forge, and Gabriel worried that taking Dominic along was making the son a refugee in the father's dry country.

And yet, upon reaching the arrival gate, he was glad he was doing it.

There was a heightened sense of peril these days in traveling—you passed through electronic surveillance, your luggage x-rayed by attendants as though it was a kind of physical exam to indicate your worthiness to fly. It slowed things down, for sure, and Gabriel must have drawn the attention of security, as his increasing nervousness at being late could have been taken for something more profound and menacing, given a guard with issues.

Dominic, in fact, had been waiting half an hour when Gabriel arrived, a slight dark figure in sagging pants and a flannel shirt, feet propped on a duffle bag, reading a Dragonlance novel. His hug for his father was brief and awkward, but the smile seemed genuine, and the boy was not nearly as surly and reticent as most teenagers in the days of Nirvana and Pearl Jam.

He is like boys were in my time, Gabriel thought, as they merged onto I-90, headed for Chicago and south. Dominic slouched in the passenger seat, feet propped on the dashboard, fiddling with the radio dial since his old man's cassette tapes were woefully back in the day. Gabriel's rather weak joke that you could smell Gary, Indiana even with the car windows closed was met by Dominic's question as to who was Gary Indiana.

And so it continued until they had reached the windswept corridor north of Indianapolis and Gabriel tried again.

"You know I came this way a few Decembers ago," he said, "when the temperature was 60 below."

Dominic regarded him cautiously. "For real?"

The boy's eyes were his mother's, dark and vital. Gabriel looked away.

"Damn right, for real. I was with this artist friend of mine."

"Laurent Morel?" Dominic asked, surprising him. Morel was the cover artist for Dacia; Gabriel had never met the man. Still, it was a sign that Dominic knew something that could strike them a common ground.

"Naw. This was a big old guy from the Fine Arts Department where I teach. It was a strange trip, because he was talking about places being a focus of strong passion—of energy,

341

usually negative, that gathered when something ill-willed gets…
frustrated or thwarted, emerging in another place, in a surprising
fashion. And it was like the weather suggested a god was angry.
It was so cold out there, Dominic, that we were afraid the roads
might become impassable, that the car might freeze over before
we could get to shelter."

"Weather like that could kill ya," Dominic announced,
punching the radio buttons again.

"That's what we decided. So I told this guy that if the car
stalled…I was cutting him open and climbing inside him to stay
alive."

"Heh."

"Well, it felt like a prospect at the time."

Dominic looked out the window. "How cold you figure
it is out there now?" he asked, and they both laughed as a cold
wind shuddered the car and the sun broke from a dark bank of
clouds.

Dominic Rackett was taken with *Dacia*. As the car approached
Indianapolis his questions began, and Gabriel began to second-
guess himself. Dominic asked uncomfortable questions—why
a character did this when he had done this before, and why in
one scene Valentine was left-handed and in another favored his
right. Dominic's was a novelist's mind, like Gabriel wished he
had, especially since he had turned out to write novels.

Or a novel, for that matter.

As Gabriel's old Chevy cruised south on I-65, the wind
whipped over the road from west to east, and the car rocked
and tremored. Dom quizzed him about the book, and Gabriel
wondered. Here he was, pushing forty and for all intents no
closer to a second book that he had been when Dacia was released
those years ago. Had the novel been something other than the
heart's and imagination's impulse, the story he was bound to tell?
Had it been, instead, a refuge and hideaway from those things he

would have been better off facing—the staggering marriage, the unanswered memories, the strange sense of diminishment that traveled with him, no matter where he was going?

That sense of diminishment sat in the back seat of the Chevy, a kind of haze behind them as Gabriel and Dominic swept past Indianapolis and into the greener, more rolling landscape of southern Indiana. As the hills rose on either side of the road, Gabriel, to his own surprise, opened up about Trajan Bell and the childhood toward which the car was sailing. All of the stories spilled forth, and Gabriel felt like he was rehearsing them for something larger, though he could imagine nothing larger than passing this strange legacy on to his son. And yet, despite himself, he began to wonder if Dominic found it all boring and silly. And then, as he had always done for his freshman students, he began to interpret for the boy.

"So Trajan was like…this wise old man, Dom. Though I guess he was younger at that time than I am now, so he hardly qualified as some bearded gent on the mountaintop. He helped me understand a lot of things. How to interpret. How nature ran deeper than I had ever imagined. How there was a power around me that was not my own, but something that…that moved around and through me. And that it was my job to catch hold of that power. To ride it toward wherever it designed to take me. Do you understand?"

Dominic had fallen into silence in the passenger's seat. Now, his eyes on the road ahead, he answered calmly.

"Yeah, Pops, I understand. But it's not too interesting. Tell me the stories, instead. Tell me about that owl you mentioned, and about Artie and the great snow."

Gabriel had almost come to the last of the stories, the bizarre end of Trajan Bell in the corridors of OLS, when the road markers signaled the approach to Louisville. Soon the skyline emerged on the southern horizon, gray and lit fitfully in reds and greens, as though the city were approximating the holidays rather than celebrating them. Gabriel shifted in the driver's seat.

"So you haven't seen your Grandma in some time, Dom."

"I know," the boy agreed, nose pressed against the window in the gesture of a much younger child as the scaffolding on the bridge raced by them and, rounding the curve that took them by Louisville's hospitals, they sped on south through the city and into the outlying suburbs. "I see Grandma Bowers all the time, and there isn't a Grandma Mountolive any more, so I only have the two of them left."

Gabriel hunched behind the wheel and watched for the exit. He was glad that Ben's mother had found grandmother stature, he told himself. He told himself that it never hurt a child to have another grandparent who loved him, as he guided the car sullenly over the ramp and onto the last leg of the journey to Mary Rackett's...

To Mary Rackett Lull's, that is.

Dominic noticed it first as the old car bumped and hissed up Flora. "These places, Pops. They're kinda small, aren't they?"

Gabriel had to agree. And there was a certain sadness as well, he noticed, in the drab arrays of Christmas lights—some simply a string over leaf-clogged gutters, others a gaudy mixture of Santa's elves and adoring shepherds.

"We used to say," he observed to Dom as they made the last turn onto August Street, "that the sure sign of white trash was if your Christmas lights were still up and burning in March."

Dominic regarded him quizzically, and Gabriel suspected his son had never heard the term. Or if he had, it had been only applied, perhaps, to the man who steered him into Mary Lull's driveway and opened the trunk as the boy moped toward the back door and the welcomes of a grandmother who scarcely knew or regarded him.

Mary Lull's house was a watermark of holiday indifference. The festive, children's side of Christmas and Easter had always been subordinate to the Mass, and Gabriel could see that nothing had changed, not really, since he left those years ago. A bedraggled, two-foot high Christmas tree, bristling with artificial snow, perched on a small pyramid of packages. Gabriel and Dominic added their gifts to the pile, and the family settled in the living room.

Gabriel remembered this desperation of presents, now muted some by the kindly presence of Andy Lull, who seemed to have mastered the art of giving Mary center stage. The packages torn open, the four of them sat in the living room, as Gabriel received the neighborhood news, filtered and inflated through the dramatics of his mother.

After some years, the Hardys had moved, she told them. After several stagy glances at Dominic—like she was holding something back and mulling the telling—she mentioned Joey's illness, and when Gabriel assured her he knew, and yes, had visited his old friend in the last days, she said that she hoped Gabriel hadn't gotten too close to the bedside, considering how that ailment spread and all.

Before he could argue the fine points of AIDS and contagion, his mother had shifted ground again. The Bell place had been sold. She heard it was to a young couple from Ohio, both of whom would work civilian positions at Fort Knox, a few miles down the old Dixie Highway. Before she veered into the gossip about the new occupants, Gabriel returned her to the house itself, questioning her intently as Andy brought coffee from the kitchen.

"The older sister seemed rather nice, surprisingly," Mary observed, lading the coffee with yet another packet of sweetener. "Sophia was her name, I'm forgetting the last name, but of course it isn't Bell since she's been married and all. Well, she's taken away most of the belongings, and 'tis high time because that empty house has been stored with things from the '70s and I can't help but thinking that, after all those years, it must of been a fire hazard and a peril to the neighborhood."

Gabriel nodded. There was no urging her to a more rapid, less roundabout pace.

"They're moving the rest at the New Year's, and it's after

that when the young couple brings their own belongings. You know, Gabey, 'tis a shame there'll be no young boys on their bicycles, stationed out on August as a welcoming band, like there would have been back in your day."

Dominic looked at his father slyly, masking a grin.

Gabriel winked at the boy, then stood and walked to the window. Across the street, defined in the crisp gray afternoon air of a wintry mid-South, the house took on a kind of certain ordinariness, green shutters faded by almost a quarter century's neglect, the one by Trajan's darkened window dangling from a single hinge.

He turned to find his son looking at him, as Mary rattled on about other, unfamiliar neighbors. Andy Lull, her attentive and doting audience, nodded eagerly and delightedly at the stories he must have already heard.

✳✳✳

Gabriel surprised Dominic in the midst of childhood belongings.

Leaving the table early during a lackluster dinner, the boy had descended to the basement, and when Gabriel followed, he found his son nosing through a footlocker, the old Lord of the Rings poster spread out before him, fractured plastic model statues of Frankenstein and the Wolf Man pinning down its corners.

"God, Pops, you were a geek back in the day," Dominic observed merrily, lifting aloft a rubber-banded stack of baseball cards. "This is the only thing in the chest that wouldn't get your ass kicked for nerdiness at my school."

"Kind of old school, wasn't I?" Gabriel asked.

"No, Pops. You aren't cool enough for old school."

Gabriel stood over the boy, absorbing the comment. Thumbing through the baseball cards, Dominic looked up at him at last.

"We're goin' over there, aren't we?"

"Over where, Dom?"

"That house across the street. The one you and Grandma were talking about."

"You're a pretty smart boy, Dominic. But we can't go in there, you know, and it's useless to patrol the yard and look in the windows. Even a little creepy, when it comes down to it."

Dominic looked down at the poster. "What is this? Somethin you did yourself?"

"Oh, hardly. That's the old Barbara Remington poster. Was on The Fellowship of the Ring when it first came out."

"They didn't have good artists back then? I mean, there was the classical ones like Rembrandt and stuff, but dang."

Gabriel laughed. "I don't go back to Rembrandt, Dom."

The boy chuckled. "I didn't mean it that way. It's just...but it isn't important. So why not?"

"Why not...."

"Go over there. Visit that house you're thinking about."

"It isn't that simple, Dominic. It's...."

And he stopped, baffled by why it wasn't that simple.

Gabriel had started the trip south with mysteries in mind. And then, for the sake of the boy sprawled on his old basement floor amid childhood keepsakes of thirty years past, he had set it aside—the whole deep purpose of the journey home, the quest and the search for the last of Trajan Bell.

Only to have Dominic bring it back to him. Indeed, to encourage the mysteries. It all seemed plotted in that old way of dreams and myths, where the hero sets out on the journey and along the way to his destination—dragon or princess or Holy Grail—meets a number of Helpers. Wise old man, talking animals, and here, past Gabriel's imagination, was the Divine Child of his own engendering. He had listened to Petasos well enough to know: the Divine Child came to the hero, not always as a child, but sometimes as an elf, or an animal, a wandering ne'er-do-well or a suddenly discovered jewel. In whatever form the child sees light, he represents the childlike forces in our lives. When part of our consciousness appears too one-sided, he appears on the road or sprawled over maps and monsters and posters, anticipating the achievement of wholeness. The Divine Child represents our creativity, our inherent genius.

Or then, quite simply, Gabriel Rackett might be on the edge of corrupting his only begotten son.

"I never broke into a place before, Pops," Dominic urged, his stage whisper just the right combination of menace and comedy.

"Nor are you starting now."

"You sound like Dr. Mountolive, Pops."

Gabriel crouched conspiratorially by his son. "That's what you call Ben?"

Dominic thumbed the neck rivets on Frankenstein's Monster. "This isn't a Frankenstein, right?"

"Right. Frankenstein's the guy who made him."

"But you made this one, right, Pops?"

"I...I beg your pardon?"

Dominic lifted the model to the light. "You didn't paint it too well, Pops. You must have been just a kid."

Now Gabriel sat on the floor by the boy. "Eleven or twelve," he said. "I don't make too many monsters these days."

Dominic laughed. "Naaah. Just books you make, right?"

And then, into the embarrassed silence, the boy made the offer again.

"I say we go over there. There are good stories over there for the having, Pops. And you're the kind of guy to tell them, and you know I'm right."

***

The discussion, of course, did not end there. Into the hours of the 24th it went, Gabriel resisting, Dominic insisting, as the boy's inclination for mischief gradually mastered his father's wavering sense of what was proper after all.

Christmas Eve progressed at a slow, almost monotonous pace. Dominic spent the day in front of the ancient Lull television, watching as the seasonal phantoms fluttered on the screen. He felt like he was awakening to something, and though the day was sleepy and the dust motes climbed hypnotically the sunstruck picture window in his grandmother's living room, Dominic was attentive to the hush around him.

Perhaps it had been wishful thinking. Perhaps a teenaged sense of the dramatic and of adventure. But the night before, he had risen from the sofa that the Lulls had set up for his makeshift bed and crept to the window above the television. Looking out over August Way, he marked the strange incline leading up to the Bell House. It almost seemed to him that someone had decked the ramp for the holiday, that some kind of ivy or vine had entangled the railing.

Somehow, it appeared that the light from the streetlamp was spilling onto the northmost window of the little house. It looked to impressionable eyes—to the imaginings of a boy who was schooled on heroic fantasy and his father's childhood stories—as though a light in the house was on, though Dominic's grandmother had assured them that Trajan's surviving sister was clearing the house for the new residents, that the power and water had been shut off accordingly.   And yet he wanted there to be a light—a light and a mystery—and the prospect had kept him up until late hours.

But now it was afternoon, and Andy Lull clattered in the kitchen, as Mary napped and, hidden behind the half-closed door of his childhood room, his father was at work on something. Passing down the hall and headed toward the basement again, Dominic could not help but look in the room, where he saw Gabriel at the typewriter, typing paper and legal pads spread over the desk, a manuscript of yellowed pages littered on the bed, as though he was putting together a complex and incomplete puzzle.

For some reason he would remember the colors later on. The yellow and white sheets cast together in the room, and a neater pile of yellowed typescript, clamped together on the desk, as though the color in them was a convergence of all the words his father had gathered in the room. Later, when all the papers were gathered together, he looked at them long and hard, as though that would be his contribution, would be all of his part.

12/24

Dear Jazzie,

I know you will be thinking that this letter should go to Dominic. I know as well that Ben is probably looking over your shoulder as you read this—hello, Ben—part of him curious, as his line of work makes him curious, and part of him past simple, mild irritation and into justifiable husband's anger.

It is you, however, that I have to tell, because I believe I won't be talking to you for a while after this, though nothing about these letters and our last several years has ever been certain. You always said I sacrificed the truth to the poetry, Jazz, but of course for me, the truth was the poetry, so if I make ominous sounds about departures... well, part of it is because it's time for those sounds, it's that point in the story.

I have almost finished one thing. I have another thing after it to finish. Dominic will understand what I am talking about—if not right away, then at some time up the road, when all the surety of youth catches up to the fact that life is really complex; when he starts giving up the contradictions, mysteries, and doubts for some irritable reaching after fact and reason.

Then he'll cut through the shadows of this letter, and he will be able to explain it to you.

At least I hope he will. I hope he doesn't grow up dining on shadows, like his old man.

Whatever comes to pass, he'll be returning with papers. You'll get the rest after the holidays, including a story about a Civil War reunion that has occupied me for years—I suppose "occupy" is the best word. I didn't know I was doing this, or I'd have brought them all with me. Between the two of you, you can decide what to do with them. I'm finished, and though I'm not sorted, my hands are clean.

Love,

Gabriel

Lark
A Story by Trajan Bell

1.

He was early by his reckoning. And he hoped that, for once, his reckoning was right.

As his driver, General, steered the shay down Broadway, mindful of the tilt and tremor of the little carriage, Tom Lark leaned back, told himself to be calm.

After all, she would not leave the station without him.

She had no place to go, if you thought about it.

Already traffic, by carriage and by foot, was crossing the wide street to the Grand Hotel, closest to the terminal. The streets were bedraggled, almost sad, the banners draped optimistically along the southern thoroughfare were sodden with last night's rain, and the morning's haze had given way to a defeated afternoon sunlight. From here, over the noise of the crowd and the clatter of carriages, the hiss of arriving trains rose out of the humid air like something emerging, slowly and secretly, from an underworld.

Out of all this bustle, once again she surfaced in his thoughts: a beautiful girl, familiar only through grainy photographs, known to him only for the last two years. His most vexed imaginings pictured her vanishing into the shadows of a railway terminal, into all the dangers of a large city at a festive time.

Tom Lark started to dwell on disasters, fashioning ghostly assailants out of the steamy terminal air.

Then caught himself.

You are at it again, he told himself.

Slowly, with an infusion of logic and good common sense, he began to soothe his misgivings. And, as a kind of brace to his jostled nerves, a rear guard to beleaguered speculations, he reached for the flask in his pocket, pulled at the whiskey, and muttered soothing nonsense to the horse, to old General, to the close air around the terminal.

The crowds were gathering at Tenth and Broadway. The trains were in full arrival.

It had always struck Tom that Louisville's Union Station was an indeterminate place. Not just your average railway terminal caught between arrivals and departures. That would have been enough, of course: there was something rootless about a railway station. But Union was a puzzlement of cathedral and town house. It was like that architect from up east had started with good intentions and a hopeful blueprint, that he had come down to Louisville imagining this station as heart of a growing city and a new prosperity. Then, halfway through the planning, it was like he had given up, brought the building to a compromise between vision and stone, and settled for a decent but undistinguished effort at just finishing the thing. The rose window on the station's Broadway side rarely caught direct sun, hovering above the business of trains and passengers like a milky, cataracted eye.

At this time of day, the terminal seemed to absorb the light. For the space of an hour, the building would seem more complex, marbling as it began to shadow Ninth Street with its confusion of towers.

Approaching one o'clock. Generally the midpoint in the station's busy schedule.

But not this evening, and not this week. Trains had been descending on the station since the early morning hours, and bands and assemblies and the long wind of welcoming speeches had filled the domed terminal since ten in the morning. The regular trains were filled to overflowing, filled so that a number of additional arrivals--*sections*, they called them--would flock into the city throughout the day.

Hallie was to arrive on the fifth Florida section—a special train, preposterously named, that would skirt the Gulf Coast, passing through New Orleans and Memphis before it came north into the here and now.

Scheduled arrival, sometime between 1:30 and 2:00. But that, of course, was subject to variety.

Tom consulted his watch. Found that, as he had suspected, it had lost twenty minutes to the clock in the Ninth Street tower. He had been wise, he guessed, to set out for appointments early. Hallie should be arriving shortly now, and far more gentlemanly to wait a while for your own daughter than to have her stand in a terminal, south of an unfamiliar city, alone and perhaps a little uncertain.

The others would come into town later. Some by train at this very spot, others at the smaller terminals or, like they did in his childhood, disembarking from the steamboats at the docks. Their way of getting here was not as important as the fact that, in the hours to come, they would all be together again. Those of Tom's friends who had stayed in the city would be joined by those who had left. He would see the wanderers once more. *The comrades of his terrible misspent youth*, he thought with a smile.

Comrades in arms.

Now, on the eve of the Grand Reunion, when the remnants of a marvelous defeated army would convene on his city for melancholy celebrations, Tom Lark could not help but feel a strange sense of dread.

Perhaps it was remembering the war, or whatever passed for remembering in his spotty recollections. Or perhaps it was seeing the aftermath of that other, more quiet war— thirty-five years of passing time, and the casualties inflicted on a band of young men who had become grayer, more bent, more absent of thought and gaze...

Infandum, regina, iubes renovare dolorum.

You ask, my queen, to relive unspeakable sorrows...

The old line from Vergil he had translated and never gotten right emerged from the whiskey and the welter of his thoughts. It was where Aeneas starts the story in Carthage, where he begins to tell Queen Dido about the Trojan horse and the city burning...

Tom Lark smiled at himself. An old man quoting a dead language on the threshhold of a new century. Quoting Vergil in the midst of a railway terminal, no less.

How suitable, he thought.

Because I am a remnant, you see.

I am residue. In an odd admixture of past and future, of regret and dread, there is no time in which I live, no moment in which I dwell.

Be of good cheer, he told himself, tightening the cap on the flask.

We are here not to celebrate the war, but our survival of it.

And to that purpose, Hallie is coming home.

***

Tom Lark had once been described as "unfailingly handsome " by Maggie Murtagh, the wife of his best friend. The word "unfailingly" had troubled him then, but it seemed well chosen to those who would have recognized him--a lean, gray-haired figure in the shadows of the station interiors, still straight and lively of step into his early sixties. His only disfigurement beyond those of age was a dull scar tracing the left side of his forehead, half masked by his abundance of hair.

Of course, he did wear an unseasonably heavy wool coat for this warming weather, and if you were to move too close to him you would catch the smell of whiskey mingled with sweat and musty wool.

You might even begin to wonder if he were preserved more by alcohol than by charm and good luck.

Tom was well into his flask already. Belle of Jefferson: a bourbon named for a steamboat. *Well, that vessel has left the docks, he imagined. I am a bit to the shaggy side of lucid, but I am still right steady on my feet.*

But the light in the terminal was beginning to change. It seemed somehow heightened and vivid, the rose window shedding a strange prismatic glow onto the arriving trains.

He needed to stop. Two drinks from the edge of bewilderment, he guessed, and unless Ed arrived soon, all logistics would fall to his command.

Taking a deep breath, Tom checked his watch again.

It was the same time it had been before, he observed ironically. What could you expect, after all, from a G.A.R. timepiece facing down a huge Confederate reunion? And what, after all, was a schedule, in the midst of all this surge and confusion?

Ed Murtagh would be here shortly.

Ed would make the arrangements; set the schedules as he had always done.

Bring out of this mess something that resembled order.

The hiss of a Florida train disrupted his thoughts, as the passengers began to disembark and mill upon the platform. Never before had Tom seen such assemblages of gray--dress uniforms the likes of which his regiment had never taken afield, coupled with the gray and white of beard and brow, as though the arrivals had spent years learning to match their uniforms. It struck him that he knew nobody on the platform, that despite his enduring sense that the war and its memory were intimate and personal things, there was a whole army of aging boys, a dwindling generation, for whom this war was equally personal, equally particular.

These were Tennessee regiments, by their banners. Tom recalled that the third section of the Florida train was supposed to pass through east Tennessee on its way north, carrying veterans from Chattanooga, from Franklin. He looked in vain for those who would have served with him at Knoxville, or Chickamauga in the year that followed, but these men seemed to have fought either west or east of him, on one side of the Appalachians or the other and in battles the histories recorded with more attention and glory than those in his own tattered sevice.

And yet, they had all arrived at the same spot. The train seemed to belch forth a cargo of ancients and amputees, more pinned sleeves than Tom had seen outside a tailor's shop, and the watery smell of coal burning was laced now with old men's sweat and chewing tobacco.

Among them were a number of younger people. Men mostly, and of course the town would turn out events in great number for the sons of veterans. Some of the younger men

357

wore Confederate dress uniforms--reasonably authentic, if you went by the *Harper's* sketches.

For a moment, it could beguile your attentions. For a moment it could be forty years ago, on a landing where boys awaited trains that would usher them away to Manassas or Shiloh. So it appeared until you remembered the truth of it--that by the time the Confederacy had thought up and agreed on standard uniforms, they didn't have the money to issue them.

So this masquerade in Union Station was just that--an artificial feast on the leavings of a Lost Cause that none of these boys remembered. Instead, the memories lay in the bent men beside them--portly or doddering or frail. Old men who, if you looked at them right and under the forgiving haze of the Belle of Jefferson, still gave indications of an old glory, their white hair cloudy and decrepitly grand.

Among all of these men there were women as well, widows and daughters sometimes unescorted by men, yet ladies no doubt by their bearing and demeanor. The younger ones (he guessed) were twentieth-century women, from what he had heard about that breed.

Hallie Lark would be in that number. Would know of the war no more than what her father had told her.

But what she remembered—-and, for that matter, what he remembered—-was anyone's guess.

It was one of the few suspenses of this afternoon in late May, as the remnants of a storied, vanquished army gathered in a town that had, oddly enough, fought against them and, even more oddly, allied with them after their defeat.

It was the subject for a book sometime, Tom Lark speculated.

But not his book.

The time had passed for that.

The Tennesseans had nearly all disembarked by now, ancients milling with their descendants in a bleary search for sign and banner. One twenty by the terminal clock, his own watch reading one now.

He reset the old timepiece. Another losing battle.

The fourth and fifth sections of the Florida train were due any minute. The fifth would bring a more exotic crew, having dragged the Gulf before heading north. Louisiana regiments with all those silly uniforms. And of course since it had passed through New Orleans and Memphis, all kinds of camp followers, from horse traders to blacklegs to whores and panel thieves, as though Louisville didn't have her fill of them to begin with.

And his daughter would be among that crowd, if nothing had changed since her reply to his letter.

For a moment, his thoughts stirred protectively. He could imagine her, the dupe of every scam and hoodwink from Orleans Parish to the southern outskirts of Louisville.

Or so he told himself, his worries spinning stories around a girl he had not seen since autumn.

Now he looked into the windows of the empty train, a great heaving thing at rest after a long northwest journey, the glass smudged and spattered with a thousand miles of dust and rain.

A whiff of roses, odd in the steamy air, reached him above the watery smell of coal. For a moment the train seemed to hover in mist and fractured light, as though he dreamed it, as though the air was taking its substance away.

Near the front of the second car, a solitary face remained in the window.

A weathered man, seasoned but not actually old. A bearded face in profile, too tall for the compartment and staring toward the front of the car with that kind of attentiveness that let you know he knew he was being watched. That he was used to being watched, when you came right down to it.

Something about the man was familiar. Something that hinted at the edge of Tom's memory, something that failed to surface amid the hiss and shudder of another arriving train. Tom glanced up the track, recognized the New Orleans train, upon which his daughter was scheduled to arrive...

And then, as though he was summoned to do so, he turned back to the man in the window.

Who had moved, ever so slightly, to regard the station with a flat and listless stare.

Tom was too far away to be sure, but he could almost swear that the man's eyes were black. The bright, glittering black of a gun barrel or an Appalachian night.

Why he continued to watch, Tom had no idea. But finally, as though he had been waiting for the opportune moment, the passenger fixed his eyes upon the elderly man on the platform...

The bearded man grinned, and Tom started to smile in response...

Until he saw in the heart of that grin something cold and feline, almost predatory, as though the man was sizing him up hungrily, waiting for a sudden movement or a sign of fear.

Then the man turned full to face Tom Lark, his features catching the strained light of the terminal...

His finger traced over the dusty window glass, forming oiled and silvery letters like the track of a snail.

And just before those letters vanished in a surprising glare of light from the station's rose window, the left side of the man's head blossomed in blood, in fragment of bone, in the gray of ruined tissue and brain.

Tom Lark caught his breath. Staggered on the platform. Blinked and stepped forward, as a hand clutched his shoulder from behind.

He wheeled, staggered.

His horror swept into relief, as though he had been pulled from the path of an oncoming train. The warmth of the whiskey rushed back: he was settled, less sober, looking into the blue and startled eyes of his daughter.

✳✳✳

The light in the terminal seemed to compose.

Hallie was more lovely than even a doting father remembered, her hair a loose arrangement of braids that had weathered the train ride magnificently, the inherited English cream and rose of her skin a legacy from her long-dead mother.

His memory balked, the man in the train fading and resurging like a drowned face on the surface of the water. He fought his way back from the vision, settled himself on thoughts of his daughter.

Returned her gaze, her smile.

Phantoms of old age and a head wound, he told himself, and took in the girl.

Hallie was dressed a bit young, and in an old-fashioned way, as though she had expected her home town to be farther behind the times and had decided to fit in: a shirtwaist with gigot sleeves and a long velvet skirt that remarked her to observant eyes as a daughter rather than a bride or sweetheart.

But it was the daughter Tom Lark remembered, of course: the child of his old age, at sixteen ill-matched with a sixty-year-old father, fresh from Madame Delamater's finishing school and fully ready to hide for a summer under the shadow of his protective wings. As he approached her, Tom found himself wondering foolishly about what she would think, his vanity frail on the platform, fearing that observers might see her as granddaughter rather than the daughter she was.

Pale blue those eyes, like the horizon out at sea as a storm scuds out of the way and leaves only water and light. He started as she met his gaze: forty years of spotted recollections, of fits of abstraction and too-frequent washes of bourbon could not take away the memory of eyes like that, her mother staring at him amid shadow and evergreen at the edge of forsaken mountains.

Ghosts, he was already finding out, returned in all kinds of ways.

And Halcyon Lark was also a mystery in the presence and flesh.

"*Bonjour, Papá,*" she said softly, her French laced with New Orleans and a whiff of Fourth Street Louisville.

He felt his heart swell and rise to a greeting, but like all fathers in the most public of places, he kept quiet, his eyes filling with her.

With all of this mulling and memory, he was unprepared for an encroaching world of sunlight and steam and crowds. And as they left the station, stepped out into the heavy afternoon air, the beggars milled around them. As they usually did, of course, but given the reunion, in much larger numbers this time. You could see it came as a shock to Hallie—grizzled men on wheel carts and crutches, amputees, the lame and the halt, and those who seemed all physically normal but could scarcely hide some turmoil or infirmity that lay in the depths of their brains.

He guided her swiftly, even roughly through the ragged crowd, stepping around a blind man who pivoted hungrily toward the sound of their passing, then shouldering aside a man on crutches so that his shaken daughter could reach the carriage unimpeded.

It may have seemed heartless to her, but there comes a time when *Shiloh* or *Petersburg* become beggar's cries rather than places in your memory, and you have to shunt off the voices just to get on with things. But the girl wasn't used to it. She stopped on the street, and the beggars were on her like street arabs, their hands extended, each mouthing his list of regiments or battles—either side of the war, it didn't matter at this distance and in this town.

Hallie was quite bowled over by it. The poise she had shown on the landing scattered, and for the first time those long yellow braids seemed to unravel a bit. One of the beggars—a big man and very insistent, too young to have been born in the time of the battles he named—stood directly in front of her, shaking his hand fitfully, his palm extended and emphatically.

Almost absently, as though she were fumbling for her keys in the dark, Hallie opened her little drab pocketbook, produced a handful of bills. She offered them to the beggar, who examined them in shock. He moved closer to her, rising to full height, and Tom stepped between the two of them, saying something awkward and immemorable about courtesy and hospitality, about ladies and honor.

The beggar regarded him now, flat eyes sizing up this new adversary, reckoning the prospects of force. The man stepped back, said, "I know you. Cap'n Lark, ain't you? Two sides at Saltville?"

Tom pushed against the beggar. It felt for a moment as though he had fallen into the man, and he reeled under the meaty, fulsome odor of dirty flesh and stale wine. They stood there on Broadway, leaning into each other like the sides of a gable, and then the beggar gave way. Tom's hand moved reflexively to his belt, brushing a recollected gun, and he said something about ordinances and how the man better be moving.

It was like the crowd parted and receded around them.

He found himself by his daughter, safe behind General in the passenger seat of the little shay. The spine of the black man's white shirt darkened with the first signs of sweat as he guided the carriage east on Broadway. Calmly, almost like he had fulfilled a municipal duty, the beggar pushed the back of the shay softly, almost as an afterthought, and waded back into the crowd. The horses picked up speed, the sounds of the station receded, and Tom was left alone to make conversation with his daughter.

It was a moment he had dreaded and yearned for simultaneously.

Tom Lark kept silent as the carriage turned onto Eighth Street, past a dozen or so of Morgan's Raiders, to judge by the familiarity of their faces and the sense of entitlement every man from the Bluegrass puts on when he comes to Louisville. They were leaning against a barouche, talking to two gaudily dressed women.

Tom nodded to, or rather *at* one of the disembarking cavalrymen. The man in the train haunted him, and he struggled for purchase, for a way to understand and settle it all.

Four times, maybe five since the War, something untoward had glimmered in his vision. Out of the ordinary, downright unnatural.

The curtain framing an open window turning in a breeze he could not feel, resolving itself into female form...

A large dog, the size of a horse, stalking across East Green Street as he wobbled home in the early hours after a night's drinking with Gideon Douglas...

And there had been others—shadows, reflections in unsettled pools, something in a barge's lights at midriver—that threatened to become something vital, corporeal. That hinted at blood and bone and indifference, perhaps even malice.

Yandell Roberts, the family physician, had attributed the dog's appearing to *bedazzlements from an old head wound, augmented by inordinate spirits*. But by *spirits*, of course, the man had meant bourbon and gin, and the young man had scolded Tom with a dry medical wit. Something about *hair of the dog* and *the whole article*...

But this had been different. Before, the apparitions had seemed tangible, corporeal. The man in the window had hovered between substance and nothingness, had seemed comfortable there, and had no intention of choosing flesh or illusion. And something about the vision--*this* vision in the muddy window--had charged Tom Lark in a way he had thought buried for years and irrecoverable.

He had not felt this way since Saltville--the strange, almost exotic rush of blood that was part to do with the mystery of the apparition, part with the return of his daughter. Part, he supposed, with the puzzle of the scrawled letters on the dusty window, but most of all with something else he did not and could not understand.

By habit, he checked his watch as well.

Two o'clock.

Had the watch rushed ahead?

It could not be past one-thirty by his own hazy reckoning. Masking something that unsettled him, something uncoiling in his stomach, Tom shook the watch and held it to his ear.

"And *that* fierce engine is supposed to tell you something, Papá?" Hallie observed merrily. "Trust a Yankee timepiece to bewilder a Rebel reunion."

Despite himself, Tom was smiling now. The man and the light and the smeared window were fading to the back of memory, and even as he tried to recollect them, the consoling means of the Belle of Jefferson were making them faint, pushing them out of recall. He was now at the edge of believing his own explanations, and at any rate, there were more pressing things than an old man's fancies, he told himself.

After all, Doctor Roberts had spoken of the phantom limb.

According to the wartime observations of a Union physician, an S. Weir Mitchell, it seems that amputees in his care had a remembrance of a lost limb, still feeling the same sensations in the missing part. And Tom Lark wondered if, in some fashion, lost memories returned to someone with a head wound, if it was another form of phantom that the wounded could not leave behind.

Hallie, after a downpour of chatter he had disregarded with a constant nodding, had now fallen into silence. Without looking at her, Tom Lark was sure she was regarding the houses south of Broadway, the bell tower of St. Louis Bertrand now rising over the rooftops, guiding her toward the home she had not seen since the Christmas holidays.

Hallie would be home. The best of the Reunion would be that he would have his daughter with him.

"You'd best take siesta when we arrive," he urged his daughter as the carriage passed through the shadowy intersection at Sixth and Breckinridge. "We're to attend General Gordon's speech this evening, and then the first of the fireworks, if indeed the weather permits pyrotechnic. And then, of course, Morning Prayer at the Cathedral, and tomorrow's picnic down by the House of Refuge, where you can admire the new monument, erected for this very occasion..."

He knew he was going on.

Now it was Hallie who was silent. Steadying her hat, she looked over her shoulder into the northward rise of Sixth Street, its vanishing point somewhere the other side of Broadway, where haze and a rising mist descended from the overcast skyline of brick and stone.

"Good," she said softly, and for a moment Tom Lark thought it was approval of fireworks or General Gordon. He smiled, prepared to tell her more about the events, about the gathering at Bennett Young's after the display...

But the look on her face was relieved, not anticipatory.

"Good," she repeated. "I was afeared he'd follow."

"Who?" Tom was instantly alert. A battlefield readiness coursed through him, and he found himself glaring into the low, shimmering tendrils of mist, expecting monsters or Union raiders.

"Never mind, Papá. Just a bold man on the train. I said nothing because... well, because he was forward but not outlandishly so. He did not deserve your bearlike vengeances."

Hallie laughed, and Tom Lark regarded his daughter closely. Time had been when such a statement demanded explanation, but Hallie was sixteen now, almost a year of boarding school behind her, and the father in him warred with common sense. Whoever it was—whether passenger on the train or forward blood at the landing—she had dealt with the problem.

She had dealt with it. He was certain.

And yet there was a strange kind of yearning in her relieved laughter, as though two incompatible things lay balanced in her thoughts.

He was unsure why, if she had 'dealt with the matter', she had mentioned the encounter at all.

All said and done, Tom Lark was unsure whether his daughter's mention of this forward man was a call for her father's protection or some kind of shadowy challenge.

2.

Concordia Latin School was an experiment. In a gabled monstrosity due west of the city center, on two floors of slanted light and dust and piled books, a strange, almost comical man named Bedivere Aurelius Lark had tried to bring a classical education to the sprawl of a fast-growing Kentucky river town.

Bedivere Lark was Tom's father, and his goal was not the least of his comedies.

Bedivere Lark was a transplanted Yankee whose affected British accent and airs led you to believe that there must be a job worthy of him somewhere up or down the river, although that job would never be in Louisville, and it might be beneath his dignity to go and find it. His eyes were light blue and edged with vacancy, his beard trimmed and curled and white like that on the bust of a barrack emperor. He had come to Louisville from Vermont in the early 40s, selling books and patent medicines out of a storefront on Market Street, raising and educating three sons while he made his fortune.

Concordia was his brainchild, his fondest notion. With enough education to straighten his grammar and prefer the roundabout to the direct, Bedivere Lark established the school because he *envisioned the ancient tongue rescued from the Church of Rome*, a sort of Protestant version of the old cathedral schools, where philosophy and rhetoric and the "light of the ancients" would shine over the shadowy, slighted Midwest.

And if the light ever shone there, truly and luminous, it was before Tom's time as instructor of Latin.

The school opened its doors around 1850, in a building on Ninth Street where it would grow, flourish, decline and die. Bedivere and his two oldest sons, fancifully named Lancelot and Galahad, joined with a local hero, a young man named Fitzgerald Gault, to make up Concordia's first faculty. In addition to Latin, the school taught English, French, geography, trigonometry, and geometry, the teachers sometimes only a textbook page ahead of the class in their knowledge, the tuition an audacious twenty dollars for a six month term.

Concordia might well have prospered on the other side of the ocean, might even have done passably well along the East Coast in a place like Boston or New York or Philadelphia. But this was Louisville, where riverboats and commerce in tobacco and whiskey were the schooling among a people scarcely a generation away from buckskinned trappers and the taking of scalps. Bedivere Lark had to stand against a prevailing attitude—that no real wisdom could be found in books—which he considered the defense of the illiterate.

Common sense, they told him. *What our boys need ain't book learning, but good old common sense.*

He understood what they meant by *common sense*— what anyone surely understands if he lives more than a month among Kentuckians. *Common sense* was whatever thinking agreed with theirs. Bedivere vowed to himself to change this, but he was never given the time.

Right from the first, Concordia had trouble drawing students, especially when the 1850s brought the rise of public schools to Louisville. Right from the first, the local newspapers began to snipe away at the impractical education offered by the Ninth Street Salon. Left on his own, training a handful of students for the Lord could only know what career or enterprise, Bedivere Lark's finances were in decline by Concordia's third year. Far from skimming the cream of the scholars, the school began to harbor the second sons of wealthy families, rogues and idlers and out and out simpletons from the spreading business community.

Faced with the prospect of shallow pockets, the faculty could afford only a single addition to its number.

That, of course, was Tom Lark. Educated at a fanciful New England college, with no intentions of returning south, he had been shipwrecked in the straits of his family, summoned home to a place that was not really home, and assigned sole charge of Concordia's Latin instruction—all of this well after the school's instruction had begun to suffer.

He would always remember disembarking at Union Station into the clinging steam of a Louisville August, would always associate heat and mugginess with that arrival, and no less with that dismal and pervading sense of failure that assailed him every time he thought of Louisville.

His own failure, of course. Not that of the city. *Facilis descensus Averno*, as the poet says: "Easy is the descent to Avernus: night and day the door of gloomy Dis stands open; but to take back your steps and pass out to the upper air, that is the work! That is the labor!" And from that platform he sank into the same pursuits, the same studies as the others.

Soon, as though substituting the fashionable for the classical might bring in survival money, Concordia became known as the heart of prevailing notions. Even before Tom's appointment to his father's faculty, the school had entertained all fashionable thoughts—from Transcendentalism and Unitarianism to the painful bigotries of the Know-Nothings, and finally, even as he stood upon that Union Station platform, Latin grammar in hand, the question of secession. Concordia was the place to go to debate the more volatile issues of the times. And it was this last great controversy, when the country divided, that Concordia, too, became a place of discord.

But in later years, when he thought of the school, he remembered it harmonious and lovely. When he imagined the classroom, the boys were always together.

He might have told his daughter about the hazy light in the old building, the smell of new wood and wax and lemon, and always the dance of dust motes in the high windows. How he would stand at the front of the class, half man, half lectern to their drowsy eyes, filling their collective heads with notions.

Oh, he knew good and well that the classroom he recalled did not match with the facts. The Douglas twins were two years younger than Ed and Cato and Gabriel, and while the younger boys fumbled through Caesar the older were studying Horace and Vergil. The books varied as much as the boys, but from a distance, from forty years, all blended into a scene that might or should have been.

He never minded, then and there, that memory works that way. He was never a stickler for order and procedure. When Cato Younger, his name a jest in any Latin class, got the order of words in the *Commentaries* all wrong...

Omnia Gallia divisa est in tres partes...

Tom Lark would nod at the lectern and let it go, because the details were not important, it was the spirit and the heroism recovered, the ancient times that mattered, not the word order or the verb tense or even the way the light spilled onto the polished desks. It was something more abstract and heartfelt that moved him then. A ghost of Rome translated to America in the mid-South at mid-century, when even though they did not know it, the whole country was preparing for the greatest of conflicts.

The issue of slavery was of complete indifference to Tom Lark, never mind his father's abolitionist notions and Fitz Gault's championing of "the peculiar institution". Black faces, to be honest, were indistinguishable to him, as they were to most white men of that country and time. And like most white men of that country and time (South and North, despite what the North would proclaim later) Tom adhered to what he thought was self-evident—-that the black man needs years of shepherding and guidance before he is able to set himself amidst the flower of humanity.

But despite an indifference to slavery, he was certain of one thing: a knowledge held more intimately than his Unionist family could possibly understand, even though his father had come from northern parts a generation back. He knew from his own time in school, from his stay in deep New England, that Southrons and Yankees were races apart, that his classmates had considered him one of their number only when it availed them, and not for a breath longer.

It was this knowledge that made him decide, in the early spring of 1861, when recruiters came up from the South and down from the North, that his future lay with the Confederacy. Fitz Gault, the son of a family with substantial land holdings, was off to Tennessee soon after that state seceded, and Tom's departure months later had truly nothing to do with the path the dashing, aristocratic Gault had chosen in the days preceding Sumter.

But it was Tom whom the schoolboys followed out.

To the great chagrin of the Unionist Bedivere Lark, a great number of his students left Concordia in the spring of 1861, following his rebellious son south in a strange children's crusade, heartbreaking if it were not dirt common in that charged, historical year, so that after a while, when you heard of it happening in New England, in Michigan or Texas, you had hardened yourself to its foolishness and waste.

A dozen of them left the city.

Eight were alive when the war ended.

And though Tom Lark would speak of the survivors, would have promised his daughter a chance at meeting five of them, there were four among them whom he would not mention—those who fell at Shiloh, Chickamauga, Chattanooga and Saltville.

This he recalled as the smell of kerosene rose, oddly from the rainy street, mixed with the faint whiff of lavender and rosemary, as though a lady was passing below, carrying an oil lamp like the image of a light-bearing goddess.

Then the horse whickered outside the window. The muffled hoofbeat of an animal not his own, catching his ear as though the sound had reached him through rain or over a stretch of water.

Tom Lark lurched to the window, and sure enough, at the edge of sight, a horse and rider stood beneath a gaslight. All of his thought, all of his bourbon and memory fled him before the man astride the horse.

Thin and gangling, his legs outlined against the pale flanks of the horse, he was dressed poorly for bad weather, his light, almost translucent jacket no match for the driving rain. It took only a moment to notice that the rain was not falling on the man, but through him. Even from this height and through the veil of glass, you could tell that he was dry, that the rain puddling the muddy road around him and his horse was also drenching the ground beneath them, as though they were made of mist or cloud.1 `

Then the man looked at Tom Lark, who recognized the face at once, the obscene smile glimpsed through the train window. The mounted man made a gesture: a crude movement with his right hand and a sudden, grotesque turn of his neck. As though he held a rope in it and was strangling himself.

The man laughed, the laughter rose over the rustle of the rain, and now Tom Lark remembered, remembered more deeply this time. He shut the window, and gazed at the guttering flame of the lamp, his thoughts inexplicably intent upon his daughter.

Because there were others he dared not mention. And one of them, it seemed, had arrived impossibly.

3.

By '64 Tom Lark had known the shape of the future.

The bunch he had gathered with him—-the Douglases, Gabriel Harme, Ed Caine, the whole lot of them—had been stripped from him by the fortunes of war. Abel Douglas had been the first, for they had lost him at Shiloh, and it galled Tom when some of the city officials, the privileged few of Louisville, waved the bloody flag and showed forth their Shiloh wounds, while he was full certain they had not been there. And as they mourned the Cause and enlarged on their limps, it always came back to him that Abel Douglas did not see eighteen, that somewhere in western Tennessee he lay out of mind and past recollection, the long years shadowing his brief garland...

He thought of Abel like that, like the boy Keats or Hyacinthus, dead long enough to have passed from mourning into a kind of gauzy beauty. It was his kind of death that was the subject of the thousands of odes and ballads published south of the Ohio for almost four decades—the commemorative poems that were on display, in pamphlets and in ceremonial volumes, throughout the city this week.

The others had been different. Gideon Douglas had survived his brother by almost a year, dying of dysentery at the siege of Vicksburg. No doubt in those last days of fever and watery bowels and incessant, overwhelming thirst, young Gideon had longed for his brother's death, for the good clean stroke of a minié ball he did not see coming. All this yearning as he melted into his own stinking fluids, the Union cannon rumbling his death knell in barrages more and more intermittent.

But Tom did not know this for sure. Gideon's was a death relayed in letters, distanced by miles and by the irreparable gap between words.

The other two, Gabriel and Ed, he lost at Chickamauga. He liked to think that the statue commemorated them both. The artilleryman with his ramrod, the cavalry man at parade rest. But he found it hard to think of them, much less speak about them.

It was the cannon again that undid them both.

Acoustic shadow, they called it.

371

There is a phenomenon in hilly terrain, primed by the right season and the right weather, and even the right time of day—or so the historians told him. Sound, it seems, can issue forth from one place, be heard half a mile or even two miles away, and yet be inaudible in the intervening space between creation and hearing. Like gaps in memory, he thought, or the spaces between words.

General Pope, the Union commander at Chancellorsville, had suffered from acoustic shadow. On the second night of the battle, the artillery on his flank began to fire on moving Confederate troops—at first videttes of cavalry, and then, in the early morning hours, a sizeable column of infantry. Pope did not hear the cannon fire, did not know of Stonewall Jackson's audacious march around the western end of his lines until it was too late to turn back the Southrons, almost too late to avoid capture or worse.

It was the story they always told about the phenomenon. A story that echoed, submerged, and rose again around a string of battles that followed in the next two years. And it was not the last time that a defending army—at Chickamauga, Tom Lark's own army, division, and company—did not hear it coming, awaited a movement on low ground, far away, only to be taken from the thickets on a flank or to the rear.

Tom had been there when the Yanks overran them. He remembered Ed waving the ramrod vainly at the rush of black jackets, because the blue was black in the bottom of night, believe me, and he remembered Gabriel, sent to the encampment with messages from the outriding cavalry, carving his way with saber back toward his horse, and the roil of blade and gunbarrel interposing, a darkness between the young man and safety, and escape.

And then a sudden light, his own head snapped back as if, at full tilt, he had collided with the solid heart of night.

He took to the mountains after the battle. Like to never come down from them. Combing the western foothills of Appalachia, shell-shattered and nebulous, he must have crossed a hundred miles by the time that the year had turned and the spring come again. Parts of that wandering still returned to him, but he was not sure whether he remembered them or dreamed them out of his terrible wound.

He remembered houses on stilts, rickety in the early winter rains. Remembered pitching a tent beneath one of them, a tent in cold December shadows, clustered eyes regarding him from the shadows above. Raw eggs, unleavened bread, a small jug of whiskey set outside his tent to greet him when he wakened, as though the folks above wanted him sustained but not sober, as though the drunkenness would somehow keep him alive.

And at last—probably January or early February—out of this tiered and frozen limbo emerged a pale, almost waxen figure, his glittery eyes and blanched broadcloth rendering him ghostly even forty years ago, before the surrender and the hanging.

Ferguson, then. And Ferguson now.

For Tom Lark could have sworn it was Ferguson, glimpsed in the train window, again under the lamp.

✳✳✳

Partisan or guerrilla, depending on your side. Even outlaw, because by March of '64, when Tom Lark was seeing the shape of the future, Champ Ferguson had kicked himself clear of recognizable allegiance, haunting the mountains of east Tennessee and western Virginia, emerging from brake or hollow to join up with this regiment or that—all Confederate regiments, but none of them graced by his silence and menace.

Ferguson was a rough-looking man of striking and rather prepossessing appearance, more than six feet in height and powerfully built. His complexion was florid, and his hair jet-black, crowning his head with thick curls. He had one peculiarity of feature which Tom had seen in only two or three other men, and each of these was, like himself, a man of despotic will and fearless, ferocious temper. The pupil and iris of the eye was of nearly the same color and, except to the closest inspection, seemed perfectly blended. His personal adventures, combats, and encounters were innumerable. Some of his escapes, when assailed by great odds, were almost incredible and could be explained only by his great bodily strength, activities, adroitness in the use of his weapons, and savage energy.

Tom got a story as he rode north with Ferguson, but whether it was the story, he never learned. Like a bandit chieftain, he had obscure origins: some place in north central Tennessee called Calfkiller Creek, for God's sake. He was forty already, perhaps the oldest commander under whom Tom Lark had served, drawn to the war by the claim, never substantiated, that his wife and daughter had been "disgraced" by a party of Union sympathizers—thugs, men only distinguishable from the thugs that followed the Confederate cause by the colors under which they rode.

Ferguson had ridden with General Morgan in the '62 December Raid into Kentucky, but Morgan for all his looting and destruction had drawn the line at Ferguson's kind of doings. At the bodies left in the fields impaled by dried corn stalks, at the backwoodsman's riding in tearful joy to the next battle, the next burning, the next requisition of horses for the Provisional Government of Kentucky.

So Ferguson had come east, into the Appalachian foothills with an actual bounty on his head and by that time three-dozen killings by his own hand, not to mention the Yankees he had dispatched in skirmish and fire fight. For Morgan was right, for all his foolishness and Lexington affectations of chivalry: Ferguson was in the war to settle scores. His wife and daughter, he insisted. But when you settle one score, you just stir up another. So it kept going, like a bad Highland Scots blood ballad, and somehow Tom Lark, dazed and with no place to go, not really, was swept into it and carried north into Virginia.

It was not a chapter of his history that Hallie knew about. He supposed he could have told her part of it—the first parts, anyway, before Champ took them up to join General Felix Robertson's brigade. But even those parts Tom had kept quiet, because he was not sure he had understood them himself.

Had he gone along out of fear? Perhaps he had, because Ferguson was enormous, menacing, and said to be capable of anything. Or was it a fear not of Ferguson but of a loss of bearing, a fear of a geography in which the compass points were moving and the landscape always seemed to promise something that had not yet arrived?

Whatever the case, it did not bear repeating. And as '64 evolved in all its bloodiness and loss, the events became blurred in Tom Lark's memory. He wondered now if he saw them all that clearly forty years ago, when he came out of the mountains with Ferguson.

They traveled west as he recalled. Two days on foot, leading their horses, both ending with the sun in their faces, and snaking in and out of the mountains like a dark creekbed, rising unnaturally and then descending through the foothills into level, low country—East Tennessee and Kentucky, western Virginia—until Lark lost his bearings.

Of the Jackson Garner and Dallas Beatty murders he had no recollection, but after the War the Nashville papers filled up with the testimony, with Ferguson's crimes and the arguments for prosecution and defense, and something about those stories came to him, something of East Tennessee, of a brace of cabins and Champ stalking the ground outside a doorway, long-haired and bearded, not cropped and shaven as he would be a year in Federal custody, looking like a twisted Light of the World, like Jesus knocking...

Then instead he remembered or imagined Champ like some fury, the scuffed LeMat cradled in his hand like a watch he was reading the hands of, his grimed finger slipped through the trigger guard, his left hand pulling the back of the boy's (Garner's? Beatty's?) head toward him, the barrel of the LeMat sheathed in the boy's mouth as the gun kicked once with a dull snap, the branch of a distant tree sheared loose.

He thought, for a moment, that he himself had held the head of the struggling boy while Champ pulled the trigger. But it was too horrible to hold in memory for long.

For what might a man do with his brain shocked and jostled? How might he acquiesce? Comply to keep an unstable peace? Compromise with a violent figure that hovered between humanity and something more abstract, almost iconic?

And yet none of it was enough for evidence, but the next memory was, of course it was, and had it not been for the long lying in at the Medical Institute on Chestnut Street, Tom Lark would have gone south and given testimony there in Nashville in the autumn of '65, despite his fears that his hands were bloody as well.

He would testify not for Garner, not for Beatty.

But for Saltville, and the sanitary hospital.

***

October '64, and most everyone knew that it was over, everything west of the Appalachians secure in Union hands, and to the east of the mountains, the Confederates burrowed behind earthworks, in towns, in strange pockets of the landscape where shadows tilted and sound dropped away.

It was all rear guard in the mountains, the lost-cause tactics of burning rails, of ambush and raid.

But some were at home, here in this rocky wildness. Tom Lark became convinced, as the year went on, that the outbreak of the War three years ago had marked no change in the way Champ Ferguson did things, that he had moved from mountain feud and retribution straight into the conflict, seeing daily life as guerrilla war. His band, which as much as Lark could figure, numbered between 50 and 100 men, the figure ranging widely depending on the weather, the county, and the regular commander they had joined with.

At Saltville they were around seventy or eighty, attached once again to Felix Robertson's brigade, and ordered to hold the rail depot against a Union sweep east up from the foothills. Tom tried to figure the sense of it: something deeper than intuition and judgment told him this was the last full year of fighting, and even the lives of Ed and Gabriel, spent so near the war's ending, seemed distant and incongruous—something he had read about rather than something he would have to explain.

But Ferguson was hot for the enterprise. There was, it seemed, a lieutenant in the advancing Union brigade— preposterously, a Lieutenant Smith whose first name Tom never heard. This Smith had done Champ wrong back before the war: a dispute over property or liquor or women? It was hard to gather from the veiled and dramatic threats. Tom wondered if Champ himself remembered the nature of the injury, remembered anything more than injury was done. But that seemed absurd somehow, like a stern backwoods God was holding them all accountable for forgotten sins.

Best to trust your chieftain, he decided, marveling how "chieftain", rather than "captain" or "commander", seemed to be the word he chose.

They joined Robertson's brigade south of the depot. The

air had snapped autumnal and chill, and Tom's head wound was throbbing, the faint scent of unseasonal honeysuckle reaching him from God knows where and the rumble of guns from the foothills. The rain misted and dazzled; they left their horses with the regimental drovers and the sutlers' wagons, proceeding by foot toward Saltville as they heard the sounds of the battle already engaged.

Engaged and dying away, because when Ferguson's column reached the field, the armies had broken. Tracks jimmied, wrecked by one or the other brigade in passage and retreat, the station house smoldering and the shot-riddled water tower dripping the last of its contents onto the sodden ties and cinders. The Confederates held the depot, for what it was worth.

Yet Ferguson did not stop. Hair tied back like a Lakota warrior, black eyes dead where the pupil had swallowed the iris, the chieftain asked around, badgered and intimidated—first a wounded infantryman, then a colonel who, stunned and subdued, his oak leaf insignia torn from his collar and clutched tightly in his hand—until he found out where the field hospital lay. Then he dropped the informers, led by a cold indifference toward a settled smoke in a cluster of cedar.

Tom had never seen anything like it. And never again until once, off the coast of Cuba, he saw a shark glide out of a feeding, trailing its own blood in the water, following the cloud billowing from its own wound, jackknifing into the tunnel of its throat...

But that was a year away, and even that he was not sure he remembered.

There was Ferguson nonetheless, stalking down the needled path back toward the horses, pistol nestled in his hand, confident beneath knowing where he was headed, and Tom Lark, repelled by the pale broadcloth bobbing like a spectre on the path ahead of him, followed in spite of himself.

***

The hospital was on the railroad, about nine miles from Abingdon on a school campus. It was called Emory and Henry

College, but Tom Lark thought of Concordia as they rode up to the buildings.

Three stories of hospital, the Yankee troops on the second and third floor, the upstairs reached only by two stairways. Beyond it an open field sanitary station and a log cabin all of which served as hospital for the Negro troops who had begun to fill the Union ranks that summer.

Ferguson knew where he was headed, but at the first stairwell a sentry—-an Irishman named Conroy, as Tom recalled—-stood in his path, and not for coaxing or reason or threat would he step aside. So calmly Ferguson led his men back down the stairs and up the other flight, where the guard stepped aside just for the look of the chieftain.

Tom was standing at the doorway when Ferguson approached Lieutenant Smith, sat on the bedside of the wounded Yankee officer, muttered something to him, scarcely audible, almost confessional, then pointed the gun at the young man's head and pulled the trigger. Down the same stairwell he swaggered, brushing past the thunderstruck surgeon, a Doctor Murfree who gave damning evidence a year later at the trial, and into the yard. Snatching up another pistol from one of his men, he walked across the grounds toward the cabin, firing into the recumbent bodies as he went.

Tom remembered the last glimpse before Champ entered the cabin. How he turned and, aiming at yet another of the colored soldiers, fired one last time, the flicker of the gun barrel, the flinch of the body, then the sound catching up across the long field and the pistol going off again and again in the planked and gabled shadows.

***

It was all he could have told them at Ferguson's trial. The written testimony, sworn and dictated in the presence of a lawyer, had reached the courthouse in Nashville two weeks from the day it was written. It had taken, according to some reports, scarcely an hour for the defense to discredit the best part of Tom's story.

After all, a man with a head wound. The distance of a year. The fact that poor Lieutenant Lark was unfit for thought and travel...

But then the other testimonies. A Lieutenant Carter of the 11th Michigan. Orange Sells and Harry Shocker, two troopers from the 12th Ohio. Stories dovetailed with stories, and Tom's first-hand account from the Confederate side. There was a kind of consensus that came from it all, and slowly Tom's version of the story rose out of the murk of evidence again, like a creature the military tribunal had imagined was mythical, even fanciful, but now, given support and corroboration, had became altogether too real.

You could sense the changes in the hot September courtroom, as incalculable to the mind as a slow shift in temperature, and yet you could feel it along the skin, you could smell it in a difficult tile of the air toward autumn. Nashville, a city the Advocate had maintained all along was loyal to the South, was revealed as a city conquered, in which the slightest loyalty to Dixie scattered conveniently and pragmatically before the apparatus of law and the barrel of the Sharps carbine.

So when Ferguson's defense made its summation, the case was already decided. The Advocate's closing statement had been an indictment of stories, how the South had fabled itself into ruin, telling a tale for the benefit of Southern women who now, half ghostly and half virginal, haunted the recesses of smaller houses and governed their growing sons toward nothingness. They had killed off a third of a generation, or so the Advocate seemed to say, and whether the "they" was Southern womanhood or whether it was the stories they told, no listener was absolutely sure.

Against this argument, the defense mustered little more than the old truths. A Captain Goodwin reminded all present how easy it would be "for a man to live with his fellow men, correcting all evils and promoting all good, had we remained as created. If our reason," he said, "were always, as in our first ancestors before the transgression, clear and perfect, unruffled by passion, unclouded by prejudice, unimpaired by disease or intemperance, the task would be pleasant and easy; we would need no other guide but this."

And here Tom Lark, his head throbbing from a wound he could not remember, took in the words and considered, for a moment, how they had everything and nothing to do with him. Two weeks later, when Champ Ferguson was found guilty and sentenced to be hanged, Tom Lark had forgotten even more. Already back in Louisville, reading the verdict in the distanced typescript of the local papers, he followed the progress toward the gallows, and, on the 21st of October, read of the execution, which took place scarcely ten days after the sentencing.

By then, the trial itself had become blurred, almost hallucinatory. The world of Tom Lark's memory commingled with fancy, with the evidence of the senses, until what he recalled of late '65 was a series of fragments, strung together by dreams and supposes.

4.

Acoustic shadow again.

If such a phenomenon could happen with sound, Tom Lark now figured, perhaps other energies could leap over space and time. Perhaps it was memory, he thought, or his eyes. But perhaps it was an old and seething hostility that, unable to die when Ferguson climbed the scaffold and dropped through the trap door, had hurdled years to settle on this place.

And it was this that he thought when, descending the stairwell at his daughter's summons, he found Hallie seated in the parlor before the chessboard, her opponent sitting with his back to the landing, playing the white pieces, long hair tied, mottled and dirty like the tail of a horse.

Tom had a terribe premonition of who it was.

For a moment, the stairs seemed to tilt, his head throbbed, and a strange, rumbling light swept by on the street outside, as though a train rerouted and derailed was thundering over a trackless street, was brushing the edge of his property. Tom clutched the banister, assured himself it cannot be, because...

...it could not be.

Now the light in the room flared, and he saw the rope burns purpling the back of the man's neck, and the sharp, metallic stink of rats commingled with old decay, and for a moment Tom Lark's stomach lurched, his eyesight fluttered, and the stairs collapsed to a shadowy, rain-sodden road and the lantern weaving in the hand of the foremost rider, the rain spattering the dusty leather of his saddle.

There are four of them, always four. And always a mournful feeling. Like he has lost someone or something important. Like the world is ending in a stormy night, and the long-haired rider at the front of the party will drive them on forever into hell's mountains.

Then the light returned, reassuring light, and his daughter rising from her seat, offering her hand to her teetering father.

Her caller stood behind her, black hat clutched politely in his pale hands.

"May I be of assistance, Mister Lark?" he asked, and Hallie hastened to make the introductions that neither man needed.

"You surely recall Mister Campion, Papá."—-her accent proper on the last syllable, Tom noticed—-"here to make apologies for... the abruptness of our railway station encounter."

Tom steadied, allowed himself to be guided to a chair. He closed his eyes, rested the back of his head against the antimacassar as the room settled. Strangely, the light in the parlor sputtered: the urgent, quivering sound of a dying insect against the window class, and Tom clenched his eyelids tightly, thought through the encounter as his daughter called him again and again, softly at first, and then with rising concern.

He opened his eyes to see the rough but not unkind face of this Campion hovering over him.

"Again, sir," the younger man offered. "May I assist you?"

He lifted Tom from the chair, steadied him. His hands were cold.

"'Tis an old war wound, Mister Campion," Hallie explained, and immediately Lark felt a sense of intrusion, like his daughter was talking out of school. "Sometimes my papá has a kind of... dizziness about him."

"Well the war has haunted the best of men," Campion replied gently, fixing Tom Lark with a stare that might have been mistaken for probing and sympathetic, were it not for a glitter in the depths of his eyes: something you'd expect to see down the sight of a gun rather than in the gaze of a confidante.

Campion's skin mottled and dulled, and the air filled with a whiff of pine and ordure. Lark grabbed the arms of his chair, staggered up as the room swam and buzzed.

Campion's eyes became opaque. Gently he guided Hallie Lark to a corner of the parlor, the gesture one of confidence, of concern. Stationed by the window, he whispered to the attentive girl, whose worried eyes flickered back to her father now and then.

And Campion's whisper tumbled into a pocket of sound, carried surprisingly across the room.

It's a thing that happens with such injury, Miss Lark. A head wound jostles the imagining. I ain't no alienist, mind you, but I hear tell that living with such damage is pretty near like them dreams a body has, where he wakes up or thinks he does, and all the time he's still dreaming. And it's when something horrible rises out of what he thinks is his everyday world, but he's still dreaming, you see?

And they say as well that a head wound jostles the memory. I have seen cases of men in my own father's party— veterans like your father here—who cease to remember the most gruesome things about the War, like the sunken road at Sharpsburg or them trenches at Petersburg. So maybe there's something that his head is holding back, Miss Lark. But I don't know. I ain't a doctor.

Tom leaned against the banister, uncertain of what he was hearing or even whether he was hearing it.

And what is more, Miss Lark, I have heard tell that the memory skips over the worst you done. There was a whole bunch of men—good men otherwise—who massacred them colored boys at the Battle of the Crater, and them folks didn't remember slaughtering the prisoners until years after, I hear tell, when they would startle awake in the heart of the night screaming at what was done because they had done it themselves. Now I don't know of your father, and of his service in the War, but then you ain't so sure yourself, I figure, and perhaps uncovering the dead...perhaps raising them ghosts...

And Campion paused and looked across the room at Tom Lark, and he smiled and his eyes narrowed, and his pale jacket roiled like an eddy of smoke...

...well, perhaps raising them ghosts would undo him. And what would be the purpose in that?

"Beg your pardon, Mister Campion?" Lark asked, cursing himself silently when his voice shook.

Those glittering eyes turned back to him, fixed him.

"Merely soothing your troubled daughter, Mister Lark," Campion replied. "Reckon it's hard on a girl to come back from school and all, finding her father a bit...haunted?"

So the threat was in play. Tom watched the afternoon sunlight redden the street.

Or perhaps there was no threat at all. Perhaps it was indeed a Mister Campion in his parlor, drawn to the reunion and the Lark house by circumstance. Perhaps he was all concern and innocence, and perhaps—and this was the worst of Tom Lark's chain of supposings—the threat he posed was all the conjury of an old man with a forty-year head wound.

Whatever the case, it would be improper for Campion to escort Hallie Lark to the fireworks—to escort her *anywhere*—on such short acquaintance. That much her father knew, though ill-acquainted with the guardianship of daughters almost grown.

So *no*, he told Hallie Lark, finding her more disappointed than he had hoped she would be, but more compliant than he had feared. His eye on Campion as he whispered to his daughter at the foot of the stairs, Tom assured Hallie that, were Mister Campion's intentions honorable and were he to stay in the city a spell, that he might be welcome to call on Miss Lark, chaperoned of course in this very parlor, for tea and for another game of chess.

Not that he meant it, of course. He offered the prospect as a kind of peace, maintaining that Campion might even escort Hallie to events in the town after a somewhat longer familiarity (though "familiarity" was not the word he wanted, sounding too forward, too... well, familiar). It was a peace of concessions, then.

Like the one he had made years ago in the mountains.

For Tom Lark was afraid that Hallie was too modern. No doubt she found this slow dance of permissions and visitations to be rather quaint. But where honor was concerned, sometimes the old ways were the best.

And yet he was surprised at the sting of the word "honor". To remember how Gabriel Harme and Ed Caine, the

Douglas brothers and the few survivors had followed their schoolmaster out on a song of honor, and how so many had not seen their twentieth year.

The honor of the old ways. Allegiance and fealty. But blood feud, vendetta, weregild as well. Tom Lark knew all the terms for honor, all the guises it took. And an honor of pure justice, and an honor of steadfast loyalties, and how the two of them commingled, hard to distinguish, like the silt and slow water where a river reaches the sea at last.

Yandell Roberts was once again peopling the parlor with phantoms, and Tom resented his daughter's absence.

After all, he had invited the young physician for brandy and cigars, his hopes that Hallie would catch the eye of the handsome doctor, and that he might catch her fancy in return. And that such an encounter might deflect her thoughts from the pale man who had stalked their parlor on the previous day.

But here they sat, the two of them, the bottle between them and the lamp low, Hallie having claimed headache a scant hour before the doctor's arrival, and retiring to her room with apologies indistinguishable from a warning not to be disturbed.

And here sat Dr. Roberts, having expected lovely and female entertainment, only to receive the gruff company of a man his father's age. Son of a Confederate veteran himself, the young doctor had the leisure to practice, to research, and unfortunately to burden Tom Lark with speculative tedium, because Yandell Roberts could find no other subject of conversation beyond that of medical advances. Vaccines for the lockjaw and diphtheria, for typhoid and malaria, the acetyl salicyclic acid that was the modern-day nostrum— good for what ails you, like a medicine show elixir. And there was the strange device of the German Roentgen, enabling the physician to see bone beneath unbroken skin.

At first Lark marveled at these discoveries, agreeing with the young doctor that, yes indeed, countless more young men would have lived to swell the numbers of these convening veterans had disease and limited science not taken casualties on the fields of the War Remembered. But as Roberts continued his lover's serenade to science and progress, to the sweeping of superstition and atavism back into shadows, Lark's attention wavered on an erratic current. He had heard this dance tune before.

Recognized it so well, in fact, that he was not surprised when Yandell Roberts, his long, handsome face partially obscured from the declining sunlight in the western windows, moved to the inevitable next step, the one no man of science could quite shake loose, and the one Tom Lark had expected since the conversation had turned to advances.

"But some people say..." Doctor Roberts began, and drew forth the usual stories. General Bull Nelson haunting the Galt House where Jeff Davis (not the President, mind you, but a Yankee general of the same name) shot him in an altercation over a point of honor. The Mitchell woman in Frankfort, pining the rest of her days for General John Bell Hood, her true love who had seen to the vanishment of her true husband in his command down in Texas...

"And I am sure," he concluded with an ironic smile, "that the Reunion here will be peopled with the dead as well as the living."

"You've heard more stories, then, Doctor Roberts?"

"One always hears stories, Mister Lark. Because your ghosts are, quite simply, your guilts. We are haunted by the done and the undone, by what might have been or might have been avoided. You have spoken to me on occasion of your troubling dreams, those regarding the guerrilla chieftain, Captain..."

"Ferguson. Yes. Champ Ferguson."

Roberts relit his cigar, which he had let die during his long ode to science. "Your Ferguson is a good example, Mister Lark. Tried as a criminal, as a mass murderer, despite his claims that it was all done in legitimate service. Now that debate still rages, does it not?"

Tom Lark remembered. His hands recoiled briefly, spilling the brandy as they recalled, in the way that the body recollects old or practiced movements, a sudden and violent lurching...

He almost heard the crack of the revolver.

"Ferguson's gone, Doctor Roberts," he insisted, masking the tremor in his voice. "Long gone, and the verdict in."

"If it's ever gone, Mister Lark. If a final verdict ever comes in. Because, you know, I've heard tell. Power of suggestion, mind you, but I've heard it told."

And Yandell Roberts, enlightened scientist but lover, it seems, of the dark, insistent stories that survive because we need them, recounted what he had heard regarding the strange aftermath of the Ferguson trial. Using it, of course, as an example for the alienist's power of suggestion, the tactics of voudon, all the magic of the primitive still dormant in us that awakened in trauma or crisis. That was the reason, he explained, and in that, it was not unlike the phantom limb condition that fascinated the good doctor so— the ancient fears still shuddering, though reason and science and enlightenment had severed them from what we used to call the soul.

But all this while, something in Tom Lark attended to the story he did not know. For Ferguson's execution, on 20 October 1865, did not mark an end to his story, but stood as a midpoint in a chain of aftermaths and killings.

One of the prosecutors. That was when they said it started. Barricaded somehow into the smokehouse next to his summer kitchen up in Southern Indiana, the charred and furrowed wall about his corpse a sign that he had continued clawing for escape, probably after he ceased to agonize or feel or even to know, and the smokehouse smoldering for two days afterwards, a savage smell drifting into Kentucky on the back of a northerly wind...

And two witnesses for the State, Doctor Roberts maintained, or so the story continued, found bizarre deaths at the far reaches of the country and the remaining century— one in 1867, who hanged himself in a Sacramento loft, and another forty years later, almost to the day, found in a New Hampshire barn, impaled and mutilated by dried cornstalks, an act that had become one of Ferguson's signs in his war-long rampage through the foothills. And though one would think, as Tom Lark certainly thought, that as those arrayed in court against the Captain were dying out here at the brink of the 20th century, that Ferguson's ghost might rest at last...

It turned out that the stories Yandell Roberts had heard all operated by a different mythology.

For in 1899 there was the death of a young girl— inexplicable, according to Roberts. Daughter of one of the judges, found dead in a schoolhouse in east Tennessee, the back of her head a shambles from the shotgun barrel of a LeMat revolver, the wall behind her spattered, the weapon still clutched obscenely in her teeth in a last and bizarre rictus of surprise, as though even in this suicidal moment she had not seen it coming.

"Do you not suppose you *would*, though, Doctor Roberts?" Tom insisted, his cigar burnt low enough at last to snuff and discard. "Do you not imagine that she would have expected the impact of the shell?"

"I've seen it happen," Yandell Roberts insisted. "A half dozen times in my life, I suspect, I've been called in to autopsy apparent self-slaughter. Four of them veterans of the War, mind you. All of them men, and though I believe that women undo themselves, they do not seem to do it by gun."

"And yet this time it was? By gun, I mean?"

"That's what they say, Tom. But you know it might only be story. But as the story ended, for each and every one of them, there was a look of surprise and dismay and bereavement in those unclosed eyes, as if they had learned in the last split second when the shell crashed into the back of their heads...as if they learned that, somehow, they had not hit the target they were aiming at. But as I have said, it may be only story."

$$*** $$

They drank yet another glass of brandy together, and Doctor Roberts, noticing his host's continual glances toward the head of the stairs, settled on the first polite occasion to take his leave. Tom Lark watched the doctor climb into his big, expensive barouche, then headed uneasily up the stairs toward his daughter's room, the last swallow of brandy burning sweet and oily on the back of his throat.

He clutched the banister as he ascended, thinking all the while of displacement. Phantom limb, acoustic shadow, the appearance of ghosts—-all of them the surfacing of something born elsewhere and in another form entirely, passing through presence to absence and back. He thought as well of the look of astonishment on the faces of suicides—-

how what they thought they controlled was never what they expected. So his thoughts ran ahead of him, to his daughter, whom he had sent to be raised in a distant country under the watch of others.

His head swam, and he stopped mid-flight on the stairway. Perhaps now he mourned more than the time he lost in those damaged months with Ferguson. Perhaps he had undertaken more or had let more happen than he remembered or wanted to remember. But his forgetfulness when it came to his daughter...that he could still amend.

He figured that it was time to get to know Miss Hallie Lark.

Her door rattled at his soft knock. No answer, even to a more insistent rapping. Then, taking a deep breath, Tom Lark opened the door to find the window open and Hallie somewhere else, removed into the rainy night.

Nor did the letter soothe his concern:

My dear Papá,

I am certain you will have no occasion to worry over this letter, since no doubt you will pore over medical matters all the time there are recitals by the River and fireworks at the Boys' Home. I understand that the Reunion is a time for recollection and for talk, nor would the company of your silly girl do aught to enliven reminiscence. For you see, those of us who do not remember—younger folk such as Mister Campion and myself—can only provide a kind of heedless audience to that wisdom we can only understand when we come to your age. For us, you see, it is a time to enjoy the sights of a city that, frankly, we barely know.

You have said yourself, Papá, that given time and inclination, Mister Campion might prove a promising caller to a young woman. I know that such occasions were arranged in your day by the parents of the girl in question, but in a time when sons look to a future mapped out by the progresses of science, and when daughters are entrusted to most capable hands for schooling in far-off places, you certainly should understand that people my age have made wise and resolute decisions in our young lives already, and that my choice to accompany Mister Campion on the town has within it a guarantee of prudence.

We shall be in a crowd and communally supervised, as it were, and if you are reading this letter, it means only that you and Dr. Roberts made a shorter evening of your conversation, and you may expect your daughter's immediate return. I understand that the River and the Boys' Home, with its new monument to our fallen troops, are both but a brief carriage ride from here.

Forgive me, father, if I sound defiant. Indeed, I am but the independent and modern girl of your striving, ambitions, and greatest hopes. I shall be home before you miss the medico.

Your devoted daughter

As the rain swept over the city for the second night running, gliding from the west off the river, through Portland and Shippingport and down from New Albany and the Knobs, it became clear to Tom Lark there would be no fireworks that evening. So at his employer's command, General steered the shay through the darkened, rain-glistening streets, north toward the sound of brass bands and cheering.

Up Tenth Street they rode, past the old hospital and across Broadway, where Union Station loomed again on their left. And once again the beggars began to gather, walking beside the carriage like an escort of the maimed and halt. The beggars followed for several blocks, the most persistent of them slowing and reluctantly shearing away by Walnut Street.

General drove the little shay past Market Street all the way to Main, and now Tom stepped out of the carriage into a crowd of elderly men, wives and daughters on their arms, a tide that swept him away from his coach toward a pavilion where, according to the signs, Generals Buckner and Gordon were to address the graying remnants of their legions. And you could see it on the faces: the old men lost in memory and the younger members of the crowds—-daughters and sons and grandchildren—-forgetting what they had been told as they all swept toward Library Hall, the auditorium and the War that glimmered in the recesses of the old men's minds.

The stories were nothing to these young ones, Tom guessed, in the face of the rain and the hovering dark.

Nor would they be to Hallie, he realized suddenly, now swimming against the tide of umbrellas and wet wool, as the rain picked up even more, sheeting across the river with a rumbling and with scattered flickers of light somewhere off to the south, and the buildings shuddering at the rumors of thunder.

For a moment Tom's memory cascaded back, and he thought of artillery, of infantry lines in conflict as you approached by cavalry. Then his thoughts anchored and returned, and wondered at fireworks in this dismal weather—how the Boys' Home grounds to the south had turned suddenly ablaze and explosive. But then, when the light steadied, broken only by occasional sputter, he knew it as the electric lamps installed for the Reunion at Jefferson and Central. The bright and modern display obscured the night sky, turning the town to an artificial festival, a sunlit world of towers and booths and emporia in which there seemed to be no longer any room for shadows.

Tom looked back through the city, at the rain glittering through the electric light, and beyond the gaudy display, this jewelry against gray sky, he thought he saw flashing lights on the southern horizon. Nor did the Edison bulbs explain the ground shaking, the muted unnatural rumble below the murmur of the crowd. He looked at his fellows, who seemed intent on the reunion, the pavilion, on getting good seats for the speeches, and the whole business unsettled him, as though after years of schooling and battle and teaching again at the War's end, after all this living he had been called to find a simple girl and his instincts had guided him in completely the opposite direction.

Now, wading upstream against the human current, he looked vainly through the netting of umbrellas for his carriage. Pushed back by the surging crowd, in some cases politely but in others insistently, Tom Lark began to feel his age—a kind of trapped, old man's silliness in the irresistible flow of things.

He kept telling himself that Hallie was safe. There were people out and about all over town. The police, generally patrolling in force of a weekend and at full strength during events such as this, were doubly vigilant because of rumors that con artists of varying stripes and skills had converged to work the town.

Or so he told himself. Unsure of what he should do next, he caught sight finally of General's white shirt as the old black man stood on the seat of the shay, looking for his employer in the eddying crowd. Tom shouted out, and wading through the last mire of bodies, climbed into the seat beside his driver and gave specific, loud instructions that General drive them home.

Now moving awkwardly into the passenger seat where he could be shielded from the rain, Tom issued further orders. General steered the carriage east, turned right onto Sixth Street, and weaved them through the multitudes, the sound of piano and brass reaching them from the Buckingham Burlesque Hall as they passed Market rose into the electric lights on Jefferson Street.

It would be all right. Tom Lark was assured of that much. He would return to the house, and the light in her room would be visible through the rain and from the road, and he would ascend the steps toward whatever kinds of amends he needed to make, and he would close all distances, providing a secure little island for his daughter in the midst of all turbulence, and there, like her schoolmaster, he would make her more profit than other daughters, than princesses who had more time for vainer hours and tutors not so careful.

Or this was what he told himself, but then, when the carriage picked up speed and rattled over the rutted dirt street south of Broadway, Tom found himself in a dark borderland between the electrical lights behind him and the flicker of the unexplained fireworks ahead.

"What is that?" he asked his driver.

General looked back over his shoulder, his broad face dripping with a new wave of rain. "What's *what*, sir?"

"The light over there. Like a southern aurora."

"Don't see much light, sir. And I don't know from no auroras. Maybe it's the moon off'n the rain."

It was nearly too much for Tom Lark's patience. He had never raised his voice to General—indeed, prided himself on speaking to his Negroes rationally and on equal footing—but it was becoming too much for him, and he snapped at the old driver, who shrugged, nodded, and steered the shay toward the house.

Which was still.

Which lay in complete unruffled darkness.

"Stygian, ain't it?" General asked, and Tom almost smiled, despite his anxiety.

Funny what your people picked up just by brushing against you.

Surely Hallie was in the house. Had gone to bed early.

So he had General pull the carriage to the front of the house, wait as he went inside and swept over the rooms in a vain, cursory search for his daughter. Then back out the door, his instructions to General more urgent, as his concern turned to worry and now danced on the edge of panic as the carriage rumbled away from the city, headed toward a pale light General swore he did not see and Tom Lark baffled by that insistence.

Past the new park and onto Third Street, down a busy and elegant suburban thoroughfare that tonight was quiet beneath the muffle of rain. The rumbling he had heard by the river was becoming more insistent on the grounds of the Boys' Home, and he was sure now that the fireworks were on display, that he would find his daughter safe in the cascading light...

Until they passed the covered wheel at the northern gates of the institution.

✳✳✳

At the western edge of the Boys' Home property lay the new monument to the Confederate Dead. The tall granite obelisk, crowned by the bronze figure of an infantryman staring resolutely north, a cavalryman and an artillery soldier facing east and west at its base. Scarcely six years old, erected as a response to a Federal Army reunion in 1895, it was perfect as a southern focal point for the events planned throughout the city.

At night it took on an even more eerie cast, like a solitary pillar from some ancient, ruinous temple. And the quiet around it made the approach that much stranger, Tom looking about him for the signs of festival and fire...

Seeing instead the Great Incendiary Apparatus, as it had been advertised when purchased in late winter, useless in the heavy rain.

Ixion's Wheel, they called it. After the man doomed to wander for kin-slaying only to be taken in by Zeus himself, who punished him by strapping him to a celestial torture wheel when the ungrateful guest tried to seduce the queen of the gods. This present device was a kind of Ferris wheel of fire, turning rapidly when propelled by the fireworks at its spokes.

It lay dormant now, covered in oilcloth. And passing beside it in the carriage, Tom realized at last that the light guiding him here was a foxfire, a fata morgana, and he sat back helpless in the shay, the water coursing over the canvas roof like it pooled and cascaded on the great wheel.

Then the light rose again, and for a moment, like in the flutter of artillery fire, the landscape blazed and he saw a forking road, black and impossibly level, branching at the foot of the monument, and lights rushed up both roads like lamps on ships running at unearthly speed, and the choking smell of oil or kerosene rife in the air, and buildings where Tom Lark had never imagined buildings, larger and taller than those he knew and impersonal in design like geometry rising out of the earth...

And he knew he was at the brink of something, somewhere at the edge of wonders, and that this all had nothing to do with the past, and then the light fell, tumbling back into fitful moonlight and glittering rain, and the only sound now was the rush of water across the roof of the shay, and he was baffled, struck with the confusing and terrible wonder of something he had glimpsed but knew he would never recognize...

And General repeating, softly at first but more and more insistently *no Mister Lark, I don't reckon you oughter get closer to that statue*, and then Tom following his driver's gaze toward the monument.

General's hand rested on his shoulder now, tugging him back into the carriage, but he was wrestling free, his boots sinking into the waterlogged ground, dragging his steps like he walked through a nightmare. He approached the monument, glimpsing the statue atop it in the sourceless light, the bronze man gazing vigilant northwards, while

General's desperate call faded behind him in the rush of the rain...

But the artilleryman, the eastern statue at the monument's base, held something in its extended arms.

The long dress, draped sodden over the bronze ramrod like a dismal flag. Her drenched hair dangling limp like dark cloth in an uncanny light and her arms, once delicate and lovely as he held them on the train platform, now drooped lifelessly, surrendered to the rain.

Four

I saw pale kings and princes too,
Pale warriors, death-pale were they all;
They cried—'La Belle Dame sans Merci
Thee hath in thrall!'

I saw their starved lips in the gloom,
With horrid warning gapèd wide,
And I awoke and found me here,
On the cold hill's side.

"Orfeo"

A Study in Depressive Behavior

Benjamin Mountolive

Prefatory Remarks

There is a moment in the life of a practicing psychologist when he calls to task all the theories he has learned, trying to find the answer implicit in all his experience. Where does the discipline leave off being therapeutic and become philosophical, speculative—at worst, a kind of fashionable New Age? And how, if at all, are the genuine curative properties of the science—those areas in which it might probe, re-order, and better the living of our lives—to be distinguished from all the party games that pass in its name?

This is the problem that confronted me as I returned to practice after a long stay as a university professor in upstate New

York. The return was unavoidable: the exceptional case of a chronically depressed subject, whose father vanished, apparently, in an abandoned house while the boy stood on a cellar landing, awaiting a return that never came.

Intellectual and professional curiosity aside, my calling was almost personal, given the poignant case of a young man, now in his early twenties, who had been haunted by abandonment—whether real or imagined—for nearly a decade. It was a case that cried out for the intervention of analysis and mythic insight: a journey to the psychic underworld to retrieve the damaged soul.

$$***$$

Almost immediately, I confronted the fact that, over the years, my studies had led me farther and farther from the office, the counseling session, the client—the whole experience of the clinician. Nor was it long before I wondered if, indeed, I could recover that experience or, ultimately, if there was an experience there to recover at all.

Poetry, once, and also the telling of stories, once served as the way we worked through our inner conflicts. Myth and fiction were the grand arenas where our imaginations worked, up against larger and less manageable forces in our experience. As such, they provided some escape, some consolation. But perhaps their time is over, in an age when the more direct and precise vocabulary of science, though it misses the old suggestions of metaphor.

And yet there is something to story, after all, even if it takes the everyday form of the case study. Freud and Jung both realized this at their best, and perhaps it is why client histories figure so prominently in their work. Scientific findings that peer into what used to be called the soul cannot escape so easily the ancient assurances of story, its ability to brush against what is yet to be identified and explained. Story should be thanked, of course, for giving us our forms: it is the place to start and the place within which we can stand, to examine and interpret and comprehend.

However, story is only story at the end of the day. The work of analysis is not simply "what happens next"; instead, it is an array of descriptive states of being, basic powers at work in the psyche. The images of a dream are representations of something more abstract. A furtive adventure to a house with boarded windows, an agonizing wait at the head of the stair, a father who vanished by one device or another—all speak to a primal sense of exclusion and distance and even abandonment.

Under the analytical lens, the scenes of childhood are not taken either as images, or linked into developmental narrative, but become examples of more theoretical moments and instants—-occasions that, as analysts, we believe may apply to the most exotic of lives. Under the lens of a good analyst, events do not tell a story but expose a structure. We take this structure, of course, and fit the recounted events to it. There is, after all, very often a source of malaise, a constant, a gesture of the mind that applies to other events across time, to the many stories of the analysand, illumining the one essential truth that troubles him.

So then, the attempts of the boy's father to excel as a novelist, his obsession over dead friends, his hot and cold relationship with his only son—-all these unite, somehow, as manifestations of a single root principle in the trauma of the subject's life. His world, then—indeed, anyone's world—-becomes a marked road in the dark, headed toward a destination and mapped clearly, but shady at its margins, requiring the headlight beam of the analyst to negotiate the grades and the curves. I, then, provide the function of consciousness, you might say. I am the voice and eyes and ears of reason, seeing abstractions, structures and laws.

With this in mind, I present the case of Young Orpheus—a study in depressive behavior. It does, I believe, indicate a continuing use for the form of story in psychological diagnosis and treatment, and I hope it is nott too derivative of the famous, almost literary case studies of my predecessors and forefathers. Orpheus' loss, descent into the Underworld, and return to the surface is still a good analogy for both the experience of depression and the undertaking of therapeutic analysis.

As we all know, Orpheus descended into the Underworld to retrieve his wife, Eurydice, following her untimely death. His song charmed Hades, the God of the Dead, into relinquishing the shade of the girl, on the condition that Orpheus, while guiding her back to the land of the living, not look back to see if she is following. Orpheus, of course, looks back at the edge of emerging, and Eurydice, who has been following all along, vanishes, leaving him bereft.

The story is a rather simple allegory, but useful for those who internalize it, who see it for the parable it is. As Joseph Campbell reminds us, it is simply a fact that all the gods are imagined, are part of our psyche, and that all mythology is about ourselves. No less Orpheus: one goes under to retrieve what has been lost, does work to retrieve it, then emerges, neither looking back nor revisiting the complexes, because looking back is regression, is counter-intuitive, is against the cure.

Of course, Orpheus' is not the story for everyone, but nevertheless, some can profit and heal from it. For it is often profitable, ultimately, to cast oneself in heroic dimensions. If the Underworld is negotiable, so is therapy. If the bride is retrievable, so is the health of the psyche.

These were the premises with which I approached the case of "Orfeo", a New England graduate student under treatment for depression. The success of the counseling was remarkable, and yet a pair of significant ethical issues must be addressed at the outset of this essay.

First of all, I had formed a close acquaintance with the subject over a number of years and in a non-professional capacity. Whether or not this previous association forced Orfeo into what Freud has termed "secondary revision", manifested in the patient's particular way of behavior toward the analyst, is an issue subject to debate; however, thirty years of experience in analysis may do a great deal to countervail any compromise to objectivity.

Perhaps more suspect is the fact that the heart of this essay rests upon a somewhat imaginative employment of transcripts, the purity of which I have tried to restore by removing virtually any possibility that the identity of the young man might be uncovered; furthermore, I have been advised by a copyright attorney that the activities traced through this account are legally uncompromised, regardless of ethical questions that might be raised over a number of events in Orfeo's story. All of that, of course, assumes the truth of any of the events recounted by the client.

Background

Orfeo was a twenty-four year male at the time of these consultations, the only child of an exceptionally intelligent mother and an admittedly talented, if irresponsible and erratic, father, who is worthy of extensive mention only because his story is a significant factor in the story of his son.

The parents had lived apart since Orfeo was a toddler. The mother, true to her gifts and ambitions, undertook a successful career as a university professor, relocated and remarried, while the father, himself an academic of sorts, drifted through a series of adjunct posts in the upper Midwest.

Orfeo had suffered for a decade with sporadic depression. Second-hand report had established that the episodes involved a combination of obsessive reading, isolating behavior, and in more recent years, binge drinking in excess of the general undergraduate indulgence. In the "up" stages of this cycle Orfeo was charming and productive; indeed, a number of his acquaintances were heard to comment on his physical and personal attractiveness. Indeed, such had been almost a universal verdict until the Christmas of 19__, when his father disappeared on a mysterious trip to Kentucky, in circumstances complicated by the fact that Orfeo was with him on that trip. At the time, I assured the young man that such behavior was typical of his father, that even a kind of fleeing the scene of the accident, given immature character, was not out of the question.

Orfeo, however, insisted that his father had disappeared—had vanished, as it were, from the face of the earth, completely and literally. This, of course, was a fanciful explanation even for one who was only fifteen at the time, but when Orfeo insisted upon it almost a decade later, it could be construed as a position he held against all evidence, a serious lapse from realism. It was then he was first urged under my care, for consultation in the spring and summer of 2000. The sessions were intermittent because of the client's occasional resistance, but the progress made in consultation should be evident from the following transcripts. Please note the following:

1. The documents below are edited solely for the purposes of preserving the privacy of the subject, the focus of the condition, and a kind of narrative continuity.

2. The primary focus of each session is that of Orfeo's "self-narration", guided, as it were, by the commentary of the clinician, both in the recorded conversation and in the resultant text, as an array of notes to the stories.

INITIAL

PSYCHIATRIC ASSESSMENT

Identifying information:

Date:

DOB:22 June 1977

Name: *D.R. (referred to as "Orfeo" in transcript and accompanying documentation)*

Parent(s)/Guardian(s): *G.R. (whereabouts unknown)*Father

J.B.M (university professor) Mother

Current Intake/Comprehensive assessment material reviewed by reporter: ☐Yes ☐No

Current status:

Referred by mother, whose professional opinion detected a number of abnormalities. Client lives alone, employee of small town book store, indications of incipient alcoholism, recreational drug use, frequent bouts of depression. Vivid, haunting

nightmares that bleed over into a kind of hallucinatory mid-state between sleep and waking, in which client is unable to distinguish dream from the everyday (c. Green & McCreery on the metachoric experience, i.e. lucid and false dreaming).

Presenting problem (consumer statements and clinical impressions)*: Client maintains there is nothing out of the ordinary with his situations. He is, according to his account, a "slow waker," and believes that false dreaming has yet to impair his capacity to function meaningfully in his environs.*

Historical data reviewed:

Family:

Medical: *No significant physical or pharmaceutical issues known in the case of the parents. Paternal grandmother (M.C.L.) reputedly addicted # of prescriptions meds, 1st Librium and Valium, then progressing to more* recent varieties of anti-depressants, the names of which she refused to share with Orfeo's mother, out of long-standing estrangement.

Psychiatric/Mental health: *Paternal grandmother displays, according to Client's mother, characteristics of borderline NPD (see Masterson, 1981). According to Client's mother, father displayed some of the same characteristics, or, very possibly, those of BP disorder (see Zanarini et. al. 1998; Gardner & Cowdry, 1985)*

Drug and alcohol:

Paternal grandparents: *Alcohol (grandfather); alcohol, prescription drugs (grandmother)*

Father: *Alcohol, cannabis*

Patient:

Medical: *Excellent physical health*

Medication: *Mild anti-depressants (currently Paxil®)*

Psychiatric/Mental health: *Intermittent mild depression. Erratic behavior toward family and friends; abandonment fears; withdrawal. This feeling self-characterized as "emptiness" (DSM-III-R).*

Drug and alcohol: *Alcohol; cannabis; possible (though unadmitted) "experiment" with peyote and hallucinogens.*

Mental status exam:

At the moment, Client's basic diagnosis suggests a number of possibilities, none of which seem to cause the client discomfort or unhappiness. Attending therapy, however, is uncomfortable, which might indicate a resistance to authority/authority figures characteristic of his father and bearing further examination.

Clinical summary: *Mother's initial assessment, though professional, was in need of secondary support. Initial conversations w/ client tend to concur with* mother's provisional diagnoses and/or therapeutic approaches.

Diagnosis:

Axis IDepression, bipolar disorder (?)

Axis IIBPD (?) NPD (?)

Axis IIINormal

Axis IVModerate difficulty in social/ familial functioning.

Axis VGAF (current)36GAF (past year)56

Psychiatric problem list:

Depression is most pressing of Client's clinical problems. Client is resistant to medication.

Consumer strengths and resources:

Excellent and perceptive support system through Client's mother, a qualified professional in the psychiatric field.

Recommendations:

Consensus between Counselor and family that traditional analysis—the time-honored "talking cure"—constitutes optimal immediate option.

Prognosis:

A vexing but hardly impossible combination of syndromes. A year of regular analytical sessions should leave client fully engaged with real environs, and productively and happily so.

Psychiatrist signature and credentials:

Benjamin Mountolive, M.D. PsyD. Ph.D.

Clinician's Note: *The following transcript begins with a segment of a conversation between the clinician and the client. This exchange is included with the text to illustrate some of the issues the sessions intended to address, and also to indicate that the initial weather between client and clinician was, at best, testy.*

BM: And there is something you continue to believe, [Orfeo]. That your father is not going to return, despite the fact that after eight years, and with you on the premises at the time, that there is no evidence of foul play involved in his disappearance?

Orfeo: Come on. A five-year disappearance has foul play involved in it somehow. Whether it's that he was carted off, done in, or just simply disappeared, it's foul play by any standard unless you're the police.

BM: What do you mean, 'simply disappeared,' [Orfeo]?

Orfeo: What I say, Ben. I mean what I say.

BM: Rather elusive there, [Orfeo].

Orfeo: What's elusive about meaning what you say? Isn't that the least elusive thing of all?

BM: You are very much indeed like your father.

Orfeo: You mean disappeared?

BM: No. I mean what I say. But tell me, [Orfeo]. Tell me what is wrong with this way of explaining. You came back to your grandmother's house before dawn, having searched the B___ premises for the father you expected would turn up, and you lay down on the sofa while your grandparents were still sleeping. Is that right? Pretty much right?

Orfeo: That's the outside of it, Ben. And I went into his old bedroom, hoping he'd be there even though I was pretty much sure he wouldn't be. I was there among his childhood keepsakes. It was strange, because I was about the age he was when he collected them.
BM: How did that make you feel, [Orfeo]?

Orfeo: Like I said. Strange.

BM: Can you....

Orfeo: ...be more specific? Not fuckin' likely. It just felt like I was connected to him in a way that I hadn't been connected before.

[Inaudible].

BM: Well, however indefinite that might seem, maybe this is what was happening with you that night, and maybe this is the place to start the conversation. Will you listen to my version of things, [Orfeo]? [Orfeo]?

Orfeo: (Inaudible)
BM: Will you? I'm sorry, I....

Orfeo: Listen to mine first, Ben. Just listen to mine. Don't be giving me your version of things before you got something to build a version on.
    Willing to hear me out? Or are we here to decide the story before it's told?
    [A signal from the clinician follows, a gesture meaning to imply that all was welcome, that the client be put at ease to tell his story the way he thought he was telling it.]
    Don't wave it away before you've heard it, Ben. It's hard enough to remember all of it without your distractions.
    But it started in my father's room. It was his old room, on

August Street.

I remember it was lazy evening, early Christmas Eve. And the sunlight was carrying dust motes, encouraging me to sleep.

It was hot in the house. The way old people make a house hot, closing all the windows and raising the heat about five degrees above what's comfortable for the rest of us. And I was sitting in Pops' room, looking through his kid stuff, which they had deposited in a box in the back of the closet, and thinking how one box wouldn't make a start on my music alone. I could hear the snap of typewriter keys against paper in the adjacent room. Hear the keys stopping, the slow breath of time when I waited for my father to come for me.

He found me with his belongings all spread out on the floor. Plastic models, posters, frayed paperbacks and baseball cards. Disposable childhood, was what it was, things bought on the cheap because he couldn't afford the better versions, then put away for keepsakes like they were going to last. Of course they were already frail, but they were still fascinating, like artifacts from another world.

And I read the manuscript later. The ones he left. Read how he claimed I persuaded him into what happened next. But I think it was already mapped out when he came into the room, and despite what you're thinking there can be two versions of the same intentions——versions not that far from each other and still a little different so that they amount to the same thing, no matter who started what and for what reason.

You might say we wanted to share the story.

So the way I remember it, he was behind what happened that night. But I'm not attaching blame, and if you'd love for me to do that, well so be it, because I'm not and won't and can't, do you understand?

Do you?

He had told me part of the T_____ business. Some of their wanderings. A little about the Halloween adventure. It was only later that the letters to Ma filled in some of the gaps. When I was putting the papers together, you know? I saw the background then, and the histories, the bruised reputations. So I knew part of it—not all of it, but enough to steer by as it got late Christmas Eve, and I waited in my father's old room, shutting off the lights and lying back on the bed, checking out his spattered black light paint that had made a constellation on the ceiling thirty years ago.

Well, the stars he made up were still shining then, and I suppose that whoever has my grandma's house now, whoever lives in August Acres, may have noticed that there's a whole other heaven on the ceiling when the lights go out, and I hope it's a kid that notices, because instead of restoring or replacing the ceiling, it would be a kid who would count the stars. Who would steer by them.

BM: *(Inaudible).*

Orfeo: Whatever. We snuck out of the house when it was fully dark, and I thought that someone had to be at the B___ place, because it seemed decked out for Christmas. The old ramp that led up to the front door was green with what looked like holly and ivy, parts of it almost black in the yellowed glare of the streetlight. From where I stood at my grandmother's window, the leaves looked sharp, almost bladed. And I passed off the menace of the leaves into thinking that someone was there, and despite my father insisting that, no, it was part of the haunting of the place, I kept thinking that until we were at the ramp itself and could look into the picture window at the front of the house. Then you could see how the light fell in over nothing, and all of a sudden breaking in there seemed a lot less dangerous, a lot more like a simple adventure.

It was strange, because as we crossed the street it was like one of us was leading for a minute, and then it was the other. My father walked ahead of me most of the time, in that ancient blue overcoat of his, a pillowcase slung over his shoulder, weighed down with something or other, so that it looked like a makeshift knapsack, a gnome's gunny from a fairy tale. At first, as we approached the incline, I thought he was set on guiding us straight through the front door and into the house, but he turned and moved along the north side of the house, along an old wooden privacy fence to the back of the property like he was sure, completely sure where he was headed. And I'm thinking: how could he know? And: it's got to have changed over the years.

Sure enough, when he gets back there, the fence line is overgrown, and we're passing through husks of grass and dried branches, making enough sound to wake the dead, I was thinking. Then he reaches the corner of the lot, and I hear him swear under his breath.

"Who in the world would have mended the damn fence?" he goes, and then he's setting his shoulder against one of the boards, and pushing. I come up beside him, about to tell him that maybe we should call it a night, that maybe it wasn't meant to be. But then he opens the gnome's gunny and produces a crowbar. And he levers it into the fence planking, and the board gives way, the nails in it screeching as the crowbar tugs them from the wood. And there was this smell—curious because it was winter, of course, but the smell of decay under the smell of smoke, and he turns around and helps me through the gap in the planks.

Now I was beginning to worry. I had an idea in my head that as long as we didn't knock anything down or in, like a door or a window, that entering the house wasn't illegal. I know now that it was trespassing no matter what, but the house was silent and so was the night, and when the window opened it smelled like paint and old tobacco rushing out to greet us, and Pops laced his fingers to give me a stirrup for a lift up...well I knew we weren't going back then. And I mounted the hands and the windowsill, and I took a deep breath as I climbed into the close dark.

Progress Note

Recipient Name: *"Orfeo"*

Date of Service (m/d/yy)*:*

Type of Service:*Consultation*

Length of Service:*1 hour*

Treatment goals addressed*: Establishing trust in Clinician as authority figure/guide. Attempted transferring of analytical work to the Client instead of Clinician. In short, Orfeo was asked to address "what the story means."*

> *Active interventions provided as specified on treatment plan and an interpretation of how recipient responded to intervention(s):*
>
> *Encouragement to analyze resisted, if not outright rejected. Client continues to press clinician to analyze narration, insisting "it is your job."*
>
> **Recipient's progress towards treatment goals:** *Initial misgivings and hostility toward therapy not abated.*
>
> **Other clinically relevant information:**
>
> **Signature of provider and credentials:**
>
> Benjamin Mountolive, M.D. PsyD. Ph.D.

Clinician's Note: *The second session, two weeks later, occurred at the continuous urging of the clinician. Orfeo did not show for the scheduled appointment, which I took as a further expression of his reluctance to pursue the matters we had engaged upon. Nonetheless, I knew where he could be found: a brief and authoritative contact with his university brought him back to the offices the next week.*

Sometimes the role of analyst is—and, indeed, must be—paternal, especially on the occasions when a stable paternal figure is absent from the client history.

Orfeo entered like a truant student or a prodigal son, so the first exchanges between the two of us were guarded, even testy. I had contemplated addressing the manuscript that figured in the strange events of that now-distant December; however, I had second thoughts upon viewing the client's demeanor, and instead approached the session through the customary tactic of simple, open-ended questioning. "What comes to mind?" was followed by second, more specific line of questioning, in which we focused on the story Orfeo had been telling when I adjourned the last session. "You left us climbing into the B___ House on that Christmas Eve. What comes to your mind about that time? That moment? What do you remember happening next?"

When the client proved resistant still, my questioning took us to the resistance itself. "When we were together last, you seemed most sure of the story you were telling, and reasonably sure of its meaning. What's happened, do you think, to shake your certainty in the last two weeks or so?"

By now, I was scarcely directing him. And yet, for over half of our allotted time, Orfeo defied all and any suggestions to interpret his story, or indeed, even to continue it. It was as if we stood at the margins of shadows ourselves—that is to say, stalled at the brink of our journey into Orfeo's hidden psyche.

So I retraced our steps. I asked Orfeo more about meeting his father at the airport, about their trip in the car together down from Chicago, and about his waiting that long afternoon for the night of Christmas Eve. Each time I tried to cast light on other events and situations, particular circumstances, thoughts and feelings.

I felt like Orpheus myself, descending to return with the dead.

The retrieval brought us full circle, as it usually does. Now, once again, the client stood, in his memory, at the windowsill, peering into the dark house, having reached after fact and reason with little success. That, of course, was where I could aid him, as his analytic guide. His surface consciousness. He was back to the point where I had left him, schooled by my questions and, of course, by his own memory. It was a simple step to the story's resumption—a step he seemed to make with less fear now, and with less reluctance:

✳✳✳

Orfeo:... no, not at all. The darkness didn't hold any real terror

417

for me. After all, even from the back yard, you could see the street lamp through the picture window. And except for one bedroom I looked into as we passed down the hall, the other windows were without curtains, like they were bare to the world or something.

It was a familiar kind of darkness, I guess you could call it. That kind where your main danger was tripping over something rather than meeting something, if you see what I'm saying. And so, after Pops produces this flashlight, we could pass pretty safely down the little corridor toward the living room, where the streetlamp was all golden light pooled on the floor, and Pops takes his breath in, and he says, I'm shutting off the flash now.

So we're standing in the hallway, and I move behind Pops like I am getting ready to have him defend me from something. But the living room was pretty much empty—a couple of collapsed cardboard boxes, and seeing them there, the only thing lying on a threadbare carpet, made the room look that much more empty. Not like the emptiness we would see at the bottom of the stairs, in the basement where it all opened up and happened.

Because the basement was where we were headed now, through a cramped kitchen that smelled of dust and tobacco and old bacon, and something turned nasty in the air. It was December, and no doubt they had shut off the heat in this house for months or years, but it was stifling on the tiles. A back window was letting an uneven light into the kitchen, and you could look out a window over the sink and see the yard we had come through to get here, the bare branches on the trees waving like they were flagging down a ride.

Pops stepped on a little landing where three doors faced each other—the back door into the desolate garden, the side door into a garage that was no longer a garage, had never been a garage, and the door in front of us, leading to a basement that neither of us had traveled, though Pops said he had dreamed of it once while he was awake, if that made sense at all. What did make sense is that we were standing at the top of a flight of stairs, and Pops crouched there for a moment. I could see him all frozen in moonlight, drained of color like a Civil War photograph. He looked diminished: almost my size, and I remembered how long it had been since I saw him.

***

Clinician's Note: *"I remembered how long it had been since I saw him." It had been almost half a year, since the previous summer vacation, to be exact. This brief comment was more significant to my trained ears than anything to do with the story Orfeo was telling, although the story itself had bearing on this truth. The father had exploited the son's eagerness to make contact, to reunite, and had enlisted the boy in a hare-brained escapade that was a misdemeanor at best. I began to think that it should have been Orfeo's father "on the couch"—-that this was about an attempt to redirect a kidnapped childhood, and that Orfeo had suffered for this indulgence.*

Oddly, Orfeo did not dwell on the potential abusiveness of the situation. Indeed, he never even indicated that he perceived it—-no doubt a testimony to its embeddedness and his repression.

***

Orfeo: So Pops tells me that Miss V_____ had kept all kinds of junk in the garage, and it felt like an accident when he says it aloud. I suppose the sound of his own voice startled him, caught him up short, on account of he starts to turn on the flashlight and then it's like he thinks better of it, like bringing more light from the outside wasn't the way down and through this world, if you know what I'm saying...

***

Clinician's Note: *And of course, as a clinician, I did know what he was saying. Orfeo saw the world into which he was descending as a* kind of self-contained entity. Like so many in their early years—-and like most boys, especially, I say without condescension—-he hovered between obeying the rules of the place and somehow rising or standing above them, which he no doubt thought would be the privilege of adulthood. As a reader can see, Orfeo credited his father with some kind of symbolic wisdom, understood the refusal to turn on the flashlight as a kind of mystical submission to the experiences that the father claimed had created him. It was the same kind of thing that, as a young teen himself, the father had undertaken with the guidance (and perhaps more questionable influences) of the long-dead man whose house the two of them were exploring. Nor would it have been wise for me—at least not at that juncture—to introduce the possibility that Orfeo's father risked breaking their necks in the darkness for the indulgent adventure of living out his so-called defining myth.

But I knew the myths of descent. Knew them better than the man at the head of the stairs. Knew how all the heroes approached their dark and defining underground journeys, and I can tell you that Orfeo's father was bound for that basement because of a limited number of reasons. For judgment or vision, to visit ghosts or to retrieve something or someone, or perhaps (and I say this after passing acquaintance with both Orfeo and his father) just a simple and, frankly, rather shallow curiosity. Perhaps the motive contained elements of all these desires and lonely impulses, and perhaps this minor novelist and part-time teacher, knowing enough myth to indict him, identified with all the great underground voyagers— with Gilgamesh or Orpheus, Odysseus or Aeneas or Dante. Perhaps he thought that the country of his memory would answer questions or yield him riches. Or perhaps, in that undisciplined and scarred imagination, the venture was lifted out of a simple burglary of a musty vacant house in a Midwest suburb. Maybe Orfeo's father saw a meaning in the darkness at the foot of the stairs.

Whatever, it was fascinating and absurd, and just a little bit pitiful.

✳✳✳

Orfeo: We stood at the head of the stairs, Pops and me. And it's now of all times that he turns off the flashlight, and it's now I am looking down this flight of stairs into nothing, and you can't even see stair past the third or fourth step. It was like a wall of absolute black after that. So I hold on to the rail, you know, and start to descend, but then he holds me back, and he's saying "not yet" in a whisper that feels almost…dangerous, it is so quiet otherwise. He whispers, "Don't let it rise into words just yet," and I'm thinking, "This is a place where my senses don't apply." Now I wonder if it is like that in all those sensory deprivation experiments, where they put you in the Lilly Tank and after a while you start making things up, or having visions, or whatever you'd call it once you start seeing, hearing, and smelling things.

So Pops is saying not yet, and his hand is on my shoulder for a second, then he takes it away all sudden and fast. I remember thinking, "Well, there's still touch, we haven't passed into a world where touch falls away." But then it was like the other senses came back when I called on them, and I grip the railing tightly as I descend. From somewhere down in the darkness there's a whiff of clay and moss, and by now I had it figured that the way down into the basement was going to be easy compared to the way coming back up.

So, like I said, I went down there. And the only light I carried with me was on the fluorescent dial of my watch. But right about then, just like it was answering my thoughts or something, the darkness in front of me starts to layer. And then you could see ordinary dark—the dark you thought was the dark to begin with—giving way to a dark that was deeper, like mottling out on a pond, where you can see from the surface that some parts of the water stretch down further than others… oh, you know what I mean by that, and it's the point at which your eyesight fails entirely and, when you think about it later, your words fail when you try to get them around the idea. And it's almost like you blink and the layers change places, and I felt like we were traveling through the darkness and ending up in a kind of makeshift light. Damn, but it's hard to put the words around it, but it was kind of like thinking you were going into a place and taking a few steps, only to find out you were going out of the place you thought you were going into.

So it was down the steps, like I said, and the dark rising up to meet us. All the time, mind you, Pops has not turned on the flashlight. So I'm clinging to the railing like the stuff from a shipwreck in a storm... what do you call it?

Flotsam. That's right.

And I'm taking the steps one by one and thinking of a moment in some Steven King novel where the steps you are on just fall away into a drop on hand-made spikes, and it was like Pops knew the worst of that fear, like he's had them himself, because before I know it, he's past me and ahead of me. Now I got my hand on his back, and I'm steering more by the touch of him than by sight or hearing, and then his back seems more solid and still, and my guess is that right then we had reached the foot of the stairs.

✳✳✳

Clinician's Note: *The account above was broken on a number of occasions, by questions, by my requests for more clarity, more detail. Orfeo, however, resisted any analysis of his own. When I stopped him to reflect on what something meant (his father's eccentric use or non-use of the flashlight, for example, or his own odd description of "layered darkness") he kept to the story, to the sights and the sounds and the smells of his memory. The account felt rehearsed, the phrasing carefully chosen as if he had memorized it all, or as if he did not trust a departure from his senses, as though they were his only anchor in the world.*

No wonder that those who supposedly appeared in the basement of the old B_____ house were no surprise to me, and the very fact that they appeared was a sure sign they should be brought out into the light. But they should be unmasked, also, so that we no longer had to glimpse them through the dark glass of memory and desire.

But I did not know that as Orfeo concluded the session with the following part of the story, and his telling passed into the realm of shadow and dream and myth.

***

Orfeo: The basement of this house couldn't have been all that large, unless the house followed the rules you hear about icebergs—that only a little lies on the surface, while most of it is deep, out of your sight and reckoning. But from the beginning, when Pops and I went down there, you could feel a kind of largeness to the place—drafts of watery-smelling cold air in a space where you'd never expect drafts.

There was really no light down there. T_____ had boarded up the high windows at ground level, so not even a slant of moon got in. So I extended my hands, felt for the wall and found it.

Then the wall began to suck me in.

I went wrist-deep and started yelling. I tried to pull away. It closed softly on my wrist like dough or clay, and I shouted again and tugged free. Pops is shouting, "what? what?"

And no, I have no idea why he still didn't turn on the flashlight. It turned out all right, I guess… forget about it.

But in that instant I pulled free, and I was on the floor, and collecting myself, and standing, and turning about in the dark that had almost swallowed me. Now it surprised me that I could pick up shapes in the shadows as we moved through the basement, though we still were steering largely by touch and smell. All of a sudden, there's this doorway, again the smell of water, this time laced with old laundry detergent. And Pops tells me to stay put at the doorway, and he leaves me with the flashlight and the orders not to use it. And of course I'm thinking what good is it, then. Not to mention, don't leave me here where the walls are hungry. But surely he knew what he was doing, because I'm here to tell this, aren't I?

Anyway, he moves on into the recesses of the basement, and

it isn't long before I hear him headed back.

He says there's one more door up to the right, and that the place is laid out in this odd fashion, that it wasn't like the basements of his dead friends Del and Joey, though he'd imagined that all the houses on August were built to the same floor plan. Go figure, he says, but I'm thinking all kinds of horrors, like bodies walled up in that spongy wall like something in a Poe story....

I know. But what else can I compare it to? It was like a world you read about, not one you live in. Like the one in the old man's stories.

Of course I mean T_____. I would never refer to Pops as "the old man."

No. Doesn't mean that I don't think Pops wrote them. I don't know what I think. He wrote the novel, though. I know that much.

But I'm thinking of the stories, and how T_____ is this solitary man who lives with his mother past the time you're supposed to do that, and I'm thinking of the Bates Motel, and of Dahmer and John Wayne Gacy, because none of those were that long before and we had been warned against them, and it wasn't like Pops' day when growing up was safe and sunny, now was it?

There was this smell rising out of the stale soap, and you could tell that something had turned down there. And I was remembering that part in The Odyssey where he sets out a bowl of blood so the ghosts can talk.

No. I don't know what that means. Why the fuck do you keep asking what it means? Isn't it your job to find out?

(Inaudible. Long pause.)

Well, I know this much. Thinking about the other stories makes what I went through a little more interesting when I remember it now. But stories don't always feel so good when you're in the middle of them.

Then again, feeling that pain or fear or even panic...That's sometimes the thing that gives the story meaning, isn't it? Maybe that smell wasn't rotting or rats... maybe it was sorrow, pure and simple. Maybe that's your meaning. Maybe I really was smelling tears, and thinking of T_____ and his mother, of the story I didn't know until `later when I read Pops' manuscript.

But then again, when I read about them in the manuscript, it was like "is that all?" And this sorrow, mind you, was something larger and deeper than a house could contain.

And I stood in the same spot, and it was like the story stopped until Pops puts his hands on my shoulders and he says "See there?" but I didn't see anything. I didn't even know what I was supposed to be seeing or looking for. And he braces me, and his grip tightens on my arm, and he goes, "Right there. The arch." And I'm not seeing it. And he shakes me just a little. Now something takes shape. I could see an arch there, or just about. So I nod my head, and his grip loosens and he pats me on the shoulder. Then he asks if I can make out details, but no, it was still just an arch, though I knew that if you had an arch you were headed through it.

XXXII

Clinician's Note: *The next session was postponed past the week I wanted, on past the second week for which I was prepared to settle, simply because (I told myself) of the Memorial Day holiday. We had ended the second session in Orfeo's long account of his entrance, with his father, into an abandoned house across the street from where that father had grown up. It was an event that struck me as at best trespass, at worst out and out breaking and entering.*

Neither of these crimes was beyond Orfeo's father, of course—a man who, as it turned out, was seeking to raise the ghost of his own literary career out of another man's tomb, so to speak. And yet Orfeo had been of an impressionable age, his father notably absent in his formative years; in short, he displayed all the tendencies and vulnerabilities that would have enabled an emotionally thwarted man such as his father to exploit his own son, to assure obedience down to the very details in which the son saw what he was supposed to see. It seemed encouraging, however, that Orfeo had resisted his father's command to "recognize details" in the hallucinatory arch. In essence, Orfeo was not buying into some paternal reality—not seeing everything his father was telling him to see.

The significance of this resistance cannot be underestimated.

The wedge between father and son provided an opportunity for what I could only call a constructive intervention. At this moment, I found it both professionally and ethically possible to introduce the issue of manuscript piracy—the father's sin that had been visited on the son for over eight years.

✳✳✳

BM: I think it's time we address something, [Orfeo].
Orfeo: I know where you're headed, and it's a lot more complicated than you think.
BM: Oh, I'm not passing judgment. I never judge.
Orfeo: I don't believe that.
BM: And yet you're more than willing to believe that those stories are your father's own.
Orfeo: You've always had it in for him, haven't you?
BM: Of course not.
Orfeo: Yes you have. This goes way back and you know it.

✳✳✳

Clinician's Note: *What I knew indeed was that "way back" was hardly an apt description for the time period covered by Orfeo's therapy. In his understandable defensiveness (his father's metaphorical and symbolic absence having become disturbingly literal on the very night he was recounting in therapy), Orfeo was no doubt projecting a mixture of trust and resentment onto his clinician. Needless to say, the issue of plagiarism—one could say, of literary grave-robbing—that had tainted the reputation of Orfeo's father did not merit burdening his son, whose insistence on telling the rest of the story suggested a larger need. In short, if Orfeo was to be helped or healed in any fashion, the story would have to be finished, the last tale told. With that in mind, I suggested we drop the issue of the manuscript, and that Orfeo continue his account of the Christmas Eve in question.*

***

Orfeo: Fair enough, Doctor. But don't make me stop to interpret, all right? Like I said last time, it's your job to analyze.

We kept walking on, into the darkness. The arch drifted ahead of us, like it was moving back, receding, keeping us at a distance or something. I kept my hand on Pops' shoulder—I was reaching up, clinging to him as I followed him, and my arm was getting tired, because remember I was thirteen and not so tall. And Pops isn't saying anything (well, not much), and I close my eyes—I swear to God I closed them—and I see, in a kind of after-image, a tiled floor at my feet. The draft had become a wind by now, a wind in my face, and I suspected I had crossed into something, like that moment when you are falling off into sleep and you could pull yourself back into wakefulness but you don't. Your mind and body give way to the dark, and then you are tumbling into a kind of cloudy light.

And that was in the direction we were headed, forward and down, and soon it was pretty obvious how incredibly huge this basement was turning out to be, because we are passing through pockets of cold air and continuing to walk, and sometimes the cold would break around you and sometimes pass clean through you. And sometimes it would even stop and dwell inside you for a minute like a second heart, and when it did that, this awful sorrow would settle on you. It couldn't have been more than a few seconds, but it felt permanent, it felt like the space of years.

Then there was a scuttling ahead of me, like something rushing out from underfoot and bound for even more darkness, if you could imagine that. And maybe it was just that my eyes were wanting to make up for the evidence of senses—maybe that was it, after all—but I start seeing things in front of me now, vivid things, flutters of light like a strobe at a club or like an after-image when you come out of the sun and a full snow, or when someone's clocked you and you're seeing stars. And in the midst of this, I think I see Pops standing on a smooth floor tiled in huge squares of black and white, all like there was no color left in the universe, only shades.

So it was then that I closed my eyes again.

Oh, sometime since the last time I closed them and saw the tiles and all...I don't remember when I'd opened them. It doesn't make much difference, really. I wasn't seeing with my eyes.

At any rate, the shapes around me begin to become more solid—human forms, or something near to human, not quite complete but suggesting at flesh by angles and lines—and it was creepy to imagine that we were on the edge of not being alone down there.

Because we were and we weren't alone.

Yes, I'm trying to explain it, god damn it!

We were and weren't alone, but we also were and weren't. The cold crush of sand or snow under my feet, the shuffling as I brushed it out of my path. And it was terribly cold down in that cellar, and I knew we'd moved into some labyrinth or recesses underground, and that Pops was perhaps the only living soul who might have been here before and might have been aware of where we were headed.

Now the ground under us began to rise, to slope up in a kind of steep incline. It led us, finally, through the arch itself, and now, thanks to a faint light from the other side of the thing, I figured I could begin to read the inscription that Pops was talking about before, that he wanted me to read so badly.

But of course I couldn't. I'd only had one year of Latin. Couldn't read it even if I'd known the words, because all those Roman inscriptions are full of abbreviations. And I had no idea what the letters were short for.

So I asked Pops. And it turns out he couldn't read the Latin either. Was hoping I could. Said that was part of the reason he wanted me down here, which didn't make sense on account of I had been the one to urge us down there, hadn't I? And how would he have known to begin with that the inscription was down here? Or the arch?

But there were images, carvings up and down the supports of the arch—what they call the abutment, I found out later.

There was a boy afloat above this weird geometrical relief, like he was flying over crystals or over some snow-covered city. There was a man perched on a bridge, and some kind of form in more shallow relief behind him so it looked like a ghost or something, or somebody creeping out of the fog and up to no good. And there was a couple, seated in the middle of these cloudy, lonely shapes, and they were playing chess among what looked liked men and what looked like angels, I figured. And finally there was this man hoisting the body of this girl into the arms of another man, who did not seem to be spirit or flesh, but was something else altogether, something I could not figure.

But the images were inscribed, and one year's Latin was barely enough for me to understand. "Hibernus", "Vernus", "Aestivus", under the couple playing chess, and "Autumnus" was the last one. So I figured it was a calendar or just scenes of the seasons, like winter with an icy beard, blowing on the edge of an old map.

That's what I thought until I read the stories. Until I came to realize that the images had been set years ago, to await us coming here.

And that wasn't all that was waiting for us. Because the ground sloped upward more steeply, and something glittered under my feet, like I was walking on ice or glass, so that I'm wondering now where the light is coming from. Then I see it above us, a steady light high on a hill, like in all those near-death experiences they talk about on cable TV, so I'm thinking, no thank you, I'll stay in the basement.

Then I see Pops is up there ahead of me, motioning me on without looking back, and I'm wondering how he even knows I'm behind him.

Now the light up there begins to spread out, and Pops calls to me and says, I know you're behind me, D_____, and that's why I'm not looking back, and it was like he had read my mind. And more than that, it was like by not looking back he was carrying me, like he was bearing up for a little space beneath some kind of heavy burden. And I knew it was my part to follow, because following would make the load lighter, and there was no danger he would take me somewhere that he thought he couldn't get me out of.

***

Of course it looked like Dacia. How could it not?

You had the mountainous slopes. You had darkness behind us, and light ahead; like Orlando, Valentine, and Jack must have seen as they climbed toward the princess in the novel you never read.

No, you didn't. And that is why you can't speak to his stories—why you can't tell me where T_____ leaves off and Pops begins, and maybe where Pops leaves off as well. I don't have to defend him——he's beyond my defending and your attacking right now.

***

Clinician's Note: *Here the projection intensifies. Orfeo wants his analyst to share a kind of adulation of his father, to move off task. It is here that the veil parts and the repressed begins to return.*

***

Orfeo: No. I'll tell you the rest of the story.

Because I followed him, and the two of us climbed beyond most anything I knew or recognized, scaling up that mountainside, and up there in the light, like dust motes at first, then the size of flies, then of reeling birds, there are these dark shapes come out of the glow, and for a minute I am thinking they are angels, perhaps like the ones somebody carved on the arch back there.

It all looked inviting from where we were, and of course everything in me is rushing up toward that summit. I'm thinking if I get there I'm going to see it all clearly for a change.

But I got there, and I didn't.

Up there the light was so brilliant that everything vanished into the glare. Only a few minutes before—or maybe even an hour, I lost track and the watch had stopped—I couldn't find Pops in the darkness. And now I am struggling to find him in the light.

And I get the feeling that the light is even more brilliant the higher up you go, because it's almost blinding me here, blazing out of this dark wall that is riddled with holes so you're seeing a black space with light erupting from all sides of it, and I could only imagine what it would be like if the wall was down, and I figured it would be unbearable. I know what I'm telling you flies in the face of everything you taught me about science, about physics especially, but I could make out a closed door in the middle of that wall, framed in this rectangle of light like the sun was about to burst loose from behind it. And the door itself was bending and buckling as if the light was an irresistible surge of water or wind, or like the light had weight and substance, and was pushing the door free of its hinges.

I try and look around it, but this wall goes on for as far as I can see. It was all black and porous with tendrils of heatless flame licking over it and through it like those waves of gas you see rising off the surface of the sun in deep-space photographs, curling and crusting over the dark surfaces and giving them an outline so that the light was making things gather shape. You'd think the wall would sear you when you touched it, but I touched it and it didn't: it was cold, and the whole place was cold as the Christmas Eve outside the B_____ House, and that was the only thing that kept reminding me that we were not in another place and in another world, but right next to where Pops had grown up—forty-seven of his steps from his door to T_____'s doorway, he said he had measured. Knowing there was night and winter and Christmas and August Acres not a long throw from me… well, back then it gave me confidence. When I think about it now, though, it unsettles me, on account of I know there are whole worlds of secrets right under the surfaces of things and sometimes those secrets rise up, like monsters out of the water.

Anyway, I feel Pops's hand on my shoulder, and I turn to him in all that confusion of dark and light, and there he is, shorter than I knew he was, way shorter, and then he's his usual size again and he never stayed the same. It changed while he stood there and talked to me.

"D_____," he says. "This is the point when you turn back. You needed to know all this was down here. I needed to know it, and needed to know you knew it."

Or it was something like that. Something about needing and knowing. For what I remember, that's pretty close to the words. He was telling me I could go back if I wanted to.

But right then he brings up the stories for the first time. The stories you're so fired up about because of all your intellectual honesty, and I bet at the end of the day the story you're gonna tell will have questions in it, too.

Let me finish. You absolutely know I'm right.

And those stories, Pops tells me... those stories are beams of love, he says. Like all stories are. And they blessed you, he said, and they cursed you as they blessed you...

And yes, he said it exactly like that, and even if I don't recall the tone of voice like you want me to, those were the words he used—exactly the ones—and when the exact words stop meaning something, well, I guess that's blessing and cursing at the same time as well.

Pops told me once that stories heal you as they damage you. Like people do. And stories heal you in the very places they damage you as well. And roll your eyes all you like, and go ahead and smirk like irony is the only story, because it isn't, you know, and just because you get the joke doesn't mean you're any smarter than someone who doesn't get it. Because maybe, just maybe, you find the wrong things funny.

✳✳✳

Clinician's Note: *Stepping from my objective role as clinician, I* *must confess that I was taken aback by Orfeo's outburst. I can only assume that this bizarre tirade manifested, quite simply, that the client had reached a point in analysis where it was therapeutically helpful to turn on me, where the psyche itches and irritates in the process of healing.*

That in and of itself was understandable. But what Orfeo claimed to see after that last exchange between father and son, before the door of his imagination opened into the room he dreamed out of these stories, out of the remembered traumas and the people involved in them—what he claimed to see was so persistently imagined that for a moment I found myself concerned for his basic sanity. After I had calmed him sufficiently—or so I thought—he continued with the outlandish account, stepping out of his father's world of glassy mountains and fairytale fancies into a hallucinatory interior we had yet to visit together.

✳✳✳

Orfeo: At any rate, Pops opens the door. When the light settles, there they were, seated above the table with the board on it, like the summer carving on the arch. The woman faced us, and for a moment, I actually thought it was Ma, because she did that thing with her shoulders Ma does when she's surprised, you know? But she was half hid by the shadows so I was guessing by the body, by her posture and all. And then the woman bends, and she looks older, looks the age of Gramma L___, and there were these spots on her hands—I saw them clearly—when she reached out to move the white bishop.

And then the hand above the chess piece darkens, and it looks older and older. Like a tree root resting on the pointed top of the bishop, poising a gnarled finger on the miter before she let it go, committed to her move.

It was like she wanted to crush the piece before she released it.

And the man seated across from her, mantled like some kind of predatory bird over the black pieces.... well, he keeps his face turned away from us.

I found myself drawn to the game, which I guess was strange. I mean, considering I had walked through an otherworld to reach this blinding crest of shadow and light, here I was thinking about a chess match, the most ordinary thing on the planet, considering the glassy mountain and the flying boys and the gathering ghosts I had already been through.

And the pieces were all over the place, like they sometimes seem to be in a match between masters, where you can't imagine the strategies above the board. I couldn't figure the endgame, and I guess they were either so much better than me that I was too dumb to catch on, or it was chaos and nobody was sure where it was headed.

Now the man with his back to us lifts the black knight— the one left on the board, because he had lost the other.

I knew it was T_____ without being told. It was like the light collapsed all around him and he was absorbing it all into himself, drawing it in. And the back of his pale jacket was boiling with shadows and light.

It was only now, for the very first time, that I'm wondering why Pops brought me here to begin with. I didn't stop to study it, though.

I got a good idea now. He had to put me in danger in order to protect me.

And you're wrong. That does not make it "all about him." It makes it about me, damn it.

Let me finish.

✳✳✳

Clinician's Note: *Whatever really happened on that Christmas Eve, the recollection of it was traumatic to Orfeo. Whether that night marked a final abandonment by an unreliable father or whether something else happened and the boy, years later, projected his own issues of abandonment onto that occasion, it is difficult to say. Nonetheless, we must consider the story as "real" at some level; that at* *least it deals with Orfeo's problems of self-identity and authenticity. As a consequence, the way he told the story (and the end that story reaches) represents his attempt to master repressed memory and hostility, and to leave behind the memories of childhood damage. Neither magic nor mythology features in the end of this tale—just the simple and profound apparatus of analysis.*

✳✳✳

So they both have their backs to me—T_____ and Pops—and it was like I was in this tableau or something, and Pops moves between me and T_____ like he's guarding me, but all it really does is makes me lose sight of T_____ behind him, and that makes things a little more confusing and a little more scary.

So T_____ spoke first, and his voice all doubled in sound like they do for monsters in movies now and then, but it's not particularly frightening, not really, but maybe that was on account of you couldn't see him. And he's saying: I didn't call you here. At least I tried not to.

And Pops goes "I know that. I came on my own, T_____."

And T_____'s all "But you brought the boy…"

And Pops "It wasn't for your sake, but for mine."

And T_____ "But weren't you…"

And Pops not letting him finish, but saying "No, because he's with me, and because of even more, T_____. Because I can be sure you did not mean harm."

I look around Pops, trying to catch a glimpse of T_____, and the old woman is gone now. It's the three of us only, and for some reason that felt right.

No. I don't fuckin know why! Let me finish the damned story, awright?

Good. Good.

Because this is right where T_____ says, "I tried very hard."

And Pops, "We all did, T_____. We all do."

T_____ pushes away from the table and stands up. He's still got his back to me, mind you. Then why did you bring the boy?' he asks my father. "What for your sake does this boy provide?"

It was kinda like a catechism, I guess. And right then I was on the outside of things, and it was like another game of chess beginning, this time between T_____ and Pops, where you could tell that a lot of things were afoot even if the two of them seemed to be standing there, facing away from me, doing next to nothing.

"He's an end to the story, T_____," Pops says at last. "And he's the story's end."

So T_____ stares off into the light. I wish I'd got a good look at him, but I guess we have to rely on the description Pops gave us in the manuscript, and nothing I saw really contradicts what was in the story. But I'll confess it was hard to say, because T_____ was all blurred in light and that pale jacket of his was always churning and changing shape.

"I didn't want your ruination, G_____," he says. "I kept back from it."

And shapes started coming out of the light in front of us— branches bending and twisting, tree trunks leaning over a natural arch of foliage, but it wasn't natural as much as conjured, rising out of a fog of light the way forms take shape in marble under a sculptor's hand.

But T_____ said, "I did not seek your ruination, and It was an executor I wanted. Someone to settle this part of an estate I did not have. And of course you were the choice, G_____. I had told you my stories in your growing up, and you had figured some of them for yourself. And there was nothing after that novel, was there? I knew you'd dried yourself. You had the poetry in you, but not the grand theme. So why not more stories of mine? Stories to help you. Because I thought..."

And Pops raises his hand. "You thought I'd 'do the right thing'. That's it, isn't it? It was a loaded gun you left me..."

And T_____'s voice getting all strange and faraway, like it was...was displaced, all of a sudden. And he's saying, "no, G_____, that's not it," and Pops telling him to stop, that nobody calls him by that shortened version of his name, not any more.

Oh, it was a mess, it was. It was a nightmare.

No, not a literal nightmare, god damn it.

I was wide awake.

And now T_____ is standing up, and he's moved to the other side of the board. And he's playing the white pieces, if they really are white. Because they're more ivory, I'd say, or more pale, if pale was a color. And his hair is all in this brilliant fog that is tumbling over his shoulders so you can't see his features and you don't know whether to be afraid of him or drawn to him... or both.

Then Pops turns to me, and he looks tired, very tired, but happy.

Yes, I said "happy."

And he says to me, D_____, you were there when my stories began, though you don't remember it. Now I want you to turn around and go back the way we came, because you've seen everything you're supposed to see...

And all the time T_____ is saying, It was not like that, G____, until it became a chorus in the back of my father's instructions.

✳✳✳

It was later on, when I looked at the stories, that things started making sense. It was that second story—do you remember it?

Probably not.

Well, anyway Pops insisted there was a code to it, it was why of all of them, he was nervous over publishing it as it stood, because he wasn't sure he understood the code, you see.

I think I figured it out, though.

It had to do with something T_____ had let loose. It was the dark side of that Tibetan boy in the story, and so later on when Pops talked about his friend Joey and what Joey had seen... well it got him to the edge of something. It's what brought him back to Louisville over those holidays.

Though why he brought me back I was never that sure.

Whatever his reasons, they didn't hold now, and he sits down behind the black pieces and faces off against T_____ or the October Man or Champ Ferguson or whoever it was lost in the light and facing him. And I'm thinking, Pops doesn't know how to play, he barely knows how the pieces move…

And that's when he says, "You go on, D_____. I'll be right behind you."

And I look across the chessboard into that web of light, and the two black glittering eyes at the heart of it. I didn't want to leave Pops there, because it seemed like T_____ was transforming, like the old woman had done, and it was hard to tell where T_____ left off and the others began.

And "Go," Pops is saying, "Go back D_____," so, being the good son, I turn and head away, and I'm still thinking on how lonely and dangerous it is for him in that place, so I stop and I start to turn around, and he says, "No, don't look back. I'm behind you. I'm coming," and it's dark in front of me now, and warmer, as though the light behind me was bottled and contained and could not illumine a bigger place, and it occurs to me that I had forgotten how cold it was in there.

How I got to the stairs I couldn't tell you. I think I closed my eyes and I ran into things, but all of a sudden I bark my shin on the bottommost stair, and Pops calls "go on!" from behind me, and "don't look back!" and his voice is all muted like I'm hearing it through walls or remembering it.

At the top of the steps I turned. I waited for him. Figured from the sound that he was a good distance behind me. But he didn't show, and he still didn't show. And I sat down on the topmost stair to wait.

And I know what you're going to say. Because the next thing I remember was I'm seated at his desk in Gramma's house. His old desk. That horrible psychedelic Tolken poster on the wall, and Christmas Day rushing in so suddenly that it was like the sun broke into the house and ambushed me.

The stories were on the desk. Held together by those binder clips he always used to collect his work. All of it was freshly typed, crisp as something he'd send off to his agent, I bet. That was when I first started thumbing through it, and when he didn't show that day nor the next, and Gramma slipped right into full drama and sent me back to Ma, remember? And I read it on the plane coming home…it was in that accordion folder, remember? And I think it was then that I started to understand what happened to me.

Well, that's not true. It's when I started to understand that there was a story to what happened to me. A pattern. A meaning.

Though I'll be damned if I can figure it out yet.

But I do know this much: that for a long time, while I wondered if I looked back too soon, I was really wasting energy. Because if I'd turned around at any time—as I came down the mountain or through the darkness or up the stairs, or any time since in the years that followed… I would still not have seen him coming.

XXXIII

Progress Note

Recipient Name: *"Orfeo"*

Date of Service (m/d/yy):

Type of Service: *Consultation*

Length of Service:

Treatment goals addressed:

Active interventions provided as specified on treatment plan and an interpretation of how recipient

responded to intervention(s):

Recipient's progress towards treatment goals: *Recipient terminated service.*

Other clinically relevant information: *Recipient moved out of parents' home, quit graduate school, took up job in the service economy (see attached notes)*

Signature of provider and credentials:

Benjamin Mountolive, M.D. PsyD. Ph.D.

It was not long until Orfeo broke off consultation altogether. He ceased to return calls from our offices, and when his mother approached him in late summer on my behalf, urging him to return to an analysis that was, quite frankly, on the verge of significant breakthroughs, she, too, was dismissed with the reasoning that his "story said it all" and that, if he "needed confession", he "could find it at St. Mary's" (a small, college-related Catholic church in the town where he now lives).

It was an odd thing to say, because at the end of the day, Orfeo had "confessed" very little. Insistently, he stayed with his story—whether it was ultimately dream or reverie or simply tall tale, it was difficult to tell from my perspective. Nonetheless, training an experienced analytical lens upon that story uncovers a number of observations that, one might say, rescue success from an evidently failed analysis.

The story itself—its movement through shadows, through a basement, its archetypal setting at midwinter and on a holiday notorious for situational depression—is a feast for archetypal analysis, and indicates that Orfeo was descending into his own shadowy underworld with the hope and intent of bringing something out, bringing something "to light," as they say. Again, admittedly there is a poignancy in a child's waiting at the top of the stairs for a father who would never join him, but was not Orfeo waiting as well for "the answer," the authority figure, the male role model to emerge out of a darkness that must be equated with his subconscious? One can only entertain hope that eventually Orfeo will find all those models of behavior, either dormant in himself or alive and well in the family, friends, and mentors who surround him.

In some ways it is a disappointment that therapy did not continue, for Orfeo dropped away from his own advanced studies to work as a clerk in a small, privately owned bookstore. On the other hand, it is an encouragement that his mother reports a kind of global "lifting of spirits," and perhaps it would be immodest to draw the conclusion that a brief, truncated analysis had started his search in the right direction. And yet it might be a single factor among several—an apparent interest in Eastern mythology, and simply having lived through and past the existential anguish of one's late teens and early twenties. All of this might have occasioned a more temperate approach to life.

The issue of his father's alleged plagiarism is another matter, and one that will unfortunately be left uninvestigated. Though G_____ R_____ has not been seen since that eventful Christmas almost fifteen years ago, he covered his tracks before he and Orfeo returned to that childhood home: the freshness and uniformity of the paper upon which the stories were written indicates a last recopying, an obscuring of their earlier origins. Furthermore, Orfeo's assertion that he "read the manuscript on the plane ride home" has little to no credence, as his mother, who met him at the airport, assures me that the manuscript was not in his possession.

Two of the stories have appeared in print: "Giuoco Piano" and "The Isle is Fill'd with Noyses." Both appeared under Orfeo's father's name, and in popular genre magazines. There is talk of a compilation, to be presented to G_____ R_____'s old agent later this year. It is, ultimately, a situation that will no doubt remain unexamined, since I have been told by reliable sources that ethical compromises such as these are not alien to the creation of fiction; some of these sources argue, with equal vehemence, that journalism, history, and even psychological case studies are more gravely compromised.

Orfeo now lives a contented if solitary existence. His contact with his family is sporadic but civil. Physically, psychologically, and ethically, he has passed through more perilous waters than many of his contemporaries, and can be considered a useful, if ordinary, member of his community. We are thankful to have played a part, albeit small, in his recovery.

CODA: DOMINIC

There was that story about Muchukunda, the Hindu warrior king. He helps to win a great battle, joining up on the side of the gods against the demons, and instead of doing the good and noble cycle-of-life thing, where he returns to the community and creates a more just society, he's tired. He's heavy tired, and goes into this cave, it seems, with the intention of sleeping until he's rested—a prospect that he figures will take ages at least. In gratitude, the gods promise him a long rest, assuring him that anyone who disturbs him will be burned to ashes by the fire emanating from his body.

Well, it turns out that the god Krishna is in a struggle as well with the bandit king Kalayavana. Krishna goes into Muchukunda's cave, and Yavana pursues him, intent on the god knows what. Well, Yavana sees Muchukunda lying there asleep and mistakes him for Krishna, kicks at the sleeper, awakens him, and gets pretty much incinerated for the trespass.

Well, Muchukunda wonders why *he* doesn't burn to a

447

crisp as well. Krishna gives him the resumè, the credentials, and Muchukunda remembers the prophecy and bows before the god, saying, "Your words are deeper than the sound of thunder, and the earth sinks under the weight of your foot. Though the demons fled before my radiance, I cannot stand in your light. Show favor on me, and remove me from all evil, you who are ocean, mountain, the river, forest, who are earth, sky, air, water, and fire, who are mind, intelligence, the constant thing, life and the lord of life—the soul and all that is beyond it."

He goes on and on, of course, with the names and deeds and titles of the god, but you get the general picture. All of this, of course, leading to Muchukunda's petition to Krishna: it seems that the king has been whirled through the world too long, confusing pains and pleasures, the temporary with the everlasting, the evidence of senses with the truth.

What he wanted, then, was rest. Wanted out of illusions, out of the world of birth and death and suffering, which ends in a facedown with the king of the ghosts.

Or the *queen* of the ghosts, whom he greets in twilight in her form as a large, white owl. Because I have a different version of the story.

At any rate, Muchukunda comes to Krishna with a plea, a desire to be free of all sensory objects, emotions, and existence. The god promises him a rebirth into a distinguished family, a memory of all former lives, and a direct pathway to freedom.

Now here comes the good part. When Muchukunda steps out of that cave and into the sunlight, he notices all the people around him, and he notices that they are…smaller in stature.

Like the whole world is diminished after his brush with the god. It isn't that it's less, but that Muchukunda is *more*.

That's my story and I'm sticking to it.

✱✱✱

You know, I keep thinking I saw my father.

There was an Otter Creek down where Pops lived. In fact,

it was the name of the little stream that flowed behind August Acres, where he came up. But there is another Otter Creek, which is really a river, that flows right by the little shop I work at, on its way to Lake Champlain. And of course, after Pops's story of that lake—how he and my mother rowed on it and stirred up something in its depths, he thought—I have thought about that lake, and about that water a lot.

At night I dream of him sometimes, his voice tumbling out of the trees by that little river. He's singing something as I dream him as a rustle of wind passing from branch to branch, shaking leaves as he goes. The tune is something I almost recognize, but I'm nowhere near hearing the words.

It's all about displacement. Deflection. About a month ago, I received an email, sent to me by mistake—I'm guessing the man got the numbers backwards in my screen name. Was emailing his son, telling the boy how proud he was of him.

Wrong address but to the right place, I figured. I've read it a few times.

As to the right place: it's odd to work in a bookshop, as I was never the reader, at least as a kid, that either Pops or my mother would have wanted me to be. I took up chess and music, but wasn't that good with the music, and was put off from chess when I saw that my father found it disturbing and oddly repellent. Put it off as jealousy at first, since he didn't play.

Now, of course, I know different.

I did end up reading *Dacia*, of course, but never really got it. All those slopes and tombs and transfigured fairy tales. It seemed too strange and otherworldly to me—even after the events of Christmas Eve.

It was the stories that caught my attention, after all. The way they all seemed to start in the here and now, in a world I recognized, and moved into a strangeness I recognized. It was kind of like the way things went in the Bell house, on the night Pops vanished.

And that's what I thought about, when I took my own first looks at those stories.

I thought they were Pops' to begin with. But the pages were a giveaway, even to a teen-aged boy who had never been that observant. Wasn't at all like I told Ben. Some of the pages were yellowed and brittle, while others were smooth, crisp on the edges, and altogether new. I could tell where Pops had worked on the manuscript most recently, and that some of the pages were old past the time that he had been writing.

So I knew it was Trajan to begin with.

But where his story left off and where Pops' began...well, it was pretty much a mystery then, and largely a mystery now. Pops had gathered it all together—all kinds of pages, it turned out, from those written on an old typewriter to some dot matrix pages, and some even in yellow legal pad, where part of the handwriting was Pops's, I could tell, because the "z"s were crossed like Gramma Lull's and he'd always spoken about how she taught him that.

All the papers were in a kind of order. Stories in stories in stories.

The last one wasn't finished. Not yet, anyway.

Ben always thought that I came back to Grammas and found a spanking new manuscript. Fueled his belief that Pops had lifted it all, had typed it all up so as to cover his plagiarism.

I know better. Some of it was his.

But I had an even better idea when I saw it, though, as to why Pops had taken me down on the night journey.

It was to see the transfer. To find my place at the end of the story.

$$***$$

My mother was all questions when she met me at the plane. What happened, where he was, and then when my answers were no better than my grandparents' or those of the police, she started asking the *whys*.

Saw the manuscript in the big accordion file. Promised she'd stay mum about how suspicious it looked, and as far as I know, she always has.

I think some things had come to pass with her. I think it was his vanishment that made her realize she was still sweet on Pops. It's how we love invisible things, I suppose, because the lure of the unseen lets us ponder its insides, lets us stretch and compress it and fit it to our imaginations...

So that when we come out of the cave, the people look diminished.

***

Barry Green is not a bad sort, despite what Ma says about Pops's coming to fear him more than rely on him.

After I published the first two stories, he's taken an interest in putting everything together in a single volume, a kind of "last words of Gabriel Rackett" anthology, though he doesn't call it that, and, when all is said and done, Pops's splash was too small for some kind of memorial volume.

I think he's doing it to help me along. Not that there's royalties in short stories, but helping me along nonetheless.

There are fragments to look at. Scattered papers that fit in the gaps between stories—Pops's own account of growing up, and the things he told me and those he told Ma, who's told me later when I asked about them. I'm stringing them all together like beads or strands of weaving.

Nobody stole from anybody, I'm thinking. Everyone just passed it on, for good or ill.

***

Grampa Bowers has this place up against the lake. Not 50 miles from here.

They're too old to take care of it themselves. But my aunt and her husband, and sometimes my uncle...well, they come up there.

And Ma and Ben. And sometimes Ma alone.

I took a girl up there now and then for a while. A nice girl named Peri, or at least she seemed nice at the time. But it didn't work out.

Still, the cabin is a good place and sometimes I go up there alone.

Which is where it really happened. The one time I was sure I saw the old man.

The first time I went to the cottage after Peri and I broke up. I was there, all inconsolable. Peri had claimed it was the drink and the drink alone that had split us, but I was certain that deeper things were at the cause of it, and that less whiskey would not make the fundamentals better.

So the lake was a refuge, George Dickel and Jack Daniels and myself getting away. But I left those gentlemen ashore when I went out on the water, because I might have been a drunk then, but a drunken fool I wasn't quite. And the strange thing about refuges…you hide in the midst of the thing you're running from, and…

Too much analyzing. Here was the story.

I took a rowboat out on the lake. No more than a scull, actually—the kind of boat that always made me think of that great story about the Irish poet who's at a séance in London, where one of the other fellas claims to see a scull in a vision, and the poet's all *was it gory-locked and grimacing?* until he finds out the guy is from Oxford where a scull is a boat, and that he's just remembering his rowing days. A rowboat probably a lot like this one…

Which could become a ghost in the right light.

I was conceived on this lake—not in a scull, of course, but in the aftermath of Pops's and Ma's venture out on the water looking for Champ the monster. And as I rowed I was thinking of the convergence of names, how there was Champ in the lake and in the story I'd been buried in, and how they both came up out of the shadows. But mainly I was thinking about how nothing was matching up or making sense in the daily world.

I felt like old Muchukunda, *whirled around in the circle of earthly existence.*

Anyway, the lake was still. Pops always claimed that he and Ma had rowed over it through the sound of cicadas, but the only noise I was hearing was the revving of a faraway powerboat, like everything had fled the lake but us and our machineries.

Out in the water, barely in sight of any shore, it can be tranquil and large and just a little indifferent, so I didn't row out that far. Just kept to the near shoreline, at the old stone's throw, and though there were places where the shelf drops off into much deeper water, for the most part it's safe, especially for a strong swimmer in a life jacket.

A drunk but not a drunken fool. Remember?

I couldn't have been in *less* peril, frankly, and when I passed over a dark stretch of water, I let her run and benched the oars, drifting to a stop pretty readily. The powerboat had faded out of earshot and it was a lot like it was, I figured, when old Champlain himself explored the region.

And in that stillness I feel the boat rise a bit in the water, like a wave had taken it up.

And there he was. Maybe three feet or so below the surface, Pops is floating face up and smiling, his arms crossed over his chest like on the sarcophagus of a pharaoh or a crusading knight.

In his smile was a song and a serenity, not quite a giving over, you know, as much as a glimpse into the depths of things where I doubt he is finding peace but I am pretty sure he is finding poetry, wherever and whatever he was. I kept the oars benched and I watched him, adrift in midwater between surface and depths.

And he sank back, still smiling, without a goodbye or a farewell, which makes me think that the time for that hasn't come yet. But the smile allowed everything, and embraced it as well, and when the cabin came in sight, I felt as though I had come in a circle, and eyes were watching me—Ma's eyes, and Pops, and Trajan, and the watchers before the three of them, everyone looking on as the boat scudded to shore and I came home.

About the Author

Over the past 25 years, Michael Williams has written a number of strange novels, from the early Weasel's Luck and Galen Beknighted in the best-selling DRAGONLANCE series to the more recent lyrical and experimental Arcady, singled out for praise by Locus and Asimov's magazines. In Trajan's Arch, his eleventh novel, stories fold into stories and a boy grows up with ghostly mentors, and the recently published Vine mingles Greek tragedy and urban legend, as a local dramatic production in a small city goes humorously, then horrifically, awry.

Trajan's Arch and Vine are two of the books in Williams's highly anticipated City Quartet, to be joined in 2018 by Dominic's Ghosts and Tattered Men.

Williams was born in Louisville, Kentucky, and spent much of his childhood in the south central part of the state, the red-dirt gothic home of Appalachian foothills and stories of Confederate guerrillas. Through good luck and a roundabout journey he made his way through through New England, New York, Wisconsin, Britain and Ireland, and has ended up less than thirty miles from where he began. He has a Ph.D. in Humanities, and teaches at the University of Louisville, where he focuses on the he Modern Fantastic in fiction and film. He is married, and has two grown sons.

www.ingramcontent.com/pod-product-compliance
Lightning Source LLC
Chambersburg PA
CBHW021840010726
47493CB00005B/1485